"Can't You Tell A Waltz From An Obstacle Race?

Why, I feel like a marionette who's gotten her strings all tangled up."

Indeed, Richard held her so stiffly and moved in such a jerky, disconnected fashion, that Jennifer twice stumbled over his feet and had to clutch his arm more tightly to steady herself.

She tipped her head backward in order to study Richard's face for a moment. "Shall I tell you what I think? I think that we two are used to dealing with each other on the basis of the several roles we play. Why, this must be the first chance we've had to face each other simply as man and woman."

Richard smiled sheepishly.

Jennifer giggled and unconsciously snuggled a little deeper into his arms. "And you see how much nicer it is like this, with neither of us kicking up a row? Though having become used to the old system, no doubt we'll soon feel as surfeited with this one as a cat in a dairy." She looked up mischievously at her partner, only to find him smiling down at her in a way that made her feel positively breathless...

Letter Of Intent

Letter Of Intent

LESLIE REID

WARNER BOOKS

A Warner Communications Company

WARNER BOOKS EDITION

This Warner Books Edition is published by arrangement with
Wildstar Books, a division of the Adele Leone Agency, Inc.

Warner Books, Inc.
666 Fifth Avenue
New York, N.Y. 10103

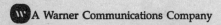A Warner Communications Company

Printed in the United States of America

First Printing: November, 1987

10 9 8 7 6 5 4 3 2 1

For someone who understands the significance
of signing a letter of intent

I would like to thank Alison S. Reid for suggesting the title for this book.

I would also like to thank Paul Soter for providing the definition of letter of intent and for other pertinent legal advice, and the Stanford University libraries for their invaluable collections, which include the original documents that suggested the idea for this story.

LETTER OF INTENT: Customarily employed to reduce to writing a preliminary understanding of parties who intend to enter into a contract.

—*Black's Law Dictionary*

Chapter 1

JENNIFER SOMERS stuffed another fold of the pea-green traveling cloak carefully beneath her and eased slowly back down onto the seat of the coach. She stroked the soft material dazedly for a few minutes and then permitted herself a tiny sigh as her body began once more to ache at every jolt of the vehicle. Still, she supposed there was very little one could do to counteract the seemingly execrable conditions of the roads in America—at least not after the more than twenty days that had been required so far to forge a passage north from Savannah. Thank heavens for her physical well-being that they were finally nearing their destination, Jennifer thought, as they began to negotiate the descent to the river. Although aside from that minor consideration, she had to admit that she'd enjoyed every moment of the journey thus far, not least because she'd fortunately been provided with the most unfailingly cheerful and tireless companion imaginable.

She pulled her gaze away from the window to watch her father, who was chatting comfortably with a matron from Boston. With his open, friendly manner, easy speech, and modest, if fashionable, attire, Jonathan Somers could almost have been called unremarkable. In fact, his daughter was nearly certain that none of their fellow passengers had the slightest idea that the gentleman who'd kept them all so well entertained during the trip possessed a title that harked back to the time when Greater Britain and Less Britain were two separate countries, as well as an income that was usually referred to in reverential whispers.

Unfortunately, his wealth wasn't the only reason that Lord Somers, Earl of Arundel, was the favorite subject upon which the gossip mongers liked to chew. It was far more likely, Jennifer knew, to be what her father affectionately termed his "projects" and what his detractors referred to privately as "Somers's crack-brained schemes" that provided the tidbits satisfying even to the most jaded town palates. Last year, for example, it had been sheep. Indeed, only the persistent war with France had convinced Lord Somers not to cross the Channel to secure a few specimens from Rambouillet. In the end, he'd been forced to make do with several fine pairs of merinos that he'd obtained in a circuitous, if no less hazardous, fashion from Spain and then happily set to breeding on his estate in West Sussex beneath Ducton Downs.

Jennifer smiled fondly at her father and stifled an impulse to call his attention to his disordered locks. This urge she felt to take care of him was ridiculous, she reminded herself, tucking her own bright red curls into place beneath her straw bonnet instead. He would doubtless think himself more capable of looking after his affairs than his twenty-year-old daughter, regardless of how self-reliant he'd raised her to be. It was only that no matter how much time they spent contentedly in each other's company, she still couldn't fathom the way his mind worked or when he unearthed the numerous snippets of information with which he sprinkled his conversation. On the trip between Savannah and Charleston he'd shared his impression of the status of land transportation in this year 1811; when they'd stopped because one of the horses threw a shoe between Charleston and Philadelphia, he'd volunteered to point out the thoroughbraces and other niceties of the vehicle's construction; and now he was describing the ferry on which they were apparently to cross the Hudson River to New York City.

Of course, none of this would have seemed remarkable even to Jennifer if she hadn't known that four months ago her father had no understanding of the roads and certainly less of the rigors of travel in the United States. It had all started one day in May when they'd been seated in the library of their London residence, Jennifer deliciously absorbed in Miss Austen's *Sense and Sensibility* and her father poring over his beloved history books. She was just on the point of deciding to lay aside the novel in favor of some afternoon refreshment when her parent seemed to echo her thoughts.

"Water," he declared firmly, looking inordinately pleased at this remark.

"Yes, I was thinking of tea myself," Jennifer agreed.

"Not tea water," her father objected a trifle impatiently. "Land water. Irrigation. Aqueducts. In short, canals."

Observing the sudden fervent light in her father's eyes, Jennifer pulled the footstool a little closer and settled herself happily in anticipation of the discourse that she knew would follow.

"Did you know," Lord Somers began slowly, "that in the thirteenth century B.C. there was an extensive canal and storage system for irrigation constructed along the Nile by Rameses II?" He carelessly tapped the stack of books he'd been consulting so that they promptly threatened to topple over. "And in the seventh century B.C.," he continued, as Jennifer reluctantly dragged her attention back to the conversation at hand, "the greatest water system in the world was an aqueduct that conveyed water to the royal city of Nineveh. Amazing example of hydraulic engineering," he confided. "They built a series of dams and sluices to regulate and catch the water before it reached the city: open masonry channels sealed against leakage with a mixture of sand and broken limestone. Amazing," he repeated, shaking his head in disbelief.

He stopped to tug at his neck cloth in the characteristic gesture that Jennifer had long since fondly decided must somehow help ease the flood of words that invariably accompanied the discovery of what would become his latest project. "You see, it's irrigation I'm interested in primarily. Why, after a heavy rain the sheep will nearly drown in the lower meadows one week and then the next the grass will be so dry the damned beasts must think they're eating sticks.

Got to devise some way to drain the flats and then save and share the water all around. Building a canal's the perfect answer,'' he concluded, smiling happily either at his conclusion or at the prospect it presented.

Jennifer smiled back. It was simply impossible for her not to find his enthusiasm wholly contagious, even though she knew that the same tendency had often earned her father such derogatory epithets as ''Simpleton Somers'' and ''Jonathan Jackpudding'' from certain members of Society.

Since she was also well versed in the second stage of any of his adventures, she paused for only a moment to digest the foregoing information before asking tentatively, ''Are we to go to Egypt, then?''

Lord Somers took no notice of the fact that his daughter had, as usual, assumed that she was to be included in his plans. Instead, he rose from his chair and favored her with a disgusted look before observing, ''Thought I schooled you to cultivate logical thinking? If I can read about the cursed places, why ever would I want to bother going to them as well? Not the least reason for that that I can see. The whole idea is to go somewhere I can't read up on and discover for myself what it's about. Do you take my point?''

Jennifer wisely refrained from asking her father how he expected to be able to identify such a mysterious destination and merely nodded her head. Everything is revealed to the true believer in due course, a mystic had once told her. Happily, this was a philosophy to which Lord Somers, too, was inclined to subscribe, perhaps in part because he was accustomed to his daughter forming his entire audience. Jennifer waited patiently, as ever, for him to continue— content to be the recipient of his confidences and unconsciously guarding him from any immediate negative response as closely as she was used to keeping her own confidences entirely from most others.

''Thought we'd go to America,'' he offered at last. ''Do you remember that man we met a few years back at Walter Scott's: Aaron Burr? Nasty looking, with a face as cold as a flounder? The one who got himself mixed up in all that trouble over invading Mexico to free the colonists? Do you know, it turned out that that was just a pretext; the real issue was that the silly fellow tried to recruit a private army to overthrow President Jefferson, take over the Congress, and then set up a new government. What was it he kept telling us that evening?''

'' 'Small morals were not meant for great men','' Jennifer supplied dryly.

''That's it. Convenient bit of lip wisdom, don't you think? Like to learn the full particulars sometime. After all, you don't bring a fellow up on trial for treason—even if he did get off without paying the shot—if you don't suspect he's playing a deep game. But at any rate, do you remember Burr mentioning the company he'd founded? Peculiar idea to have them conduct banking and also be charged with supplying drinking water to New York City. Still, it occurred to me at the time that a letter of introduction might prove useful—if I ever wanted to visit America, that is.'' He pulled open a drawer in the elegant writing table that served as his desk and rummaged through it for a minute before triumphantly producing a sheet written in a bold hand. ''We'll start there, I think, since it seems to be the perfect answer to my needs of the moment. Then perhaps later there'll be an opportunity to investigate one or two other notions I have in mind.''

''But do you think we can sail into New York directly?'' Jennifer raised the delicate brows over her green eyes and shot a dubious look at her father. ''As I recall, relations between our two countries are rather strained at the moment, to put it nicely. Why, I'm sure I read the other day that most people think it's merely a matter of time before British cruisers and American frigates have a set-to practically in the city harbor.''

Lord Somers lounged back precariously against the slender desk and regarded his daughter with a good deal more approval. ''There! I knew you could tease the sense out of the thing if you tried. No point in thinking to pass yourself off as a caper-wit, my dear. Besides, one in the family's quite enough.'' He indulged in a hearty laugh at the expense of his own well-known reputation. ''Not that I care a jot what anyone may think of me, but I won't surround myself with bores or fools. And that includes my relatives.'' He tried without much success to affix a stern expression on his face as he addressed the sole person who could honestly claim a blood tie. "Not much good at playing tyrant, am I?" Jennifer smiled at him. "Or parent either, for that matter," he relented a moment later, seeing his daughter's amused response. "Pure selfishness, that's what it is: Encouraging you forever to say what's on your mind merely so I could safely do likewise; hiring private tutors so I'd be sure you'd have enough learning to carry on a proper conversation; and then dragging you along from place to place so I'd be provided with a decent companion. Not at all the right sort of upbringing for a young lady."

If only you'd been equally careful to encourage me to reveal what I felt in addition to what I thought, Jennifer mused to herself. But her father, long accustomed to acting as easily on his emotions as breathing, seemed curiously reluctant to separate feelings from feats and apparently believed everyone else felt exactly the same. "Oh, piffle!" she exclaimed inelegantly, pushing aside that thought once again and promptly confirming his preceding assessment. "Why, you know I can be a perfect miss if I choose. You were careful to see I had my come-out, weren't you? It's only that I find all those things like paying calls and shopping for gowns tedious beyond bearing when compared to the sort of scrapes you're likely to discover. And I'd as lief spend my time with you in—" She broke off, a grim suspicion suddenly beginning to form in her mind. She leaped up from her comfortable chair and regarded her father in dismay. "You can't mean—that is, surely you don't intend to leave me behind?"

She drew herself up to her full height and advanced toward her parent, shaking a finger threateningly at him as she spoke. "If you think for one instant that I'll let you sail off on some fine adventure without me, then you'd best reconsider, sir! Why, whatever would I do? I should have to be content with listening to Randolf Stamford bumble through yet another unwelcome proposal of marriage and devising new ways to prove myself unworthy of his attentions."

"Now that's exactly what I'm talking about," Lord Somers complained a trifle peevishly. "I'm sure we shouldn't be discussing these things as equals at all. As the parent, I should be telling you what to do and you, as the child, should be following my orders.'' He looked down at his daughter, as anyone more than five feet tall was easily able to do, and attempted a more subtle approach. ''But perhaps you've forgotten that Stamford will inherit a very handsome income when he reaches his majority?''

''What? When he's so everlastingly fond of reminding me of that fact himself? Now if he only stood to inherit a few brains, I shouldn't quibble in the least,'' she admitted slyly. ''But then, I'm confident you wouldn't wish on me a future peopled with bores and fools—especially since you've only just claimed that you would never gladly suffer the same fate yourself,'' she pointed out with admirable logic.

Lord Somers pulled her into a rough hug and gracefully admitted defeat. ''Well done, brat,'' he conceded. ''I own I should be glad of your company after all. Besides, no doubt there'll be time enough to come up with another solution to this little dilemma.''

Jennifer snuggled deeper into her father's arms, too relieved now that the threat had passed to pay much attention to his last remark. Then she slipped happily into her customary role once more. Smiling up into his face, she asked in a curious voice, ''How do you think it best for us to proceed, sir?''

One of the traits Jennifer admired most about her father, and consciously strived to emulate, was the way he wasn't afraid to admit when he didn't know something. In fact, in her experience, he was indeed rare among men, for he seemed to derive as much satisfaction from the process of discovering how to solve a problem as he did from being able to offer a quick solution. What's more, he didn't make the mistake of equating a lack of knowledge with a diminution of his manhood. And unlike the other members of his sex whom Jennifer had so far encountered, Lord Somers had no trouble separating fact from opinion and wouldn't have dreamed of trying to pass the latter off as anything but personal cogitation.

She shook out her cloak and gratefully stretched her legs

as she watched the maneuverings required to load the stagecoach onto the ferry. There was, for example, the matter of arranging for their passage to New York, she recalled. Although her father had known little of what might be involved at the outset, he'd cheerfully settled down to the task of learning everything he could about the travel in the New World. Fortitude was going to prove the key, he'd informed Jennifer a few weeks after he'd begun his investigation. Given the vagaries of the weather and the fact that it appeared expedient for them to land in Savannah and then follow an overland route north, it seemed that the trip was likely to entail as much discomfort, hardship, and even danger as circling the globe.

Lord Somers had now stripped off his putty-colored walking coat and was helping the driver steady the horses, Jennifer observed. And that brought to mind another trait she admired. Her father didn't use his title and position to put himself above others. Sometimes, in fact, it seemed to her as if reminders of his wealth took him quite by surprise. For instance, when a friend—scandalized to learn his lordship was contemplating a trip of more than three weeks' duration in a crowded public conveyance—had pointed out that hiring a private coach would surely halve the time and inconvenience, Lord Somers had regarded him in astonishment. Traveling in isolated, if comfortable, splendor wasn't conducive to learning, he'd explained kindly to his guest. And since broadening his understanding was the primary motivation behind such a journey, he'd continued, he preferred not to engage in an experience so altogether different from that of ordinary people as to be practically artificial. This was not to say, however, that he ever attempted to hide his identity and pretend to be a common merchant. Particularly not when discovery of that subterfuge should leave him open to charges of being pretentious, condescending, and downright ill-bred—none of which any man of character would have the least desire to be, he'd concluded firmly.

Jennifer tied her bonnet a little more tightly and joined her father at the rail of the ferry. A stiff breeze blowing down the river ruffled the water and promised a speedy passage to the other side. Behind them, the steep cliffs of the Jersey coast brooded darkly in the lengthening shadows of late afternoon. Ahead, the slanting rays picked out rolling hills atop a shoreline that curved away to left and right before disappearing from view. Jennifer, who'd been as excited as her father at the idea of visiting America and who'd undertaken in her own way to prepare for the trip, now plucked a thick volume from her reticule and began to read aloud.

The island of Manna-hata spread wide before them, like some sweet vision of fancy, or some fair creation of industrious magic. Its hills of smiling green swelled gently one above another, crowned with lofty trees of luxuriant growth; some pointing their tapering foliage toward the clouds, which were gloriously transparent; and others loaded with a verdant burden of clambering vines, bowing their branches to the earth, that was covered with flowers.

"What's that you called the place: 'Manna-hata'?" her father asked curiously.

"Yes. It means a land flowing with milk and honey, you know," Jennifer explained. "Listen to the description of the first ship's landing—at just about this same time of year." She turned a few pages and read again.

They ate hugely, drank profusely, and slept immeasurably; and being under the especial guidance of Providence, the ship was safely conducted to the coast of America; where, after sundry unimportant touchings and standings off and on, she at length, on the fourth day of September, entered that majestic bay which at this day expands its ample bosom before the city of New York, and which had never before been visited by any European.

" 'Drank profusely'? 'Ample bosom'? Strange sort of book I appear to have bought you," Lord Somers wondered aloud.

Jennifer looked up, a mischievous smile on her face. "Oh, I wasn't referring to *The Picture of New York*," she admitted. "Not that I didn't find the information . . . useful . . . just a trifle dull. No, this is called *A History of New York from the Beginnings of the World to the End of the Dutch Dynasty* and claims to contain 'an account of its discovery and settlement, with its internal policies, manners, customs, wars, etc.' The writer is given as one Diedrich Knickerbocker, but the bookseller told me the author is really someone named Washington Irving and that he intended to parody the very same book we originally purchased. I thought that between the two, you see, we'd at least discover the full story—and be highly entertained as well!"

"I should think so," her father agreed. " 'Ample bosom' indeed! Still, I should have known you'd find a way to inject some humor into the proceedings." He reached over to give one of her curls an affectionate tweak. "The thing I like most about you, my dear," he volunteered, echoing the direction of Jennifer's earlier thoughts, "is that you're so consistently unpredictable and take such delight in confounding everyone's expectations. I mean, here you are, not much bigger than a child and yet mad as fire if anyone dares treat you as one—and then off you go and behave like a perfect babe at the first opportunity!"

As if to emphasize the foregoing point, the stout matron who was continuing on to Boston chose that moment to take her leave of the Somerses, and Jennifer was only able to avoid being patted on the head like a schoolchild by dint of much practice. But after the stagecoach had deposited them at the corner of Courtland Street and turned north on Broadway, she promptly banished from her mind the dark thoughts inevitably produced by people who dealt with her as if she were a mere girl of thirteen.

She was allotted only a few minutes to gaze up the wide avenue bordered by poplars that she'd read stretched from the tip of Manhattan to the northern limits of the city at Canal Street. By that time her father had secured a porter, helped load their trunks and cases onto his pushcart, and announced that they might as well walk the two blocks to the hotel.

Jennifer had eagerly undertaken to prime herself for her exposure to America by steeping her mind in as wide a variety of reading material as she could bring to hand. Therefore, she was now able to point out to her father that the Broad-way, as it used to be called, was one of the only streets in the city able to boast pavement along most of its length. And that fact was all the more impressive, she informed him, when one learned that until a few years ago the building of sidewalks along the road to accommodate foot traffic had been up to the discretion of the individual property owner.

"Don't seem to have improved much," Lord Somers observed bluntly. He flashed Jennifer a good-natured smile as he strove to keep his balance on the cobblestones while avoiding the buttermilk cart a street vendor had just thrust in his path. "Good God, look at that!" he exclaimed. He stopped so suddenly that his daughter collided with his back and then had to be steadied by a helpful arm.

Jennifer followed the direction the finger at the end of that arm was pointing and smiled. What distinguished this pile of refuse from the several others they'd circumvented along their route was the pair of large and rather fierce-looking pigs that was busily engaged in scavenging among the scraps. Of course, now that it had been brought to their attention, the smell of the street at once became overwhelming. As if by prearrangement, father and daughter with one movement raised scented handkerchiefs to their faces and quickened their pace.

A few minutes later they arrived in front of the City Hotel, an imposing, four-story, red brick building extending the entire length of the block below Cedar Street. Fashionable shops filled the ground floor facing Broadway, unlike the taverns that seemed more commonly to occupy that position. What's more, Jennifer whispered to her father, the hotel took enormous pride in such innovations as a slate roof, said to be the first in the country, and the shutters that had replaced curtains at the windows.

Lord Somers, for his part, was more interested in exploring the wine cellar for which his daughter had noted the establishment was equally famous. First, however, there was the business of their arrival to be attended to, and he set himself accordingly to that task. Why was it, Jennifer wondered yet again, that people initially assumed her father to be someone of little consequence? True, his brown hair and eyes and medium build were certainly not remarkable. But anyone who also noted his confident bearing or encountered his perfect manners should easily have been able to place him among the cream of polite society. Perhaps, she mused, it was on account of his predilection for traveling without servants or for wearing clothing that was superbly tailored, if far more modest than fashion decreed.

She had inherited both tendencies, Jennifer admitted, tucking a stray thread into her stylishly short kid gloves. Unfortunately, in her view, she'd also inherited the diminutive stature and disproportionately curvacious figure of the woman she dimly remembered as her mother. Lizzy Fairfield had been the belle of the season in 1790, so outrageously beautiful that it was rumored two gentlemen who'd never seen her had once fought a duel for the right to be the first to pay her his compliments. Nevertheless, after the night she met Jonathan Somers, her heart had been decidedly caught— and not merely by his fortune, since she was quite comfortably situated in that respect herself. No, Jennifer knew, theirs had been purely a love match, and they had continued openly—and most unfashionably—to adore each other for the few years allowed them until Lizzy had died trying to give her three-year-old daughter a brother.

Jennifer turned just in time to witness a startling, if familiar, change come over the hotel manager as he finally realized the identities of his latest guests. To be sure, Mr. Willard promised in honeyed tones, Lord Somers's rooms had already been prepared for his arrival. Perhaps he and his daughter would care to be shown there forthwith and then, perhaps, a late tea might be arranged for them by his partner?

This suggestion proved agreeable to his lordship, and they were at once directed to spacious adjoining chambers on the third floor. After washing off the evidence of their travels as best she could, Jennifer changed into a simple gown of white Indian muslin embroidered with tiny green leaves at the cuffs and hem. Then she paused to collect her father, and together they descended to the dining room.

There they were greeted personally by Mr. Jennings and shown to a table by a window overlooking Broadway. The room was light and airy, with a high ceiling and graceful proportions. In a few minutes their host returned bearing a bottle of the fine Madeira which he advised Lord Somers was called The Eliza, after the ship that had brought it into port. This he accompanied by several plates of assorted biscuits and cakes and a pot of strong China tea. Clearly, Jennifer decided, the man who supervised the hotel's provender and liquid refreshments had thought her far too young for sherry. She sighed. Being taken for a mere girl alternately amused and angered her, as her father was well aware. Now, for example, he'd as usual anticipated just such a development. After tasting the Madeira and complimenting Mr. Jennings on its quality, his lordship pronounced himself inclined to sample one or two of the sweeter wines as well. A bottle of Amontillado was immediately produced, and soon Jennifer was able to join in a toast to their safe arrival in New York.

A friendly silence fell between father and daughter. To be sure, except for a vague similarity in their features and the difference in their ages, a casual onlooker might have taken them for husband and wife instead, so content did they appear to be in each other's company. The same thought had crossed Jennifer's mind as well. Putting down her glass, she propped her chin in one hand, examined her father for a moment, and then asked gently, "Do you ever miss Mama?"

"Every day," he confessed. "I don't suppose you remember her very well? No, I thought not. Well, she was absolutely devoted to you. She always thought it a virtual miracle that she'd managed to produce a daughter. She even confessed to me once that she felt having children was a privilege and that everyone ought to be obliged to prove themselves worthy before being allowed to do so. She wouldn't let you be thrust off into the care of maids and governesses either, but insisted on doing everything herself. In fact, I'm certain that's how you come by your mischievous ways, because Lizzy used to spend hours crawling around on the floor inventing games for the two of you and having a perfectly marvelous time. Of course, she never let the least hint of such behavior escape the walls of the nursery. Outwardly, she was the picture of the fashionable young wife and mother. It was only in private that one realized the contradiction." Lord Somers cocked his head at his daughter. "You're very like her in that respect, you know—though I'm afraid you're not as careful as she was to keep up at least the pretense of respectability."

"And who was it who taught me to dislike pretense so very much, I wonder?" Jennifer inquired innocently.

Her father laughed. "In that connection, perhaps we'd best think about how you're to keep yourself occupied for the next several days. After all, even the New World believes in some of the old customs, I understand, and thus you'll scarcely be able to go traipsing around the city alone—much as I'm certain you long to do. We shall have to find a maid—if not a companion of sorts—to accompany you. Now, there's no point in protesting," he said quickly as Jennifer opened her mouth. "I mean to see we start things out right and proper, at any rate, before you have your way with them!"

Jennifer attempted unsuccessfully to look every inch the obedient daughter. "Whatever you say, Papa," she said in a chaste voice. "You, I take it, shall be busy elsewhere?" she asked, hoping to change the subject.

Lord Somers nodded. "Yes, I expect to pay a visit to the Manhattan Company. That is," he paused, wrinkling his brow anxiously, "assuming the directors received the letter I sent announcing my intention to call. I never did get an answer, you know."

"Perhaps the omission was only on account of the same difficulties in shipping that complicated our arrival here," Jennifer suggested.

"Yes, that must be it," her father agreed in relief. "Besides, even if the letter didn't arrive, I'm sure I can't see how my presence would prove the least inconvenience to anyone."

Chapter 2

L ORD SOMERS was unfortunately wide of the mark in assessing the effect his visit might have on the directors of the Manhattan Company. Had his letter, in fact, ever arrived, his lordship would no doubt have been most cordially received by those gentlemen. As it was, however, the news of his arrival had long since gone astray in the worsening tensions between England and the United States. Barely two weeks earlier, the incident everyone had predicted had finally come to pass. Practically in the city harbor, the USS *President* had suddenly been attacked by HM man-of-war *Little Belt*. Naturally, the American ship had retaliated, dismasting the sloop and leaving it near sinking with eighteen dead and forty wounded in an unlikely display of naval power. Talk of Commodore Rogers's surprising victory had claimed the public's attention, and speculation about the extent of the reparations the British would be forced to make had dominated conversation ever since.

The youngest of the thirteen directors of Mr. Burr's company would surely have welcomed the luxury of being distracted in such a fashion from a consideration of his present difficulties. At the moment, though, Richard Avery was seated in his study attempting dispassionately to figure out how he was to keep the management of his household from crashing about his ears. He shifted back and forth in a fruitless attempt to settle his long frame into a fashionable but uncomfortable Chippendale chair. Then he ran a hand through his thick, dark hair and allowed the eyes some people disparagingly referred to as mahogany-colored to close tiredly for a minute. He tapped the bridge of his aquiline nose with a well-shaped finger and let out a small sigh. The tutor he'd retained without actually meeting him was two days overdue, and Richard was beginning to question the wisdom of having hired a man who was already proving so unreliable. And that very morning, his normally long-suffering housekeeper had informed him that she was at her wit's end. It had been one thing when the twins were little to give them each a biscuit and set them to playing happily on the kitchen floor while she attended to her duties, Mrs. Booth reminded him. But now that they were nine years old, George and Caroline weren't so easily shabbed off, and she didn't have time both to attend to them and to her work as well. It was clear to her, at any rate, that they needed a proper governess—not a ninny like the last one, either—and the sooner her employer recognized that fact the better, Mrs. Booth had announced, fixing him with an implacable look before sailing out of the room.

Not that he was inclined to dispute either his housekeeper's advice or her opinion of the unfortunate Miss Pennycott's character, Richard admitted. He walked over to the bookcase, pulled out a leather-bound volume of Charles Lamb's essays extolling the virtues of London, and stared at it blindly for a few moments before sliding it back onto the shelf. He must have been daft ever to have thought that moderate schooling and a strict upbringing would have prepared Miss Pennycott for the rigors of managing two inquisitive yet well-behaved children. No, not daft—desperate, Richard conceded, casting himself back into the chair and thrumming his fingers on its arm. And even though she'd succeeded for a while in keeping pace with the twins' lively intelligence, Miss Pennycott's nerves had been overset in the process. What's more, she found herself quite unable to adjust to the hurly-burly atmosphere of New York, she'd admitted to him, before she bolted back to the safety of her parents' country home.

Following Miss Pennycott's departure a month ago, Richard had spent a considerable amount of time pondering the attributes of the person he required to fill her position. It should be someone who knew Greek and Latin, certainly, and had a solid grounding in the classics, as well as an

understanding of French, mathematics, and possibly politics. Someone intimately acquainted with English institu-
tions and thought would be ideal, Richard had decided,
being a confirmed admirer of those things himself.

London-born, Cambridge-educated Andrew Plummer had
seemed perfect, and he'd responded to the invitation to
come to New York with the correct degree of enthusiasm to
encourage Richard to feel he'd made the right choice. And
if it didn't immediately occur to him that he'd selected
Plummer precisely because the man seemed to have reached
the pinnacle to which his own strict upbringing, Columbia
education, and exacting parents had schooled Richard to
aspire, that was perhaps just as well. He'd so long ago been
convinced that a conservative outlook and stolid attitude
were appropriate for a man of business and infinitely more
suitable than the dashing and impetuous romantic he'd once
fancied he'd like to become, that he'd nearly forgotten he'd
ever acted—or wished to be—any other way. But he occasionally still found that he slipped without warning into a
pleasant daydream where his life was ruled by emotion
instead of only by common sense, and he now made an
effort to pull his thoughts back to the matter at hand.

Once Mr. Plummer was established, he reminded himself
briskly, he and the faithful Mrs. Booth could share the
remaining responsibilities between them and bring peace
again to the household. If the damned fellow would just
arrive, that is, Richard thought in irritation, beginning once
more to drum a march upon the chair with his fingers.

Indeed, his mind was so occupied by playing through the
first conversation he planned to have with Mr. Plummer,
that when his butler entered and advised him that a gentleman had come to call, Richard scarcely heard the name
announced in his haste to greet the tutor.

"Delighted!" he exclaimed, rising to pump his visitor's
hand vigorously. "Been expecting you for two days!"

"Then you did get my letter?" Lord Somers said in
relief. "Yes, we encountered a bit of a delay outside of
Philadelphia."

"Well, never mind, never mind," Richard said, urging
his guest toward a chair. "Let's begin at once, shall we?

Now, I thought we could start with a little Latin—maybe review one of Caesar's campaigns—before anything else.'' He tilted his head expectantly in the direction of his visitor.

Lord Somers appeared somewhat disconcerted by this suggestion. True, his host seemed normal enough: tall and dark, well dressed, with deep brown eyes and regular features that most people wouldn't have hesitated to call handsome. Still, his greeting had appeared so unrestrained, even to one used to the worst of sycophants, that it prompted his lordship to wonder what manner of intelligence lurked behind the man's imposing exterior and enviable good looks. "I'd have thought it would make more sense to begin with scientific theory," he offered carefully after a minute.

His host drew back and seemed to grow even taller in his chair, if that were possible. "I'm sure I don't see the slightest need for that sort of approach," he observed in a cold voice. "Leastways, not when dealing with children."

"With children—?" Lord Somers echoed, considerably taken aback at being so rudely identified. "Now, just a moment—"

"George and Caroline are not to be exposed to those ridiculous modern ideas," his host interrupted. "Especially not when anyone of sense knows that such things are simply tarradiddles."

There was a brief silence. "Who," Lord Somers asked at last, "are George and Caroline?"

"Why, my children, of course. See here, Plummer—"

"The name, I'm afraid, is Somers. Oh, I see—you've mistaken me for someone else," Lord Somers realized, as his host's remarks began to fall into place. "A tutor, perhaps? Well, awfully sorry to disappoint you. I'm Jonathan Somers. Came to see your waterworks—? I take it you didn't get my letter after all, then?" He watched his companion shake his head dumbly. "No matter—happy to explain," he offered, and promptly proceeded to do so.

His host's face turned a dusky red once he realized the full extent of the error he'd made. "But where's Plummer?" Richard wondered dazedly nevertheless. "He was to have arrived on the stage from Philadelphia."

Lord Somers brightened. "Would that be one Andrew

Plummer? Yes, I believe he did get on at Philadelphia. But the poor fellow didn't look at all well by the time we reached New York. I shouldn't wonder, you know, if he wasn't coming down with a touch of influenza,'' he confided. "But then, no doubt you'll be hearing from him shortly."

Richard Avery looked stunned at this new information. "You mean to tell me you took the stagecoach to the city yourself?" he said unsteadily. He gave himself a shake as if he were a spaniel emerging from a pond in what was clearly an attempt to rally his wits. "But how have you come to call on me here instead of at the Manhattan Company?" he asked more sensibly.

"Oh, they were kind enough to direct me to your house," Lord Somers explained, before adding somewhat apologetically, "I was rather insistent, you see. I'm afraid that I exhausted my patience on the journey to New York and was so eager to become acquainted with your amazing enterprise that I couldn't bear to wait even one more day before throwing myself on your hospitality. Indeed, my daughter often warns me that I shall be called to order for such unbridled enthusiasm."

At this point, Richard, who was inclined to feel some sympathy for this last remark, also began to feel enough like himself to ring for a reviving pot of coffee. "You're traveling with your family, I take it?" he asked politely. He poured out two cups and offered cream and sugar to his guest.

"In a manner of speaking," Lord Somers said, "since Jennifer is my only family. But then, she's such an invaluable companion that I sometimes tend to forget she's my daughter altogether and simply admire her for her resourcefulness and curiosity. I'm sure you'll agree that such qualities are ever to be cultivated in one's offspring—?"

"Oh, indeed—just as long as they're tempered by sufficient amounts of obedience and virtue," Richard said, as if reading from a well-rehearsed script about what children ought to be like. He hesitated, conscious of a fleeting and unreasonable desire to press his guest for more information about his own unlikely sounding daughter. "But come now—perhaps we should turn to what it is you wish to learn about our water system and leave this elevated discussion for another time," he urged politely instead. Whereupon, Lord Somers, needing no further encouragement, pulled his chair closer and began to speak.

At approximately the same time as Lord Somers was bending his host's ear, Jennifer was endeavoring to make use of the very qualities for which he had so recently commended her. She was perched on the window seat in her room observing the street scene below and considering how best to deal with the matter of finding a companion. Not that she should actually be required to do anything about it at all, she admitted, since before her father had departed he'd announced his intention of seeking assistance from the hotel management in locating a suitable person to act as her maid. The problem was, whomever they suggested was bound to be someone infintely proper and just as equally dull, Jennifer thought glumly. It wasn't even that she objected to the custom that required ladies to be accompanied on their various outings. In fact, although she was fairly unconventional in her thoughts and actions in private, when in public she saw no need to ride roughshod over accepted modes of behavior merely for the sake of doing so. For one thing, it seemed to her that such blatant flaunting of socie-ty's dictums served only to land one promptly in the center of attention, thus making it harder than before to do as one wished. Therefore, she was accustomed to keeping her own counsel regarding her feelings about such rules—much as she'd learned to do with her other emotions as well. And for another thing, she'd long ago discerned from her father's example that one shouldn't be in a rush to dismiss all rules wholesale without first attempting to determine if there wasn't some sensible reason for the rule's existence in the first place—that reason often providing the key to how to circumvent the rule itself.

Thank heavens, for instance, that Lord Somers had seen easily through the tradition barring ladies from acquiring a serious education in the expectation that they should get married and therefore have no need to use any sort of esoteric learning to support either themselves or their fami-lies. But suppose, he'd postulated as he presented his daughter with a copy of Ovid, that she didn't marry? And even supposing that she did, he had to confess that he failed to see anything inconsistent between developing one's mind and learning how to get on in the world. After all, he'd reasoned, learning how to think could just as easily be applied to the difficulties of running a household as to those, say, of exporting woolens—could it not?

Now, Jennifer knew perfectly well that behind the admonition not to venture on the town unescorted lay the fact that the city streets were dangerous to men and women alike from thieves, pickpockets, and all manner of others ready to prey on the unsuspecting. Then, too, a lady also had to guard against an attack on her virtue that might be avoided by traveling tandem. And from what she'd seen so far, both rationales seemed to make as much sense in New York as they did in London. But even as this thought occurred to her, Jennifer was pulling a green velvet spencer with a white silk collar over her frock and covering her curls with a matching bonnet. Surely there wouldn't be any harm in walking over to nearby Trinity Church for just a few minutes, she told herself. Besides, she'd been mewed up in her room the entire morning and needed some fresh air to clear her brain.

Slipping quietly down the stairs, Jennifer gained the door of the hotel and turned the corner onto Thames Street without being stopped or questioned. Her black slippers crunched a few early fall leaves as she swung open the iron gate at the entrance to the church's graveyard and began wandering among the tumbled stones. If she had to be chaperoned by someone, at least she'd want the woman to be a familiar of the real city, she decided, her mind returning of its own accord to its earlier cogitations. Someone who knew its secret byways intimately and could share its hidden stories with her. She paused to peer at the inscription on one of the newer grave markers. And if she had to choose, she'd prefer her companion to have a sense of humor and not be afraid to speak her mind—traits, she admitted wryly, that she possessed in no small measure herself and valued equally highly in others.

"Watch where you're stepping," a voice warned, breaking abruptly into Jennifer's thoughts. She turned to see a strange girl about her own age frowning heavily at her across the graveyard. "That's Mr. Hamilton's grave you're trodding on," the girl told her. "Killed in a duel he was, you know. Now, if it was that damned Burr who shot him you was walking over, I wouldn't give a fig. Mr. Hamilton was a real gentleman, though—refused so much as to take aim! And then what does that slyboots Burr do but shoot him through the heart just the same! Well, I fancy that's what comes of being properly raised. But if you ask me, Hamilton was a bobbing-block himself to think good manners any way to deal with a certified lowlife like Burr!"

Jennifer hesitated, caught between marveling at how often Mr. Burr's name seemed to crop up and wishing to know more about the speaker herself. She walked toward where the girl leaned against the fence along Broadway. The latter was dressed in a white cotton chemise covered by an apron, her pale blond hair crowned by a mobcap. Next to her stood a little cart on which sat a few baskets of late strawberries.

"Are you selling those?" Jennifer asked unnecessarily, pointing at a basket in an attempt to prolong the conversation. The girl had a remarkably plain face, she noted. Still, the gleam in the brown eyes that now seemed to be regarding her in a measuring way gave promise of more than ordinary intelligence.

"Yes, indeed, miss," the girl answered in a tone of exaggerated patience. "Girls pushing carts on the streets are generally in the business of selling something," she pointed out in deliberate accents. "This week it's berries, next week maybe melons, and another time pears."

"And how is—business?"

"Right enough, considering a powerful lot of fools still think fruits and vegetables are poison. It always seems the cholera comes to the city when this stuff's around, you see." The girl stopped for a minute to rub her upper lip with a stubby finger before saying slowly, "Though I think it must be from the sludge everyone uses for washing. Why, the whole world knows bad water brings on sickness."

Jennifer, who'd never thought much about it one way or another before, now paused to consider the matter. "I daresay you may be right," she said thoughtfully. "But what do you do in the wintertime when there isn't any fruit, if I may ask?"

"Oh, sometimes I sell tea or chocolate or try to get a place somewhere cleaning rooms or as a maid for a while." The girl jerked her head in the direction of the City Hotel.

This information caused something to fall neatly into place in Jennifer's brain. "Do you mind if I ask your name?" she said after a moment.

"What's to mind? Ask away, if you like. It's Molly— Molly Danhope."

"Pleased to meet you, Molly. I'm Jennifer Somers, and I believe I may have a little proposition to set before you," Jennifer began eagerly. "My father and I are visiting New York for several months, perhaps for the whole winter. We're staying at the hotel for the moment, though we may lease a house if we stay very long. My father is here on business, you see. Unfortunately, we didn't spare a thought as to how I should manage while he's engaged. What I mean is, I need someone who can accompany me around town—someone who knows the city like her own house and how to get by in it. Well, it occurs to me that you'd be perfect for the role! You could share my room, like a maid, and I'd see you got a fair salary. Of course, I'm not altogether sure how much such a person ought to be paid, but I promise to find out immediately. Why, whatever's the matter?" she asked in dismay as Molly began to shake her head back and forth. "I thought you said you needed to find employment for the winter, didn't you?"

"I may be a bit down on my luck, but I'm not about to hire out as someone's personal servant," Molly objected, setting her thin lips into a firm line.

"But you wouldn't really be my servant—you'd be more of a companion," Jennifer corrected hastily. "I only said 'like a maid' because that's what other people will naturally assume that you are. Between ourselves, however, we can agree that you're not to tend to me in the least—besides, I hate such fussing!—and that we'll be on as equal terms as possible. Well, what do you think?" she urged when the girl still didn't answer.

In response, Molly shot another calculating look at her. "I think there's something havey-cavey about all this," she said bluntly at last. "Appears to me the hotel would be happy to supply you with a proper maid. Strikes me as crackbrained that you'd want to go hire some girl you'd never met until today off the street instead.''

"But that's just it—I don't want a 'proper maid,'" Jennifer said in exasperation. "I want someone who won't always be throwing a damper on my plans."

"Only wish I could be sure you're not touched in your upper works," Molly muttered under her breath. "Still, one penny's as good as another, I suppose," she continued as if to herself. "All right—I'll do it! And you may give me a little blunt on account—to buy a few clothes and such," she directed, holding out a hand.

"Capital!" Jennifer exclaimed happily. She opened her reticule and stuffed whatever bills it contained at Molly, either feeling she was trustworthy enough—or herself desperate enough—to take such a risk. "And you'll join us for dinner at three, then, after my father—" She broke off.

Molly looked calmly at her new employer. "Forgot about him, didn't you?" she noted with some pleasure. "Appears to me you have the harder task. I've merely to look the part—you've to convince him that I'm the one you need for the job."

"Oh, poof!" Jennifer attempted, wrinkling her brow a little all the same. "Leave it to me to come up with some shift or other."

"My pleasure," Molly told her in all sincerity.

A good thirty minutes before the appointed hour, Jennifer sat in her room awaiting Molly's arrival. Or rather, she was waiting to see if the girl showed up at all, she admitted silently, as she crossed to the window for the third time and peered up and down the street. Not that she thought she'd been wrong in arranging for Molly to enter her employ. It was just that the agreement had been struck hastily, and it had only occurred to her later that she'd neglected to learn such important information as the details about Molly's background and family, for instance. Why, she wasn't even sure of her age, Jennifer realized with a start. Any one of these matters might be reason enough for her father to reject her choice. And despite her self-possessed air and decisive manner, she was well aware that the decisions she made with such outward ease were usually the result of long and careful deliberation.

Needless to say, Jennifer was a good deal relieved when a knock on the door interrupted this train of thought. Opening it, she discovered Molly standing on the threshold with a small case beside her. What's more, the girl looked every inch the well-bred companion. Her clothes were a slightly simpler version of Jennifer's own: a striped cotton dress, muslin cap with tippet and attached collar, a reticule with a single tassel, and black slippers. And she wore those new garments as easily as if they were her usual garb, for if truth be told, she'd been raised in a properly genteel fashion in a household whose main difficulties had been monetary—not moral—in nature. As if she understood exactly what was passing through Jennifer's mind, Molly now tilted her head to one side and asked, "Will I do?"

"Admirably!" Jennifer exclaimed, practically pulling her into the room. "This shall be your couch, and you may put your things in the wardrobe over there." She curled into a chair and watched Molly unpack her clothing and necessities and lay them out in an unhurried fashion. "Are you always so calm?" she asked curiously after a few minutes.

"Most often. Never did see the need for dashing about. And fretting doesn't ever seem to improve on things either, does it?"

"No," Jennifer admitted, seeing the sense of this observation even though, in contrast, she knew she appeared to have a far more impulsive nature than Molly. "Shall we join my father, then?" she asked at last. "I believe he's already descended."

Lord Somers was indeed seated at one of the long common tables in the dining room. These were shared by the hotel's guests and whichever of the city's men of business had chosen to partake of the simple fare that day. This arrangement suited his lordship to perfection, since at every meal he was thus thrown cheek by jowl next to someone new and could spend his time happily feeding his endless curiosity about people and things. This afternoon, however, he planned to devote himself to making the acquaintance of his daughter's new companion.

Their introduction was momentarily halted by the arrival

of the food. Dinner at the City Hotel consisted of at least a dozen plainly cooked dishes that might on any day include venison, wild turkey, duck, lobster, crabs, oysters, and pigeon. These were accompanied by local vegetables and fruits, and everything was offered in large serving dishes from which the guests helped themselves.

Lord Somers handed a platter of boiled potatoes across the table to Molly and smiled at her in a friendly fashion. Now, when Jennifer had presented her father as "Lord Somers," Molly had been momentarily taken aback. But she'd hidden her surprise beneath the clatter of the china, save for raising an eyebrow at Jennifer and whispering, "Something else you forgot about?" It wasn't that she was afraid of the gentry either, since her own upbringing had been happily beyond reproach, only that like most people in America, she held the upper class a little in awe. Still, she thought to herself as she examined his lordship's face, he looked ordinary enough—almost simple, some would say— not pompous or condescending, and his easy acceptance of her was certainly encouraging. In fact, Molly, who was a long way from simple herself, had just begun to wonder how much he knew of the circumstances surrounding her hiring when Lord Somers chose to broach that subject himself.

"Jennifer tells me she met you outside the churchyard," he began politely. "Were you enjoying an outing in the city, too?"

Clearly his lordship hadn't yet been told very much, Molly realized. She toyed for a moment with a piece of beef on her plate, glanced briefly at Jennifer for support, and then deciding there was no help for it, plunged in. "No." She shook her head. "I was selling strawberries," she said, hoping Lord Somers was a man who appreciated plain speaking.

"Oh, then you're a street vendor?" he asked. His lordship, Molly noted, not only appeared nonplussed by this news but actually looked a good deal more intrigued than he had a few moments before. "Fascinating work, I should think," he continued, casting what she was startled to note could only be called an envious look at her. "Why, I warrant you must see all manner of extraordinary things."

Molly nodded. Then, like many before her who'd been exposed to Lord Somers's gentle probing and genuine interest, she found herself opening up further. "I'm half English myself," she offered. "My dad was an officer who came over to fight in the Uprising and then stayed on after. I guess we got to be too much for him, though—there's five of us, you see. Anyhow, he took off for the Western Territories a couple years back." She shrugged her shoulders in her calm way. "Guess he's still out there somewhere. Leastways, we haven't heard so much as a peep from him since."

"And I take it you weren't exactly trained to seek any meaningful employment, of course, so you began selling fruit to bring in a little money?" Lord Somers asked. "And a very useful service such people provide, too. Only this morning I learned that water vendors fill their hogsheads at the Tea Water Pump and then peddle the stuff around town for a penny a gallon. Why, I'm confident that anyone resourceful enough to pursue such a profession would be exactly the sort of person I'd want as my daughter's companion." He smiled impartially from Jennifer to Molly and then back again. "Indeed, it seems a capital arrangement all around. Now tell me—have you decided where you'll begin your explorations?"

"We haven't yet had time to consider," Jennifer confessed, wondering why she'd ever doubted that her father would readily accept her choice of attendant. "I think I should like to walk around a bit to start—perhaps along Broadway and a few of the others streets. And what are your plans?"

"I believe Avery said tomorrow he'd take me to see The Collect—that's the freshwater pond where most of the city's drinking water comes from. The Manhattan Company has sunk a well nearby and built a reservoir to store the water."

Molly sniffed. "Wouldn't exactly call it drinkable, though," she said. "There's plenty of people none too happy with the stuff they try to pass off as fit to use. Then, too, there's days when you'll be forced to go without any water altogether because of trouble with the pipes or some such nonsense." She turned toward Jennifer. "You recall my saying that I thought dirty water brought on sickness? Well, there's a lot of folks who think the last dose of yellow fever was caused by bad water supplied by the Manhattan Company. Did your Mr. Avery think to mention that, I wonder?''

"No," Lord Somers admitted. "But the poor fellow wasn't himself, after all. When I first arrived, he mistook me for the tutor he was expecting! I gather his household's been in a bit of a tear lately, and that's proving a distraction. Still, he strikes me as the sort who usually prides himself on never losing control. Very proper, you know—quite tediously so," he confided. "Why, I'm dashed if I could discover a single particle of humor in the man. Wonder what his children are like? Must be devilishly hard on the little brats, him being a widower," he mused, before calling himself to order once again. "Still, I suppose the state of his family's nothing to the point. Seemed an intelligent enough fellow, nevertheless. Said he'd even put his mind to thinking about what else I should see now that I'm in America."

"Then it looks as if we've both spent the day in a profitable fashion," Jennifer observed. She helped herself to a baked pear. Then, holding her spoon up and waving it about like a flag, she said, "And I, for one, am perfectly confident that things will continue to go off without a hitch."

True to Jennifer's prediction, nothing untoward occurred in the next week to mar either her pleasure or that of her father. Indeed, the two dedicated themselves separately, but with equal diligence, to becoming devotees of New York. Their days soon fell into a satisfying pattern. After breakfasting together, Jennifer and Molly would set off on their explorations and Lord Somers would deliver himself into Mr. Avery's hands, ready to prove accommodating to that gentleman's program for the day. Then the three would reassemble at the hotel later in the afternoon, at which time they would take the opportunity to share their impressions of the city and its inhabitants.

They were thus happily engaged the following Friday. Jennifer had just finished pouring out tea for everyone in their private sitting room and was nibbling on a slice of poppyseed cake. "I declare I must by now be a hardened nationalist, for truly, I find this to be the most amazing town,'' she exclaimed happily, trying to review in her mind everything she'd seen in the preceding five days. ''Of course, it's the contrasts we see that I think must be primarily responsible for my good feelings. Why, one day we walked the entire length of Broadway to the old stone bridge over the canal, and beyond there was nothing much at all save a few farms and some apple orchards. Yet at this end of the street, there are numerous stately houses and fashionable shops marching one after another down the west side and soon, apparently, up the east side as well.''

Jennifer paused to wash down the cake with a few sips from her steaming cup. ''Do you know,'' she continued thoughtfully after a moment, ''I've decided that nearly everything one needs can be found on the streets themselves.'' She smiled at Molly. ''Why, along with people selling fruit or water there are others hawking oysters or clams, hot gingerbread, sweet potatoes, and buttermilk. And whatever the vendors don't offer from their pushcarts you can usually find in one of the public markets. I've seen chimney sweeps soliciting customers and a man offering cattails and other marsh grasses for stuffing mattresses, and I've watched someone named Potpye Palmer compete with the pigs by hauling away garbage in his cart. I understand that even important business dealings are sometimes conducted on the streets! Apparently there's a buttonwood tree on Wall Street where Molly tells me men used to gather to buy and trade public stocks, although now they conduct their business mostly at a nearby coffeehouse.''

Indeed, both Jennifer and her father had had numerous occasions already to applaud the day Molly had joined their little family. It was she who'd pointed out the elegant house facing Hanover Square that had belonged to the infamous Captain Kidd before he was sent to England to be tried and hanged for piracy. It was Molly who knew that the first paving stones in the city had been laid in Stone Street because a Dutch brewer's wife had objected to the dust raised by passing wagons. And it was also she who could name the King's Arms as the tavern that had served as

Benedict Arnold's quarters after he'd deserted the American cause.

There appeared to be only one limitation to Molly's endless store of knowledge. She'd never been outside the main populated area of the city concentrated on the southern tip of the island. The stone bridge that she and Jennifer had visited marked the northern boundary of her travels. Lacking the money and the means to do so, she'd never ventured up to Manhattan-ville near the Harlem River, for instance, or seen Greenwich, where those who were able fled to avoid the epidemics that swept through New York with unfortunate regularity.

Those particular outlying districts were presently on Lord Somers's mind. That morning, Richard Avery had described the latest scheme the Common Council had devised for the development of Manhattan. "This new plan will mean a lot of changes for the city—and apparently for the Manhattan Company as well, if they're to continue to supply the city's drinking water," his lordship explained. "You see, they mean to divide all the rest of the island above Fourteenth Street into rectangular blocks separated by wide avenues running north to south, some even extending as far as Harlem."

Jennifer twirled one of her curls slowly around a finger as she was prone to do when thinking deeply about a particular subject. "It doesn't sound very humane somehow to cut everything up into neat little boxes," she objected at last. "I prefer things in a bit of a jumble myself. Still, I suppose there will be parks and places for people to walk and enjoy the view of the rivers?"

Lord Somers shook his head. "Not more than five parks are indicated, I believe. Now, Avery told me there was an earlier plan that provided for many more squares and plazas and included a broad promenade sweeping the island's perimeter so as to guarantee that the riverbanks would be retained for the use of pedestrains—like cities on the Continent, you know. For some reason, though, the first plan was set aside and this man John Randel was hired to come up with a new one."

"Only five parks—? But whatever are people to do?" Jennifer asked.

Molly sniffed loudly. "Have Randel brought up on charges of trespassing, for one thing. Happens every time he tries to finish his survey work," she said with considerable satisfaction. "So often, in fact, that the Council finally had to pass a law saying that he had to be allowed to enter a person's property."

"Won't do much good in the long haul, I expect," Lord Somers put in. He tilted back in his chair and stared thoughtfully at the ceiling. "Things are changing in New York. Why, they've even started to drain The Collect by enlarging the present canal and extending it all the way from the East River to the Hudson. It's nearly filled in already. Too bad, too. Avery said when he was a boy he used to go fishing on it in summer and skating on it in winter. He and his pals even used to dream about taking canoes and paddling along the canal, since it was rumored to be navigable the entire way."

Molly nodded her head knowingly. "That ain't the only rumor about The Collect," she confided. "It's also supposed to be home for several hideous sea monsters that like to carry off unsuspecting people who wander too close. No one even knows how deep it is. One time, during the Revolution, a strange creature was said to have risen up and snatched a Hessian soldier right off the bank! My dad even insisted he'd seen it once, but then he was probably in his cups like all the other folk who claim likewise. Anyway, I always thought that those were just stories to scare children and keep them respectful and all."

Jennifer laughed. "Oh, I'm sure Mr. Avery would never resort to such tactics with his children. But then," she allowed, turning toward her father, "you seem to have discovered another side to the man at last, wouldn't you say?"

"Yes," Lord Somers agreed. "At any rate, he seems to have had the same wild fancies as any normal child. And yet, at first I'd have assured you that the man had never been a boy at all, since to all appearances he's now nothing but a right stickler. Yes, he's a strange fish, to be sure. But then, you'll soon have the opportunity to judge for yourself," he told his daughter. "Mr. Avery has invited the two of us to take Sunday dinner with him."

"Indeed? Ah, but then doubtless Mr. Avery thinks extending such an invitation to strangers in the city the only proper thing to do," Jennifer said, her eyes twinkling. "Nevertheless, I shall look forward to it with pleasure, I promise. And you may be sure I mean to discover, if I can, whatever became of that young hopeful who dreamt about adventuring in a canoe."

Chapter 3

B Y MID-AFTERNOON on Sunday, Richard Avery would have been delighted to set off to sea in whatever manner of craft he could call to hand—anything, in fact, but have to admit that he still hadn't solved the problem of what to do about his children. He simply wasn't used to feeling so altogether powerless, he thought, as he selected a neck cloth. Though it was that damned fellow Andrew Plummer who was mainly to blame, he reminded himself. Two days after Lord Somers's first visit to him, and true to that gentleman's predictions, Richard had finally received a note from the tutor. He was most dreadfully ill, Plummer had written, and was now being bled for the third time in the hope of stemming off the development of brain fever. In addition, he'd continued, he'd rapidly come to the conclusion that the air in the city was decidedly unhealthy and that he'd best return to Philadelphia as soon as possible if he wanted to retain even a shred of his health. He was frightfully sorry to have to turn down Mr. Avery's very kind offer after all, but what other choice did he have?

Richard stepped back impatiently to survey his appearance in the mirror: clawhammer tailcoat of gray-blue cloth, buff waistcoat and breeches, plain white cambric shirt, and low-heeled black shoes. What choice indeed, he fumed, giving his watch fob a sharp tug. Why, it was outrageous that he should feel at sixes and sevens, as Mrs. Booth had phrased it, over such a simple matter. If truth be told, however, Richard wasn't aware of feeling anything other than at a standstill lately when it came to George and Caroline. And that was certainly a confusing development, since he'd originally wanted children with a fierceness that had taken him completely by surprise. It was only after his wife had died of yellow fever, leaving the babies solely in his care, that he'd discovered what an enormous gulf lay between loving someone and being able to express that sentiment freely.

In fact, it wasn't until long after she'd been claimed by the same epidemic that had taken his parents that Richard had been able to admit he hadn't strictly loved his wife. He'd been extremely fond of her, of course, but theirs had been a marriage arranged for the mutual convenience of two families, rather than a match born of a great passion between two people. Richard draped the snowy neck cloth around his collar and then began to twist it expertly into a firm knot. Indeed, if someone had asked, he'd have had to confess that he shrank from strong emotions of any kind, Richard thought, his fingers slowing. And it wasn't that he'd ever actually ceased to feel, but rather he'd recognized that the expression of feelings—by himself or anyone else— left him feeling confused and vulnerable. But somehow he'd moved from a reluctance to display his emotions to an unwillingness to acknowledge them at all, so that his manner had by this time become the stiff mask that had prompted Lord Somers to term him a right stickler. All that remained on the surface was an unwavering sense of rectitude, beneath which simmered a warm, loving nature which he appeared to be having increasing difficulty associating with himself.

Not that anyone could claim he hadn't discharged his responsibilities as far as the twins were concerned, for example, Richard told himself now, giving his neck cloth a last adjustment. Why, he'd given them every advantage he'd thought they ought to enjoy. But it was as if every time he made a decision for their supposed benefit, based on the way he thought things ought to be, they drew a little farther away from him. Oh, there was no question about whether or not they were dutiful children who treated him with the respect owed a father—of that he was certain. He was far less certain, though, if they even knew he cared for them, since he found himself singularly unable to demonstrate that fact. And what was worse, he hadn't the least idea if there was any love lost for him beneath their dutiful demeanor. Sometimes he could very nearly imagine they appeared to be afraid of him, and yet he hadn't any desire to encourage that attitude.

Richard exited his bedroom and slowly crossed to the sitting room to await his guests. He was certain that Lord Somers would never have encountered that situation with his own child. Why, the man had to be the least pretentious fellow he'd ever met. The one afternoon they'd happened across the twins on their way to the schoolroom, his lordship had shaken George's hand, bowed to Caroline, and then immediately offered to take them for a drive to Rickett's Amphitheatre to see a circus performance. Richard had only been able to stand aside—stiff and self-conscious as usual—while his guest treated his children as if he'd known them forever. And how the devil had his lordship, after only a few days in New York, managed to hear of an entertainment that he knew nothing about? Of course, even had he known, he wouldn't necessarily have consented to allowing the twins to attend, much less actually thought to take them there himself. Still, it was clear that Lord Somers possessed the very knack of easy acquaintance that he would dearly love to acquire, and Richard felt himself beginning to wonder whether his daughter shared the same skill and what other facets of her character he might soon discover.

Curiously enough, Jennifer's mind was turning in a remarkably similar direction. She and her father were seated in a hired hack for the short drive to Richard Avery's house in Wall Street. This convention Lord Somers had for once insisted upon in deference to the occasion, if not to their host's preference for form above all things. Her first glimpse of his house certainly supported the notion that Mr. Avery put a great deal of store in appearances. Either that or he was a secret lover of beautiful things, Jennifer mused—a trait that hardly seemed to fit the impression she'd drawn of him to date. No. 30 Wall Street was three stories high, well proportioned, and built in a lovely Greek Revival style, with a marble façade and a central doorway topped by a pediment surmounted by four graceful columns.

Father and daughter were admitted at once by the butler and led up the stairs to meet their host. Everything was precisely as she'd imagined it would be, Jennifer noted amusedly, from the Sheraton chairs in the hallway to the portraits by Joshua Reynolds on the wall. It was almost as if someone had determined what was necessary to furnish a house in the first style and then had simply ordered the appropriate number of items. There wasn't a single personal touch anywhere that she could see, nor anything even a hair out of place that might offer a clue to the character of the building's inhabitants.

No, she reconsidered. There was an untidy bowl of wild roses on a pedestal table in the room that had either been arranged by an inexpert hand or by someone conscious of the same lack of individuality she'd already noted. Jennifer was momentarily distracted by wondering who that mysterious person might be when she was brought back to the present by her father's voice.

"Allow me to present my daughter Jennifer," Lord Somers was saying.

"Charmed," Richard Avery murmured, bowing politely over her hand before motioning them to be seated.

Jennifer settled gratefully into a chair. At least now they were on eye level so she wouldn't have to get a crick in her neck by conversing with a man who towered easily three-quarters of a foot above her. Their host's attire was as fashionable as his residence, she observed. Nevertheless, it seemed to her that he wore his clothes as impersonally as if they were some kind of uniform. And yet, she admitted, if he acted even half as self-possessed as he looked, the combination would be altogether devastating. He was certainly handsome enough to carry it off, she thought, taking in the way his dark hair curled attractively over his forehead and the tiny, disarming cleft in his chin. And how was it that her father had overlooked mentioning that important fact to her? But then, thinking this a business arrangement, he'd probably judged it of no account, she decided in a burst of generosity. And could it be that Mr. Avery only seemed ill at ease at the moment precisely because she was staring at him in such a very ill-bred fashion? That possibility having been admitted, she moved at once to see if she couldn't rectify the situation.

"You certainly have a lovely house, sir," she told her host, smiling at him in a way that made her emerald eyes seem to sparkle.

Richard, who'd indeed been unable to keep from shifting uncomfortably under Jennifer's steady gaze, now relaxed a trifle. "Thank you," he acknowledged politely. "I must admit that it appears to suit my needs very well. Actually, I believe it's one of the oldest houses in the city," he informed his guests as he regained a little of his confidence. Why, dashed if he was going to let some tiny slip of a girl make a cake out of him in his own home just by looking sideways at him, he vowed silently. Even if she was the most gorgeous thing he'd been fortunate enough to lay eyes on in the last twelvemonth—with that incredible red hair and a figure that was ridiculous on such a little woman but which no doubt made men at once itch to gather her into their arms. Good heavens, he corrected hastily, whatever was he about, thinking of a lady he'd only just met in such an unlikely manner? "It used to belong to a Dutch family named Vandervoot—one of the two hundred richest families in New York in those days—though naturally I've had the whole thing redone to suit the current styles," he went on, in an attempt to channel his thoughts in a more suitable direction. He paused to study Jennifer's fashionable Regency dress: a high-waisted affair finished at the throat with a collar cut in points and rising above slightly padded shoulders trimmed with epaulets and long, tight-fitting sleeves. "I can see that you, Lady Somers, are clearly a woman who appreciates the necessity of keeping à la mode," he observed pointedly. He settled back in his chair to observe the effect of this jab, feeling rather pleased at his recovery and at the same time alternately irritated and intrigued by the woman who'd obliged him to exert such effort.

Now, Jennifer greatly disliked being referred to as Lady Somers, since most people tended to treat the title as if it had more importance than the person who possessed it. What's more, she'd chosen her gown precisely in the hope of mocking the tendency of certain individuals to accept outward appearance in place of the substance of a thing itself. She favored Richard Avery with a second, closer look. Possibly there was more to the man than she'd initially thought, she realized, feeling unaccountably cheered by that notion, far more charitably disposed toward her host, and already curious to learn what the outcome of yet another round might reveal about him. Luckily for all present, perhaps, Lord Somers chose that moment to inquire whether they weren't to meet the twins.

"Yes, indeed," Richard said. "I arranged with Mrs. Booth to have them ready when you arrived."

Why, he refers to them as if they were pieces of meat to be inspected before purchase instead of flesh-and-blood creatures, Jennifer realized in disappointment. Still, she admitted a few minutes later as the twins entered silently, he wasn't far wrong, since they seemed utterly unlike real children at all. They were attractive enough little things, with their matching blond curls, blue eyes, and sturdy bodies. For a moment, she even imagined she detected a hint of devilry in one twin's eyes and a set of dimples on the other. But that suspicion vanished as soon as their father started to speak. What poor solemn brats they are, Jennifer thought, examining the boy's formal double-breasted suit and the girl's plain cotton frock with its tired satin sash.

"Lady Somers, I'd like you to meet my children—George and Caroline," Richard Avery said. "Now, come and say how do you do," he directed them.

As if they were babies, Jennifer thought, rather taken aback by a discovery she'd so often made in regard to herself. And was that a look that seemed to echo her opinion flashing between the twins? "Oh, lovely!" she exclaimed a minute later as Caroline stepped forward and thrust a scarlet rose at her in one chubby fist. "Was this your own idea?" she asked in a gentle voice. The girl raised her head just long enough to nod shyly before dropping her eyes back down to watch one foot nudge a bird in the design of the Aubusson carpet. "And are you also responsible for the charming flower arrangment?"

"Mrs. Booth helped," George piped up. "But I cut 'em and Caro stuck 'em in place. We had ever so many more, but they wouldn't all fit," he offered. He and Jennifer both turned to consider the bowl on the table, which was, in fact, noticeably overcrowded.

"No doubt you'll do better next time," Richard advised. *There, now I've done it again,* he realized with an inward groan as the children shrank back at this criticism. *And yet I don't mean to be so harsh. In fact, I feel quite differently—it just somehow comes out as orders about what the twins ought to do or how they should behave. No wonder my manner puts them off,* he admitted sadly. "Away with you two upstairs for your dinner, then," he suggested in a kinder tone.

This time, Jennifer saw a look pass unmistakably between the two children. "Please, sir, may we eat in the back room with Mrs. Booth instead?" George asked, planting his feet solidly apart as if to gather courage for this request. *So that's who their ally is in the house,* Jennifer noted.

"Very well," their father agreed. "But see that you're both on your best behavior, and mind you don't get in her way," he couldn't forebear adding. "And straight to bed afterward—is that understood?"

The children nodded in unison and then quickly sketched their good-byes before escaping in what Jennifer would have been prompt to describe as a relieved manner. Good heavens—if he wasn't talking to them as if they were still in leading strings, he was ordering them about as if they were little martinets, she thought, turning around once again to examine her host. But surely it was unusual for a parent to switch back and forth that way, wasn't it? Could it be that he didn't really know how to treat them at all, she wondered. "It's too bad the children aren't going to be dining with us," she observed, having immediately decided to test the waters. "I was quite looking forward to getting to know them a little. Aren't you in the habit of taking your meals together with them?''

Richard regarded her in surprise. ''But surely that's not appropriate? At least, not when company's present. Ordinarily, of course, they'd have their meals in the schoolroom with their governess.''

''I'm afraid Jennifer was used to somewhat different treatment,'' Lord Somers admitted. ''After my wife died, you see, I was loathe to be left too much alone, and I found her babyish chattering to be a distraction at first, and then later a comfort. Still,'' he said companionably to his host, ''I scarcely think such a breach of etiquette could be considered more than a simple peccadillo—do you?''

Fortunately, perhaps, the other gentleman was spared the necessity of answering this question by the arrival of the butler to announce that dinner was served. Shortly thereafter, the three were seated in the rather severe dining room, enjoying the first course of what turned out to be an altogether elaborate meal.

Jennifer took a sip of bouillon. ''I take it you named your children after the Prince and Princess of Wales?'' she asked politely. Richard nodded. ''Indeed, I warrant the Prince Regent is judged by many to be an outstanding model of a certain kind of behavior,'' she continued somewhat ambiguously. ''Are you, then, a lover of all things British?''

''For the most part,'' Richard admitted. He laid down his spoon—the better, apparently, to regard her earnestly before asking, ''Surely you'll admit that the English constitution is the most perfect ever devised?''

''Why, how odd that you should think so—particularly when one might say that your own country went to war against that same document in order, supposedly, to establish a better one,'' she observed. ''Indeed, I have to own that I've already proven myself a ready convert to the American cause, because I find this country a complete marvel. And besides,'' she added, in an effort to inject a little humor into the situation, ''you don't mean to pretend that it isn't a French chef—and not an English one—that you've got hidden away in the kitchen? I'm positive this couldn't be the product of one of *my* countrymen, after all,'' she said, waving her arm in the direction of the dishes covering the table.

''Tush, Jennifer,'' her father cautioned quietly. He helped himself to some chicken in cream sauce and a generous portion of marrow pudding. ''Why, Prinny himself has a frog for a cook,'' he offered, nicely confirming his daughter's suspicion that that practice, too, was one their host sought to imitate. ''And at any rate, the Americans don't follow our lead in all things. Why, they're years ahead of us in the development of this water system, for instance. How much pipe was it you told me your company has laid so far?''

Richard waved a dish of beef collops aside before replying proudly, ''More than twenty-five miles. And I believe we now supply water to almost three thousand families.'' He turned toward Jennifer to gauge the effect of his statement, and promptly became distracted by admiring the way the light from the chandelier made her red curls look positively aflame.

''Indeed? And what do your customers think of your service?'' she inquired in an interested voice. ''Are they one and all happy with your product, I wonder?'' She picked up her crystal water glass and held it up to the light, studying it for a long moment before deliberately taking a small, considering sip.

Richard had to admit that he wasn't feeling altogether unaffected by the sight of the lovely woman seated opposite him. And though he'd earlier been quick to discount her as a mere slip of a girl, that same youthful energy held its own attraction to someone who'd become accustomed to a more stolid existence. That fact, coupled with what he'd been just as quick to conclude was a genuine—and very flattering— curiosity about his business affairs, encouraged him at this point to answer a good deal more candidly than he might have otherwise.

''Naturally there have been problems from time to time,'' he admitted, returning Jennifer's level gaze with one of his own. ''We haven't yet perfected the type of bored-wood pipe we employ to carry the water, for one thing. But even so, I think the system we've devised must be preferable to the one Joseph Browne proposed.'' He looked at Lord Somers but continued to speak as if framing his words for Jennifer's benefit. ''As I may already have told you, Dr. Browne suggested damming the Bronx River and then pumping the water into reservoirs built on the north end of Manhattan. The trouble is, the people who need the water all live at the other end of the island, and his scheme would have necessitated laying many more miles of pipe than we have at present. And the more pipe, the more problems, as I'm sure you can appreciate.''

The arrival of the second course brought a brief hiatus to the conversation. After recommending the scalloped oysters and mutton ragout in particular, Richard helped himself to some of those same dishes before continuing. ''But there's another idea that may prove the best of them all,'' he said, pushing a carrot around on his plate before popping it into his mouth and chewing thoughtfully. ''I don't believe I mentioned it yet, but there's a movement that started about six years back that advocates building a canal from Albany to connect to Lake Erie at Buffalo. It would open up a major navigable east-west water route and also allow the waters to drain into the Hudson River and, thus, to New York City. The mayor, De Witt Clinton, and several others propose—''

''A canal?'' Lord Somers interrupted, laying down his fork and leaning forward excitedly. ''Now, that's more like it! We've a few of our own started in England, you know, though they're nothing much to speak of yet. The Regent's Canal Company.'' He gave a disparaging snort that might have been meant as a laugh. ''A bunch of unskilled nobodies who don't understand the first rudiments of engineering! But this plan for a canal from Lake Erie sounds as if it has the makings of a proper enterprise!''

By this point, despite her earlier and rather harsh assessment of how Richard Avery treated his children, Jennifer had to admit that she'd found the man to be a good deal more intriguing than she'd expected. And though it would have been easy to have let herself be swayed in his favor on account of his looks—precisely as she supposed many men tended to have been with her—the contradictions she'd already perceived in him were what had mainly captured her interest and made her feel compelled to learn more about him. "And what do you think of Mayor Clinton's proposal?" she therefore inquired now.

Richard considered the question for a moment before replying. "I think it would ultimately prove beneficial to commerce," he said at last in his stiff fashion. "And being a businessman, of course, I support whatever will most effectively serve to stimulate trade."

Jennifer looked a little more respectfully at the speaker for the neat way in which, purposefully or not, he'd avoided answering her question directly. "Given your support of trade, your preference for formality—shall we say?—and your opinion of our constitution, you must be a member of what I understand is called the English Party, then?" she ventured. When he seemed to hesitate overlong before answering, she decided to assist him by asking helpfully, "You would consider yourself a Federalist, sir, would you not?"

Richard shook his head. "I wouldn't call myself a member of any organized political party," he admitted at last, "though it's true I find more to sympathize with in the ideas and practices of the Federalists than with those of the present administration. Nevertheless, I'm not at all interested in politics per se. When I have the time, I prefer to devote myself to activities aimed at the social betterment of my fellow men."

"How commendable," Jennifer observed. She smiled in a manner sure to diffuse any notion that her response might have been less than perfectly sincere. "And how is it that you accomplish that worthy task, I wonder?" she prodded gently again.

Her host unbent sufficiently to preen a little beneath his praise. "I am a member of the Washington Benevolent Society—named after our first president, you know. Although it's true that many of the founders were Federalists themselves, membership in the society isn't restricted to those who share that background. In fact, we encourage all manner of merchants, shopkeepers, and even former officers who fought in the Revolution to join our cause. Why, last year to commemorate Washington's birthday, we held a parade in which more than 2,000 of our members marched in celebration!''

"Yet, I must confess there's something that puzzles me in all this, sir,'' Jennifer said. "How is it that on the one hand you can belong to a group that reveres a patriot like Washington and appears to emphasize a love of country, and on the other hand feel such a strong tie to England that you would seemingly like to see that same country become merely her handmaiden?'' She sat back and allowed a look of girlish confusion to steal over her face. "But then, no doubt I've managed to get the whole thing messed up in my mind,'' she admitted prettily.

That statement, however, could have been applied more aptly to her host just then. For one thing, Richard was hardly used to detailing his personal beliefs in public— partly out of fear that others might find his ideas absurd or ill formed, but mostly because he rarely took the time to hammer out exactly what it was he truly thought. What's more, when he actually did engage in such rare discussions, it was scarcely to be considered that there might be a lady present. And the fact that he now found himself squarely in the middle of the very same uneasy sort of conversation, and with a woman at that, was proving terribly disconcerting to him indeed.

He took a deep breath and resorted to the formal, reserved manner that was his refuge on those occasions when he felt himself to have arrived at point nonplus. "Doubtless you're a trifle befuddled,'' he told Jennifer in a condescending tone. "But then, women so often seem unable to grasp the intricacies of politics,'' he added, in an ill-advised attempt to regain the upper hand. Indeed, had he paused to analyze his reaction, Richard might have discovered that he was also used to having members of the fair sex admire him for his supposed expertise in realms to which they weren't generally privy themselves. As it was, however, he now found himself confronted by a woman who not only acted unimpressed by his knowledge, but one whom he was apparently—if unreasonably—longing to enchant by firing her with an appreciation of his finer qualities.

Lord Somers, who'd been watching the interaction between his daughter and his host with his usual interest, now observed that it was clearly time to intercede, and conversation soon shifted to more desultory topics. Nevertheless, when the Somerses departed an hour or so later, Jennifer couldn't resist asking her father whether he'd revised his opinion of Richard Avery. They were strolling along Wall Street in the direction of Broadway, admiring the elegant buildings that lined both sides of the road. Lord Somers stopped to point out the location of the Manhattan Company before responding.

"I like the man," he said simply at last. "Now, I know I called him a queer fish and a high stickler," he continued as Jennifer raised an eyebrow at him. "But just because the fellow thinks a little differently than I do doesn't mean we can't get on together. In fact, I wonder if it wouldn't do you a world of good to learn the knack of being at home with others besides me. And without forever trying to expose their faults to them, either—even if it is with the idea that it will prove beneficial. I know it may come as a shock to you, my love, but you ain't the only person longheaded enough to understand how matters lie."

"Stuff!" Jennifer replied good-naturedly. "You can't think me such a moonling that I don't see that someone needs to send Mr. Avery to the rightabout—and soon! Why, not only is he the stiffest thing in nature, but he also doesn't treat his children as kindly as one might a lap dog, his politics are hopelessly muddled, and he appears to be too much of a widgeon to figure a way out of his tangled coil!" *And blister it if even so, I don't find him a dashedly attractive man—perhaps because I've the tiniest suspicion that he wishes to be other than a high stickler himself,* she added silently.

Lord Somers clicked his tongue several times in a thoughtful manner before responding, "And you, naturally, consider yourself a prime hand at such things—on account of your vast experience?" He raised a hand to forestall his daughter's quick answer to that question. "You may be surprised to learn that I tend, for the most part, to agree with you, my dear. But you, in turn, must at least grant that the man's honest and never once attempted merely to wrap things up in clean linen for us. And I wouldn't, if I were you, make the mistake of thinking him a coward, either. I think you'll discover that once Mr. Avery understands a situation thoroughly and what needs doing, he won't be slow to bring himself up to the mark and attend to it before you can say whiffler.''

Observing that his remarks had given Jennifer something to chew over, Lord Somers declined for the moment to press his daughter further on her reaction to Richard Avery as a man, and instead seized the opportunity to turn the conversation back to a topic closer to his own heart. "Damned if I ain't determined to beat up all quarters till I tease out every morsel of information about this idea of building a canal to Lake Erie,'' he told her. "How far away is Albany, I wonder, and how does one go about getting there?'' he continued as if to himself. "Got to put my hands on a proper map.''

"There now, Papa—don't fall into a pelter,'' Jennifer advised calmly. "No doubt our host of this evening would be happy to accommodate you.''

"Of course!'' his lordship exclaimed in relief. "Must be dicked in the nob not to have thought of that myself! Why, bless me if I won't put the question to him next time we meet.''

Accordingly, the following afternoon, Lord Somers presented himself at Richard Avery's house with the full intent of satisfying his curiosity on the matter of building a canal to Lake Erie. Richard's mind, however, was occupied with a rather different matter, which he'd only just resolved to bring to his lordship's attention. For the past week, ever since Andrew Plummer's untimely defection, Richard had been unsuccessfully tossing about possible solutions to the problem of what to do about his children's upbringing and education. Clearly, he needed to locate a governess—a tutor simply wouldn't suffice. But how and where he was to discover the superior sort of person he desired was by now causing him to gnash his teeth in frustration. What's more, since meeting Lord Somers he'd been persuaded that in addition to his other requirements, the individual in question definitely had to be English as well. Surely only an Englishwoman would possess the unconscious good breeding he so dearly admired.

Take Jennifer Somers, for instance, he mused, firmly pushing aside the temptation to daydream about that lady. Now, although she'd obviously been allowed far too much latitude in developing her own ideas and was altogether too forward, to his taste, in expressing them, she never appeared to hesitate when confronted by questions of etiquette or conscience. And it was that same unquestioning ability to apply one's values to one's life that Richard wished to inculcate in his children—along with the proper values, too, of course. And why had he seemingly never considered that the proper relationship between the sexes could be a most pleasant situation? he found himself wondering quite irrelevantly. He'd even be willing to concede somewhat on the subject of the twins' education, he continued determinedly once again, since it was unlikely, he knew, that most women would have developed the expertise in the higher realms of learning that he'd originally specified. Nevertheless, having finally devised a potential solution to his problem, Richard had promptly determined to enlist Lord Somers's assistance in bringing it to pass. Surely among his vast acquaintance his lordship would know someone—possibly a spinster or a woman in reduced circumstances—who'd be inclined to accept an invitation to his employment, Richard reasoned. And so it was with the idea of soliciting suggestions for the position of his children's governess that he eagerly awaited his guest.

Unfortunately, Lord Somers's enthusiasm for his own project swept aside all other considerations for some time after his arrival. Pressed for more information about the canal from Lake Erie, Richard obligingly shared what little he knew of the enterprise. Then he produced several maps showing the area from New York all the way west to Indian Territory and much of Lower Canada, and the two proceeded to pore over these documents together.

At last Richard sat back and regarded his lordship thoughtfully. "There's a fairly well-established route to the area, if you truly mean to go there yourself," he said, tapping the place on the map between Lake Ontario and Lake Erie. "It's mostly by water, but I'm convinced that that would be to your liking, would it not? Very well, then," he continued at his guest's nod, "here's what you would do." The two men hunched over the map again, following Richard's finger as he traced the journey. "You'd begin by taking the steamboat up the Hudson River to Albany; that should take about a day and a half, assuming you don't fetch up on shore with a broken paddle wheel. Then I'm afraid you have to go overland to Schenectady for about fifteen miles. There's no stage; most people hire a horse and ride the turnpike road. Next, you'll need about five days for the keelboat trip up the Mohawk River to Utica, and then three more to reach Oswego. Then you switch to a sailing boat for the trip along the Oswego River to Lewiston—say, another three days—and you've arrived at the outlet of Lake Ontario. If all goes well, it should take you about two weeks to complete the trip. From Lewiston, it's a simple matter to travel down to Buffalo and Lake Erie, though no doubt you'll want to explore Niagara Falls before doing so. I understand the drop of water over the cliffs is a stunning spectacle and not to be missed."

Richard hesitated for a moment, tapping the map again thoughtfully as he pondered how to raise the problem that had come to mind as he spoke. "I should warn you, however, that I've heard the area's in a very unsettled state at the moment. No, it's not on account of the Indians," he said with a smile, anticipating Lord Somers's first question. "Though I'm certain they're involved somehow. It's the British," he offered more soberly. "You see, being so close to Canada there, on one side of the river is an American fort and directly across on the other bank is a British one. A lot of people think that if we do end up going to war with England, the hostilities may very well begin precisely where you're headed. And since you're English, you can see how that might prove a complication, should anything develop along those lines. Of course, I'm sure you can provide quite nicely for yourself, but it occurs to me that you might want to reconsider whether to expose your daughter to possible danger.''

"Precisely what's occurred to me," Lord Somers confessed. "Only not on account of the risk. Why, Jennifer wouldn't spare a straw for such a thought! Child after my own heart, you know." He smiled proudly for a moment before tilting back in his chair and continuing in a more contemplative tone. "Starting to feel guilty about carting her around with me every place I go. Well, it can't be entirely good for her—I don't like it all that much myself, on occasion. Besides, high time she settled down somewhere and stopped living like a gypsy. There've been offers of marriage, of course, but so far she claims she can't see how she'd find that alternative anything but beastly dull." He hesitated. "Most times I'm glad of her company, but once in a while," he admitted, "I've an urge to hie myself off on my own without having to spare a thought to such excess baggage as children.''

"I know exactly what you mean," Richard agreed, sternly mastering the impulse to seek details of the aforementioned proposals, as well as to explore the unexpectedly strong feeling of jealousy that that news had promptly aroused. "Just when I thought I had things sewn up all right and tight regarding George and Caroline, some fool has to go poke a hole in my nice little scheme and the whole damned thing collapses! That fellow Plummer left me in a pretty pickle, I must say. In fact, I was rather hoping you'd be so kind as to suggest a way out of it," he said, and promptly proceeded to outline his desire to locate an English governess for the twins.

Lord Somers tilted even farther back in his chair and thrummed one arm of it with his fingers in an unconscious parody of his host. "Sensible idea," he agreed when Richard had finished. "Plenty of women schooled in the classics who'd be happy to accept a place in your household. Why, my own clergyman in Sussex has four daughters, any one of whom would be perfect for your needs. Trouble is, they're in England. Well, bound to have the devil's own time making the crossing, you know, what with the way things stand. Too bad there ain't a girl hereabouts already who'd suit the purpose—"

He broke off suddenly, allowing his chair to come back to the floor with a crash that caused Richard nearly to fall out of his own in turn. "Sorry, dear boy," his lordship apologized hastily. "But fancy I've just thought of a way to solve both our problems at once." He offered his host a broad smile that plainly indicated he was feeling decidedly pleased with himself. "Quite simple, really. Well, no question but that we should appoint Jennifer your new governess!"

Chapter 4

RICHARD GOGGLED unabashedly at his guest and appeared to be having inordinate difficulty finding his tongue. "Lady Somers?" he managed to sputter at last. "Whatever can you be thinking of, man?" he wondered, thrusting aside both his usual reserve and his secret awe of Lord Somers's title in one breath.

His lordship seemed unperturbed at being addressed in such a casual manner. "It makes absolute good sense to me," he pointed out. "Perhaps I should tell you a little more about her education. She reads Greek and Latin with ease and is as familiar with the writings of Cicero as those of Homer; she can converse easily in Italian or French and often writes poetry in the latter; she has studied the great thinkers and would willingly argue that Descartes is a better philosopher than a mathematician; she understands the principles of Euclid's science as well as Newton's, and she has a thorough background in, and a dedicated appreciation for, all of the finer arts." He paused for a moment to ascertain the effect of this speech. "In short," he concluded, hoping to drive his point home, "Jennifer has been far better schooled than most men, as I'm sure you'll admit, and is infinitely qualified to become a governess.''

Richard held up his hands as if to ward off another onslaught from the same direction as the first. "It isn't your daughter's qualifications I doubt, but rather the suitability of even considering her to fill that role." He turned his gesture into a shrug of his shoulders. "Why, I'd have to be daft to think that she'd actually entertain the idea in the first place." And in the second place, she's so much more beautiful and so clearly different from other women that she'd doubtless prove a major disruption to a household that prided itself on order amd moderation, he realized with a shudder, before continuing aloud. "And in the third, er, second place—'' He paused, casting about for a tactful way of phrasing his last reason for hesitating to embrace his lordship's plan.

"Jennifer ain't exactly the sort of person you had in mind?" Lord Somers supplied calmly himself. "No need to pull punches with me. Besides, I'm in a perfect position to know that she can be willful and stubborn and opinionated in the extreme. Probably should lay the whole blame right at my door, after all. But I'd still sooner confess to encouraging her to think for herself than have to own I'd raised some milk-and-water miss who had hysterics at the first sight of a cloud on the horizon," he declared proudly. Then, recollecting that such reasoning would scarcely help persuade his very proper host of his purpose, he abruptly changed tactics.

"It isn't as if this is meant to be the final solution to your problem," he reminded Richard. "Perhaps you could view it as a temporary measure that would conveniently alleviate both our concerns for a little while, at least. And then, too," he continued, noting that his companion seemed to be softening a trifle, "you'd be doing me an enormous favor, don't forget. Why, where would Jennifer stay otherwise? I couldn't allow her to remain at the hotel the whole time I'm gone, and it don't seem to make sense to lease a house just for her and Molly—er, her companion. Besides, I'd feel much better knowing she was safely under your watchful eye," he said winningly. Not that Jennifer would necessarily ever be inclined to do as she was told, he thought glumly.

"I promise she can be quite biddable," he said nevertheless, more as if wishing to be convinced of that fact himself than anything else. Of course, there was another equally important fact that his lordship had conveniently decided to ignore entirely, and that was whether it was strictly proper to place his daughter even temporarily in the care of a strange gentleman. He had to admit that the arrangement could only be called tenuous, at best—particularly when he'd already begun to wonder if there didn't seem to be a spark of attraction between Jennifer and Richard Avery. "And what's more, she adores children," he went on now, trying a different approach. "You saw yourself how she took to the twins like a gosling to the pond from the very first."

"That's true," Richard admitted, brightening somewhat. "At least this way George and Caroline would have the benefit of edifying company." *And so would I,* he added silently. Even though he'd already guessed that Jennifer might prove a weighty distraction, he'd also felt an unexpected thrill at Lord Somers's suggestion that she reside in his house, and the mere recognition of these conflicting emotions had begun to make him feel distinctly—if rather pleasantly—confused.

Lord Somers, who had struggled to keep his face expressionless as he pictured his irrepressible daughter in the role of arbiter of learning, continued to regard his host with polite interest while trying to imagine what the devil the man would say next.

"Lady Somers would probably enjoy the opportunity to keep herself occupied in such a wholesome fashion," Richard observed stoutly, as if to oblige his lordship.

That remark promptly caused Lord Somers to marvel at his host's lack of acumen as well as to let out a loud snort. This last he managed to turn into a credible fit of coughing and a request for something to clear his throat. After a bottle of Madeira had been produced and a glass given into his lordship's grateful hands, a brief silence ensued while the two men allowed the wine to take effect.

"What puzzles me," Richard began, "is how you imagine that your daughter can be persuaded to remain here. It seems to me that if she thinks settling down and running a household would be tedious in the extreme, she'd be bound to find caring for two nine-year-olds infinitely worse.'' He stopped with some reluctance just short of inquiring directly about either that lady's current romantic situation or her views on the concept of marriage in general. ''Why, you could almost say that such a situation would have all the disadvantages of being married and none of the advantages,'' he observed pointedly instead.

Could say, but wouldn't, since that's exactly what Jennifer's likely to think, Lord Somers reflected. And the perfect excuse not to tell her anything at all about having proposed that she act as the twin's governess, he realized slowly. He took another generous swallow of Madeira and resisted the impulse to tilt back in his chair again to consider the matter properly. Say only that he'd arrange for her to stay with Molly at Avery's house while he was gone, he mused. Time enough for her to discover her new responsibilities—and his duplicity—once he was safely far away. What's more, he decided generously, after stealing a sidelong glance at his host, won't trouble the poor fellow's conscience by making him privy to this little scheme. Far better for him to bear alone the brunt of Jennifer's anger when she learned that he meant to leave her behind—and learned of his deception too, if it came to that. And having reached the foregoing decision, his lordship settled down happily to expressing a steady appreciation of his host's excellent wine cellar.

It was indeed prudent that Lord Somers had sought to fortify himself for the task of confronting his daughter. In fact, no sooner was their little group assembled for a late tea in a private sitting room than he promptly blurted out both the news of his imminent departure for Lake Erie and the announcement that Jennifer and Molly were to settle at No. 30 Wall Street until he returned.

Jennifer's initial reaction, however, wasn't quite what he'd expected. She merely stared at him for a long moment without speaking and then, leaning forward, took a deep sniff as if to test the air. ''Oh, I see,'' she said in a patient voice, ''you're a bit up in the world at present, that's all.''

''Certainly not,'' Lord Somers denied indignantly. He

swallowed a hiccough that threatened to give the lie to that statement and attempted to rally his senses. "Why, it's perfectly proper that Mr. Avery should invite you to stay at his house," he said, generously altering the facts as needed to fit his purpose. "Even with Molly here, it isn't appropriate for you two to remain at the hotel while I'm away, you know."

"It's not the propriety of the invitation that interests me," Jennifer said, dismissing that notion with a careless wave of her hand. "Besides, I wouldn't expect anything else from an upright like Mr. Avery." She narrowed her eyes and considered her father carefully. "It couldn't be that the man's confessed to being smitten by me? Or possibly that you've taken a fancy to throw me at his head?"

Lord Somers shook his own head vigorously back and forth. "The thought never occurred to me," he said altogether truthfully. "Besides, you must know you're not to the fellow's taste."

Jennifer relaxed a trifle in her chair. "Well, after our conversation Sunday, I'd have been surprised to hear he thought me a perfect match," she admitted with a tiny smile. But if her father wasn't intent on her tying the knot with Mr. Avery, surely there was only one other reason he'd be longing to get her off his hands? "Then I guess," she said slowly as if it were painful to get the words out, "it must be that you've simply tired of my company and long for a little pleasure unfettered by the likes of me."

Now, this statement was so close to the truth that it made Lord Somers squirm uncomfortably. In addition, it was said in such a straightforward manner without the least touch of self-pity that his lordship found himself hard-pressed not to volunteer immediately the very information he'd previously determined to keep hidden from his daughter. And in order to maintain that resolve, he realized he'd have to own up to his real feelings after all.

"I haven't grown tired of you in the least, my love," Lord Somers told her. He reached over to press Jennifer's hands in his before continuing in an earnest voice. "It's only that we're so much in each other's pockets that I thought you truly wouldn't mind a few weeks apart. I won't be gone more than two months at the outside, I promise. And in the meantime, you can take the opportunity of assisting Mr. Avery in recognizing those areas in his character and his thinking that want improvement.''

At this point, Molly, who'd sat quietly through the preceding exchange, gave one of her disparaging sniffs. ''From what I hear, you'd best plan on half a year's absence at least, then, if we're to make any headway in that department,'' she observed.

Jennifer laughed. ''Oh, very well, Papa—have your little holiday,'' she said. ''I shall content myself with seeking to discover the pleasures of domesticity.'' She smiled impishly at her father. ''Only don't think everyone involved won't hold you responsible if poor Mr. Avery discovers that he no longer enjoys either peace or pride once I've joined his household.''

Precisely what I'm afraid of, Lord Somers admitted, before pushing that thought firmly out of his mind.

Thankfully for all concerned, the next several days were taken up with preparations for Lord Somers's trip because he was anxious to depart before the week was out. Normally, he would have become totally absorbed in completing the necessary arrangements for the trip. This time, however, even the anticipation of his first steamboat ride had failed to dispel all his misgivings about leaving his daughter behind. Hoping to clear his thoughts, he decided to go for a walk late one afternoon. And a few minutes later, he quietly exited the hotel and turned south on Broadway, heading for the tip of the island.

It wasn't that he was regretting his decision, he thought as he strolled past Trinity Church. If anything, he'd been more than honest finally to have admitted that the life he and Jennifer had been leading couldn't—or, possibly, shouldn't—go on forever. But that wasn't to say that he suddenly expected her to settle down to a conventional existence, either. He paused to admire the silhouette made by the church's tower against the early evening sky, his eyes crinkling in amusement as he tried to imagine his daughter ever leading what most people would call a normal life.

He'd thought it important enough, however, to expose her to yet another possibility of how to make one's way in the world. That way, when she finally did make a decision, she might feel as if she actually understood what she was choosing and believe that she had a real choice to make.

Lord Somers resumed his meandering pace. If only the circumstances were different, he thought wistfully. Ordinarily, Richard Avery wouldn't have been his first choice for either chaperone or companion—or his second choice either, for that matter. He only hoped that the man wouldn't take his role too seriously. Of course, he admitted, crossing the street toward Bowling Green, there was scarcely any danger of that happening, given Jennifer's temperament. Indeed, he was counting on her unfailing sense of humor to carry her through whatever difficulties she might encounter, he realized. He pulled open the iron gate and strolled over to the far side of the park facing the Government House.

Why, what about the time she'd almost gotten married, his lordship recalled, claiming a seat on a convenient bench. There'd been that dashing Austrian with the name no one could pronounce and boasting a title as long as his arm who'd begged her to run away with him to Europe. She'd accepted, too, and the invitations had even been sent when the damned fellow without warning decamped, and they'd discovered he already had a perfectly good wife and a baby neatly stashed away in his castle. Most women wouldn't have ventured forth in public for a full month at least after having been left practically at the church door. But Jennifer had merely laughed and said that since she fancied she was a handful enough by herself, it was just as well the silly man hadn't found himself saddled with two wives after all.

Lord Somers idly watched a pair of carriages traverse the circular drive in front of the building. Yes, Jennifer certainly was a complete hand at times, to put it bluntly, and he was pleasantly looking forward to not having to spend his spare time extricating her from some scrape or other. Liar, he confessed cheerfully a moment later. No doubt he'd be wondering what basket she'd landed in no matter where he was. He rose from his seat and began to amble back across the park. What was it Caroline Lamb had once told him? Oh, yes—truth, she'd said, is what one thinks at the moment. And right now, if truth be told, his lordship had to admit he expected sorely to be missing Jennifer's company on his journey.

Similar thoughts were passing through Jennifer's mind, though not, it was true, for the same reasons. She and Molly were closeted in her room at the hotel, engaged in packing her clothing in preparation for removing to Mr. Avery's house the following day. Jennifer, however, being somewhat distracted and having little patience at the best of times for that tedious task, had been satisfied with throwing things haphazardly into a trunk. Molly, therefore, was now calmly removing the crumpled items one by one from the first trunk, refolding them, and stacking them neatly into a second trunk.

Much to her relief, Jennifer had finally given up the pretense of assisting in the proceedings and had curled into a chair to watch instead. "I wish I didn't feel so uneasy about this arrangement," she confessed after a few minutes, winding a blue satin ribbon around one finger until Molly plucked it away from her. "Oh, I know it's only for a short while and it isn't as if I'm being abandoned forever. Why, I warrant Papa even feels guilty leaving me to Mr. Avery's ministrations—though he'd scarcely be likely to admit it." She paused to nibble at a fingernail, a habit she suddenly remembered that she'd outgrown before she was ten. "That's the trouble, you see. I know what I feel, and I can pretty much guess how Papa feels, but I haven't a clue as to what Mr. Avery feels about our coming to stay with him. Of course, I doubt he truly knows what he feels himself; he probably has it all confused with what he thinks he ought to feel."

She straightened up in her chair, looking a trifle alarmed. "I certainly hope he doesn't imagine he's supposed to act as my guardian and approve all my decisions. No, I'm convinced Papa wouldn't have been so unwise," she said firmly. "Still, I wonder how much freedom I'll be allowed, don't you? How will he treat me, do you suppose?" she asked, clearly not expecting an answer. "Of course, he doesn't seem to have distinguished himself in dealing with his own children, so I probably shouldn't expect any better myself. Nevertheless, I won't stand for him treating me as if I'm not yet out of the nursery or, worse still, as if because I'm a woman I've no more sense than a pea goose. And I warn you, Molly," she said, jumping up from her chair with sudden energy, "if Mr. Avery is so misguided as to imagine that he holds the reins in this arrangement, he'll soon discover that he has an altogether fractious mare at the end of them!"

Molly, who privately thought it rather a waste of time to mount a defense without knowing the enemy's strength, so to speak, wisely held her tongue. Taking in Jennifer's defiant pose—feet spread, arms akimbo—she merely nodded. "Yes," she agreed sympathetically, "no doubt the poor devil will."

Lord Somers's departure the next morning provided a welcome, if temporary, distraction for all concerned. He had booked passage to Albany on Robert Fulton's newest steamboat, the *Paragon*. The huge vessel was nearly 200 feet long and dwarfed the Hudson River dock where she was moored to receive passengers. She was fitted with a pair of masts, but even without sails, his lordship had confided, she'd make between five and six miles per hour upstream. The boat had been described as an entire floating town, his lordship announced, where one could enjoy the best wines, all manner of delicacies, and even ice cream in the hot season.

"I was a little worried at first about the safety of the thing," Lord Somers confessed. "Oh, not the boat itself—she's solid as they come." He thumped a wooden rail as if to attest to the fact. "But things have changed since Fulton's first steamboat took to the waters five years ago. You see, the men who earn their living on the river quite properly recognized the steamboat as a threat. Initially, they sought to discredit the *Clermont*, claiming she was dangerous and warning that the engine might explode at any moment. When they weren't successful in making the boat unpopular, they then actually attempted to disable her. Whole scores of

men would pile into their sloops and run the steamboat
down; several times they even managed to knock off the
paddle wheel.''

Jennifer peered down at the huge wheel, which was
enclosed by a protective structure of heavy timbers. ''I take
it this was the solution?''

''Yes, and it's proven most effective, I understand. Though
you could almost take such hostility as a measure of how
popular the boats have become for river travel. In fact,
Fulton's been granted exclusive rights to operate steamboats
on the Hudson. Only now, I hear, people are incensed that
he's been given a virtual monopoly—especially since he
didn't invent the concept of steam travel in the first place
and thus has neither a legal nor moral right to claim sole
ownership.'' His lordship looked down at Jennifer for a
moment. ''It appears that many people are now throwing
their support to another steam line in the hope of advocating
free and unrestricted travel. But then, as we know,'' he
added with a smile, ''no one ever takes kindly to having
their choice taken away and being told what to do instead.''

This final remark echoed in Jennifer's head long after
she'd waved good-bye and watched the huge vessel move
off, sounding much like the description her father had
related of the *Clermont*: a devil in a sawmill. And despite
her earlier resolution, she was painfully conscious of feeling
young and unsure of herself when the hack pulled to a stop
in front of the house in Wall Street and the owner himself
came out to welcome them.

Richard bowed politely when Jennifer introduced Molly
as her companion, and then motioned them toward the door,
taking refuge in his formal role as host in order to cover up
the pleasure he felt on seeing Jennifer again. ''I trust Lord
Somers embarked smoothly?'' he inquired.

''Yes, thank you,'' Jennifer said, ''though I believe—''
She broke off in surprise as she entered the hallway and
found a half dozen strangers inside the door to witness her
arrival. And that circumstance, coupled with her bewilderment at discovering she wasn't as unaffected by the sight of
Mr. Avery as she'd thought she would be, caused her
suddenly to appear at a loss for words.

"You were saying—?" Richard prompted after a moment.

"Oh, yes, I believe—That is to say—Well, I believe this is rather unexpected," she managed lamely at last.

Richard looked puzzled. "Indeed? Why, I'd have thought you'd expect to meet the rest of the staff."

"Oh, to be sure," Jennifer agreed in a tentative way.

"Well, then, this is Mrs. Booth, my housekeeper," Richard began, indicating a plump, motherly looking woman of about fifty. She had row after row of tightly wound curls that lay like little gray sausages beneath her lace cap, and a pair of soft brown eyes that regarded Jennifer with kindly speculation.

"And this is Ellen, her assistant," Richard went on, moving down the line. "Sydney, who cares for the carriages and horses and helps with the grounds; Walters, our butler. And this—this is Monsieur Fouquet, our valued chef."

"Mademoiselle," Monsieur Fouquet murmured, bending to kiss her hand with true Gallic grace. He was a tiny, elflike man of approximately Jennifer's height, whose fluttering movements and darting eyes reminded her of an exotic bird in a cage.

"Ah, Monsieur Fouquet," she said prettily in his native language. "Perhaps one day you'll be so kind as to show me the secret of making a proper meringue? I understand only a Frenchman is artist enough to have mastered those troublesome confections."

The chef's face broke into a delighted smile. "With pleasure, mademoiselle," he assured her in French. "My own creations are so light they almost seem ready to float away." He cast an admiring look at Jennifer. "Besides, nothing would be too much trouble for a lady who speaks my language like an angel!"

At this point, Richard was startled to feel a sharp, unexpected stab of what could only have been called jealousy at the immediate rapport that had clearly been established between his guest and his chef. What's more, since his own French was of the schoolboy variety and he'd barely followed the gist of the preceding exchange, he now sought to regain control of the conversation. "Fine, fine," he said abruptly, turning toward Jennifer. "No doubt you'll want to get settled in your rooms, first of all. George and Caroline are upstairs waiting for you in the schoolroom, I understand. Just let Mrs. Booth know if you require anything and when you wish her to arrange for the twins' dinner.''

Jennifer refrained from commenting upon her host's odd speech until they'd been shown to their apartment on the second floor. While Molly calmly assumed the task of unpacking and shaking out the same items she'd only just packed the day before, Jennifer once again perched on a corner of the bed beside her to watch. "Didn't you think it strange that Mr. Avery kept referring to how I was to see to the children's needs and even to bespeak their meals?'' she asked at last.

Molly paused for a moment, her head on one side, to consider the question. "Probably he thinks that because you're a woman you're bound to be experienced in such things—or at least interested in them," she observed in a dry voice.

"I wonder," Jennifer said slowly. "After all, he's scarcely the sort to admit that someone—especially a woman—might know more than he does about anything.''

"Maybe the man's just tired of making all the decisions," Molly said, beginning to grow somewhat tired of Jennifer's constant desire to discuss every little event. "No doubt you're making too much of the whole affair anyway," she sniffed. "You do tend to overthink things, you know."

Jennifer regarded her in surprise. "Do I? Yes, I expect you're quite right," she admitted with a laugh. "Well then, what do *you* think of our host, I wonder?''

"Oh, no question but that he's a very attractive man," Molly said at once. "And it's probably a good thing he don't seem to have the nerve for it, or he'd be a perfect heartbreaker, I'm sure." She shot a sudden, calculating look at her friend. "It ain't like you to be subtle," she observed bluntly, "so you might as well tell me if you've taken a notion to set your cap at him.''

"No, no—nothing of the sort," Jennifer protested hastily. "I merely wished to garner another woman's opinion, that's all. I promise I shan't offer another word on the subject.

Let's go and find the twins instead and see what they have to say about our arrival.''

But trying to get George and Caroline to say anything at all proved to be a more difficult task than Jennifer had imagined. She and Molly located the schoolroom easily enough. It was a large, light chamber on the third floor furnished rather sparsely with a sturdy table and chairs, a couple of shelves of books, a handsome globe, and a box of what looked like discarded baby toys. The twins had apparently been kneeling at the window, following the goings-on in Wall Street below. But despite the pleasant picture the children made, with the sunlight streaming down upon their already golden hair and expectant faces, the atmosphere in the room was anything but cozy, Jennifer decided as they crossed the floor toward the twins. There was nothing on the walls save a couple of mediocre prints entitled "Virtue" and "Obedience," and the place had the same lifeless quality as the rest of the house. Obviously, no special accommodation had been made for the room's young occupants, Jennifer noted in irritation, wondering absently how she could even think she might be attracted to a man who had his own children's interests so far from his heart.

"Hello there," she greeted the twins in a friendly fashion. They bobbed silently in return. "This is Molly, my—ah—companion." The children bobbed a second greeting. "I take it your father must have told you we're to live with you for a little while?" she pressed on. "I must say I'm looking forward to getting to know you both better. I'm sure we'll get on famously, aren't you? Have you been watching the passersby?" she continued, in a determined attempt to put an end to her monologue. "I like to do the same thing myself, you know. Have you seen anything curious today?"

The children shook their heads until Caroline suddenly tugged George's sleeve and whispered something. "Well," he admitted at last, "we did wonder about her." He leaned over to point down at the woman in the street.

"Why, that's Prickly Peg," Molly said calmly, after she saw where they were looking. "It's not her real name, of course. We all have pet names on the street. Makes us feel a bit more like a family, you see. Old Peg sells pineapples, and they have little prickers on their skins, so that's where she gets her name. The fruit's grand, though. It comes all the way from some islands south of here where it's warm all the time."

The twins looked a good deal more interested than before, Jennifer observed, and they regarded Molly with new respect, too. "Would you like to try a pineapple with your dinner?" she asked. Two sets of blond curls bounced vigorously in assent. "Very well," she said with a smile. She opened her reticule and handed a coin to Molly. "If you'd be so kind?"

George, who apparently watched everything with a very keen eye, now appeared to wrestle with himself. "Is she really your friend? Why'd she used to sell things on the street then—she did, didn't she?" he blurted out.

Jennifer paused for a moment to consider how to phrase her words. She didn't actually wish to set the children against anything their father might have taught them, but only to expose them to new ways of looking at things and, she hoped, to prompt them to question what they were told by others—especially adults. "Well, it's not unusual for someone to do several different things in life when they're growing up," she began, "particularly when circumstances might require them to earn a living. And it doesn't matter to me that Molly was once a street vendor. You see, I believe that you like someone for who they are, not for what they do. So even though selling fruit as Molly used to do is not, perhaps, a very elevated profession, it's certainly not a dishonorable one either. There's no point that I can see in putting up false barriers between people because one comes from, say, a wealthy family and the other from a poorer family where everyone must work to keep food on the table. Do you understand a little?"

Although her speech had clearly given him a good deal to think about, George nodded slowly. That's enough for one day, Jennifer decided, remembering how it felt to have discovered a new idea and not yet have had time to work it through. Therefore, she set herself to the task of arranging for their dinner. And before another half hour had passed, the four were able to settle down at the table, which Jennifer had asked to be pulled in front of the fireplace.

The meal turned out to be a very congenial affair. For one thing, Jennifer was accustomed to talking to children as easily and in as straightforward a manner as she did everyone else. And Molly, used to a large family herself, approached the twins with the tolerant air of a wise older sister. Apparently the two had never enjoyed such warmhearted treatment before, because even shy little Caroline seemed to blossom. In fact, she became bold enough to ask Jennifer's companion what her street name had been, and then to giggle delightedly when she heard it was Mulberry Molly, on account of the fruit she used to sell. They had just finished sampling the pineapple—which George had promptly called nasty tasting but which Caroline had pronounced lovely—and were watching the shadows made by the firelight dancing on the walls of the room.

Caroline gave a small, contented sigh. "You're ever so much nicer than Miss Pennycott," she told Jennifer.

Jennifer laughed. "Thank you, I think. And who, if I may ask, was Miss Pennycott?"

"Our governess. She wasn't mean exactly, but I think we made her nervous," Caroline confided. "She told us she was going away to her parents' house for a long rest."

"Perhaps she wasn't used to young children," Jennifer suggested.

"But Papa said you weren't used to children, and it doesn't look as if we make you nervous," George pointed out.

Jennifer laughed again. "Ah, but then I'm not a governess, you see."

The twins regarded her with identical confused expressions. "But Papa told us you'd be teaching us our lessons," Caroline said in a puzzled voice.

"And he said we were to work hard and see if we couldn't manage to learn something from you," George volunteered.

Jennifer shot a quick look at Molly, primarily to steady her own nerves, which were suddenly threatening to become overset. "You must have gotten it wrong," she said finally.

"Perhaps he just meant that I'd look in from time to time to see how you were progressing."

"No," George said, shaking his head. He continued as if reading from a prepared speech. "He said that since Miss Pennycott had gone and Mr. Plummer hadn't arrived, you were to be our governess while you were staying here. He said you had a good education, and even though you might act strangely at times, we're to mind you and do whatever you tell us."

A governess? Jennifer slumped back in her chair, her mind reeling with such irrelevancies as who the mysterious Mr. Plummer might be and why he hadn't turned up. But more important, she realized, was how this infamous scheme had been concocted and why she hadn't known about it until now, much less agreed to take part in it.

Since the information she required could obviously be obtained from only one source, Jennifer had to content herself with resolving to confront her host first thing the next day. For the moment, she rallied sufficiently to say sternly that since she was to be in charge, the children were to prepare at once for bed. Her twinkling eyes advertised that she was only pretending to be gruff, however, and the twins stumbled over each other to win the distinction of being first under the covers.

Needless to say, Jennifer passed a very restless night. Early the following morning, she descended to the dining room to break her fast and to await Richard Avery's arrival. The latter project was unsuccessful, however, since that gentleman had apparently resolved not to interrupt his usual routine by exchanging pleasantries with his guests. Very well, Jennifer decided, she would go find him instead—and not with the intention of sharing a few casual remarks about the weather, either.

Accordingly, a few minutes later, she knocked on the door of the study. Entering in response to an invitation to do so, she discovered Mr. Avery seated behind his desk, perusing some papers. And if any of his acquaintances might have observed that he looked just a shade less than perfectly turned out, Jennifer herself was too wrought up to notice. True, she was conscious of feeling more than a little uneasy about confronting him on his home ground, so to speak, and somewhat shy at finding herself alone with him for the first time, in addition. Nevertheless, she was determined not to dwell on either of those emotions in order to get to the heart of the matter as quickly as possible. Therefore, she advanced across the floor and planted herself squarely in front of him. Then, having decided to dispense with the preliminaries, she offered him a cold look and demanded, "Now, what is all this foolishness about my acting as the twins' governess?"

Richard, who had looked up when Jennifer entered the room only to find himself promptly distracted first by the fact that there was a woman in the room he liked to think of as his sanctum and second by her ravishing appearance, now froze. Jennifer's abrupt manner immediately chased all such charitable thoughts from his head, however, and galvanzied him to marshal a response in kind. "Foolishness—?" he exclaimed. "Why, I'll have you know that it was your father's idea," he informed her in an equally blunt way. "Surely he must have told you that I wasn't at all inclined to agree at first. No?" His expression changed to one of bewilderment. "Well, then no doubt he at least mentioned that I'd only allowed myself to be persuaded because the tutor I'd hired had begged off—and also because he insisted I'd be doing him an enormous favor to take you off his hands and offer you an opportunity to settle down a little by acting in that capacity for the children. He didn't? Well, just what the devil *did* he say?" he asked in exasperation.

"Nothing," Jennifer admitted, shaking her head from side to side. "Only that you'd been kind enough to invite us to stay here while he was away."

"Oh." Richard appeared somewhat mollified by this information. "Well, I can't think why he didn't discuss it with you."

I can, Jennifer thought grimly to herself. Without question, her father had recognized that if she might have disliked the notion of playing governess, she was certain to be infuriated when she discovered that that activity was meant to render her sober and responsible as well. And although he'd never indicated to her that he judged those same qualities in need of improvement or even that he thought them indispensable to getting on in the world, he'd clearly suffered some sort of attack of conscience before his departure. Now, she was apparently expected to reap the consequences of his belated, if well-meaning, attempt to become a model parent and to set her on the correct pathway of life, Jennifer realized. And that being the case, she immediately determined to make the best of it and, in the process, to learn whether she might not turn it to her advantage.

"Oh, doubtless he was too busy with his preparations and it slipped his mind," she invented. "Truly, it doesn't matter in the least to me. I was only surprised, is all. In fact, now that I think of it, it seems an altogether interesting idea," she said truthfully in a more enthusiastic voice.

"It does?" Richard said in surprise, having as much trouble adjusting to her sudden change of mood as he'd earlier had accommodating himself to her mere presence. "Well, in that case, perhaps we should arrange to discuss the particular course of study the twins are to follow," he suggested.

Jennifer considered for a moment. "Give me a few days to begin to feel comfortable with them, and vice versa, and to get a sense of what they already know," she decided. "And I think we ought to start slowly," she added, flashing a disarmingly brilliant smile at Richard. "After all, as Demosthenes said, 'Small opportunities are often the beginning of great enterprises.'" And leaving him to ponder that observation, she turned and swept briskly out of the room.

After her departure, Richard collapsed deeper into his chair, feeling as exhausted as he used to after winning a footrace at Eton. Clearly, he hadn't reckoned on the energy that would be required to deal with his guest on even the simplest of matters. *Really, these emotional palpitations are most unsettling,* he thought, and he sincerely hoped they weren't going to continue. *I simply won't allow it,* he told himself. *And what's more, I won't let Jennifer Somers disrupt my life and lead my household on some pretty dance. Of that,* he promised the empty room, *you may be perfectly certain.*

Chapter 5

DESPITE HER oft-expressed preference for the unconventional, Jennifer harbored a practical side as well. What's more, she did not—as many others apparently did—find the two tendencies contradictory, or even mutually exclusive. If anything, she felt her ability to deal with the problems of everyday life in a competent manner both prepared her to recognize the extraordinary when she encountered it and also ensured that she possessed the freedom and the insight to enjoy the experience to the utmost. The process was not necessarily a conscious one, however. That is to say, she wasn't in the habit of reminding herself that now such-and-so would be opportune or efficacious, and then carefully orchestrating her actions accordingly. Instead, everything had been molded together to such a degree that it was often impossible for her to separate intent from outcome, decision from action. And even when she actually paused long enough to resolve how she ought to proceed, it was more with the idea of framing how she might mentally approach a particular situation than determining in advance what specific steps she might take within that context; the latter she was content to allow circumstances to dictate instead.

Therefore, when she'd announced to Richard Avery that she wanted a couple of days to become acquainted with the twins, she'd had no preconceived notion of how she was to go about accomplishing that task. And although the situation in which she now found herself had initially come as something of a shock, it was primarily her assigned role as the twins' governess that felt uncomfortable. She did indeed like children very much, as her father had said, and had frequently bemoaned the fate that had allotted her no brothers and sisters. To Jennifer, the chief attraction of children lay in the fact that they were usually the only people who acted as spontaneously as she did herself, without making a giant distinction between purpose and performance. And if anything, it was precisely George and Caroline's apparent inability to do and say what they wished without first considering its correctness that set them remarkably apart from others their own age.

Never had she known two nine-year-olds who acted less childlike and more like a pair of little automatons than George and Caroline, Jennifer decided three days later. This phenomenon, she'd quickly realized, was mainly the result of their heads having been stuffed with such an endless number of cautions and strictures that they seemed able to produce a convenient reason for not doing anything she'd proposed. Moreover, the author of that list of prohibitions was none other than their father. And although he apparently always couched his instructions in terms that showed he was properly solicitous of the twins' well-being, such generalities also indicated his reluctance to take the more personal interest in them of a normal, caring parent.

"Don't you want to walk to the Columbia Garden for an ice cream?" Jennifer would suggest.

"Oh, yes," the twins would answer eagerly, and then invariably add something like, "But Papa doesn't allow us to eat sweets in the middle of the day."

Or, "Wouldn't you like to visit the new panorama in Greenwich Street?" Jennifer would wonder.

"Very much," George and Caroline would assure her, before saying sadly, "But Papa says we're only to go to see things that are said to be educational and broadening."

Certainly it wasn't surprising, therefore, that when Jennifer finally kept her appointment to discuss the subject of the children's education, she came prepared to discuss the form of it as well. She found Richard Avery as usual in his study, poring over what seemed to be an inexhaustible stream of papers that kept him busy at all hours when he wasn't actually at work in his office. In fact, when he raised his head as she entered the room, Jennifer was struck by how bone weary he looked. The tiny lines around his eyes and mouth seemed to have deepened even in the short time since she'd arrived at No. 30 Wall Street, though they did give his handsome face a new distinction and a sort of individuality it had heretofore seemed to lack. Why, she hadn't spared a thought to his life outside the house, she realized somewhat guiltily as she sat down, nor considered whether her mere presence in that same household might have proven problematic to the orderly existence that she suspected he preferred. But to be honest, it wasn't only that she wondered if she might have been acting in an uncaring fashion that now prompted Jennifer to reconsider her behavior. Rather, she'd already begun to perceive that there was something vulnerable about her host—some elusive inconsistency which, despite his controlled exterior and his best efforts to disguise it, had definitely captured her interest. And the sudden recognition that she was really longing for a way to prove herself a helpmate—not just a thorn in his side, as she'd once threatened—made her feel vulnerable and a little shy herself, in turn.

Richard had actually been in the midst of worrying over the latest scurrilous attack on the Manhattan Company's ability to provide drinking water for the city's inhabitants. Already, the flow in some of the original wooden mains laid only a few years before had been almost completely shut off by the growth of tree roots, and the pipes were in urgent need of repair. In addition, it now appeared that a new pump engine would soon be required and installation would temporarily interrupt service altogether—a situtation of which the company's critics were bound to make the most. In fact, Richard had been wondering distractedly if this time that criticism might not take the form of some physical protest when Jennifer's appearance provided him with another, if rather more enjoyable, distraction.

She was wearing a morning dress of some kind of twilled stuff in a clear jonquil color that wrapped to one side and fastened snugly down the front with a row of tiny, covered buttons. The lightest wisps of swansdown edged the sleeves and collar and trailed across the garment to descend and

circle the hem. Even the high neckline and properly circumspect cut of the gown couldn't negate the fact that it showed
off the wearer's admirable figure quite—admirably. Indeed,
Richard was happily caught up in observing how the severi-
ty of the style was very nicely offset by the silly fluff of
feather trimming when he realized with a start that his guest
had just asked him a question.

"I beg your pardon," he said, rubbing a hand across his
brow in a gesture of unfeigned weariness. "I'm afraid I
wasn't attending. You were saying?" he asked politely.

"I was only wondering if you were ready to entertain my
suggestions for the twins' curriculum," Jennifer repeated in
a similar tone. *And also why your oh-so-formal manner
always makes me feel curiously reluctant to speak,* she
thought to herself, *much as I'd like to risk breaking through
that careful reserve to inquire what's troubling you.* "Very
well, then," she said in response to his nod. "I think we
can safely pursue all the ordinary subjects such as Latin and
Greek and grammar and so forth. To these I would add a
little French and Italian—conversation only, at first—and
some history—concentrating on the modern rather than
strictly on the ancient periods. My idea, you see," she
continued more enthusiastically, "is, insofar as possible, to
set those studies within the context of life here in America.
For example, what better way to learn the history of, say,
your country's fight for independence than to visit the sites
of some of its famous battles?" She moved impatiently to
the edge of her chair, looking at him in an earnest way that
he found utterly appealing. "You see," she rushed on,
"I've discovered that the twins know very little about this
wondrous city and even less about anyone outside the walls
of their house. And it's my feeling that unless they're able
to understand how the smaller pieces function—how their
lives and those of other people fit into the larger picture—
that they'll never be able to deal with the world and
successfully make a place for themselves in it. Don't you
agree?"

"Er, yes," Richard admitted, thinking it would have been
difficult for any right-minded person to have found much
with which to disagree in that little speech. That fact alone,

given what he already knew about the character of the speaker, caused him to feel a momentary flash of uneasiness. Still, her purpose seemed clear and reasonable enough—quite what he might even have suggested himself—so surely it didn't signify that her methods sounded a trifle out of the ordinary, he told himself. Indeed, he was considerably relieved to think that the question of what to do about the twins was apparently to be resolved so easily.

If truth be told, however, Richard was somewhat embarrassed to discover how little difference it actually made to him in the end what Jennifer suggested the twins ought to study or how. He'd already perceived that she was approaching the matter with what he'd judged to be the proper amount of deliberation and that she appeared to have as solid a grasp of the issue as he'd ever had himself. Therefore, he'd rapidly decided that it only made sense to place the matter in her hands, and this he was prepared to do at once. If he'd been willing to admit it, however, the businesslike approach he'd selected very neatly concealed a second more compelling, though far less rational, purpose: how to discover a reason for him to spend some time with Jennifer regularly on a personal, if not an intimate, basis. Of course, if he'd dared to ask, that lady would doubtless have assured him that he didn't need to manufacture a pretext to share her company. But the fact remained that such an arrangement was the only one in which he could imagine feeling comfortable to any extent. And having unfortunately had a good deal more experience in dealing with papers than people, he promptly made the miskake of concluding that one could handle them in the same dry fashion, if need be.

"By all means, go along just as you wish," he advised Jennifer in such an unemotional manner that it made her stare at him in surprise. "No need even to bother me with the details. I'm confident that you must know my general feelings about such things. Well then, all I ask is that you don't encourage George and Caroline to act in any way that could be considered unseemly or injurious to their best interests and that you meet with me every week to report the news of their progress," he finished. Then, without waiting

for her response—or, possibly, feeling one wasn't necessary—
he lowered his eyes back to the papers in front of him.

Recognizing that gesture as a dismissal, Jennifer rose and
walked slowly toward the door of the room. She was all at
once aware of feeling a trifle disappointed by the outcome of
the interview. In the first place, the impersonal manner Mr.
Avery had employed when talking about the twins seemed
to dash a momentary hope that he might prove a loving
father after all. And in the second place, he hadn't appeared
all that much more interested in talking with her, either. In
fact, save for his initial reaction when she'd entered the
study, he'd appeared determined to adhere both to his
habitual demeanor and to his customary routine, insofar as
possible, without allowing her to alter those circumstances
by a single degree. Surely he hadn't given the slightest hint
that he found her attractive or her company enjoyable,
Jennifer reminded herself. Or could it be that he hadn't yet
stopped to consider his feelings, or even perhaps that he
couldn't—or didn't know how to—recognize them? she
wondered. This last thought made her feel considerably
more optimistic, and before closing the door, she cast a look
of quiet sympathy at the gentleman bent over his desk. Then
she shook her head at what she hoped was only his stubborn
foolishness, and at the same time smiled inwardly at her
own folly in feeling drawn toward a man who so far
appeared to be a decidedly unacceptable partner.

Although Jennifer had to admit being surprised at Richard
Avery's ready acquiescence, she wasn't about to quarrel
with having so effortlessly achieved her goals. Therefore, in
the days that followed, she quickly took advantage of the
authority with which he'd vested her to arrange life in the
schoolroom to her satisfaction.

They chose their studies from either Latin or Greek,
natural science or mathematics, grammar or composition,
history or philosophy, French or Italian. But that was where
any resemblance to regular lessons ended. As she'd told the
twins' father, Jennifer was convinced that information couldn't,
or shouldn't, exist in a vacuum; the children needed to be
able readily to discuss and to understand what they'd learned,

as well as to comprehend that what they studied wasn't merely isolated but integral to the context of their lives. Thus, while in the morning they might first read one of Caesar's campaigns in the ordinary way, as Richard Avery had requested, they were also just as likely to spend the afternoon acting out the battle itself. Or if they had consulted a geology text after breakfast, they might find themselves near teatime strolling along the Hudson and examining the strata in the cliffs on the opposite side of the river.

Each of the four took a different sort of pleasure in these exercises, and in turn, each seemed to derive a unique benefit from them. Timid little Caroline was gently but firmly informed that she had to take her own part and couldn't rely on her brother to represent her any longer. Still, she continued to be too shy to do so until the day they were discussing Greek mythology. Struck by the sudden realization that it might be speaking aloud of which the girl was afraid, Jennifer produced the working end of a mop, plopped it on Caroline's head, and ordered her to act out the role of Medusa. That suggestion was happily seized upon, and soon the child was standing on the schoolroom table, waving her arms vigorously about, and emitting a series of chilling, unearthly moans. So amazing was her performance that Perseus and his two companions were quite unable to cut off her head as they were supposed to because George, Molly, and Jennifer couldn't stop laughing long enough to raise a hand. And after that day, Caroline had been a good deal less reluctant to add her voice—and sometimes even her words—to the general conversation.

It had taken Jennifer a bit longer to figure out what made her uneasy about Caroline's brother, however. In fact, it wasn't until they decided to visit the house at No. 1 Cherry Street on the corner of Franklin Square, where Washington had lived when he was president, that she began to have an idea where the problem lay. They'd been admiring the three-story, colonial-style mansion and had just begun discussing the first years after the country had officially become the United States.

"Papa said George Washington wrote the Constitution," George volunteered proudly.

Jennifer shook her head. "No," she corrected, "he helped draft it, to be sure, but I believe Thomas Jefferson and President Madison are generally credited with being its chief authors."

George looked confused. "But Papa told me he wrote it, and he wouldn't lie."

"Of course he wouldn't," Jennifer agreed. And how many times, she realized, did George punctuate his sentences with "Papa said," or "Papa told us"? It was as if in this way he was able to include his father in the conversation, even though he wasn't present, and to make himself believe their lives were more intimately connected than Jennifer knew them to be. But was it also that he needed to make him into a hero, to place him on a pedestal as well? For certainly, by seeing him as an authority, as the giver of information, as someone who knew everything, George was creating an idealized vision of the man whom, she suspected, he knew in his heart was a far from perfect parent.

"When we get home, I'll show you the passage in your history book that describes how the Constitution was composed, and you can see for yourself what role Washington played," Jennifer said. She knelt down in front of George, forcing him to look at her while she spoke. "Think of it this way," she began. "You make mistakes, don't you? Well then, why would you believe that when you grow up you wouldn't continue to make a mistake once in a while? It's no catastrophe, you know. Your father was simply wrong, that's all. It doesn't suddenly make him an ogre or even a bad man. Perhaps he didn't understand your question, or he really thought he knew the truth. Or perhaps," she said softly, with a flash of inspiration, "he needed to feel that he was the one person who could answer your question. But it really doesn't matter very much what his reasons were, though—does it?"

George hesitated for a moment. "I'm glad he didn't know," he blurted out, immediately looking as if he ought to feel guilty for voicing that thought.

Jennifer laughed. "I quite agree," she confided. "Why, just imagine how relieved I am to know that since you grant your father can be wrong on occasion, I don't have to worry so much if I should happen to make a mistake, too,'' she said, neatly putting herself in George's place and hoping he noticed the substitution.

In fact, as the days passed, Jennifer often put herself in the twins' place and came to realize more clearly how very different their upbringing was from the way her own had been. Watching George and Caroline, she felt almost as if she were literally seeing how she might have turned out herself—if her father had been a more conventional sort of person, that is, or possibly if circumstances hadn't convinced him to act otherwise. The twins, she decided, were a perfect example of what could happen to children raised by someone who had all the right intentions but who resisted throwing his heart into the bargain.

The question of precisely where Richard Avery's heart lay was one to which Jennifer had to admit she'd already begun to devote a good deal of attention. Ordinarily, that development would have been unusual enough, given that in her experience the situation was far more commonly reversed, and also that she'd never anticipated finding herself so definitely intrigued by a man like Mr. Avery. To be perfectly honest, though, Jennifer wasn't in the habit of spending much time pondering the state of her own heart, either. That is to say, she easily accepted the notion that she might one day marry and have a family. Still, that prospect had always seemed to exist somewhere in the far-off future, and the particulars of who, when, and where remained definitely fuzzy at best. And for someone with an impetuous and emotional nature, Jennifer had nevertheless proven surprisingly restrained about bestowing her affections on a mere anybody—though whether that tendency was the product of design or coincidence, even the lady herself probably couldn't have said for certain.

By the time her next meeting with her host arrived nearly a week later, Jennifer found herself eagerly anticipating the chance to fill in her picture of him with additional personal details—and blithely unaware that he had the identical purpose in mind. She chose to believe, however, that her real errand was to discuss the progress of the twin's schooling instead, though it wasn't altogether clear if in private she might have admitted that that was only a giant subterfuge. And since, morever, this was the selfsame excuse that Richard had already seized upon, the interview seemed destined to follow a somewhat rocky course.

They met again in the study, just as dusk began to fall. Her host was obviously used to thinking this room his exclusive domain, Jennifer noted, and had therefore chosen to conduct what he'd assuredly term part of the household business in it. She would have preferred a more neutral setting, she thought to herself. But wait a minute—why was she suddenly phrasing things as if the two of them were adversaries when they were actually on the same side, so to speak, as far as the twins were concerned? And then, despite her assurances to George that it didn't matter why his father always insisted on assuming the role of savant, she promptly decided to see if she couldn't discover what his reasons might be after all.

"Good afternoon," she observed in what she thought of as her company voice. "It gets dark so early these days— don't you think? Why not light a fire to brighten things up a little, and offer me a glass of sherry to warm my insides as well?" she suggested.

Unfortunately, Richard had been thinking of undertaking those very activities himself. Thus, he immediately felt grumpy at having had the initiative so quickly plucked from his grasp and also at having had his feeling of being in control so neatly dashed to bits, besides. "Just what I was thinking," he said sulkily. Things weren't going at all the way he'd imagined they would, he realized in irritation. And as he set about accomplishing the aforementioned tasks, he couldn't refrain from trying to figure out how it was that his beautiful guest inevitably seemed to put him out of sorts. He had to admit that she looked lovely today, in a pale green gown embroidered here and there with what looked like weeping willows. If only her conversation were as refined as her clothing, he found himself thinking wistfully.

"No need that I can see to pull a long face and act cross merely because I happened to read your mind," Jennifer pointed out somewhat tactlessly, quite as if she had.

"I wasn't," Richard argued, and then stopped abruptly

when he saw that he'd only managed to confirm her statement. "Oh, well, perhaps you're right," he allowed.

The very trait that you endeavor so assiduously to cultivate yourself, Jennifer thought. This time, however, she wisely held back from commenting to that effect, and sought to direct the conversation along what she felt would be more profitable channels. "Perhaps," she agreed. She tossed Richard a teasing smile and was relieved when he grudgingly gave her a small one in return. "Do you know," she continued in a thoughtful voice, "this business about being right is altogether too tricky, to my way of thinking. For instance, I'm fairly confident that the method I've chosen for George and Caroline's studies shall prove beneficial. Of course, if I should discover that I'm wrong, I wouldn't have any qualms about admitting it, and then at once trying another tack." Seeing that her host was regarding her politely but without that light of recognition in his eyes which she'd expected to discover, she adjusted her approach to one that was considerably less subtle. "I do think it's important for children to see that adults can admit when they've made a mistake—don't you? Otherwise, I would imagine they'd become reluctant to own up whenever they found they were wrong for fear of being chastised for something that I, for one, consider a normal part of learning and of life—don't you?" she repeated.

Richard, who'd clearly never stopped to consider the matter except in the abstract, hesitated for a minute. "Yes, I suppose that's true," he said finally. "But surely you'll grant that it's important that children be given correct information?"

"Oh, indeed I do," Jennifer assured him. "But merely wishing to be thought—or trying to give the appearance of being—forever right isn't exactly synonymous with striving to be accurate in what one says, you know."

"Yes, I see—although I must confess that I don't think I ever separated the two in my mind before."

Jennifer nodded understandingly. "Well, ofttimes people don't," she acknowledged. "The thing is, it seems to me it's all the more crucial to make such distinctions when children are involved. For instance, when George discovered you'd been mistaken in telling him that Washington wrote the Constitution, he very nearly thought you'd purposefully lied.''

"He didn't—? I mean, he did—?" Richard asked in confusion. "Oh, dear—I never meant to steer the boy wrong, I promise. It's only that so often it appears that what's important is that George have an answer to his question right away—and that *I* be the one to provide it. And although I don't exactly set out to fabricate an answer, sometimes when I'm not altogether certain of the facts, I don't bother to check beforehand or, I see now, even to indicate that I'm not perfectly sure." He paused to consider this point for a moment, and then seeing the sympathetic look on his guest's face, he added a trifle lamely, "He looks up to me so very much, you see. Why, sometimes I confess I allow myself to be persauded that I really am the perfect hero he prefers to think me. His attitude is highly flattering, after all, and I'm sure you'll agree I'd have to be less than human not to be seduced by it on occasion."

Privately Jennifer might have hoped for such a candid revelation, but she never would have permitted herself to expect one. Nevertheless, she hastily smothered her surprise at that development and promptly offered a few positive remarks to show that she was properly deserving of Richard's continued confidence. Clearly, a new dimension had been added to their relationship with this exchange, she decided happily. And though they soon moved on to discuss less personal topics, both were aware of the congenial atmosphere that had been established between them that persisted for the remainder of the interview. And that fact, together with the promise of future talks and the opportunity for increased intimacy they'd no doubt offer, caused the two participants to feel highly pleased with one another and almost unreasonably cheerful, too.

It was that same sort of intimate, loving contact with her father that Jennifer missed most of all since his departure, and until now the atmosphere in the Avery household had scarcely been calculated to compensate for that loss. Indeed, she was repeatedly conscious of feeling somewhat like a felon for using George and Caroline as a bulwark both against her own loneliness and against the coldness of life at No. 30 Wall Street. She derived an infinite amount of pleasure from peeling off the layers of reserve one by one from the twins to reveal the sweet creatures beneath, who were not only obviously in need of loving attention but also just as obviously afraid to ask for it. Or was it, she wondered, that they thought they might not get it even if they did ask?

That the two were totally unused to any outward show of affection Jennifer had discovered quite by accident. A few days after her arrival, they had gathered one morning in the schoolroom as usual. After a half hour or so, she noticed that Caroline looked very tired and was holding her head carefully as if it pained her to move it. When she inquired if something was the matter, the girl admitted that she'd been awake half the night with the toothache, and opened her mouth to point at the spot where a molar was pushing through a swollen, reddened gum.

Jennifer at once asked Molly to find the tincture of laudanum that she used to relieve various minor pains. Then without thinking, she gathered the child into her arms and began stroking her hair and rocking her back and forth, murmuring sympathetically, in an effort to make her feel better. But Caroline didn't know how to respond to such tender treatment, she quickly realized, for the poor thing sat stiff and uncomfortable in her lap, silently enduring her attentions, instead of snuggling happily against her breast as Jennifer fully expected her to do. Obviously, she couldn't force the girl to enjoy even the least measure of physical contact that she considered normal between adult and child in the same household. And just because she was used to being stroked affectionately herself, Jennifer admitted, it wasn't fair to subject either of the children to such intimacy if they didn't invite it. Perhaps when they'd known each other longer, or after they'd become accustomed to thinking it a possibility, they might start to reach for her hand on the street or even to ask for a goodnight kiss, she thought wistfully.

Such wishes didn't seem to hamper Molly's relationship with George and Caroline, however, Jennifer admitted with a touch of jealousy, though doubtless it was her position as something more than friend and less than teacher that assisted her in this respect. Molly's family had been a very close one, and so she, too, was used to a healthy dose of touching and caressing. More often than not, Molly's affection for the twins took the form of tousling their hair or poking them in the ribs, and their growing regard for her seemed to find a comfortable outlet in equally informal gestures. Though if anything, she had proven a more exacting taskmistress than Jennifer, for she didn't hesitate scornfully to term George a widgeon if he seemed slow to grasp a point or briskly to call Caroline to order for not attending to her lessons. And thus, Jennifer found that as the days passed, Molly's alternate cajoling and berating in some indefinable way began to help meld the four together into the semblance of a family.

The growing intimacy between his two children and his two guests wasn't completely lost on Richard Avery. The fact that he was still away from the house much of the time and saw the twins infrequently hadn't changed. But now, when he did feel like visiting with them, he discovered that he couldn't always expect them simply to appear at his request. More often than not, he'd inquire as to their whereabouts only to be informed by Mrs. Booth that they'd taken a walk to the Battery or be advised by Walters that the group had borrowed the carriage to drive to Greenwich. They seemed always to be busy now, and their plans rarely included him.

Indeed, one Saturday morning, Richard found himself with several hours of free time to fill and an empty house. And as he stood in the doorway of the schoolroom, gazing about at the changes that had been wrought by someone since he'd last ventured into that realm, he began to admit that that same person might be responsible for the recent alteration in his feelings as well. Colorful crayon drawings were tacked all over one wall, and on another were several hand-painted papier-mâché masks of various animals, as far as he could tell. A couple of wooden flutes, a small drum, and a pair of cymbals heaped on one side of the table accounted for the strange sounds he'd lately heard emanating from the floor above his head like a slightly demented chorus. And a chessboard set up on the opposite side of the table with a game in progress attested to the children's participation in mental, as well as physical, exercise.

Richard walked slowly down the stairs and hesitated outside his study. It couldn't be that he resented Jennifer Somers's presence, he thought as he toyed idly with the doorknob. No, he decided, it was rather that he was beginning to resent the time she was able to spend with the twins, as well as what he felt sure must by now be her considerable influence over them. And what's more, he admitted, wasn't he just a tiny bit jealous of the twins' claim to her time and attention? And why didn't Jennifer think to invite him along on these outings, or the twins imagine that he might enjoy such an invitation? he wondered, feeling somewhat sorry for himself. He was actually beginning to feel left out as well, he realized with a start, and that sensation was so novel to one who prided himself on being in control of every situation that for a few minutes he could do little more than peck reluctantly around its edges the way a hungry bird might a piece of spoiled meat.

He shook himself briskly as if to get rid of the dust accumulated by standing too long in the same place. Still, that was no reason why he needed to allow matters to remain as they were, he reminded himself. And after inquiring about the destination for today's outing, he set out to see whether he couldn't intercept the rest of his household at someplace called the Fly Market.

It was amazing how narrowly circumscribed his own life had become of late, Richard thought. Why, he'd be surprised if he could recall the last time he'd ventured farther than the end of the block, where the offices of the Manhattan Company were located. He hadn't even known there was a public market on Pearl Street scarcely a five-minute walk from his door, and he honestly couldn't attribute that oversight to anything other than lack of interest, he realized.

The Fly Market turned out to be an elaborate affair occupying the entire narrow block along Maiden Lane between Pearl and Water streets. As Richard wandered among stalls offering imported herbs and spices, all manner of produce, beef, and pork, and a variety of delicious-looking confections, he began to admit that not only hadn't he known the source of the food that appeared daily on his table, but that he'd also only a slim chance at best of locating anyone within the vast confines of the market.

Luckily, just when he was about to give notice to quit, he heard a happy shriek that sounded strangely familiar from somewhere close by. Following the sound, he turned a corner and abruptly came face to face with his two children, who were dancing excitedly beside a large tub.

Jennifer was not only surprised at encountering Richard Avery so unexpectedly, but also at discovering that she felt so immoderately happy about it, as well. For a moment, she tried to pretend that she was glad primarily for the children's sake, and that she was merely curious to see how he would behave outside the confines of his orderly little world, particularly after their recent conversation. And since she was quite unable to sort out her emotions, she was only able to smother her confusion in the end by steadfastly concentrating on her two charges. Even their father's sudden appearance—which once would have rendered them as sober and formal as he—was unable to dampen the twins' pleasure this time, she observed with some satisfaction. In fact, Jennifer was obliged to stifle a laugh at his expression when the two children scarcely hesitated before grabbing his hands and dragging him over to the tub of sea water in which a large number of fish were thrashing about, and then loudly imploring his help in selecting one for Monsieur Fouquet to cook for dinner.

Whether it was because of the unexpectedness of this request or because of the unusual surroundings Jennifer couldn't be certain, but for once Richard Avery was clearly at a pass. He, too, was having a little trouble acting any way other than flustered at finding himself in public with Jennifer for the first time. Thank God they weren't alone, he thought fervently, feeling certain that it was only on account of the other people present that he hadn't turned tail and run at the last second. Nevertheless, he was fleetingly conscious first of how unpolished he must surely appear, and second that he was probably the only one of the group to whom such a ridiculous thought had occurred. He smiled ruefully, looked rather helplessly from Jennifer to Molly and back again, and then shrugged his shoulders. "I'm afraid I haven't any idea," he began in an apologetic voice. "Perhaps one of you—?"

"Now, the first thing to look for," Molly took up smoothly, "is for a fish that's still swimming heartily around and not sunk to the bottom and just lying there." She leaned over the tub to poke at one or two candidates in a way that made them leap out of the water and made Caroline shriek again in delight. "And you want it to have a nice fresh color—not all mottled-looking—and bright, clear eyes, too. I think that one should do nicely," she concluded, indicating her choice to the fishmonger. The two children watched somewhat less happily as the man hauled the fish out of the tub, knocked it casually on the head, and then wrapped it up in brown paper after it had stopped flopping all over the table.

George bravely took charge of their purchase, and the group started slowly toward home, pausing now and then to examine the contents of the stalls along the way. Richard, Jennifer noted approvingly, seemed in no particular hurry but was quite content to wander at the children's pace, his daughter's hand still tucked trustingly in his. Was he actually beginning to come to his senses and alter his attitude toward the twins, or was this merely a temporary aberration? she wondered. The thought that it seemed much easier to think of him as a father than as a man did occur to her, but she attempted without much success to push it out of her mind. After all, she'd already started to think of them as a family, so why did it make her feel so embarrassed suddenly to imagine herself in the role of the twins' mother? Wasn't it, perhaps, the realization that she would literally assume that role if she were to marry Mr. Avery that now threatened to make the blood rush to her cheeks? So in order to cover her confusion for the second time that afternoon, she asked curiously, "And what do you make of the Fly Market, sir?"

"Amazing," Richard pronounced in a convincing voice. "But I have one question." He looked around to ensure that they couldn't be overheard and then whispered, "Where are the flys?"

At this, the rest of the group went off into whoops of laughter that lasted several minutes. Finally, Jennifer recovered sufficiently to take note of the injured look that had appeared on the speaker's face, and to recommend that George relate the story Molly had told them earlier.

George hesitated for a moment and then waved his arm in the direction of the stalls. "All this used to be a meadow with a creek running through it," he began shyly. "It was always a bit dampish, so the Dutch named it a *vlai*, which was their word for valley or wet ground." He looked at Jennifer, who smiled encouragingly, before continuing. "There was a market here even in those days, and after awhile the people began to call it the '*vlai* market' or 'valley market.' And pretty soon '*vlai*' got changed somehow to 'fly,' and it's been the Fly Market for ever so long now." He regarded his father in a kindly manner, and then informed him, "So you see there aren't really any flys—at least, no more than usual."

"I see," Richard said. He, too, caught Jennifer's eye for a moment to show her that he had kept their earlier conversation in mind during the outing. "Thank you, George," he told him gravely. "That was a most edifying—er, educational— story, to be sure, and I'm altogether grateful for the benefit of your wisdom on the subject, and Molly's."

The excursion to the Fly Market had apparently been to Richard's liking because in the following weeks he occasionally joined the group on other, similar outings. When they saw that their father could actually be interested in such innocent diversions, George and Caroline began clamoring to invite him along on every occasion. But even though he'd several times demonstrated that he could be a considerate guest and could treat his children with a gentle tolerance of which she'd heretofore thought him incapable, Jennifer continued to feel reluctant about including him. She told herself that she was merely protecting the twins, wary that he might suddenly revert to his old ways and dash the fragile new relationship between them to pieces. And surely she was more favorably disposed toward him than before on account of this change in his demeanor and not because she might be starting to feel distinctly interested in him in a way that went far beyond what she might feel for any reasonably intelligent and attractive man. He was certainly a puzzle, she decided, and it was only the hope of understanding the complicated way his mind worked that compelled her to devote so much energy to thinking about him—wasn't it?

Nevertheless, she had to admit that she'd begun to look forward to their weekly talks together and to dress carefully and otherwise to prepare for them with a good deal more thought than if she were merely going to play governess. After that first conversation, they had been too shy for a while to do anything other than stick to a discussion of schoolroom activities. Then she'd ventured to ask about the state of his business affairs, and another time he'd inquired how she was enjoying her visit to New York. Their conversations usually lasted an hour or more and ranged over a broad spectrum of topics in the same congenial fashion they had on that initial occasion—except when the talk came around to the subject of politics.

Jennifer shook out the folds of her sage-green China crepe gown and wondered irrelevantly if Richard would notice how nicely it matched the color of her eyes and how it made her skin look like fine, polished ivory. No, she admitted, he was far more likely these days to comment on some facet of her logic than on some aspect of her costume. She smiled wryly at herself in the mirror. How strange that, having satisfied herself that he in fact concealed a keen, inquiring mind behind his dull, conservative exterior, she should now find herself actively trying to make him interested in her as a member of the opposite sex rather than as simply a casual, conversational partner. And at the same time, ironically enough, he now acted far less concerned with anything having to do with her womanhood than with her mental capacity. A fine kettle of fish to be sure, but one that she'd had no small part in creating after all, she reminded herself with a lopsided grin.

Had she but known, Richard's thoughts were running in a remarkably similar direction. He'd declined the assistance of Walters, who doubled as his valet, and was now engaged in arranging the folds of his cravat himself. From that very first dinner nearly two months before with Jennifer and Lord Somers, he had to own that he'd felt in awe of that young lady's formidable intellect. And he'd soon realized it was only pure narrow-mindedness that had caused him to be surprised that a woman was capable of devising such complex arguments as she did, much less audacious enough to voice them. Ever since then, he'd made it his goal to persuade her to think of him as an intellectual equal, and he'd attempted to steer the conversation accordingly whenever possible. Yet, almost at the same instant he did so, he'd suddenly find himself thinking about cupping her delicate face in his hands or running his fingers through the tempting mass of her curls. But because he was convinced she'd only be amused, if not actually annoyed, by such common tactics, he'd sternly mastered those impulses time and again in favor of a more high-minded approach.

Therefore, shortly after the two were seated in his study that evening, he quickly—if inadvisably—moved the discussion around to the embargo that had been instituted by former President Jefferson.

"That sort of 'peaceful coercion' is simply a disastrous policy as far as business in concerned," Richard announced confidently. He took a sip of sherry and then regarded Jennifer over the rim of this glass. "Why, it bankrupted literally hundreds of people in New England alone, and who knows when—or if—they'll recover." He shrugged his shoulders as if to punctuate that point.

"Oh, the embargo was a misguided measure, I agree— but only because it didn't go far enough," Jennifer informed him bluntly. "Surely, it was the merest sop meant to placate some of the more vocal critics of this country's policies, and a slender bolster, at best, to her already dubious reputation abroad as a nation of cowards. I've even heard it whispered that there's some secret but compelling reason why a war at this time might prove fatal to the United States—though I, for one, should never believe it," she insisted, tossing off the rest of her sherry with an expert flip of the wrist.

"Huh!" Richard temporized. He hadn't heard that argument before and actually felt a chill when he paused to consider its possible significance. "Well, if you really want to learn the truth behind all these rumors, you'd best ask the man who will be stopping here day after tomorrow,'' he advised. ''John Henry is what's known, I believe, as a 'commercial traveler.' At any rate, he moves around the country a good deal and seems to have the ear of many of those in positions of influence. Doubtless he'll be able to illuminate the current state of affairs for us, if anyone can.'' He looked meaningfully at the papers on his desk to signify the interview had come to a close.

''Very well,'' Jennifer agreed. She rose, aware of feeling disgruntled about the course the evening had taken and more than a little sulky at having allowed the conversation to be terminated so abruptly. ''Let's see whether your Mr. Henry can provide me with a more suitable sparring partner and what he can offer in the way of enlightenment, shall we say?''

Chapter 6

JENNIFER BIDED her time for the next two days with somewhat more impatience than tact for one who was, after all, a guest in the household herself. It hadn't taken her long to realize that Richard Avery's social activities were of the barest minimum necessary to protect his standing at his company and within New York society. Whether that fact was the result of inclination or necessity, on account of his long hours and the persistent demands of his job, she'd so far been unable to determine. Nevertheless, it did strike her as highly unusual that in the last month and a half there hadn't been a single dinner or even a card party to disturb the domestic routine. Perhaps such events were curtailed on account of there not being a hostess to preside over the table, she mused. No, she decided upon reflection, it was far more likely that Mr. Avery found such diversions too uncomfortable, and indulged in them only when it was clearly impossible for him to avoid doing so. Why, hadn't the one evening at which a half dozen gentlemen had arrived at the door turned out, she'd learned later from Mrs. Booth, to be merely a business discussion over several bottles of cognac? What then, she wondered, had caused her host to reverse his customary practices for the sake of this Mr. John Henry? Tonight he had asked her to join them at dinner following Mr. Henry's arrival, but he'd also blushingly solicited her assistance in arranging a dinner party in the man's honor for the following Saturday evening. To this request she'd pleasantly acceded, partly because she loved planning that sort of entertainment and also because her curiosity had been piqued at the prospect of seeing how Richard Avery would act in a purely social setting.

Jennifer stood on tiptoe to fasten a pair of ivory combs into her hair and then stepped back to observe the effect in the mirror. She was wearing a satin robe in celestial blue with a demi-train, short sleeves fastened up the front with a row of pearls, and a broad border of Vandyke lace around the hem. A tippet edged with matching lace cascaded over her shoulders, the snowy white of her hair ornaments causing her curls to appear a deeper and more luxuriant red than usual. Mr. Henry must be a man of considerable influence, she reflected, making a few minor adjustments to her scarf, given the degree of upheaval the household had experienced merely to prepare for his visit. But then, knowing the extent to which her host tended to be impressed by titles and appearances, perhaps she'd best reserve judgment until she'd at least seen the man, she reminded herself with a smile before turning away from the glass.

John Henry was certainly not very remarkable looking, Jennifer decided approximately an hour later. She studied him across the table as he chatted with his host: average height and build, dark hair, close-set eyes, and a hawklike nose that dominated his face. He dressed rather flamboyantly, though; his embroidered waistcoat, for example, was far too ornate for a simple dinner, and his fashionably high shirt collar was as unbecoming to him as it was unwarranted to the occasion, in Jennifer's opinion. What's more, he had drunk quite a lot of claret, and his apparent tendency to speak loudly had now been exaggerated by the liquor into an irritating stridency, which he punctuated by repeated thumps with one fist upon the table for emphasis whenever he felt the discussion called for it.

Unfortunately, it was readily apparent to Jennifer, at least, that Mr. Henry's favorite topic of conversation was himself. To be sure, he'd been properly polite when they'd first been introduced. As the evening wore on, however, his deferential air had become near obsequious instead, and he now positively oozed a conviviality that was totally inappropriate to the brief duration of their acquaintance. To someone like Jennifer, adept at recognizing the flattery of sycophants, his approach was nothing but a far from subtle attempt to have her think of him as an equal. Ordinarily, it would have afforded her great pleasure to have boxed his ears (verbally, of course) and dealt him a stunning set-down. But she now found herself curiously reluctant to do so. Whether she hesitated, however, because she was conscious she wasn't in her own home or because she was curious to see whether Richard Avery would observe and choose to react to such behavior himself was unclear. Nevertheless, she forced herself to endure Mr. Henry's familiarities with the patience of a hawk on the hunt, deferring to him in a way she felt must surely be obvious, while secretly calculating the best moment to go for the kill.

"Actually, I was born in Ireland," Mr. Henry was saying as an apparent prelude to detailing his entire family background to her.

"Indeed?" Jennifer murmured politely in a colorless voice.

"Yes. One of the first families, of course," he told her, swelling visibly over even that mild encouragement. "No prospects, though. Younger brother," he added by way of explanation. He paused to help himself to another measure of claret, adorning the lovely damask tablecloth in the process with a fine spray of ruby drops. "Came to America in the expectation of becoming my uncle's heir, seeing as he was old and had a considerable fortune and was unmarried besides. But it didn't turn out quite as I'd hoped." He stared darkly into his wineglass for a moment without elaborating further. "Got married instead to a French lady with a title and a bit of blunt of her own," he continued. "But then she died and left me with a couple of brats and scarcely two pennies to rub together—the rest went to her brother. Kind of like your own situation, ain't it?" he said, turning toward Richard. "Only 'pears you've managed to get the brats and the fortune and the lady with the title as well!" He gave Jennifer a rather lewd wink and then actually went so far as to clap Richard on the shoulder.

"As I told you, Lady Somers is a guest in my house while her father is away on business," that gentleman said stiffly. But although he hastened to correct Mr. Henry's impression of the situation, he felt altogether flustered at the realization that he did so primarily for the benefit of his two guests. Privately, he'd felt a tiny thrill upon hearing the arrangement Henry had outlined, and part of him longed for the chance to consider it further.

"That's right, so you did," Mr. Henry agreed cheerfully, breaking into his thoughts. "Damndest luck I've ever seen!" He favored Jennifer with a brashly admiring smile. "Now where was I? Oh, yes. Well, when I discovered I needed to earn a more substantial living, I applied to the British minister, and through his influence with the American government was appointed a captain of artillery with a command first at Portland and then outside of Boston." He gulped the remainder of his claret and twirled the glass around in his fingers for a minute. "But the military just ain't the right field for a man with as much ambition as I have," he announced. "Besides, I'd come into a bit of money myself by then, so I bought a place in Vermont near the Canadian border and for the next five years devoted myself to the study of law."

"And that, I take it, is the profession in which you now engage?" Jennifer inquired.

"No," he advised, "too much of a free thinker, I'm afraid. Lately I've set up residence near Boston and turned my hand to writing. The policies of this administration are enough to scandalize anyone of the least sensibility and foresight, so I've taken it upon myself to compose a piece now and then in the hope of illuminating those follies for the ordinary reader. And I venture to think my little essays have met with some success, since I've received assurances to that effect from no less a person than the Governor General of Canada himself."

"Mr. Henry's articles have appeared in the *Columbia Centinel* in Boston and the *American Citizen* in New York," Richard told Jennifer. "And I know they must have attracted a good deal of interest in certain quarters because they contain more than the usual modicum of truth one has come to expect in politics today."

This remark prompted Jennifer to wonder who—aside from her host—had been so impressed by the specious-sounding Mr. Henry, and also what interest an official of the British government might have in encouraging his literary activities. "But perhaps I've misunderstood," she inserted, looking prettily confused. "I thought Mr. Avery said that you were something called a 'commercial traveler.'"

John Henry chuckled in what Jennifer felt to be an unpleasant fashion. "And so I am, dear lady, in the broadest sense of the term," he assured her with another wink. "You see, I travel in order to discover those things from which I may profit, and my income—or profit—is dependent upon what I learn during those same travels. In fact, I'm currently in the midst of concluding an arrangement that should see my financial situation nicely settled at last, if all goes as I expect." He lounged back in his seat for a moment and then smiled at Jennifer in a way that made her begin to think of snakes and other crawly things. "But here, now," he said in a patronizing tone, "surely you don't want to clutter up that charming head of yours with a lot of dull talk about business and politics?"

"Indeed, they do seem a puzzle to me, on occasion," Jennifer confessed. She held her breath, hoping Richard Avery wouldn't think to object to that fantastic claim and that it wouldn't occur to John Henry to believe that a woman could behave otherwise. "For instance, the other evening we were discussing the embargo," she began, when it appeared safe to do so.

Mr. Henry's fist thumped down on the table, making the

silverware jump and clatter. "Outrageous!" he exclaimed, his cheeks flushing a dull red with emotion. "The government simply has no excuse for treating its citizens in such a cavalier manner. If you ask me, there's a limit to what decent folks will tolerate. Why, if the policy of non-intercourse hadn't been canceled, I saw plenty of evidence to indicate that those injured would unite and rise up against the administration that had treated them in such a heinous fashion."

Jennifer found she could only stare at him in horror. "Do you mean to say you thought there'd actually be a civil war?" she managed at last.

"Quite possibly," he said in a knowing voice. "Though I think the term 'revolution' might be more appropriate. It was my feeling, you see, that once such a movement had begun in the New England states, where people had suffered most from the embargo, the rest of the country would quickly come to see the advantage of replacing the present government with one like the British, which advocates unrestricted trade and personal freedom."

At this point, Jennifer forgot herself enough to exclaim, "Like the—? Why, how can you claim that England advocates free commerce when the Orders in Council specifically allow her to capture any vessel from the United States seeking to trade with any other country than England herself?"

Richard shifted uneasily in his chair at this exchange. "You know I agree with you insofar as the principle is concerned," he told Henry. "It's the practice that don't always seem right and tight. Why I must admit that it was the fear of further hostilities that persuaded me to join in drafting a resolution protesting the search and capture of vessels and the impressing and murdering of citizens by foreign—that is to say, by British—armed ships."

This statement promptly caused Jennifer to look with much more favorable eyes upon her host. *So he doesn't necessarily accept a philosophy wholesale or without questioning it after all,* she mused, delighted to have stumbled upon this proof that he harbored a thoughtful, human side to his nature as well. Indeed, she was all at once conscious of how greatly she resented the circumstances that now prevented her from gratifying an immediate desire to learn how many other chinks she might discover in that gentleman's armor. And at the same time she was startled to realize how readily she'd be willing to forego a meaningful discussion of politics—or of anything else, for that matter—if it meant she'd have the opportunity to get to know Richard Avery on a more personal basis instead.

"But surely drastic measures can be the only response to serious crimes," Mr. Henry observed coldly, breaking into her thoughts. He frowned across the table at his two companions. "Will you at least grant that desertion falls under the heading of a serious crime? And now that the number of deserters has reached more than 2,000 a year, something has to be done to rectify the situation, or there'll be no one left to serve the British navy."

"But there must be some reason why so many men have seen fit to desert," Jennifer couldn't resist arguing. "And at any rate, I still don't understand why British deserters should necessarily turn up on American ships."

"Ah, but I collect they do," Richard told her. "The money we pay sailors is relatively good, you see, and our navy supposedly at peace—quite a contrast to the conditions of service in England." He hazarded a sympathetic smile at Jennifer and felt his heart leap as she responded with one that clearly showed she was grateful for his support. *This is what I've often pictured,* he thought happily: *the two of us firmly allied against the rest of the world.*

"Now wait just a minute," Mr. Henry objected, interrupting Richard's daydream as brusquely as he had Jennifer's. He pushed back his chair with such force that it nearly overturned. Then he began striding up and down one side of the dining room, gesturing widely in accompaniment to a speech that soon threatened to become a harangue.

"How conveniently everyone forgets that the Berlin Decree declares England to be in a state of blockade and asserts that France has the right to seize and confiscate any American ships carrying British goods or touching at British ports! Given that fact, why not declare war against France instead of England?" he asked rhetorically. He gulped for air and then plunged on. "But no one seriously considers that possibility, do they? And what's worse, the United States is guilty of practically financing France's war with England—didn't President Madison undertake to purchase the Louisiana Territory just when Napoleon needed money to continue his campaigns? And if you don't believe that being ruled by Bonaparte would be a worse fate than being delivered into English hands, then you're as much a moonling as little Mr. Jimmy himself,'' he informed Richard, before collapsing once more into his chair.

"I believe it was actually James Monroe who engineered the acquisition of Louisiana when he was envoy to Paris," Richard corrected mildly. "But let's have no more talk of war or politics tonight," he urged. "After all, it isn't every evening we can count on enjoying the company of a charming woman, so doubtless we should make the most of it." Whereupon, Mr. Henry having apparently exhausted his ire, conversation was thereafter directed into more desultory channels.

Later that evening when she was changing into her nightclothes, Jennifer had time to mull over the dinner table conversation at greater length. First, she allowed herself to indulge in a pleasant fantasy whose details were sketchy but which appeared to center upon a certain gentleman. How wonderful it had felt to discover herself and Richard Avery for once in perfect accord, she remembered with a half-smile. Why, it hadn't even mattered a whit that they'd differed on a few minor points when fundamentally they appeared to agree so nicely. She wrinkled her brow a little. What had mattered somewhat, though, was the fact that Richard hadn't seemed particularly worried at the outrageous attention Mr. Henry had shown her afterward. But perhaps her conscientious host had only decided he ought to be polite to his newest guest, she told herself. Doubtless he knew she could easily handle any unwarranted advances from Mr. Henry's direction. Of course, she had to admit it wouldn't have bothered her at all to see that he could be just a tiny bit jealous of how she bestowed her favors—or on whom. Still, he probably had so little experience in that realm that he was bound to be slow to react, she decided in a burst of generosity. Fortunately, that conclusion caused her to feel a good deal more encouraged about the course matters between them seemed to be taking, though she was still curious about how long it would be before Richard might be convinced to show his hand.

Unfortunately, however, this little activity did nothing to relieve a nagging anxiety that seemed to worsen the longer she thought about Mr. Henry's remarks on the political situation. Granted, he appeared to her to be the sort of man generally given to exaggeration—particularly when in his cups—as a method of enhancing his own importance. Nevertheless, she couldn't shake off the suspicion that his predictions contained more than a grain of truth and hadn't merely been calculated to make a good impression. But it was the uncertainty of how much she ought to believe that teased at her mind as she slipped beneath the covers and pulled a warm quilt up to her chin. Moreover, that doubt seemed to raise a host of other questions besides.

Exactly what sorts of things was Mr. Henry likely to discover in his travels that might earn him a reward? Who was in a position to be interested enough in such information to pay him for obtaining it? Was he really so certain of the current political climate that he believed a whole segment of the country wouldn't just object, should war be declared on England, but would actually revolt in order to side with her against their own government?

The more she turned over these questions one after another, the more uneasy she began to feel. Surely Mr. Henry's curiosity and knowledge surpassed what would be considered ordinary. Even the notion that the man might actually be a spy in the pay of some other government— presumably England—didn't seem altogether too fantastic, she realized. In fact, once the initial shock of such a possibility had worn off, she had to admit that if he were indeed a spy, it would neatly answer all of the questions she'd posed so far and more.

Jennifer reined in her thoughts and bolted upright in bed as an even more disturbing idea occurred to her. What if it was Mr. Henry's intention to enlist Richard Avery's assistance in promoting his cause? She chewed distractedly at the corner of a fingernail. He wasn't such a very unlikely candidate either, since on the surface, at least, his sentiments were similar to the ones his guest had advocated, and he'd even admitted that he agreed with him in principle. What was to prevent Richard from being persuaded to cast aside his doubts? She nibbled anxiously around another few fingernails. But suppose, she realized slowly, it wasn't a question of what but of who was to steer him clear of falling into such a trap? And wasn't she the logical choice of someone to undertake that task, since she was a prime hand in the art of persuasion herself? And what's more, even if she hadn't privately come to a firmer understanding of her feelings for that gentleman, she'd never forgive herself for merely standing by while he was tricked into participating in some dubious scheme when she might have been able to prevent it. Certainly that was the least any ordinary human being would do for another, she decided. And the fact that she cared for Richard a good deal more than for any ordinary man had influenced her only a trifle. Surely once she'd amassed a case against Mr. Henry she'd have little difficulty exposing him and urging Richard to challenge whatever plan the man might be planning to put forth.

This line of thinking proved so steadying that Jennifer was able to spare her second hand the same ignoble treatment as the first. All she needed now was the opportunity to search Mr. Henry's room in the hope of discovering notes or a journal or some other tangible proof of his intentions. And that goal had to be accomplished, she reminded herself, before her host—consciously or not—decided to throw in his lot with that of his other guest.

She should have known better than to try and plan in advance exactly what she meant to do, Jennifer thought rather grimly late Saturday afternoon. During the preceding three days, all her spare time had been devoted to assisting in the preparations for the dinner to be held that night in Mr. Henry's honor. And whenever she'd managed to shake off the encumbrance presented by the twins' devoted attendance to her, Molly—whom she'd promptly enlisted as her coconspirator—would report, for example, that their subject was too close to the bedrooms to make an investigation feasible. Or if she learned that the two gentlemen had actually gone out, it was only to discover that no one knew when they'd return, and she was reluctant to risk being found in Mr. Henry's room without an excuse, should he suddenly materialize there himself. What's more, she'd overheard him announcing that he intended to sail for England just as soon as he could manage to book passage. No, it was clear that the only time she could be assured both of knowing his exact whereabouts and the precise duration of his absence would be that same evening while the party was taking place. Somehow she'd have to slip out while the festivities were under way and endeavor to complete her search before her own absence became remarkable.

A few hours after reaching that decision, Jennifer fidgeted impatiently as Molly fastened a spray of miniature yellow rosebuds into her topknot and then carefully loosened a few tendrils to curl against her cheeks and neck. She was wearing a rather more elaborate gown than usual in a style known as a sacque. It consisted of a yellow satin overdress brocaded with flowers in white and silver worn atop a white satin petticoat worked in delicate Chinese embroidery; short, puffed sleeves covered in fine white gauze were fastened with yellow satin bows as was the overskirt, which was edged with Valenciennes lace. Her costume had been carefully chosen to play up her beauty to best advantage, and this purpose she'd accomplished admirably, she decided. Jennifer wasn't entirely unconscious of the effect she could have on men when she chose to exert the effort. In this case, she'd dressed so as to ensure that she'd prove a decided distraction to the members of the male sex who were present that evening—the better, she told herself, to carry out the plan she'd devised. And if she was aware of wondering how one particular man would react to seeing her, and was curious to discover if he might be as vulnerable to a beautiful woman as most men, she didn't allow herself to dwell on those thoughts for long.

She clasped a strand of very large pearls that had been her mother's around her neck and looked anxiously at Molly. "We're agreed then, are we not, that when the gentlemen and the ladies separate after dinner shall be the best time for me to disappear for a while. Then I shall come to find you directly, and we shall see what we can discover about the mysterious Mr. Henry's activities.''

Molly inspected her friend's fever-bright cheeks and glittering eyes for a moment. ''No need to fall into a pelter,'' she observed calmly. ''You go hobnob with the company for a bit and put them off the scent while I get the lay of the land. That way, we'll each be doing what we're best suited for, and between us we should manage to carry the thing off very nicely indeed,'' she said in a comforting voice.

These words of encouragement followed Jennifer down the stairs and into the drawing room where the household was gathered to receive the guests. She hadn't spent much time in this room before, and was so busy looking around that she completely missed Richard Avery's sharp intake of breath and John Henry's appraising smile that followed close upon her entrance. The decor was as staid as most of the other rooms of the house and equally undistinguished—save for the large, exuberant bowl of flowers she'd arranged earlier that day. Showy stalks of white and yellow gladiolus pushed above a mass of purple heather, providing a display that was quite distinctive, Jennifer decided.

Richard, who was still struggling to regain a composure that had been delightfully shattered by Jennifer's appearance, paused to admire the way the colors of the floral arrangement complemented that lady's gown as she bent to adjust a blossom. She was certainly a magnificent creature, he thought with a pang, and he'd be quite happy to look at her forever. He sighed. There was no denying that his feelings for Jennifer were far stronger than he'd hitherto been willing to admit, and that fact was proving equally as confusing as the feelings themselves. His first instinct had been to resist confessing how much he cared, and his second to try to keep those feelings as well hidden from everyone else as he initially had from himself. To do otherwise would leave him feeling far too exposed, much as he might wish that things could be different. Putting aside these unsettling thoughts, he bestirred himself to come forward and greet Jennifer.

"Good evening," he began. "May we offer you what we call a cocktail?" He led her over to a small table set with bottles of various spirits and containers of sugar, water, and something he said was known as bitters.

Mr. Henry bowed to her as well and then confided, "You should know, dear lady, that such concoctions are also known vulgarly as 'bittered sling,' on account of the fact that they're usually made with gin. The stated purpose, you see, is to awaken the appetite, but I daresay many a poor sod's forgotten food altogether after enjoying several of these little appetizers."

Jennifer laughed and took a small sip from her glass. "Indeed, I think I can understand why. I'm not entirely certain that I like it," she admitted, hazarding another sip and then wrinkling her nose. "Still, I've no doubt that more than one of these could make me forget my manners as well as my meal."

Mr. Henry, who could be quite personable when he chose, suddenly smiled. "Ah, you've hit upon the real purpose of this ritual," he informed her, "and that is to enable a roomful of strangers to feel on the very best terms with one another quickly. Why, how else would a poor stick like Richard here be able to sail gracefully through the social intricacies of an evening such as this?" he observed, but in a jocular tone that took the sting out of what Jennifer felt to be an uncomfortably accurate assessment of their host. Nevertheless, she was surprised to find that her mind automatically began at once to manufacture excuses for Richard's behavior, and it was only because he appeared willing to let that gibe pass without comment that she was likewise able to refrain from responding.

Mr. Henry appeared to be slam up to the mark with those predictions, at least, Jennifer concluded an hour or so later. By that time, the company had swelled to a dozen and had moved on to the dining room to partake of the excellent dinner Monsieur Fouquet had prepared. Everyone seemed in a most congenial mood, although whether this was due to the cocktails or the anticipation of the delicacies to come,

Jennifer wasn't certain. She looked around at the guests as they helped themselves to a first dish of turtle soup.

Richard Avery was seated, naturally, at the head of the table. On his left was a Mrs. Westfield, the elderly and very deaf widow of one of the officers of Richard's company. Next to her and to Jennifer's right was Mrs. Westfield's brother, Major Hartley, a veteran of the Revolution. On Jennifer's other side was Benjamin Hartley, who looked to be in his early thirties and who was enduring his mother's attempts to push him into conversation with Jennifer with what she felt to be admirable patience. Mr. Henry presided at the far end of the table, just past the well-meaning Mrs. Hartley, but he was devoting his attention to the striking blond with an exceedingly low-cut gown named Sylvia Trask. Robert Trask, her rather mousey husband and apparently one of Richard's business associates, came next. He was followed by Mrs. Edward Rutland, then the senior director of the Manhattan Company himself, and finally, Miss Abigail Rutland, on Richard's right hand. The last young lady was also blond but possessed a sort of fragile ethereal style in keeping with her willowy figure and cloud of golden curls. What's more, she and her host seemed to be on very familiar terms and chatted in low voices as the soup made the round of the table. Observing the proprietary interest that Mr. Rutland appeared to be taking in this exchange, Jennifer easily deduced that fixing a match between his daughter and his colleague was that gentleman's current objective. And it was certainly an appropriate one, given the nature of their business relationship and the fact that Richard appeared disposed to favor the lady. Jennifer found that the latter discovery was a distinctly sobering one, however, and the minute she admitted its importance, she also found herself wondering whether marriage with the lovely Miss Rutland was also uppermost in Richard's mind. She didn't even attempt to deny that she was jealous of the lady's prior claim on her host. After all, she reasoned in a strangely circuitous fashion, she could scarcely justify being angry that another woman had made Richard's heart her personal property when she'd been unwilling for so long to grant that he even possessed such an organ. Why, she probably ought to be relieved at finally securing the proof she'd sought that he was as susceptible as the next man to a beautiful face and figure, she told herself. Whereupon, she proceeded to ignore the inner voice that called her three kinds of fool for trying to make herself believe such a fairy tale, and began an attempt to converse with her lefthand neighbor instead.

This effort proved moderately successful so that Jennifer was able to partake of the salmon croquettes, turbot smothered in baby smelts, a saddle of mutton, chicken roasted in herbs, and boiled potatoes. The second course featured a dish said to be the Prince Regent's favorite: veal in a wine-and-cream sauce, sprinkled with truffles and surrounded by cooked onions, new potatoes, and miniature artichokes. By the time the dessert of assorted cheeses, an apricot tart, and a veritable pyramid of syllabub and jellies was served, Jennifer had managed to extract a summary of Benjamin Hartley's upbringing and education, and had learned that he was studying the law but that he wished to go into politics.

"You see, I find the old ways simply don't address the position our country's in at the moment," Mr. Hartley was explaining to her. "And there are plenty of others already in Congress who feel as I do—men like Henry Clay, Israel Pickens, and John Harper who want to ensure that we remain truly independent and don't slip under Britain's or France's thumb. So where once they might have opposed such measures, now they support the notion of declaring war in order to preserve America's integrity. And I must say I'm inclined to agree with that sort of nationalistic attitude myself."

Mr. Henry snorted loudly. "Huh!" he exclaimed in a derisive tone. "That pack of upstarts doesn't understand the first thing about politics! Why, they're naive enough to think that merely going to war shall make this country a power to be reckoned with, when it would very likely prove a devastating blow instead!"

At this point, Richard hastily intervened in his role as host to suggest that the gentlemen withdraw to his study to continue the conversation over brandy and cigars. The ladies were encouraged to retire to the drawing room for their own entertainment before the company reassembled there approximately an hour later.

This was the moment Jennifer had been awaiting, and she had to exert considerable restraint to keep from immediately bolting out of the drawing room. She was temporarily able to overcome that desire, however, in favor of seeing what else she could discover about the younger two members of the group. Sylvia Trask, who'd had a good deal of wine with dinner and was even now calling loudly for another liqueur, had disposed herself on the seat nearest the drinks. Her pretty face had settled into a sulky pout and she made so little effort to join in the conversation that Jennifer soon decided she must be one of those women who only sparkled in the company of the opposite sex and never felt truly at ease in the presence of her own. Abigail Rutland, though, turned out to be a pleasant, if rather unstimulating, companion. And her questions regarding the length of Jennifer's visit and the nature of her position within the household clearly demonstrated an interest in defining her own relationship to the owner of that house before overlong and made Jennifer wonder again whether and to what degree Richard might reciprocate those feelings. Indeed, only the rare tonic of being once more in society after several weeks of being cooped up in virtual isolation was sufficient to distract her temporarily from dwelling on the surprising—and utterly unforeseen—realization that she had a rival, if Jennifer were to admit to a romantic interest in Richard.

But what wasn't clear to her, Jennifer admitted as she ascended the staircase a quarter hour or so later, was whether there was an informal understanding between Richard and Miss Rutland already. More than likely there was, she decided with a tiny sigh, and they'd for some reason agreed not to rush a public announcement of their engagement. Happily, Molly's solid presence at the top of the stairs interrupted this depressing train of thought and steered Jennifer back to her original purpose for the moment. The two walked over to the door of Mr. Henry's bedroom and looked carefully around.

Molly handed Jennifer a candle. "I checked to make sure you could get inside," she whisperd. "The door was locked, of course, but there was nothing to stop my solving that little problem before you arrived.''

Jennifer smothered a laugh. "How handy! Remind me to have you teach me that trick sometime,'' she whispered back. "Now, you stand guard at the landing and warn me if we're in danger of being discovered. And I'll see if I can't learn whether Mr. John Henry is up to anything more substantial than blowing his own trumpet.''

She slipped inside the room and shut the door before venturing to light the candle Molly had supplied. Then she began a hasty but thorough search of the room and its occupant's belongings. She opened the dresser and looked through the clothing in each of the drawers. She searched inside the writing table and shook out the books stacked beside the bed. She ran her hands under the mattress and even lifted up the rug to see if there were any papers beneath it. She looked in every corner of the wardrobe and got up on a chair to feel along the top. Then she stood in front of it and gazed dispiritedly around the room again. Either Mr. Henry was more circumspect than she'd imagined or there wasn't anything to find after all, she thought, turning and running her hands casually over the coats and jackets hanging up in the closet. Wait a minute—was that a lump in the inside pocket of his traveling cloak or just the fold of one of the capes? She felt slowly along the lining of the garment and then nearly yelped aloud as her hand met a thick wad of paper.

Pulling out her find, Jennifer took it over to the writing table and leafed quickly through the sheaf. It seemed to be a series of letters between Henry and several people in Canada. She moved the candle closer. The first letter was dated January 26, 1809, and her eyes widened as she began to read: "The extraordinary situation of things at this time in the neighboring state has suggested to the governor in chief the idea of employing you on a secret and confidential mission.'' She scanned quickly to where it ended by asking Henry, "... if you will have the goodness therefore to acquaint me, for His Excellency's information, whether you could make it convenient to engage in a mission of this nature and what pecuniary assistance would be requisite to

enable you to undertake it without injury to yourself." The
letter was signed by Herman W. Ryland, secretary to Sir
James Craig.

Jennifer picked up another letter, this one dated February
6, 1809, and apparently from Sir James himself. Since,
he wrote, Henry had so readily undertaken the service suggested, he requested him to proceed to Boston at his earliest
convenience. "The principal object that I recommend to
your attention," Jennifer read, "is the endeavor to obtain
the most accurate information of the true state of affairs in
that part of the Union, which from its wealth, the number of
its inhabitants, and the known intelligence and ability of
several of its leading men, must naturally possess a very
considerable influence, and will indeed probably lead the
other eastern States of America in the part that they may
take in this important crisis." Specifically, she learned,
Henry was instructed to investigate, "the state of public
opinions, both with regard to their internal politics and to
the probability of a war with England, the comparative
strength of the two great parties into which the country is
divided, and the views and designs of that which may
ultimately prevail."

So Henry was indeed a spy in the pay of England through
the office of the governor general of Canada! And despite
her suspicions to that effect, Jennifer still felt stunned to
have them so definitively confirmed. Why, the man even
had a credential signed by Governor Craig, she discovered,
turning over the document and examining the government
seal in the bottom corner. She began to read, "The bearer,
Mr. John Henry, is employed by me, and full confidence
may be placed in him—"

"Just what the devil do you think you're doing?" demanded
a loud, angry voice behind her.

Chapter 7

HER HEART pounding a retreat in her chest, Jennifer started up from her chair, twisting around at the same time in a vain effort to hide the evidence of her activities behind her skirt. "Oh, thank God it's you!" she exclaimed. She sagged back against the table and smiled in relief at the intruder.

Richard Avery's expression remained black as thunder, however. "I asked what the devil you think you're doing here," he repeated in a cold voice. He glanced around the room and then walked over to the writing table as he continued. "I decided to excuse myself from my guests for a few minutes to check on the children. And having learned that you'd proposed to do likewise, I ascended the back stairs and presented myself at their bedroom, fully expecting to enounter you at any moment. Well, imagine my surprise to find you nowhere to be seen and George and Caroline quietly sleeping away undisturbed. I happened to see Miss Danhope on the landing and came to ask if she knew where you'd fetched up. But, as I was passing the door here, I noticed a light flickering underneath and decided to investigate. Just what is this that had you so absorbed you didn't even hear me come in?" he asked. He lifted a corner of the top letter with one finger and then let it fall back onto the stack.

Jennifer steeled herself against the new tattoo her heart had begun beating and heroically refrained from immediately pressing to learn why Richard had sought out her company. "It seems your Mr. Henry has been absorbed in some interesting pursuits of his own," she informed him earnestly instead. "From what I can determine, the governor of

Canada has employed him as his agent in an effort to determine the political climate of the eastern states as well as well as current sentiment regarding the possibility of a war with England. From what he's already said and from what I've read here so far, it appears to me that he's meant to ascertain the possibility of those states siding with the British, should war be declared. But you interrupted me before I had the opportunity to read any of his reports."

Richard shrugged his shoulders disinterestedly. "Surely the man can write whatever he likes to whomever he wishes—? Frankly, I can't see any reason to get in a flame about such a trifle."

Jennifer gaped at him. "Apparently I haven't made myself clear," she managed after a moment. "But then, perhaps someone like myself—a citizen of England who has come to admire America enormously—has a different perspective on things. Granted, such actions carried out by an ordinary person might not seem so altogether outrageous if they'd been undertaken primarily because of dissatisfaction with the government and the hope of bringing its faults to light, although I'd still have argued with the methods chosen. But the man is actually a spy, being paid by another government to gather information detrimental, if not downright ruinous, to the government of the United States," she explained in deliberate tones. "What's more, he has an official credential signed by the governor general of Canada plainly attesting to that fact. He's even been supplied with a cipher to ensure that the details of his correspondence remain secret." At this point, she became so caught up in the need to convince her companion of the gravity of the situation that she laid a beseeching hand on his arm. Then, searching his face hopefully for some sign of agreement, she urged, "Richard, we must do something to stop him! At least say you'll let me copy a few of these letters so we'll have some proof of our tale?"

Richard hesitated, though if truth be told, he was probably as much affected by Jennifer's touch and her unconscious use of his Christian name as he was by her discovery. How often he'd longed to touch her himself and yet held back from doing so, he remembered. Now it was she who'd initiated the very contact he'd been wishing for, and the impetus had been politics, not the overwhelming force of his personality. How little he apparently understood women, he thought wryly, since it was clear he still had a lot to learn about this particular one, at least. "I assure you that if I truly believed this invention—which, mind you, I don't credit for a minute—I should be the first to order Mr. Henry to give an account of himself," he promised Jennifer in a level voice. "But surely you'll agree that such a demand is ridiculous, based upon these meager scraps of information— and information obtained in an altogether unseemly manner at that! So no, you certainly may not make copies of a gentleman's personal correspondence. I have my reputation to protect, after all, and the privacy of my guests to safeguard as well—concerns, I might add, which you'd do well to address a bit more carefully yourself."

Jennifer snatched her hand away as if it had touched a hot coal. "Meager scraps—?" she repeated incredulously. "Good God, but you're more thickheaded than I ever dared imagine!" She considered him again, her face taking on a mingled expression of understanding and dismay. "You don't mean to lift a finger, do you?" she said slowly at last, clearly reluctant to accept that fact. "It's entirely too disruptive to your safe little existence to have any truck with unpleasantries like treason and deceit, isn't it?"

"I shall request an interview with Mr. Henry and inquire as to his intentions as soon as possible," Richard said stiffly.

"You shall 'request,' you shall 'inquire,' " Jennifer mimicked. "For heaven's sake, I wonder if you won't be seeking permission to breathe next!" she exclaimed unkindly, promptly tossing away the last remnants of good breeding in her haste to drive her point home. "Why, the man can talk circles around you! How I ever imagined you'd be willing—and even eager—to join me in thwarting Mr. Henry's plans I'm sure I can't recall. But then, I daresay you haven't spared a moment to consider my position in all of this, have you? No, I thought not," she observed, after examining his face again. "What interest should I—a British subject—have in exposing a plot by my own government to foment a revolution in the United States, after all? Why, I expect I'd encounter enormous difficulty simply getting anyone to listen to me, much less take what I said seriously. And then to ask them to accept my word for the whole thing without being able to supply a single shred of evidence— well, surely you'll concede that that would strain most people's credulity? Your reputation, however, would be ample to overcome such doubts and to persuade even the most hardened skeptic to beware. And therefore, for some reason, I made the unfortunate mistake of assuming that together we could— Well, never mind now," she said abruptly. "My father was wrong after all, it seems," she continued almost to herself. "He said he was convinced that once you'd grasped a situation thoroughly you'd never have reason to earn the title of coward for failing to show yourself slam up to the mark. But now it appears that he—or you—is considerably wide of the mark instead," she decided, feeling not only disappointed at that conclusion but also apprehensive when she wondered how she was ever to reconcile the fact that Richard refused to act with her growing regard for him. "And though I've scant interest in applying labels or calling names," she concluded in a last attempt to goad him to respond, "I must say it's tempting to find a man who allows a distorted notion of propriety to keep him from doing anything to prevent a possible catas- trophe as contemptible as an egg thief in a henhouse!"

Jennifer paused to shuffle the letters together and replace them carefully in the pocket of Mr. Henry's traveling cloak. Then she picked up the candle and headed toward the door. "Besides," she couldn't forebear adding when Richard still didn't answer, "since you doubtless weigh a mere acquain- tance's assessment of your character less heavily than a potential partner's—such as, say, Miss Rutland's—I'm sure my opinion of you won't cause you to lose a minute's worth of sleep." She exited the room and pulled the door shut behind Richard, who'd followed her out, testing to see that it was locked even as she'd tested the waters a moment before. "And now I must say goodnight, sir. I have a great deal of thinking to do and little strength or patience left for conversing with a half-wit too stupid to know if his head is properly fastened on.'' She sketched a curtsy and then called softly for Molly before turning down the hall in the direction of her bedchamber.

Richard was left staring after her disappearing figure and trying to decide whether her parting remark referred to his guest or to him, just as she'd probably intended. He had to admit that his first impulse was to rush over and stop Jennifer and beg to know how he could climb back into her good graces. If only he weren't so cursedly slow to come to the boil, he thought bitterly. No wonder she'd formed such a lowly opinion of him when it apparently took him half again as long to reach what might in the end be the same conclusion as she. His second, if belated, impulse was to return at once to Mr. Henry's room and to peruse those letters of his in greater detail. And in point of fact, his hand was already reaching for the knob before he recalled watching Jennifer check the door to see that it was secured behind them. It did occur to him to wonder briefly how she'd gotten inside in the first place, if the door had also been locked before she'd arrived, but he knew he was scarcely likely to learn the particulars of that accomplishment without pressing her for an explanation. This he was distinctly loathe to do, however. And why was he so reluctant to take her word regarding Henry's involvement in possibly subversive activities without being able to confirm them to his own satisfaction? Sadly unable to answer any of these questions, Richard walked slowly down the stairs to rejoin his guests, each foot dragging after the other with the marked reluctance of a child approaching a distasteful chore.

Several hours later, after the Rutlands and the rest of the company had taken their leave and Mr. Henry had retired, Richard sat alone in his study going over the events of the evening again in his mind. He'd propped his elbows on the arms of his chair, laced his fingers together, and was now resting his chin on his hands and staring broodingly at the last flames of the fire dying in the grate. He listened to the small shifts and sighs of the house as it settled down for the night and thought briefly about his two children sleeping safely up-stairs in their beds and then a good deal longer about the others taking temporary shelter in his household.

Jennifer Somers was still an enigma, he had to confess, and her behavior alternately intrigued and infuriated him until at times he found himself actively wishing for her father to return and relieve him of the responsibility for her well-being. Indeed, on occasions such as this evening, he felt himself to be more a threat to her than an unofficial guardian. To be honest, he'd been altogether shocked to discover her in Henry's room going through the man's things, although when he considered for a moment, it was plain to see that that was easily something she wouldn't hesitate to do. But his objection was the same one he'd had about the political situation and Henry's remedy for it: It was the methods in both cases he'd disliked—not the motive behind the act.

He chewed meditatively on one thumb for a minute. If anyone had asked him just then about the source of his discomfort, he'd have had to admit that he appeared to be suffering from injured pride. For example, how was it that Jennifer's assessment of his character was so vastly different from his own—and that his assessment of Henry seemed so radically different from hers? He allowed himself the mo-mentary pleasure of rolling Jennifer's name around on his tongue before dragging his attention reluctantly back to the matter at hand. And even supposing that he had been taken in by the man, surely he didn't propose letting his embar-rassment over that mistake stand in the way of rectifying it?

But that was precisely where he seemed to be having the most difficulty, and also where he and Jennifer seemed to be at arm's length from one another. If only he wasn't used to making every decision based on his ridiculous notions of right and wrong—notions, he'd begun to see, that were far too rigid, moreover, to accommodate every circumstance. He knew perfectly well that he was hesitating now because he felt obliged first to confront John Henry with his suspicions and to hear his explanation before proceeding any farther.

Richard got up to poke at the fire and then cast himself back down into his chair. A minute later, he tired of that sedentary pose and began to amble restlessly around the room instead. No matter how he looked at it, he couldn't rid himself of the feeling that it would be wrong to take any action against Henry—even in the face of such convincing evidence as his letters promised to provide—unless he also let the man speak for himself. And yet at the same time, wasn't he willing to admit that any defense Henry might offer would also be suspect? He might say whatever was needed in order to put his host off the scent, knowing full well that Richard was a pure novice when it came to separating the chaff from the wheat.

Richard groaned aloud. Honestly, he was completely knocked up by this continual effort to interact with and draw conclusions about people, and he'd little energy left over to attempt to verbalize his responses and adjust his performance accordingly. Far easier to have everything neatly categorized in advance so he'd no need to fumble with such inanities as feelings. After all, he'd no recourse to slipshod methods in his business affairs, so why resort to them in his personal life? And if some change should be required in the latter, there wasn't any need to raise a hue and cry over it, was there? If he should decide to marry Abigail Rutland, for example, he intended to go about the matter in a systematic way so that the change in his circumstances produced scarcely a ripple on the surface of his life.

Why bother at all, then? he thought suddenly, his foot actually pausing mid-stride at what was for him a daring and certainly unexpected notion. True, he found her a pleasant companion and could think of no objection to making her an offer. In fact, he suspected she'd been waiting nearly a year for him to declare his intentions and he couldn't imagine why he shouldn't willingly fall in with that plan—save for a nagging worry that he might be tying the knot only because everyone, himself included, believed it was high time for him to do so. But, he admitted silently, the truth was that though he was fond of Abigail, he didn't love her, and nor was he excessively pained by the thought of losing her to another man if he himself didn't marry her. He suddenly realized, however, that such a situation would affect him a good deal more if the woman in the picture were Jennifer instead of Abigail, for hadn't he felt absurdly jealous tonight at watching her merely talking with Mr. Hartley? And this second revelation, coming as it did so close upon the heels of the first, promptly caused Richard to stagger over to his chair and then to pour himself a reviving glass of brandy.

Just when, he wondered, had he begun to cease thinking of himself as a cold fish? He took a large swallow and felt the liquor burn a path down into his chest. Wasn't it shortly after a certain young lady had accused him of that attitude that he'd resolved never to deal with others in a strictly unemotional fashion again? And wasn't he now in a worse tangle than ever, because although he'd confessed that he wouldn't be happy to continue with his life as it had been before, he wasn't always willing—and certainly not yet able—to approach it any other way? But even if Jennifer Somers had been responsible for initiating that upheaval, he meant to assure himself that he alone would be responsible for whatever direction his life might take from now on. And what better way to begin than with his interview with John Henry, since at the same time that he was discovering what the man was about he might also prove to the other interested party that he was as capable of keeping matters in check as she. Indeed, garnering that lady's good opinion seemed of paramount importance all of a sudden, he realized, aware of a steadying warmth in the region of his chest that wasn't merely the result of a superior liqueur.

Accordingly, Richard requested an interview with John Henry the next morning. His guest, he learned, had been out and about for several hours and had already booked passage on a frigate sailing for England the following day. Indeed, Henry seemed in a remarkably cheerful mood, talking expansively about the warm welcome he anticipated receiving upon his arrival in that country and referring several times by indirection to the reward he felt sure would greet his latest news of the United States.

This introduction offered Richard the opening he'd been hoping for in order to confirm that his sympathies lay along the same lines as Henry's. "It is deucedly hard, I find, for a man to remain true to his principles these days," he complained in all honesty. "It seems that everyone is perfectly willing to find fault with the government, for example, but when it comes to putting their criticisms into practice, they disappear as quickly as picnickers from a swarm of bees.''

''Not everyone,'' Henry observed knowingly. ''But then, too, there's always the question of determining the most auspicious time to act upon one's beliefs. And frankly, I don't think most people are either skillful enough or in the proper position to recognize that moment when it arrives. Clearly, what's required is one man who can become a sort of conduit through which the combined energies of a diverse group can be directed at the particular target he selects.''

''Of course,'' Richard murmued, never doubting for a moment that Mr. Henry was referring to himself.

''Besides, it isn't as if anyone in our little group is advocating raising an army,'' Henry pointed out quickly. ''In fact, our main purpose actually is to avoid any conflict at all. What we're primarily concerned with is assessing the temper of the people so that we can know, for example, that even if ordered to do so, the Connecticut militia will refuse to take up arms. Why, one might say that, if anything, our efforts promise to shorten whatever engagement does arise, because we'll not only be able to predict what resistance can be organized, but also feel confident that our efforts exemplify—rather than compromise—the very highest of principles.''

Henry's argument was indeed a powerful one, Richard had to admit again, for what man of sense wouldn't wish to avoid war altogether, if possible? But in the back of his mind, he heard Jennifer's voice saying that Henry was capable of leading him about by the nose as easily as a pig to the slaughter. And then, too, he was astute enough to recognize that there were several major issues—treason, for one—for which Henry had so far utterly failed to account. Still, he saw no reason not to give the impression that he'd been persuaded to cast his lot with that of his guest in the hope of being taken into his confidence.

''What you've just told me has greatly relieved my mind,'' Richard confessed somewhat truthfully. ''Indeed, until now I wasn't certain I could reconcile my beliefs with your methods, but I see that the two aren't really as disparate as I'd imagined.''

Henry allowed a satisfied smile to flicker across his face. ''I knew you wouldn't hesitate much longer before joining the fold! Plain as pudding you've too much sense to stick stubbornly to the roundabout when it's just as easy to make short shrift of things instead,'' he observed, echoing Richard's thoughts in a rather eerie fashion. ''Now, you should know that we appear to have reached a crucial juncture in our enterprise, and my—er—supporters to the north have urged me to withdraw to England to confer about what path it would be best to follow. When I return, I expect to have renewed my resources and to have hit upon the perfect plan to capitalize on our mutual desires,'' he concluded somewhat obscurely.

''And in the meantime—?'' Richard ventured.

''In the meantime, I think, you could consider whether any others of your acquaintance might be inclined to sympathize with our goal. It seemed to me that a few of the gentlemen I met last night showed themselves willing to play a deep game—Robert Trask and Edward Rutland, perhaps? Then once you've enlisted all possible confederates, you've nothing to do but hold yourself at the ready until I rejoin you in about two months' time, and together we can spread the toils in such a way that we'll be assured of trapping our prey!''

Similar thoughts were passing through Jennifer's mind the following morning, although Mr. Henry might have been rather surprised to discover that the target of her machinations was none other than himself. In fact, he'd neatly, if unknowingly, wrecked any further effort she might have made to study his correspondence a second time by sticking as close to his quarters as a wasp to a pot of honey. And partly because her own attempt had been forestalled, she was now all the more eager to learn the outcome of Richard Avery's attempt to bell the same cat. Therefore, she'd requested that her guardian pay a visit to the schoolroom before he did anything other than break his fast.

Richard put in an appearance on the third floor shortly

after nine o'clock. He greeted Jennifer, Molly, and the twins, and then crossed the room to see how they were occupying themselves. The four were ensconced on the cushions by the windows, busily sewing costumes for the puppet show they were planning. It was to be *The Tempest*, Caroline informed him, holding up the gown she was stitching for Miranda and pointing to the robe George had made for Prospero. The group then spent a couple of minutes conferring about how to maneuver the toy ship among the carved wooden waves, and Richard made to promise that he'd form part of the audience, before the twins allowed him and Jennifer to withdraw for a private chat.

They seated themselves rather awkwardly on opposite sides of the table, though whether this was due to the chairs being somewhat too small to accommodate an adult body or to the recollection of their last encounter, neither of them probably could have said. Jennifer was well aware that her last statement on that occasion had been to accuse Richard of being a coward. In the meantime, however, she'd had to admit hoping he'd do something to convince her to alter that opinion, and she'd been quite ready to provide him with the opportunity to do so. Nevertheless, she also wanted to guard against offering him a motive that might have more to do with securing her affection than anything else. Therefore, she resisted the pleading look in his eyes and schooled herself to treat him in as detached a fashion as she could manage. "Now then, sir," she began in a businesslike way, "I'm most curious to learn about your interview with Mr. Henry. Were you able to discover anything about the nature of his plans, I wonder—?"

If only he didn't feel so much rested on the outcome of this conversation, Richard thought. He'd been so encouraged at being invited to visit the schoolroom that he'd promptly jumped to the conclusion that it represented the chance to redeem himself in Jennifer's eyes and that that was precisely what she hoped for, too. "Well, he means to depart this afternoon in order to sail with the evening tide for England," he offered quickly, trying to quiet his nerves.

Jennifer threw him a rather disgusted look. "Not that sort

of plan! I mean his other activities—you know, the ones to which his correspondence referred? What did he offer in the way of explanation when you inquired about those secret schemes?''

"Why, nothing much. Well, that is to say, I couldn't ask about them directly," Richard corrected in a rush, "because I didn't want to put it into his head that we'd nosed him out—did I? Instead, I hit on a bright idea for gaining both his confidence and access to whatever cunning plot he might be devising," he told her, trying to look modest at his success.

Jennifer, who'd formed no great opinion to date of her companion's flair for subtlety, greeted this announcement with a sense of foreboding. "And that was—?" she prompted.

"I declared that my sympathies lay in the same direction as his and proposed that he enlist me as one of the supporters of his cause." Richard said back, a self-satisfied expression stealing over his face.

He received an altogether satisfying response as well, because Jennifer simply stared at him for a minute, her mouth indelicately half open. The first thing that crossed her mind was to wonder how she'd managed to become entangled with someone who appeared to require help in negotiating even the simplest situation in order to avoid making what she'd easily perceived would be a disastrous misstep. After all, it was one thing to feel pleasantly needed by a man whom she admired and another to feel that he was a bit of a looby at times, she admitted. Then she promptly tossed aside that unkind thought as being the product of a special case where the same man had surely little or no experience, and began instead to consider to what degree Richard was telling the truth. He did think similarly to Henry in many respects, so what if he wasn't making up an excuse about wanting to join his little political intrigue? She wished she'd had time to follow up on her earlier discovery that he didn't necessarily accept every philosophy in toto, so that by now she'd have developed a more precise understanding of what he truly thought. The second thing that occurred to her was that there never seemed to be enough time lately. What if Richard didn't prove himself the man she imagined him to be? And what if Mr. Henry went forward with some deep proposal of his own before they could spike his guns and possibly unmask him altogether? Of course, she decided, concentrating steadfastly on the latter of these possibilities, it hardly seemed he'd be likely to do so until he returned from England—and then he'd certainly be bound to gather his supporters around him and reveal his plan to them immediately. So perhaps, she realized, Richard hadn't devised such a farfetched stratagem after all.

"Splendid!" she exclaimed somewhat more warmly than he'd allowed himself to expect. "Why, you've been far more creative than I'd ever imagined," she said truthfully, "and moreover, infinitely more successful than I." She hesitated for a moment. "You see, I thought briefly about trying to get back into Mr. Henry's room to see if I couldn't at least get a look at the cipher he uses to code his reports. But since you'd specifically forbidden such action, and the man himself gave me no opportunity to do so, I haven't stepped an inch over his threshold." She paused again and then drew a tightly folded sheet from her pocket. Opening it up, she stared at Richard a trifle defiantly and then admitted, "Before you interrupted me the other night, however, and before you enjoined me not to—I'd already taken with me one tiny piece of proof I was certain Mr. Henry would never miss. Listen: 'It should therefore be the peculiar care of Great Britain to foster divisions between the north and the south; and by succeeding in this, she may carry into effect her own projects in Europe, with a total disregard for the resentments of the democrats in this country.' "

Jennifer raised her eyes to meet Richard's, and despite her usual pluck, found that quality deserting her at a great rate in the face of the thunderous look he was directing steadily down upon her. Indeed, it was no doubt fortunate that she couldn't read his thoughts just then, for Richard was rapidly trying to determine how he'd ever become attached to a woman who was clearly so little inclined to be ruled by anything other than her own strong will—or by anyone other than herself, for that matter. In fact, he nearly pleaded with her to explain at once how she'd come to act in a way that directly violated the trust he'd placed in her. "You stole the personal property of one of my guests, and after I deliberately instructed you not to—?" he said wonderingly instead, as if he couldn't believe it himself.

"No, I told you I took it before—"

"Well then, you should have put it back," he interrupted rudely. "You are a guest in his house, too, you know, and I expect you to abide by the same rules as the rest of the household. Why not admit it was pure contrariness that made you refuse to comply with my request?"

Jennifer was uncomfortably aware that there was a grain of truth in that accusation. What's more, she wasn't very happy about the poor picture Richard suddenly appeared to have drawn of her character. But she was so angry at the high-handed way he was treating her, and at the same time so anxious to correct his impression, that she inadvisably chose to fight back. "It wasn't either," she argued. "I only felt it more important to have something tangible with which to shore up our case than to follow some blind and arbitrary order."

"And you decided that you were in the best position to decide between those two, I take it? I see—something tangible," Richard said between clenched teeth. "And what, may I ask, do you find so damaging in this little epistle? Why, it's the sort of innocent drivel anyone might write," he pointed out in a disparaging voice. "So I can't see how pilfering it appears to have profited us in the least. And it's too late to return it safely now anyway." He rose from his chair and frowned sternly at Jennifer. "But I must say that what concerns me most of all is your continued denial of my right to regulate your life while you reside in my house. And given that circumstance, I promise you I plan to devote a good deal of time to considering whether it wouldn't be better all around for you to stay elsewhere until your father's return." And having thereupon thrown his glove into the ring, Richard bowed coldly at her and exited the room.

Jennifer remained staring at the door, conscious of furiously wishing her host would either live up to his word immediately or her father would suddenly appear—whichever came first she didn't much care, she told herself. This depressing prospect was interrupted by Molly, who walked over and seated herself calmly in the chair Richard had just vacated. Then, after looking closely at Jennifer's expression, she observed in a satisfied voice, "So you've taken a fancy to the man after all."

"I have not!" Jennifer said indignantly.

"Yes you have," Molly repeated firmly, "and what's more, he's obviously conceived a tenderness for you, too." She shook her head. "How you can be so knowing about complicated things and such a goose about simple ones I'm sure I can't say."

"But you must have observed that we can scarcely abide being in the same room with one another these days," Jennifer said in a sarcastic voice.

"Oh, indeed," Molly acknowledged. "And no clearer sign I know of to recognize a lasting passion than a couple who fall into dagger points whenever they happen to meet. Why, it wouldn't surprise me at all to see the two of you come to terms before another three months are out."

Although she secretly felt a happy tingle at that prospect, Jennifer wasn't about to let Molly think her merely another scheming woman when it came to matters concerning the opposite sex. Therefore, she hurried to throw a damper on speculations that were, in truth, curiously close to her own. "Not if I have anything to say about it," she vowed.

Chapter 8

BUT IF she would truly have all that much to say about whether she continue to reside at No. 30 Wall Street was, in fact, one of the questions that occupied Jennifer's mind that evening. She was not, by nature, a very domestic sort of woman. Nevertheless, when she was considerably younger, she'd discovered that doing some undemanding, repetitive task not only was relaxing in itself, but also provided a way to free her thoughts. And though she took considerable pains to hide it, she relished the time she spent ironing or mending because it was during these same tranquil hours that she'd managed to tease the sense out of many a knotty problem.

Therefore, if anyone had happened into her room just then, they'd have found the elegant—and equally unpredictable—Lady Somers, curled in a chair in front of the fire. Her feet were tucked cozily beneath a blanket, and beside her was a huge basket of socks waiting to be darned. She selected a black woolen one with a large hole and smoothed it over the polished wooden darning egg. Then she picked up a needle and began to weave new strands in one direction, tidily picking along the edges of the sock and the perimeter of her situation at the same time.

Mr. Henry had departed immediately after luncheon for the dock where his ship rested until the tide could carry it safely out of the harbor and then to England. His attitude toward Jennifer, when he'd taken his leave, had been deferential enough, she had to admit, and perfectly suitable to someone who'd spent a good deal of time in her company but who wouldn't dare presume—on the strength of that circumstance alone—that they were more than the merest of acquaintances. Yet, she still didn't entirely trust him not to make use of their meeting at some future time when it might prove troublesome to her. What's more, she recalled, her hands pausing for a moment, he'd now adopted a condescending attitude toward Richard instead, no doubt feeling confident that that gentleman would readily jump the minute he said "fetch." And she couldn't help feeling apprehensive about Richard having so casually placed himself in Henry's control by indicating that he was willing to be a party to his schemes. Why, the man hadn't used any more sense than if he were still in swaddling clothes, she thought in disgust, snapping off her thread with one quick, decisive movement.

Jennifer began working a new strand in and out through the first threads in the opposite direction. As if it wasn't just like her to be so everlastingly concerned with protecting the well-being of someone who seemed, at the moment, fully bent on wrecking her own peace of mind, she told herself irritably. Not that she really believed her host would go so far as to request that she leave his house—particularly when he'd already assured her father of his hospitality. But secretly, she couldn't help wishing that for once, the prim and proper Mr. Avery would be motivated by some more personal desire than simple duty. She was fully aware that even her sense of responsibility to the twins was no longer the primary reason she wanted to remain under that gentleman's roof. And nor would she continue to describe her purpose as one of helpfully detailing his faults to him in the hope of accomplishing their reform, she admitted.

She allowed her hands to rest for a second time in her lap. Why was she still resisting acknowledging that Molly was right? It was clear that she had indeed become attracted to Richard Avery to a degree that was proving as surprising as it was inconvenient. Falling in love was the last thing she'd ever expected to happen to her—and Richard certainly the most unlikely of paramours, besides. But then, she supposed that's why the phrase "falling in love" had been coined in the first place, because obviously no one seemed to walk deliberately or with much presence of mind into an affair of the heart. Instead, she was sure one more often plunged in wholesale, or perhaps slipped in sideways, making a great fuss the entire way. And doubtless the main comfort one could count on, she thought, giving a half-smile, was the knowledge that there was another person in exactly the same damnable predicament as oneself.

Jennifer folded the sock she'd finished darning, pulled another onto the egg, and rethreaded her needle. Was that all that was stopping her, then—the fact that she was used to easy conquests and couldn't now accept that the tables might be turned, and that for once she wasn't sure whether the gentleman in question had indeed developed a tenderness for her, as Molly insisted? True, she hadn't seen any real evidence to back up that claim, but then she'd also been scrupulously careful not to give a clue as to her own feelings—hadn't she? Of course, she reminded herself, she'd refrained from flirting or in any way openly encouraging her host to pay her court because she knew that such tactics frequently went awry when the suitor became too ardent or unreasonable. And surely such a situation would only prove infinitely troublesome if both resided in the same household, wouldn't it? Still, she suspected that that thinking was merely a convenient excuse to salvage her pride and avoid proving Molly wrong by discovering that Mr. Avery's heart was already in another lady's hands. After all, he certainly acted as if his feelings toward her were motivated by politeness rather than some ungovernable passion. And if one were to draw conclusions based solely on actions, one would have to call him a blackguard—not a beloved—for even considering dismissing her from his home, she decided with a sigh, her thoughts having come full circle again.

Apparently, Richard had had sufficient time to reconsider his decision, Jennifer discovered the next morning. She had finished her toast and was sipping a second cup of coffee when her host finally made an appearance in the dining room. He stood awkwardly behind his chair for a moment, looking everywhere but at Jennifer, and then cleared his throat.

"Er—must beg your pardon about yesterday," he mumbled, still unable to meet her eyes. "Not myself at all. Can't think what possessed me," he lied, knowing full well that it had been Jennifer's refusal to alter her behavior and fall in meekly with his plans that had set his back up. "Pray, ignore everything I said," he urged. "I don't mean to cast you out into the streets, after all. Why, who knows what deviltry you'd be liable to cause if I loosed you on an unsuspecting New York," he added with a ghost of a smile. "Besides," he went on more soberly, "things appear to be heating up a bit, and I suspect we should all keep closer to home for a while." He thrust a copy of the *New York Gazette* toward her and pointed to an article on the front page.

"Clay Elected Speaker of the House—Promises to Make U.S. Ready for War!" the headline screamed. Jennifer gave a start and began to read the article more carefully. A special session of Congress had been convened at the request of President Madison, she learned, to urge that they consider what action was needed to ensure the continued safety of the nation in the face of increasingly vigorous interference from England.

Jennifer raised her eyes from the newspaper to find that Richard had seated himself on the opposite side of the table and was watching her over the top of his coffee cup. She clutched the paper tightly, thankful to have a way to keep her hands from trembling, which they often tended to do under Richard's steady gaze. How fortunate that they had some topic on which to focus other than their last disastrous conversation in the schoolroom, she thought in relief. On that occasion, she'd come to admit that whether or not her behavior had been justified, she hadn't acquitted herself at all well. Indeed, she'd been somewhat dreading the next time they met, not so much on account of what Richard might have decided about her remaining at No. 30 Wall Street, but on what he might have begun to think about her as a woman. "What does all this mean?" she asked now. "Will there be a war?"

If truth be told, Richard had been equally nervous about facing Jennifer this morning. For one thing, he knew his threat to force her to leave the house had been completely out of proportion to her actions. And for another, he really hadn't any intention of letting a woman who fascinated him the way she did go where he couldn't keep an eye on her—even, he'd confessed privately, if she also drove him to distraction at times. He shook his head in response to her question. "Not yet," he said, and then hesitated for a moment. "Still, there's been big talk in some quarters about what our object should be, if war is declared against England. And I'm afraid that the target mentioned most often is Canada. Mr. Hartley told me the other night that Clay boasted the militia of Kentucky alone could easily take Montreal and even conquer Upper Canada as well."

Jennifer immediately looked a good deal alarmed by that information. "But isn't my father headed very close to the border? He's not in any danger, is he?"

Richard barely managed to stave off an inexplicable impulse to press Jennifer's hands reassuringly in his. "I doubt it," he said, in what he hoped was a convincing voice, before admitting, "Though, to be truthful, I wondered the same thing myself. In fact, I even went so far as to urge Lord Somers to leave you behind so that, should anything unforeseen develop, he wouldn't be obliged to attend to your safety in addition to his own.''

His companion's response was rather different than Richard had anticipated. Indeed, privately he'd imagined that such news of his concern for the young lady's well-being would not only counteract his more recent behavior to the contrary, but also would generally add to his good credit in her eyes.

''I thought you told me that my staying here was all my father's idea,'' Jennifer said suspiciously, ''and yet suddenly you confess to having played a leading role in that scenario. I may possibly grant you the right to regulate my life to a certain degree when I am within the walls of your house. Otherwise, however, what I do is purely my own affair, and I'll thank you to refrain from putting a hand in whenever the fancy strikes you—no matter how admirable your motives.'' She paused to frown at him in a way that made Richard feel at once crestfallen and decidedly uneasy, despite his superior size and the width of table between them. ''I'm altogether disappointed in you, sir, to be sure,'' she continued in an undefinable tone. ''But then, I can't fathom why I should have expected you to tell the truth or even to act any differently when my own father has had recourse to the same tactics! Yes, clearly I've misjudged you,'' she concluded, her cheeks flaming either in embarrassment or anger, Richard wasn't sure. ''But I promise it shan't happen again. And from now on I won't even trouble you for information, but shall rely on other more trustworthy and assuredly more straightforward sources instead.''

Given that warning, Richard certainly wouldn't have been surprised to find that Lady Somers had contacted the secretary of state himself. He discovered the following evening, however, that she'd apparently decided to be content with a substitute in the form of Mr. Benjamin Hartley, who had proven himself such a worthwhile companion at Richard's own dinner party.

Having returned even later than usual from his office, Richard was now wearily slumped alone at the table, eating his dinner with a none too hearty appetite. Mrs. Booth hovered between kitchen and dining room, changing the dishes and offering him tender morsels of household gossip at the same time. And it was thus he learned that Mr. Hartley had been invited to join the four occupants of the schoolroom for a generous tea that afternoon, and that the man had stayed a full hour longer, besides.

Mr. Hartley, it seemed, had the ear of someone who was actually in the War Department, Mrs. Booth related in an awed voice. And his friend had advised him—unofficially, of course—that the tactic currently favored the moment war was declared was the invasion of Canada on a broad front, concentrating at Detroit in the west, Lake Champlain in the east, and Niagara in the center. The commander of the eastern forces would probably be General Henry Dearborn, sixty-one, retired secretary of war and a veteran of the Revolution. Fifty-nine-year-old General William Hull, also a war veteran, was rumored to be under consideration for the western command. "And such a naughty imitation of that poor man Mr. Hartley gave, too," Mrs. Booth confessed. "Why, apparently he had everyone in stitches!"

Richard held up a hand and offered her a tired smile. "Wait, let me guess. Did he sit there 'baaing' and then chewing away noisily like a cow on its cud? Yes, I thought so," he said at Mrs. Booth's nod. "The general, you see, has an exceedingly long face that causes him to look unfortunately like a sheep. And then, too, I doubt anyone's ever seen the man without a wad of tobacco stuffed into his mouth."

He pushed away his plate and poured out a glass of port. What concerned him most at the moment, though, was his suspicion that Jennifer was bent on turning to some other man for assistance, if not for a more personal sort of comfort, and it appeared she'd chosen Mr. Hartley to fill that role. Not that the man didn't seem altogether willing to provide whatever was requested of him—and quite ably, too, no doubt, Richard thought glumly. Why not admit he was jealous that Jennifer had selected someone else to be the recipient of her confidences? Could it be he was afraid that even if he had shown himself deserving of that honor,

she still might have bestowed it on another man? he wondered. Clearly, much as he longed to be a bulwark against
Jennifer's fears for her father's safety, he wasn't to be
granted the opportunity yet to show it.

In fact, he realized, the war strategy Mr. Hartley had
outlined threw Lord Somers squarely into the thick of
things, just as he'd originally feared. And though Richard
was positive his lordship would prove infinitely resourceful,
should he suddenly find himself in the midst of what were
euphemistically called "difficulties," he'd just as soon help
him avoid that possibility altogether. But there really wasn't
any way he could think of to reach Lord Somers and apprise
him of the danger. And anyway, because of his situation, the
man doubtless had ample and more accurate information
than Richard himself. Yet somehow, perhaps because he'd
put the idea in the other man's mind or helped arrange for
his trip, Richard had begun to feel personally responsible
for his safety. Or was it only that he feared a certain young
lady would think it devolved on his head to account for his
actions if anything happened to her father? Well, he wasn't
about to have his behavior proscribed by the opinion of a
mere acquaintance, and a virtual girl at that, he told himself
firmly. And she'd best reconsider if she imagined he'd
actually agree to submit his decisions for prior approval
before feeling free to lift a finger, he concluded, in the spirit
of one who had firmly, if perhaps unnecessarily, determined
to delare himself his own man.

But Richard soon discovered that he needn't have decided
formally to reassert his independence, because that goal
seemed to be the same one Jennifer was intent on fostering.
Or at least, the manner she'd now adopted was as polite and
deferential as he might wish from any guest in his household, much less from a casual acquaintance. Indeed, she
neither said nor did anything untoward to provoke him, but
conducted herself in such a circumspect fashion that it
would immediately have caused anyone who knew her well
to think one of two things: Either that the error of her ways
had suddenly and magically been revealed to her, or that she
had a secret scheme in mind.

Which of those circumstances was more accurate—or even more important—Richard would have been remarkably slow to say. And if truth be told, Jennifer's new attitude had him completely muddled. As far as he could tell, she now appeared utterly indifferent toward him. When he made an observation that in the past might have evoked a heated rebuttal, she offered none save, perhaps, a disinterested shrug of her shoulders. And when he announced that he meant to accompany her and her charges on some outing and then broke his promise at the last minute, she read him no lecture and offered not the slightest hint of recrimination. Indeed, she barely seemed to recognize whether he was there or not, Richard realized. And he had to admit that he'd almost have preferred to have been drawn into another row than to be met continually by a pallidness that—studied or not—made him feel perfectly superfluous.

If Jennifer had been able, she'd have told Richard that it was precisely a superfluity of emotion that had pushed her to this pass. To begin with, there was her confusion about her real feelings toward him, the revelation that the depth of those feelings might not be shared equally between them, and her uncertainly about what either of those things might signify and which outcome she would prefer. Then on top of that had been piled her specific and urgent concern for her father's safety and her frustration at not being able to do anything about it, together with a somewhat vaguer worry about the deteriorating political situation and the threat of war with England. And on account of feeling similarly helpless and only slightly less distraught about the state of her relationship with her host, she'd cast about for something to distract her from these imaginings.

Benjamin Hartley was turning out to be a very satisfactory distraction, Jennifer thought. Flattered by the attention she'd shown him at Richard's dinner party, Mr. Hartley had lost no time responding to her invitation to tea and thereafter had presented himself at the house on a number of other occasions during the following week. And not only had he proven willing and able to supply hard-to-obtain information about the current state of affairs, but he'd also treated her interest matter-of-factly and listened to her opinions with the sort of grave courtesy she'd once hoped to discover in another gentleman. What's more, after she'd explained to him that her connection with Mr. Avery was merely one of mutual convenience, he'd been quite clear about his intentions, and surprisingly persistent, too.

Jennifer put the final touches on her cream satin slip topped by a gauzy white overdress appliquéd with satin jonquils. Tonight Mr. Hartley was escorting her and Molly to the weekly subscription dance held by the City Assembly at the same hotel where she and her father had stayed when they'd first arrived in New York. There, for a small fee, members purchased a share of the modest refreshments offered and the opportunity to engage in the minuet, the Dauphine, the Bretagne, the Louvre, the Allemand, the waltz, or any of a series of English country dances.

One thing she liked about her new escort, Jennifer had decided, was that he didn't make her feel either pressured to reciprocate his admiration or concerned about where that admiration might be leading. Of course, if she'd been willing to admit it, the primary attraction of Mr. Hartley's company lay in the fact that it wasn't complicated by the same disturbing feelings and longings as Mr. Avery's, since Jennifer felt nothing more than a sincere, friendly affection for the man. But she was so relieved first at not being obliged to confront such weighty emotions for a while, and also so delighted again at finding herself part of a congenial social set, that she probably responded to a greater degree than she might have in other circumstances. And what's more, she'd easily convinced herself that the whole situation was entirely harmless and acted, therefore, by turns so gay, witty, and altogether delightful that Mr. Hartley unfortunately now teetered on the brink of falling in love himself.

Approximately an hour after arriving at the City Hotel, Jennifer collapsed into a seat next to Molly, gratefully sipping a glass of rather warm lemonade, and recovering from having just been guided through her first Virginia reel.

"I wonder if you don't think this a very tame entertainment," Mr. Hartley was saying to her as he stood beside their chairs.

"On the contrary," Jennifer assured him. "I always find

it enjoyable to share the simple pleasures of music and dancing with such an agreeable partner. Why, I doubt I'd last very long with anyone who couldn't revel in a good romp,'' she continued, and then broke off abruptly as Molly poked her in the ribs with a sharp elbow.

Following the direction of her friend's gaze, Jennifer was surprised to discover Richard Avery standing in the doorway of the room, peering tentatively inside. He was rigged out in evening clothes that showed off his height and fine features to full advantage, she noted despite herself, aware of a queer excitement she had to own the mere presence of another man had never caused her to feel before. Richard was accompanied, in direct contrast, by a short little man whose sleepy expression made him look as if he'd just arisen from his bed. The latter had a broad, high forehead, dark blue eyes, a largish nose, and a shapely mouth, Jennifer observed, and he was dressed in the type of well-cut garments that always bespoke the finest clothiers.

''I see there's been a meeting of the Benevolent Society tonight,'' Mr. Hartley offered in a timely fashion. ''That's Gulian Verplanck, one of the founders, with Mr. Avery. No doubt they walked down from Washington Hall and decided to stop in for a drink. Verplanck's an odd sort of fish,'' he explained, assuming the two ladies would naturally wish to learn more. ''He's rich as Croesus by birth, a Federalist by inclination, and a charming rogue with a reputation to match among the fair sex.''

This last fact Jennifer and Molly were soon able to attest to themselves. Having somehow managed to pick them out in the crowd, Richard headed purposefully in their direction, his friend firmly in tow. Jennifer, who'd received a bit of a jolt both at Mr. Avery's unexpected appearance and at her now inevitable reaction on seeing him, felt her heart leap as she watched him approach, and then rapidly sink as she began to calculate her situation.

Although he'd experienced a curiously similar reaction on perceiving Jennifer in the ballroom, Richard had rapidly recovered and already arrived at a clear understanding of what he needed to do. That he wished to break up the cozy relationship between the lady and Benjamin Hartley by whatever means necessary and as soon as possible, he didn't question for a moment. His only uncertainty lay in wondering if the additional presence of her companion and his might somehow impede his desire to cast Mr. Hartley into the shade. He promptly resolved, however, to make the best of that circumstance—or to ignore it entirely.

After introductions had been made all around, a rather awkward silence descended on the group. "I'm sure I didn't know you were going to be here this evening," Richard said at last, stepping unwisely into the breach and turning toward Jennifer as he tumbled over the edge.

"Ah, but I'm sure I'm not the least surprised to discover that lapse," Mr. Verplanck put in at once. "Why, any man who troubles himself as little as you do to keep abreast of society is bound not to know whether he's standing on his head or his heels! Not that such a habit ain't forgivable, dear boy, but no lady's going to be flattered to think you've forgotten her existence," he added in a kinder tone, but to Richard's considerable discomfort, all the same.

"Quite right," Jennifer agreed pleasantly. "Besides, I'm certain I can't think of any reason I'd need to provide you with an ongoing account of my whereabouts."

"I, on the other hand, can think of at least a half dozen reasons to track your every movement without any trouble at all," Mr. Verplanck interjected, his eyes roving over Jennifer's figure with the frank appreciation of a practiced flirt. "And not the least of which is that I'd be obliged to call my friend a ridiculous slow-top for letting a gorgeous creature like you out of his sight for a single minute." At this remark, Richard looked exceedingly uncomfortable, Mr. Hartley gave a half-smile, Jennifer blushed, Molly glared at Mr. Verplanck, and he looked infinitely pleased by the sensation he'd caused. Then, apparently anxious to live up to his reputation, he promptly requested the honor of the next dance, and twirled Jennifer onto the floor.

The other two gentlemen witnessed this event wearing identical expressions of envy—though whether in response to Mr. Verplanck's luck in securing Jennifer's hand or at his matchless address, perhaps neither could truly state. Finally,

Mr. Hartley sighed and offered, "I must say that I think Gulian's perfectly right."

Richard bristled. "I beg your pardon," he said stiffly.

"You mean to tell me you don't find Lady Somers a remarkably attractive woman?" Mr. Hartley asked in surprise.

"Oh, that. Well yes, of course I do," Richard allowed. His eyes followed Jennifer longingly around the dance floor for a moment. "But then, one wants more than simply good looks in a lifelong companion, after all," he added a trifle pompously.

"Quite so. And as far as I'm concerned, the lady has everything one could wish for: a quick wit, a keen mind, and above all, a loving nature."

This statement promptly caused Molly, whose presence had been virtually forgotten during this exchange, to cast an anxious look at Richard. He, in turn, directed a hard, reappraising stare at the speaker, since these words went far beyond the mere infatuation that he'd been ready to credit to the man. "Er, indeed. Do I understand that you mean to make the lady an offer, then?" he asked with studied casualness. "After all, it would scarcely be advisable to do so without having first discussed the matter with her father, who's unfortunately not available at the moment. But then, I'm certain I needn't remind you of the proprieties," he added politely.

"If only the situation weren't so confoundly confused," Mr. Hartley agreed. "Our acquaintance has been too brief for me to be entirely certain of my feelings, and then there's the additional problem of her being British, you know."

"Yes, I suppose it would look peculiar for such an avid supporter of Clay and his warmongers to form an alliance with one of the, ah, enemy," Richard said bluntly, quite to the surprise of everyone present.

"Oh, I would never let such abstract considerations throw a damper on things if I were confident of my goal," Mr. Hartley announced in a firm voice. He shot a sudden, penetrating look at Richard. "And what, may I ask, are your intentions toward the lady?"

Would that he knew how to answer that question, Richard thought. Of course, until now he hadn't actually gotten around to recognizing it as a question at all, much less prepared himself to render a response. "I'm not perfectly certain, either," he admitted with a rueful smile. "A fine couple of dunderheads we must appear, don't you think?"

Now Molly, for one, had been privately quite entertained by the spectacle of these two bantams squaring off to see who ruled the roost—particularly when another cock seemed to be walking away with the prize while they wasted time squabbling. Still, she was considerably relieved to see Richard thrust aside his normal reserve and lose no time in asking Jennifer for the next dance. For a few moments, he seemed to find himself able to chat in a happily unself-conscious way. But then as the music began and he discovered first that his selection was a waltz, and second, that he was therefore obliged to take the lady into his arms, all his inhibitions appeared to return in a rush. Indeed, he held her so stiffly and moved in such a jerky, disconnected fashion, that Jennifer twice stumbled over his feet and had to clutch his arm more tightly to steady herself. Naturally, that action only succeeded in compounding the situation. At last, Jennifer, who was having her own problems concentrating on anything but the delightful pressure of her partner's hand on her waist, felt compelled to interrupt their progression across the floor.

"Whatever's the matter with you, sir?" she chided, giving his arm a little shake. "Can't you tell a waltz from an obstacle race? Why, I feel like a marionette who's gotten her strings all tangled up. And you were doing so well at the start, too. Come now—won't you relax a bit?" she coaxed more gently when he failed to answer. "I shan't bite, you know."

She tipped her head backward in order to study Richard's face for a moment. "Shall I tell you what I think? I think that we two are used to dealing with each other on the basis of several roles we play: you the wealthy businessman and I the titled lady; you the host and I the temporary hostess; you the employer and I the governess." Her partner's movements had slowed and become smoother as she spoke, and though he hadn't yet ventured a response, she was nonetheless encouraged to continue. "Why, this must be the first chance we've had to face each other simply as man and woman. And the problem is, we forget that that's partly what we are the whole time. Instead, we act as if each of these roles is separate and isolated from the others, rather than an integrated portion of a whole person. Surely you can do more than one thing at a time, can you not: talking and dancing, for instance?''

Richard smiled sheepishly. ''I daresay I could manage that,'' he admitted.

''There—you see how easy it is? Why, I shouldn't be surprised if we don't have you handling three or four things together before you can say 'boo' to a goose!''

He laughed. ''Well, since I don't believe I've ever said anything to a goose before, that should prove an interesting novelty.''

Jennifer giggled and unconsciously snuggled a little deeper into his arms. ''And you see how much nicer it is like this, with neither of us kicking up a row? Though having become used to the old system, no doubt we'll soon feel as surfeited with this one as a cat in a dairy.'' She looked up mischievously at her partner, only to find him smiling down at her in a way that made her feel positively breathless.

Unfortunately, Molly wasn't the only person who'd been watching the progress of Richard and Jennifer around the room, if not keeping a wary eye on the progression of their relationship as well. Although Mr. Verplanck had soon excused himself to seek out more profitable hunting grounds in the form of the devastating Sylvia Trask, Mr. Hartley appeared to be keeping careful account of every dip and turn executed by one particular couple. That is to say, he busied himself in this fashion until the arrival of Abigail and Mr. Rutland appeared likely to provide him with a new and rather more profitable occupation. This young lady had secretly admired that gentleman for some time, but she'd never encouraged his attentions first because she'd assumed that she and Richard were practically promised to one another, and second because she was certain her father wouldn't approve of such a firebrand as Mr. Hartley. A quick glance at the dance floor, however, promptly confirmed the suspicion that had been planted in her mind at the dinner party for Mr. Henry that her assumption about her future was sadly ill founded. It was perfectly clear to Abigail, at least, that Richard was utterly smitten with the beautiful Lady Somers. And being of as practical a nature as the aforementioned gentleman himself, she wasted little time bemoaning that fact and began sizing up possible replacements instead. Very well, she decided calmly, if Richard was out of the picture, she'd be quite content with Mr. Hartley. Whereupon she immediately smiled up at him and began to consider the most effective way to win that gentleman's interest and her father's blessing.

Richard, fortunately, was blissfully unaware of these various maneuverings and, having relaxed somewhat, took the opportunity to twirl Jennifer around expertly in a double turn. "You know, I shouldn't think there'd ever be the slightest danger of becoming bored with you," he told her lightly and with perfect sincerity.

Chapter 9

IN THE weeks that followed the City Assembly dance, Richard suddenly found himself propelled into the unexpected, and equally unwieldy, role of suitor. If someone had asked him to explain how he, the most rational and self-contained of men, had arrived at a state commonly known to rob even the sanest individual of his natural good sense, he would have had considerable difficulty answering. Nor could he have said why he was now clearly pursuing the hand of a woman he'd until recently thought—and to some extent still found—eminently unsuitable to become his wife.

Richard gazed rather blankly around his elegant office at the Manhattan Company and then thrummed impatiently on the arm of his chair, the sound echoing in the still room like the muffled hoofbeats of a horse on some urgent errand. Come now, he told himself briskly, this lackadaisical attitude will never do for one who is a—a what? A green-eyed monster? A lovesick swain? Or simply a tomfool? His fingers slowly ceased their cadence as he paused to examine each of these possibilities in turn.

Was he actually jealous of Benjamin Hartley or, for that matter, of Gulian Verplanck, who after meeting Jennifer Somers once had promptly announced that he meant to enter the lists for the lady's affections? Certainly, the object and single-mindedness of their respective intentions had hastily caused him to clarify his own. Still, he'd have sworn that Gulian, at least, was merely out for a romp, bent on discovering whether he couldn't add another feather to his cap with this latest conquest. And he'd even have hazarded a guess that Jennifer had readily perceived the true nature of that gentleman's suit and was now enjoying the game of cat and mouse fully as much as Verplanck himself. But Mr. Hartley was quite a different story, Richard thought a trifle uneasily, resisting the temptation to beat another tattoo upon his chair. For one thing, the man had already confessed that he was nearly determined to ask for Jennifer's hand, and it was only her father's absence that seemed to stand in the way of his doing so in short order. Why, he probably ought to be grateful that Lord Somers hadn't appeared on the scene so that the matter could be resolved—much as he'd been guilty lately of harboring quite the opposite sentiment, Richard reminded himself glumly. And for another thing, Hartley seemed perfectly willing to consider setting aside some deeply held principles of his own in order to achieve his goal. That fact alone was enough to cause Richard both to fear that the other man's suit was altogether a serious one and that he, too, might be obliged to make similar compromises if he wished to succeed.

But if Hartley didn't look on these adjustments as compromises made solely for the sake of love, why, Richard wondered, did he? Surely he wasn't so everlastingly exact in his ways that he could tolerate only one method of dealing with matters, or so all-fired set in this thinking that he could allow only one viewpoint to be heard? And yet, those errors were precisely the same ones with which Jennifer Somers had already charged him and which he'd lately come to admit had crept into his personal life—and even his relationship with the twins—as well. Why, what matter if he sacrificed part of a few so-called ideals if the result brought him greater happiness and peace of mind than the ideals had ever provided? And wasn't what was holding him back primarily the irrational worry that others would think him besotted or hardheaded? To be truthful, although he tended to give only scant thought to the current affairs of his peers—as Gulian Verplanck had recently and in such an untimely fashion reminded him—he was well aware there were a fair number of those individuals sufficiently interested in his own affairs to allot them much closer scrutiny. Besides, wasn't it still preferable to be called a dolt for learning to one's discredit that some theorem didn't serve than for never coming to that realization at all? And anyway, because a portion of the principle didn't seem to bear out, or the whole didn't always appear to hold true, that didn't mean the entire thing was worthless or wrong, did it?

Richard sat very still, his mind nibbling away excitedly at this last revelation. But why, he thought somewhat irritably, did it feel as if he'd come to the same revelation before, or that he was only acknowledging something he'd already known? Richard sighed. He could even imagine the tone of a certain young lady's voice as she chided him for rigid reasoning or read him a lesson for choosing only between the two distinct alternatives of right and wrong. Well, he admitted, Jennifer's record had certainly been impressive so far. He'd shown himself to be narrow-minded, presumptuous, and downright arrogant. Yes, all in all plenty of room for improvement, he thought rather more happily—a condition that was bound to require frequent discussions and a good deal of interaction with the young lady under his guardianship. That prospect made him face the less pleasant one of the work piled on his desk with a measure of humor he'd rarely have managed otherwise.

Unfortunately, Richard found it quite impossible to sustain that positive attitude when he considered the pivotal question of how to achieve his goal. Since he'd never attempted such a thing before, he had only a vague notion of how to initiate a courtship. In addition, the two models to which he had immediate recourse didn't promise to be of much help. Verplanck's approach, for example, was clearly suited to someone who meant to amuse himself with a casual dalliance and who was therefore prone to sprinkle his conversation with numerous references of a less than genteel nature. Apparently, though, the contrast of the man's impressive background and fortune with his often coarse double entendres tended to prove irresistible to many women because the list of those won over by said tactics was known to be lengthy, if colorful, and to include a few ladies, as well as many lightskirts. And to top it off, Gulian either seemed only mildly diverted by the suggestion that he might be damaging his reputation with this type of encounter or blissfully ignorant that any such malicious rumors were circulating at all. But since Richard had to admit that he was far too susceptible to needing the approval of others and could never hope to remain indifferent to public opinion—once he'd acknowledged its existence—he was forced to concede that the foregoing attitude simply wouldn't serve his purposes.

Nor was he particularly enamored of Mr. Hartley's approach, which as far as he could discern alternated between a sort of rapt devotion and a persistent attempt to curry favor. In the first instance, Hartley appeared inclined to hang upon Jennifer's every word as if attending an edict issued directly from on high, staring at her all the while with the stupidly hopeful expression of a puppy, which Richard personally found a trifle nauseating. And Hartley's behavior in the second instance was scarcely an improvement because he seemed too little concerned with his principles rather than his pride and repeatedly sought to prop up the latter by making little verbal forays here and there in the hope of striking a responsive chord. To be fair, it wasn't that he appeared to say only those things with which the lady was bound to agree, but rather, Richard noted, that he tended to phrase what he did say in a way that she was apt to find most agreeable. Thus, he was safely able to retain his reputation as an affable young man when another might have been condemned as a lickspittle.

But what Richard found most disconcerting of all was that, despite the differences in the two attitudes, both seemed to fit their owners as easily and comfortably as a favorite pair of boots. And just how was it that these men could each be so confident in knowing how to set about things when Richard himself had barely a clue, much less the temerity to believe that whatever stratagem he devised should be successful? It was almost as if the other two men had had the benefit of some special lesson and he'd been absent when it was taught, Richard decided, or as if they belonged to a secret club to which he'd unaccountably been denied membership. Or was it only, he wondered in a sudden burst of insight, that they were used to moving in the mainstream of society and he was not? While they were busily engaged in interacting with their fellow human beings, wasn't he far more likely to be found hidden away by himself, reduced to delivering a monologue or perhaps a soliloquy—just as he was now? No wonder he always felt as if he were floundering in a kind of vacuum without enough information or insight to make a move in any direction with the assurance of success. What else could he expect, after all, when he apparently couldn't boast a single friend eager to share feelings and impressions with him, and could think of no one anxious to offer up another viewpoint for consideration beside his own? Why, he'd even be hard-pressed to name anyone with whom he could look forward to sharing an occasional congenial chat, he realized—save, perhaps, for the very same lady he now dearly longed to make the subject of such a discussion instead. And that being the case, he was surely left with only one other logical course of action, he told himself, and one which he intended to employ at the earliest opportunity.

If Molly was surprised at being summoned in such a peremptory fashion to her landlord's study, she certainly had no intention of advertising that condition and thereby giving the man a leg up, she promised herself firmly. True, she'd suffered a momentary loss of nerve when the request had been relayed to her, and had even wondered briefly whether she ought to be begin packing her bag. Perhaps, she'd reasoned, the too-proper Mr. Avery had abruptly awakened at last to the realization that one of the ladies he was sheltering under his roof was literally a woman of the streets and he'd decided to cast her forth without further ado. Well, she promised herself, she'd be horsewhipped before she'd allow him to charge her with duplicity or even low dealing simply on account of her past and the fact that she was a trifle down on her luck at the moment—or had been until meeting Jennifer. And what's more, she continued, adopting a somewhat righteous air, she didn't mean to stir so much as an inch off the premises without first giving Mr. Avery the full benefit of her opinion regarding the dubious character of any man who'd see it as his duty to undertake such a dishonorable action.

Nevertheless, she was considerably taken aback to find that an assessment of his character was precisely what her host wished her to provide—though clearly not for the reasons she'd originally imagined.

"Tell me, Miss Danhope," he began in a somewhat oblique fashion, "do you think most people believe me to be a sympathetic sort of man?"

Molly hesitated for a moment, trying rapidly to calculate whether an honest answer was the wisest route to follow in the present situation.

"No need to wrap it up in clean linen for my sake, you know," Richard told her generously, as if reading her thoughts. "I asked you to come here today firstly because I require some information I believe you can provide, and secondly because I know you to be an upright individual rarely inclined to prevaricate—am I right?"

Molly hastily smothered an impulse to laugh and then managed to look attentive, if still puzzled, and to nod her head seriously instead.

"Yes, I thought so," he said in a satisfied voice. "So pray tell me: Would you say people tended to find me approachable?"

Molly slowly began to shake her head in the opposite direction.

"No? Well, perhaps receptive would be a better term?"

His guest continued to respond negatively to this suggestion, and her expression became even more skeptical than it had been before. "You wish me to speak plainly, do you not?" she asked at last. "Very well, then, I trust you'll understand if I don't bother to mince words. To be perfectly honest, I doubt you'd find a single soul who'd argue that you shouldn't be awarded the title of least tenderhearted fellow in all of creation. Why, good God—most times you appear to deserve as much sympathy as the rich man who constantly bemoans the lack of ways to waste his money! What's more, you don't know the first thing about being sympathetic to anyone else because you seem to understand the workings of human nature about as clearly as I do the principles of metaphysics! 'Approachable'? What twaddle! Or haven't you noticed that the members of your household are as reluctant to approach you—no matter how good their excuse—as one would a bull during high season? Your own children will readily confess to being scared to death of you, though I'll own you seem lately, at least, to have made some attempt to rectify that situation. And past time, too! But then, it probably never occurred to you that holding yourself up as an example of perfection may make you feel good, but it makes them feel only one thing—perfectly miserable! Why, they'd be as likely to confide all their little attempts and failures to you as someone who paints houses would be to a famous artist. There's just too large a gap, don't you see? And if the twins haven't been encouraged to believe you'd be willing to meet them halfway, eventually I should think they'd give up trying to make it across that chasm every time by themselves."

Molly sat back at the close of this speech and observed with some pleasure that it appeared to have had considerable effect. For one thing, her host had crumpled into his seat as if her chastisement had been accomplished with a much more substantial weapon than her tongue. And for another thing, he looked altogether stunned, though whether this was the result of what she'd told him or because of who had said it, she couldn't be certain.

"But haven't I any redeeming qualities in your eyes at

all, then?'' Richard asked at last in a plaintive voice. ''I assure you, I always mean well.''

''Ha!'' Molly scoffed. ''So you've good intentions? To my way of thinking, good intentions don't mean that,'' she said, snapping her fingers in his face. ''Who's to know what you're thinking if you persist in blundering about like an idiot or, worse still, continue on as before but convince yourself it's different because *you* know you've changed? No one can read your mind!''

''No. I guess I merely assumed that people would know I wasn't intent on causing any harm.'' He hesitated at the look on his guest's face. ''I take it you think me a perfect innocent?'' he said slowly.

''Not *perfect*,'' she observed with particular emphasis. Then, seeing that he appeared rather dashed, she allowed herself to offer him a small, encouraging smile before continuing in a kinder tone. ''It's only that you can't keep going around 'assuming' this or 'imagining' that, don't you see? You've got to pluck up your nerve and find out for sure what's on the stove instead of simply pretending that you know the contents of the pot. Otherwise, you'll have no one to blame but yourself if things don't turn out the way you want them to.'' She paused, tipping her head to one side in order to consider the man opposite her more closely. ''Do you know what I think? I think you live entirely too much in your head. And if you ask me,'' she continued, although no one had, ''you and Jennifer both suffer from a tendency to overthink every precious thing. Why, it's a pure wonder you two aren't forced to take to your beds by noon each day, given the way you carry on.''

Richard seemed all at once to turn pensive, tapping out a staccato rhythm that promptly began to make Molly feel nervous again. ''Do you find me an attractive man?'' he asked abruptly and apropos of nothing as far as she could tell.

''Who—me?'' Molly squeaked in alarm, bolting upright. ''Why, to be sure—in a general sort of way, that is,'' she amended. She was immediately conscious of her vulnerable position—not just alone for the moment with a man in his study, but as a female guest in the household, a fact she knew that many a gentleman wouldn't hesitate to seize upon, should the fancy strike him.

As if he, too, had realized how peculiar his question had sounded, Richard hastened to correct that impression. "I mean, do you think that most ladies generally would find me handsome and, ah, desirable?"

"Yes, I suppose so," Molly said dubiously, relaxing somewhat in her chair again. Then, guessing suddenly where these questions might be leading, she decided to be so obliging as to lend the poor man a hand and to speed things along at the same time. "Don't you really mean, do I think a particular young lady, whom I've reason to know rather well, believes you a suitable target at which to set her cap?"

Richard, to his infinite embarrassment, blushed vividly at his question. "Oh, all right, yes—that's what I mean!"

"Well, why the devil not say so in the first place and save us both a mess of bother?" Molly pointed out with brutal logic. She sniffed loudly in a way that made it clear what she thought of such shilly-shallying. "But since you're asking, I might as well tell you, the answer's yes."

"Er, what—?" Richard stuttered.

"Yes, I do believe that Jennifer holds a special place in her heart for you," she explained in patient accents, wondering privately if her friend hadn't been mistaken to conceive a passion for a man whose wits appeared to her, at any rate, for the most part to be entirely at sea.

This impression was unfortunately confirmed by the rather foolish expression of delight that spread over her listener's face the minute she finished speaking. "Do tell," he marveled, beaming happily at her.

"Quite," Molly acknowledged briefly. "I take it that that was the information you thought I could provide?" Her host nodded. "And now that you have it, what is it that you mean to do, I wonder?"

He stared at her confusedly. "But that's precisely what I imagined you could tell me."

"I?" Molly exclaimed in surprise. "Whyever would you think that, when I've rarely had occasion myself to tell a sweetheart from a sweet pea? But even so, I can't fathom the reason for all this hurly-burly. You've clear ground ahead of you, as far as I can see.''

It was Richard's turn to look surprised. ''Seems to me that there's a couple of other men with the same idea who are in the way. Or have you forgotten that Mr. Verplanck and Mr. Hartley are both also apparently bent on wooing Lady Somers?''

''Oh, pooh!'' Molly dismissed that threat with a careless wave of her hand. ''You don't believe that Jennifer would really treat either of them seriously, do you? Why, the first one's a whiffler and the other's a mere weanling. I'd think you'd only have to make it known that you'd tossed your hat into the ring for those two to find you'd spiked their guns quite nicely. The fact is, I wasn't sure myself why you hadn't done so before now. And what's more, I shouldn't wonder if Jennifer isn't a trifle mystified, as well.''

Richard let out a tiny groan. ''But how could I even consider mentioning my feelings, when to do so might place her in the uncomfortable position of being obliged to suffer my attentions as long as she's a guest in my household?''

Molly shot him a disgusted look. ''If you'd held back on account of not knowing whether Jennifer felt a tenderness for you, that I could understand—and even pardon. But then, I should have guessed you'd find some rule or other to keep you penned up. I'm sure I never thought I'd meet a man so awfully concerned with sticking to the niceties that he couldn't tell when to jump and when to stay. Why, I wonder you can even be certain of your heart, since as far as I can make out, you appear to have spent more time thinking about your behavior than about your beloved!''

She wound down and paused to direct another stern look at her host. He was hanging his head, however, and thinking this was the second time he'd received such a scolding, and was therefore able to escape that further censure. Molly had never had any intention of not assisting the two individuals in question toward the altar, if that's what they both wished. In fact, she wasn't even surprised at Richard's indirect request that she give him a hand in that enterprise because she'd already received a similar and far more pointed request from Abigail Rutland to the same effect. During the evening of the City Assembly dance, Abigail had suddenly shown herself interested in establishing a cozy little friendship with Molly, and had spent a good half hour chatting with her in a decidedly congenial fashion about the couples in the ballroom and their various relationships. Still, her comments had been transparent enough to lead Molly to wonder whether her companion wasn't, perhaps, seeking to establish the true extent of Jennifer's feelings toward Mr. Hartley. Indeed, she'd been just on the point of losing patience and urging Abigail toward a bit more plain speaking when the latter had apparently decided her confidences were safe enough with Molly to reach the same conclusion.

Didn't it seem to her, Abigail had inquired, that Lady Somers and Mr. Avery made an altogether perfect couple? Molly, who hadn't been able to keep from observing the difficulties that that ill-matched pair were encountering merely in trying to waltz together, thought briefly about objecting to this statement. One glance at the purposeful look in Abigail's eye, however, had been ample to prompt her to smile instead and to agree politely that such was certainly the case. To be honest, Abigail had then admitted with a self-conscious shrug of her shoulders, she'd once believed that she was the object of Mr. Avery's intentions. Still, it was plain to see that things had taken a somewhat different turn, and despite her past aspirations, she'd no intention whatsoever of standing in Lady Somers's way, Abilgail asserted prettily. For that matter, it was too bad there still appeared to be one or two other obstacles remaining in the path, she went on, staring meaningfully at Mr. Hartley, who was busy leading Jennifer out onto the dance floor. Why, she was nearly tempted to see if she couldn't try to fascinate that gentleman herself, Abigail confessed—so that the course of true love would suffer no further impediment from his continued presence, she'd amended hastily. Didn't Molly feel that to be a worthy objective and one that she'd be equally willing to promote? she inquired, following this question with a deep, romantic sigh.

Molly hadn't been slow to perceive that having clearly lost Mr. Avery's interest, Abigail now meant to secure Mr. Hartley's, and to conclude that her purpose wasn't half as

selfless as she pretended it was. Still, she'd reasoned quickly, getting rid of Mr. Hartley was precisely what was
required to offer her host a clear field, and it didn't matter in
the least to her why that objective was undertaken if it
accomplished the same goal. Therefore, she'd promptly
indicated her readiness to go along with Abigail, and tossing
her a conspiratorial smile, had inquired in low tones what
that lady had in mind. Her plan, Abigail had whispered,
was simply to make Mr. Hartley jealous by having Mr.
Avery escort her to as many of the various social functions
at which he was likely to be present as she could manage.
And thus at the same time, she'd pointed out, Mr. Avery's
constant attendance at her side would surely cause Lady
Somers to reconsider her choice of companion as well. All
Abigail required of Molly, she'd explained, was to plant the
notion in Mr. Avery's mind that the arrangement she'd
outlined would be utterly beneficial to his suit, too. After
that, she'd concluded confidently, she'd be able to handle
matters quite nicely herself.

Although it occurred to Molly to find such a scheme a
good deal more risky than Abigail did, and to wonder
whether it was advisable for her to play a role in the whole
affair at all, she also suspected that Jennifer, for one, would
never forgive her doing otherwise.

"See here, no need to take on so over a little scold," she
told Richard more gently, after rapidly reviewing the foregoing scene in her mind. "Far better to have heard it from me,
after all, than from anyone else. Now, let's consider the
situation again, shall we?" she went on in her usual,
practical fashion. "You imagine Jennifer will feel stifled by
your paying her court, and that others will believe you
unfeeling, or your actions outrageous, should you do so? It
seems to me that what's needed, then, is something to put
everyone off the scent and to make it seem that your
addresses aren't meant for Jennifer in particular." She
stopped briefly to give the appearance of chewing things over.

"I have it!" she exclaimed after a few moments. "You've
only to begin courting another young lady regularly at the
same time and the problem's solved! That way, you see,
Jennifer shan't suspect your real purpose, and no one else

will be able to predict how the wind's blowing, either. Besides, such a method will let you polish your approach and get rid of any other quirks and quarrels—don't you agree? Now then, we've only to think of someone who won't find your sudden interest in her a trifle odd.'' She paused for a minute before offering casually, ''What about Miss Rutland?''

At that suggestion, Richard, whose demeanor had under gone a rapid series of changes during the preceding speech— from dejection to curiosity and, finally, to hopefulness— looked as if he were caught on the horns of a dilemma. ''Yes,'' he agreed a bit reluctantly, ''I daresay Abigail— Miss Rutland, that is—would suit the purpose you describe. But truly, I wonder if it would be proper to use her so shamelessly for our own ends?''

''I can't see the harm, but I suppose it's all in how you look at it,'' Molly admitted, scarcely able to sort out one person's end from another any longer herself. ''What about this? You like Miss Rutland and she likes you—isn't that so? Well then, what's more natural than that you should decide to spend time with the lady in order to get to know her—and your feelings—better? It isn't as if you'll compromise her, or even your precious principles, in the process, is it?''

''No, I expect not,'' Richard admitted, brightening somewhat. ''And though I'm no great hand at such things, I trust I could manage a simple little make believe if it would ultimately help me steal a march on my rivals.''

''I certainly hope so,'' Molly said in a fervent voice.

Chapter 10

RICHARD LOST no time in putting the plan he thought he and Molly had devised into action. It had been her suggestion that he wait until she discovered where Jennifer's suitors meant to escort the two of them and then, upon learning the destination from her, make his arrangements coincide—insofar as was possible, of course. That way, she'd pointed out, he'd reap the benefit both of exposing his own activities to Jennifer's view and of keeping an eye on the progress of his competitors. And what's more, Molly had decided privately, such a method promised to capitalize most efficiently on the stratagem Abigail had invented so that Richard wouldn't be obliged to maintain the deception even one second longer than necessary and thereby run the risk of blowing the gaff, to put it bluntly.

Thus, a few days later when Jennifer related that Mr. Hartley had asked to escort her and Molly to New York's Vauxhall Garden, named for its London counterpart, for the last ball of the season, Molly hurried to convey that information to her host. Richard, she was pleased to observe, kept scrupulously to his word and promptly issued a similar invitation to Abigail Rutland. In fact, he took Molly's advice that he keep his rivals in sight so literally that he waited barely five minutes after Jennifer and that lady had departed before setting out for the Rutland's town house on lower Broadway. And in addition, he received an unexpected boost when he discovered that it was not the daunting Mr. Rutland who was to accompany them, but his rather more congenial wife instead.

It wasn't until the three were actually seated in his carriage and headed toward the famed grounds on the Bowery Road that the enormity of his undertaking was finally brought home to Richard, however, and he was temporarily struck dumb. The trio maintained a polite silence until approximately half the journey had elapsed and they'd passed the one milestone. Then, seeing that her mother had retreated into her customary role of reticent companion and her escort appeared strangely tongue-tied for one who was used to dealing with her on a friendly if not familiar basis, Abigail concluded that the task of opening the conversation was clearly to be hers. Therefore, she turned at last to Richard and smiled prettily. "Indeed, sir," she began, "I'm certain I've never heard you say that you enjoyed entertainments such as Vauxhall."

Quite right, Richard thought. "Yes, well ordinarily that's so," he admitted. "But it's been brought to my attention that a man can grow, er, imbalanced working all the time and never doing ought else. Therefore, I've determined to amend that fault before it oversets my equilibrium, and it occurred to me that you might be willing to lend a hand in that endeavor." *Here now*, he scolded himself, *you've made the evening sound about as attractive as some stodgy business arrangement.*

But Abigail was the only daughter of two doting parents who'd been blessed by her arrival late in their marriage after they'd nearly given up hope of ever having a baby. Raised by a father and mother almost too old to recall what a playful childhood should be like, she'd grown rapidly into a properly sedate young lady who looked forward to a variety of mildly pleasurable events in her life, but who was no more interested in initiating a romp than Richard. In fact, the scheme she'd undertaken with Molly's assistance was by far the most daring thing she could ever recall having done. Having long been exposed to the sober model of deportment offered by Edward Rutland, as well as the paragon of compliancy exemplified by the woman who preferred to be known as Mrs. Edward Rutland, she felt completely comfortable with what anyone else might term Mr. Avery's rather staid behavior. If anything, she was now a trifle disconcerted by the sudden discovery of a new aspect to his character, but she definitely had no intention of allowing it to cause her to miss a step, in any case.

"I should be delighted to assist you," she assured him. "I take it you haven't visited the gardens before? Well, neither has Mama, so you two must let me be your guide and agree to place yourselves in my hands for the evening."

"Oh, indeed, love," Mrs. Rutland agreed, for she rarely did anything else.

"With pleasure," Richard sighed, for he was already beginning to feel fatigued by this unaccustomed social interaction.

Therefore, for the next hour or so Abigail led her erstwhile escort and her chaperone down gravel walks decorated with ornamental trees and shrubs and through elaborate flower beds laid out around statues and marble fountains. She showed them the large equestrian figure of George Washington in the center of the grounds in front of the theater where song and dance alternated with dramatic pieces, and pointed out the orchestra enclosure hidden snugly among the trees. Together, they examined the huge apparatus used for firework displays and walked to the top of an artificial mound of earth constructed to facilitate viewing of those spectacles. They looked down at the field where balloon ascensions were the popular, daily featured event, and finally sought refuge in one of the private boxes set aside to accommodate weary guests.

After ordering a selection of cakes and some sweet wine from the vast array offered, Richard settled back in his chair, content for the moment merely to relax and to watch the passersby. *Why, I'm having quite a pleasant time*, he realized in surprise as he listened with half an ear to Abigail's description of the handsome exhibits provided on special gala days. *And it hasn't even been very difficult, either*, he decided—though no doubt that feeling was due in part to Mrs. Rutland's mitigating presence. *But Abigail is certainly a most pleasant companion, too*, he thought, throwing that lady such an unexpectedly warm and grateful smile that she positively sparkled back at him. And it was indeed fortunate that he was finding the time pass in a happy fashion after all, he admitted, since the one thing he'd discovered that he hadn't reckoned on was precisely how he expected to discover Jennifer Somers and her companions in the midst of the huge crowd that thronged Vauxhall Garden that evening.

Jennifer, however, was encountering no such difficulties, and since she hadn't known that Richard even intended to visit the garden that evening, it made her discovery all the more startling. She and Molly and Mr. Hartley had just completed a nearly identical tour of the grounds and had conceived the same desire to rest for a while and take a little refreshment. They were also headed toward the row of private boxes and were bobbing expectantly up and down through the crowd in the hope of spying an empty one they could claim for their own. A sudden break in the crush of people finally allowed them a clear view of their destination—and of the smiles exchanged by Richard and Abigail as well.

"Why, there's Mr. Avery and Miss and Mrs. Rutland," Mr. Hartley observed rather unnecessarily in a surprised voice. "Should you ladies like to join them?" he offered politely, without what might have been from anyone else a malicious intent.

"Oh, let's don't," Jennifer begged at once, sketching a pout. "It's just that he's bound to drone away over some tedious thing or other, and I don't want to spoil our nice evening," she invented. She immediately threw Molly a quelling look to forestall any possible objection from that direction.

"As you wish," Mr. Hartley agreed. "Only, I must say it doesn't look as if the man's being all that tedious tonight— leastways, Miss Rutland don't appear to think so."

No, she didn't, and neither did he, Jennifer thought somewhat confusedly. She cast a last speculative glance over her shoulder and then couldn't refrain from raising her eyebrows speakingly at her friend before turning to follow Mr. Hartley toward the refreshment booths. In fact, Mr. Avery looked as if he were having an altogether lovely time, she admitted slowly, trying unsuccessfully to resist concluding that this was a result of the company he was keeping rather than of his surroundings. But surely she wasn't mistaken about the significance of the look that had passed between those two, she decided, firmly ignoring the sad little ping her heart gave at that thought. Apparently she'd been right all along in thinking that Richard harbored a special feeling for Miss Rutland, or at least that they shared a desire to form a suitable alliance. Why, if she had a speck of proper feeling herself she'd be happy that the man appeared to be human after all, she told herself sternly. Still, she admitted a moment later, it was as ludicrous for her to try to ascribe ordinary emotions to that event as it was to pretend that she was only a disinterested observer.

It was precisely the degree of Jennifer's feelings for

Richard Avery that Mr. Hartley himself now sought to determine, although that task was complicated both by Molly's presence and by a nagging sense of impropriety at even raising the idea of matrimony without having discussed it with her father first. Upon witnessing the aforementioned exchange, he'd promptly arrived in relief at the same conclusion as Jennifer regarding the object of that gentleman's affections. Thus, he felt certain that it only remained to discover the state of her heart before removing the last real barrier that lay between him and the attainment of what he was convinced should be his goal. He waited until their little group was settled in a secluded box some distance away from the other one and supplied with a plate of pastries and a glass of champagne each before broaching the subject, which he did at last in a necessarily circuitous fashion. "I don't believe you've mentioned what your plans are after your father returns," he began, turning toward Jennifer.

She took a large, grateful sip of wine. "The problem is, I don't really know," she confessed. "I suppose we shall have to wait and see how things stand before deciding whether we can remain in New York or whether we should attempt to return to England quickly."

"And is there anything else that could induce you to prolong your visit, I wonder? Perhaps your relationship with the Avery children is such that you might be inclined to stay behind even if Lord Somers wishes to leave?" he suggested.

"No," Jennifer said firmly, shaking her head. "I've done everything I can to make their situation a bit more bearable, and have even gone so far as to point out to their father how I felt he was serving to exacerbate the already difficult strains of childhood. Not that I'm persuaded he truly understands the fears and doubts to which George and Caroline are apt to fall prey—any more than he appears to comprehend the needs of an adult heart, I might add—or that he's inclined to modify his behavior to accommodate what he doubtless sees as mere trivialities. Still, I've come to accept that exposing his faults is the most I can hope to accomplish, since I don't propose to wait around forever in order to learn whether he even means to correct them!" she concluded, with perhaps more force than was strictly called for and despite a strongly disapproving look from Molly, who nevertheless held her tongue.

And that was that, Mr. Hartley told himself dazedly. So much, apparently, for the possible threat to him posed by Richard Avery. But because he wasn't an insensitive man, he didn't stoop to gloat over that fact. "Yes, I see," he said sympathetically instead—and then, to his own surprise, hesitated. But why was he holding back now that the field was clear? That's what he'd wanted—or was it, he wondered uneasily. Hadn't he actually been somewhat relieved not to have been forced to deal with the peripheral considerations involved in pursuing the hand of a British subject, as Richard had already pointed out himself, and with which he'd now be obliged to contend if he continued on his present course? Not being any more adept than most men at changing horses in midstream, however, and also being somewhat curious—even though he wasn't an egotist—to see what her response might be, he forged ahead just the same. "Of course, I must confess that I'm not looking forward to your departure with any great pleasure," he said. "Surely you're aware, after all, that my feelings for you run deeper than those of ordinary friendship? Indeed, I'd ventured to hope that you might even have discovered you'd begun to feel likewise."

At this point, Molly nearly felt obliged to intervene as chaperone, though to be truthful, she hadn't yet had the opportunity to become fully conversant with the duties of that role. Still, she knew that one of her responsibilities must certainly be to shield Jennifer from improper advances by a member of the opposite sex. But since she was also well aware of her friend's own expertise in that realm, she was less apprehensive about how Jennifer would deal with Mr. Hartley than she might have been otherwise. Moreover, her curiosity had been piqued by this proximity to events she'd never encountered herself because of her family's reduced circumstances, and she was half inclined to allow the scene to continue to play with careful supervision, but no interruption.

"Pray, don't go any further," Jennifer begged Mr. Hartley

before Molly could make up her mind. Her cheeks had flushed a dull red when he'd started to speak, and she'd been aware of looking every direction but at him until she felt compelled to respond at last and to spare him whatever embarrassment any further inquiries might produce. "I'm sure you must know that I like you very well indeed," she said honestly, raising her head and making a point of meeting his eyes, "and I hope we shall always remain friends. But I've no intention whatsoever of forming a lasting attachment during my stay in New York," she continued in a stronger voice. "Besides, I should think it would only prove a hindrance to your political aspirations to be linked with a woman who was a citizen of the country with whom America might soon be at war—would it not?"

"Well, I daresay that might compromise me somewhat in a few people's eyes," he admitted. "But even so, I assure you I'd be more than happy to accept that challenge."

"Yes, I've no doubt that you should," Jennifer agreed before adding gently, "but I'm afraid I don't love you, you see."

"Oh." Mr. Hartley paused to digest this fact. "Probably best not to wait to consult your father about making you an offer, then?"

Jennifer quickly frowned at Molly, whom she knew would be highly amused by this question, and then was obliged to hide her own smile behind one hand. "Yes, probably better not," she said in a serious voice.

After a few moments, Mr. Hartley rallied sufficiently to shake off the disappointment that he had the tiniest suspicion he felt only because he imagined he was supposed to. "But see here—let's not let this little interlude spoil the evening, shall we?" he urged his two guests.

"I must say you're taking the news of my, er, sentiments remarkably well," Jennifer couldn't help observing, allowing herself at last to smile openly.

"No reason to cast myself off the nearest bridge, is there? Besides, I'm not altogether sure I could comfortably handle being your husband, if you want to know the truth," Mr. Hartley admitted. He stopped to give Jennifer a long, measuring look. "It seems to me, if you'll forgive my saying so, that any man willing to take on that role would either need to possess indefatigable patience, unswerving resolution, and the faith of Job—or the temperament and physical attributes of a mule!''

Molly and Jennifer laughed until their sides ached. ''Never fear—I forgive you,'' the latter managed to get out finally. ''In fact, I shouldn't be surprised if I weren't the first to agree!''

Gulian Verplanck would also probably have agreed with Mr. Hartley's assessment of the kind of man who'd seek to make Jennifer Somers his wife, except for two things: He already possessed the first three characteristics mentioned in no small measure himself, and the attainment of wedded bliss wasn't exactly what he would have described as his objective.

This wasn't to say that Gulian was in the habit of going about ruining the reputations of unwilling ladies, but only that he enjoyed the chase a good deal more than actually catching the prey. His interest lay in the sidelong glance and the billet-doux, and he was generally accounted a master in the art of wooing a woman. But in Jennifer, he'd come to admit that he finally appeared to have met his match. No sooner would he set a trap than she would neatly spring it and come up with the bait as well. If he tried to attack, she would feint; if he began to flatter, she would merely laugh; and if he attempted a sleight of hand, she'd guess the outcome before he'd even finished. In short, Gulian had found that he was now in the peculiar position of having someone play fast and loose with him as easily as he was accustomed to do. And that discovery alone had caused him to sustain interest in the game far longer than he would have ordinarily.

It also occurred to Gulian that should he ever think of settling down in a more conventional relationship, as his family often urged him to, he wouldn't find a more congenial partner than Jennifer. When he was prompted to discover whether or not to present that option to her, however, he learned—not surprisingly—that she had a good deal of trouble taking the idea seriously.

They were seated in his fashionable barouche for an afternoon drive and accompanied only by a footman. Gulian had, in Jennifer's opinion, a decidedly heavy hand on the reins, and since he also apparently felt himself unable to converse while negotiating the crowded streets, she was free to gaze around at the passing scene as they moved slowly up Broadway and then turned at the park fronting the marble edifice of City Hall and continued northward. The weather was clear and unusually mild for early December, but still crisp enough for her to be glad of the heavy blanket and the heated brick placed under her feet. She was just concluding that it was doubtless an indication of how lightly she treated her relationship with Gulian that she never felt the least bit nervous about her ability to retain the upper hand, when she observed that he'd steered the carriage onto the Boston post road and that they were now heading rapidly out of the city and into the countryside.

At first Jennifer didn't feel greatly alarmed, for there was a footman in attendance and she was almost certain that Gulian wouldn't dare have arranged to compromise a woman of her reputation as casually as he might have one of his ladybirds. But as they drove farther and farther away from the populated areas of New York, two thoughts occurred to her one after another that promptly caused her to feel a good deal more apprehensive than before. First, while there was the comfort of the footman riding silently behind her on his perch, the man was in Gulian's employ, after all, and could easily have been convinced—or paid—to ignore any attempt his employer might make to take advantage of the situation. And second, though things didn't appear too dangerous as long as they remained outdoors in the carriage, there was the question of what might happen if her escort decided to stop at some inn or other and she was left without even the footman to provide a veneer of respectability or to defend her honor if need be. Still, Jennifer told herself, there wasn't any point in raising a protest until circumstances demanded it, for to do so might only succeed in planting the idea in Gulian's mind instead.

"Allow me to congratulate you, my dear, on being brave enough to accompany such a notorious womanizer on an expedition to the wilds of Manhattan,'' Gulian observed as if he'd read her thoughts. He barely stopped himself in time from following that remark with an automatic, practiced leer.

"Oh, but it didn't require any thought at all,'' Jennifer replied innocently, attempting to ignore the painful way her heart had begun pounding at the news that her worst fears might yet come to pass. "And anyway, I shouldn't imagine even a reprobate like you would be so ill-advised as to accost a lady in broad daylight on a public road. Besides, I'm certain an open carriage wouldn't be the proper setting for a seduction by a man of your, er, talents, nor the temperature exactly conducive to that activity—leastways, not for two creatures as mindful of our comforts as we.'' She snuggled deeper into her furs and smiled up at her companion, hoping fervently that her confident façade would somehow throw him off stride.

"What a perfect little minx you are!'' he exclaimed appreciatively. "Why, blister it if I don't think you'd make a damned fine wife!''

"Well thank you, I'm sure,'' Jennifer said, pretending for the moment that his remark was meant in a general sense.

Gulian hesitated and then tossed off with apparent unconcern, "Not that you're interested in that sort of a future—?''

"Oh, I don't know that I shouldn't be at some time—'' Jennifer broke off and shot a sudden, suspicious look at the gentleman beside her. "You don't mean to tell me that you're actually considering asking my father when he returns for permission to make me an offer?'' she demanded, widening her eyes in disbelief.

Gulian's normal composure appeared a trifle ruffled by this reaction. "And what if I am?'' he said peevishly. "Nothing so awfully out of the ordinary about that, is there? Why, dozens of men must pose the same question every day. Bound to occur to me sometime or other that I ought to do likewise before overlong, don't you think?''

"Ought to—perhaps—but 'want to,' certainly never,'' Jennifer corrected promptly. "At any rate, not when I know you to be far more inclined to tender another sort of offer wherever women are concerned.''

Fortunately for Gulian, he was spared the need to marshal a further defense because just then the Buck's Horn Tavern came into view. Now, if truth be told, his only plan had been for them to rest and refresh themselves there for a while—and nothing more. Unfortunately, however, he was far more used to handling women of a rather different class than Jennifer, as she'd only a moment before pointed out. Therefore, he'd carelessly made what were clearly his normal arrangements on such occasions without giving a second thought as to how they would look to this particular guest, or to anyone else, for that matter. Poor Jennifer's heart thudded painfully as she watched the carriage disappear in the direction of the stables and the footman disappear, too—presumably to find the kitchen. And once they were greeted in a familiar fashion by the landlord and immediately led to the private parlor the man was heard to refer to as "Mr. Verplanck's usual room," she began quickly—if somewhat belatedly—to review in her mind the reasons why a lady was commonly accompanied by a chaperone.

The aforementioned chamber was comfortable enough, however, and a generous fire burned invitingly in the grate. Nevertheless, as Jennifer drew off her hat and gloves and began to warm her hands, she couldn't help noticing the candle-lit table set with an intimate dinner for two and the sofa piled with pillows that nestled conveniently in the farthest and darkest corner of the room. Perhaps, she had to admit, though she'd no idea what he expected to gain by it, her escort really meant to try and seduce her after all!

That very thought had finally presented itself to Gulian as well, not only because the setting had reminded him of how frequently it had assisted him toward that goal in the past, but also because the firelight flickered over such a lovely vision of womanhood that he was tempted to thrust prudence aside completely. He had walked behind Jennifer in order to help her remove her cloak, and as he looked down at her shining curls he suddenly realized that it would be possible for him to compel her to remove a few other garments, too, if he wished. But even as he stretched out an arm, her first words made him freeze.

"If you actually force me to say, 'Lay a hand on me and I'll scream,' I can't promise I shall be able to stop laughing," Jennifer advised lightly over her shoulder. She unfastened her cloak, slipped out of it, and laid it calmly over a chair near the fire before turning around to face her companion. "Now you're supposed to tell me that there's no one to come if I do sound the alarm—or don't you intend to carry through with this farce after all?" she asked in a voice that she managed to make sound merely curious. She looked around the room and then forced an amused expression to creep over her face. "Though I must confess I'd thought you capable of devising a much more sophisticated ruse than this. But then, possibly your other, ah, guests haven't required such elaborate inducements to cooperate as I should?"

"Oh, should you?" Gulian scoffed, throwing her a challenging look. Inwardly, however, he was conscious of a growing feeling of irritation with this woman—both for picking out his plan before he'd even been ready to acknowledge having one, and then for immediately proceeding to poke fun at it. "I think you forget that I'm a man and could easily overpower you, if I chose, and oblige you to bend to my will," he pointed out in a rather sulky voice.

"I doubt that I could very easily forget your sex, sir," Jennifer reminded him politely, "or that someone of my stature could ever feel anything but vulnerable to physical advances. Still, I can scarcely believe you'd choose to resort to such an ungentlemanly tactic. Or haven't you any experience in courting a woman who only laughs in your face? No doubt you'd expect a somewhat different reaction to the wine and the soft light and the whole tender scene—would you not? Well then, since I can promise in advance that you'll not get the response you seek—whether you cajole or coerce until doomsday comes—can't I persuade you to forego the attempt entirely and help me dispatch this delicious-looking meal instead?" She seated herself at the table and began to uncover the dishes and load her plate with an appetite that she pretended had not been impaired at all by her potential ravishment.

Gulian chuckled, his natural good humor and sense of proportion considerably restored by these commonplace actions. He threw himself into the other chair and poured out the wine. Then he took a large swallow and smiled grudgingly at his companion. "I'm sure I've never been tossed aside in favor of a baked chicken before," he complained.

Jennifer stopped nibbling delicately on a leg long enough to stare at him in a calculating manner. "Truly, I don't think it's that you mind not adding a new name to your list of conquests, if that's what you actually intended—it's only that your pride's been hurt by my having hit the nail so squarely on the head, isn't that so? And since neither of us is really interested either in damaging our good names or in establishing a more permanent arrangement—at least, not if it appears to offer even fewer advantages than the, er, short run—I can't see any need to belabor those points." She sat back and waved her chicken bone for emphasis. "Far better, to my way of thinking, to remain friends than to risk losing it all in the vain hope of discovering a deeper, more rewarding relationship through love or marriage."

"This is a new twist—you sounding the cynic. Can it be that you've received some disappointment or other during your stay in the city? Possibly, if you were to confide in me—?"

It was Jennifer's turn to laugh. "Not very likely," she assured him. "And even if something untoward had occurred, mind you, whatever do you think would induce me to confess it to a man openly termed one of the foremost gossip mongers in all of New York?" Then, seeing the injured reaction this statement had produced, she patted her companion's hand consolingly. "Dear me, I've gone and trampled all over your dignity again, and I assure you I never meant to be so careless a second time. Come now. Let's put our heads together and figure out how we're to salvage my reputation from seeming to have been compromised by this little adventure—and your honor as a gentleman, too. Surely you, having had such a vast amount of experience in such matters, after all, will be able to suggest a whole host of possibilities from which we may take our pick?" She offered him a guileless smile.

Gulian either chose not to take offense at this double-edged remark or he was feeling too worn down at this point to rise to the challenge with his usual enthusiasm. "Oh, you're probably right—as always," he sniffed, beginning to heap his own plate with a generous assortment of dainty foods. "Best look to my feed, then," he explained. "After all, can't expect me to face the dangers of nature in the raw—or of your company either, for that matter—without sufficient fortifications, can you?"

Jennifer, too, swallowed this gibe without comment. She was greatly relieved to see that the threat she'd faced in the last hour seemed to have passed, though she did wonder briefly how the afternoon might have turned out if Gulian had refused to be deterred or if she'd treated the situation as anything other than laughable and had given the slightest hint that she'd actually been afraid. "No, indeed," she said in mock seriousness, raising her glass in a salute. "In fact, I daresay you'd be well-advised to prepare for both eventualities with infinite and equal care."

Had Jennifer but known it, Richard Avery was thinking virtually identical thoughts at approximately the same time— although it was she whom he kept imagining as the victim, and not the other way 'round. He'd learned of Jennifer's outing that morning from Molly, and had even watched from behind the study curtains as her escort tucked her into the carriage in front of his footman and then tooled her away. For a while, he'd remained standing by the window, wondering idly what their destination might be and what they'd discuss or how they'd endeavor to amuse themselves during the drive. Not, Richard had reminded himself again, that his friend would ever appear at a loss, even when confronted by the redoubtable Jennifer Somers. And what's more, the man didn't seem at all affected by the attentions that Mr. Hartley continued to pay the lady, and Richard would have been surprised to hear that Gulian considered that gentleman, or any other, a serious rival.

As a matter of fact in that regard, Richard had to admit that up to now, his own nicely conceived plan to intrigue Lady Somers didn't appear to be bearing very much fruit. Since the night he'd visited Vauxhall Garden without so much as seeing that young lady, he'd escorted the ever-willing Miss Rutland and one or the other of her parents to a dance, two concerts, and an extremely dull card party, and yet hadn't been able to do anything but watch from a distance as Jennifer had what was clearly a very good time with another man. And all he could see that he'd accomplished to date was to complicate the situation further, since as far as he could tell, Abigail, her mother, and her father—and probably all others in the vicinity, as well—now appeared firmly convinced that he hovered on the verge of making her an offer. Why he or Molly hadn't anticipated such a turn of events, Richard was quite at a loss to understand. And he wasn't even perfectly certain whether Jennifer herself had observed the attention he'd paid Abigail and reached a similar conclusion. Nevertheless, he'd already resolved not to wait any longer before setting the record straight, and this he'd decided to begin that same evening.

Having made that decision, he found that at first the time passed somewhat more tolerably, if no more quickly. As the hours continued to tick by, however, he began to realize that something must have happened to keep Jennifer and her escort out so long on a mere afternoon's drive. But once he began to review the direction he'd seen them take, and then to list again their possible objectives, an unhappy and altogether alarming suspicion began to form as to where Gulian had surely been headed. After all, didn't he know full well that the long, secluded drive past the Buck's Horn Tavern, down quiet, shaded Love Lane to Chelsea, then south on the river road through Greenwich, and back to the city through Lispenard's Meadows was one of Gulian's favorite routes when accompanied by a potential paramour, Richard remembered. Still, it hardly seemed credible that Gulian intended to compromise Jennifer in such a reprehensible fashion. But there was no denying the fact that such considerations hadn't stopped him before, Richard admitted with a sinking heart. And what's more, Jennifer—unaware that the circuit was referred to as a seducer's dream and the Buck's Horn notorious as the setting of many of those seductions—might not think to raise a protest until it was too late. It was also much too late to consider chasing after them himself, Richard realized when he saw that it was close on five o'clock. He promptly damned himself for a sluggard and a fool, and within a few minutes could be seen dawdling about the front door of the house nervously awaiting Jennifer's return with the excuse of directing Sydney in cleaning the windows that faced the street.

Because there were only two pair of these, however, Sydney had already washed them three times before Gulian Verplanck's carriage turned the corner and headed in Richard's direction. But since Sydney, like the rest of the household, was fully acquainted with every intimate detail of his employer's life, he offered no objection to this make-work and, in fact, secretly hoped to be kept right where he was in order to pick up a few juicy morsels of information to share with the other servants.

Richard watched the approaching carriage a good deal more anxiously than he would have been likely to admit, though he was careful to school his expression to one of detached interest. Even so, he was somewhat taken aback to observe that driver and passenger not only seemed to be on the best of terms, but also appeared in a decidedly jovial mood as well. Just before they drew to a halt, Gulian leaned over and whispered something in Jennifer's ear that caused them both promptly to go off into whoops. In fact, it was nearly a full minute before she was able to wipe her streaming eyes and her escort to leap down and hand her out of the carrage before his footman could do so. And even then it looked to Richard as if the smallest thing would provoke another outburst and make him feel, understandably perhaps, even more on the outskirts than he did already. "I was beginning to be a trifle concerned at the length of your excursion," he began rather stiffly, after greeting the arrivals. "But I see now that I needn't have worried, for you appear to have had an enjoyable afternoon."

"Yes—save for one of the horses throwing a shoe so that we were obliged to stop and have it reshod before it fetched up lame," Jennifer said, relating the excuse she and Gulian had agreed on. "Even so, I think you could safely say that we found the whole experience to be a most diverting one," she advised, pulling a face in the direction of her escort.

"Or, at any rate, that one of us was clearly diverted," Gulian agreed with heavy emphasis.

Richard cast a puzzled look from one to the other, part of him wishing they'd leave off talking in riddles so he could learn more precisely what had occurred, and part of him fervently wishing not to hear every last detail. Still, he had to admit that Jennifer appeared to have emerged unscathed from the afternoon, and that had been his main concern, hadn't it? He turned away for a moment on the pretext of supervising Sydney's activities again as Jennifer said good-bye to her escort and sternly recommended that he seek to perfect his address—a suggestion that both seemed to find quite hilarious. Then Richard followed her inside, much to Sydney's disappointment, and once he'd closed the door behind them, cleared his throat as a means of capturing her attention.

"You certainly seem to be taking full advantage of your time in New York," Richard observed in what he thought was a noncommittal tone.

That remark immediately prompted a suspicious look from Jennifer, but she just as quickly decided it hadn't been meant in a disparaging way. "Yes," she agreed in a complacent voice, "I do appear to be having quite a social whirl, don't I?"

"Er, yes. Well, I was wondering in that connection whether you might be free to accompany me to a dinner party at the Rutlands' on Wednesday evening?" Richard managed to get out. "Since I'm practically your guardian, for the moment, I think we could safely dispense with the necessity of asking Miss Danhope to accompany us—don't you agree? And I'm certain Abigail would enjoy seeing you again, you know," he continued, without waiting for an answer.

Possibly, Jennifer allowed, though doubtless not in the guise of Richard Avery's companion. And could it be that he actually believed such an absurdity himself, she wondered, or only confusedly thought that that information should serve as some kind of inducement to her to agree?

"I should be delighted," she said nevertheless, adding

truthfully, "and I'm certain it shall prove an altogether interesting evening."

Chapter 11

MOLLY, BEING the only member of the household privy to the plans of the two people involved—and also knowing full well what Abigail's intentions were—suffered perhaps the greatest anxiety about whether the dinner party on Wednesday evening should prove a catastrophe to all concerned. Richard hadn't told her in advance that he meant to invite Jennifer to accompany him and that she wouldn't be asked along to make sure everyone's feathers didn't get mussed in the bargain. If he had, she'd have promptly warned him that the outcome of pitting two females against each other, consciously or not, was bound to be anything but pretty, and hardly likely to produce the results that he appeared to expect. Moreover, she felt certain that if Jennifer suspected he meant to drive matters to the wall by such a course of action, she was quite apt to throw a stick into the works, if just to see what would happen. It was in the hope of forestalling that response that Molly came prepared to take up the other side, if necessary, when she helped Jennifer to dress for the event. And since her own emotions rarely proved to be complicated or troublesome, and she promptly moved to untangle them if they did, Molly's demeanor contrasted strongly with Jennifer's, whose emotional nature was usually at the opposite end of the spectrum—particularly at this moment.

The latter young lady was unsuccessfully trying to twist her thick hair into a topknot and becoming increasingly exasperated as the result threatened once again to tumble about her ears. "Blast!" she exclaimed with feeling, blowing a curl out of one eye. "Do see if you can salvage this disaster, won't you?'' she begged. She watched as Molly calmly began to fasten her hair down with the aid of a few expertly placed pins. ''I'm sure I can't fathom why I should have been invited to this dinner,'' Jennifer mused. ''If you ask me, it seems totally out of keeping with our host's character. You recall our seeing him at Vauxhall Garden with Miss Rutland, don't you, and at practically every other social occasion during the last few weeks, too? Well then, if he's on such cozy terms with that young lady, whatever would prompt him to do something as contrary as suddenly to turn up at her house with me on his arm?'' She shook her head, either to check Molly's progress with her hair or in puzzlement over such inexplicable behavior. ''After all, for a man as everlastingly concerned with doing the 'right thing' as Richard Avery, that move seems entirely out of keeping—don't you think?''

Molly stepped back to survey her creation. ''Perhaps the man ain't such a stick-in-the-mud as you imagine?'' she suggested. ''And anyway, I can't understand why you're raising such a fuss over a simple meal. It's perfectly reasonable that he should escort you places while you're in his charge. Besides, it ain't as if by asking you to dinner he's asking you to marry him, after all,'' she said in a sarcastic voice.

Jennifer rose and reached for a lace scarf to drape over her shoulders before replying. ''But don't you see how Miss Rutland, at any rate, might think it tantamount to the same thing?'' she said slowly. ''I mean, I should guess by this point she'd have assumed that with all the attention he'd paid her, that she and Mr. Avery are certainly promised to one another, whether or not he's formally asked her to become his wife. So what's she to believe when I appear on the scene—that he means to make her jealous? For what purpose, if she's already been wooed and won? Or that he wishes now to break it off? For what reason, since he's obviously been devoting a good deal of time to making the match in the first place? Indeed, it's all a complete muddle to me,'' she said, shaking her head again. ''But one thing's clear, at least. This isn't at all the sort of safe, conservative move I'd have hitherto ascribed to our host.''

Molly indicated that Jennifer was to turn around slowly while she allotted a final inspection to her costume of yellow gauze with tiny raised spots of velvet. She reached out to give the skirt a gentle tug before offering a disparaging sniff that Jennifer found far from encouraging. "Well, I have heard it said that even a leopard can change its spots, if it wants to," she volunteered rather irrelevantly in her friend's view. "So perhaps you'll learn tonight if there's a speck of truth in that old saw, or whether it's only pap meant to satisfy a baby."

Jennifer was so caught up in trying to decide whether Molly's final remarks had been meant to refer to her or to her escort that at first she didn't even pay very much attention to that gentleman. This was perhaps just as well because Richard had belatedly realized first that he'd neglected to ask Mr. or Mrs. Rutland or their daughter whether he might bring someone with him, and second that, given what he'd come to believe were their expectations regarding his future and Abigail's, no one was bound to be especially pleased with his choice of companion. Miss Rutland, in particular, was likely to be mystified by such behavior, if not miffed at being treated in so casual a fashion, he acknowledged somewhat guiltily. Clearly, in attempting to demonstrate to Jennifer that there wasn't any attachment between him and Abigail, he'd once again failed to take the other young lady's feelings into account. In fact, it now looked on the surface, at least, as if he were turning from an unthinking man of business into an insensitive man-about-town. Whatever was he thinking of, flying in the face of convention and of polite society by doing something as unconventional as showing up at a dinner party with an unannounced guest? he wondered. And even though he was virtually her guardian for the time being, that didn't mean he could necessarily expect Jennifer to be welcomed on every occasion to which he chose to escort her, did it? If anything, he suspected that their reception was bound to be a trifle chilly this evening, and though he knew he probably ought to warn Jennifer of that possibility, he was decidedly afraid to bring it up.

They were bundled inside his carriage for the short drive to the Rutlands' house, for the weather had taken a distinct enough turn toward winter in the last couple of days to preclude walking. Jennifer was sitting quietly in one corner, apparently lost in thoughts that Richard would have given more than the proverbial penny to learn. "I was just thinking that it's been several weeks since we've spent any time together," she observed at last, as if reading his mind. "And I must admit that I've missed the talks we used to have about the twins' progress and similar mutual concerns. But then, you've been busy with your work and with, er, other things—"

"Yes, I have been somewhat distracted lately," Richard admitted honestly. *Well, go ahead, coward—now's your chance to tell her what it is that's caused you to be off woolgathering,* he said to himself. "And I'm afraid tonight shall offer little improvement," he said unaccountably instead, passing over that opening as if it didn't exist. "The conversation very likely will focus on business, politics, and war—or a combination of the three. I do hope you won't be overly bored."

"Why, you must have me confused with someone else, sir," Jennifer advised him in a rather brittle tone. And so much for trying to storm the man's defenses, she thought, irritated at herself for even attempting that feat. "Unless, as usual, I'm relegated to the back room for being a woman, I'd never willingly choose to keep quiet when the discussion comes around to such vital topics as those you've just mentioned. After all, if I'm to be denied the opportunity to exert any real power to change political or economic conditions, on account of my sex, at least I should be glad for an occasion on which to speak my mind frankly about what I fancy they ought to be."

Now, should he take that remark as a general statement or as a warning of what the evening might hold in store for him? Richard wondered. He was given little chance to decide, however, because by then they'd drawn up before the Rutlands' elegant house. Instead, as he helped his companion down from the carriage, he rapidly began to review in his mind what excuse he could offer for arriving at a dinner party with an unexpected—and, in this case, equally inappropriate—guest on his arm.

Fortunately for Richard, the maxims of good breeding ran strong enough in Miss Rutland's veins to overrule any possible rudeness. After one brief, surprised look at the new arrivals as they were led into the drawing room, she quickly recovered and came forward to greet them. "How happy I am that you could join us this evening," she said easily, holding out her hand to Jennifer. "Indeed, I shall count on you to keep us from being too bored by these stodgy old men and their dull talk about the state of the world," she confided. She smiled in what was plainly an artless fashion, but her words echoed Richard's so closely that the effect was the same as if they'd somehow conspired to achieve it.

In point of fact, however, save for being momentarily taken aback at Richard's turning up with Jennifer in tow, Abigail wasn't entirely displeased by that development. For one thing, she realized, continuing to smile at her guests, it might provide an opportunity for her to gauge more accurately the depth of the attachment between Jennifer and Mr. Hartley. And for another thing, she decided as she watched her father approach, Jennifer's presence might indicate to the world at large—and her parents in particular—in a rather timely fashion that Abigail was perfectly justified in looking to another man than Richard for companionship. Because both of these conclusions fitted quite nicely into the scheme she'd already concocted to win Mr. Hartley to her side, Abigail neither felt obliged to comment directly on Richard's behavior or to indicate in any way that he ought to render an account of himself to his host.

Edward Rutland, on the other hand, not being aware of his daughter's plotting and rapidly concluding that Richard wasn't acting in a way befitting a future son-in-law, felt it his duty to confront the fact of Jennifer's presence and its implications more directly. "Cooked up a bit of a surprise this evening, did you?" he said to Richard in a dry voice, raising his eyebrows speakingly. "Of course, I confess I'm as susceptible as the next man to a pretty face, so I'm sure I've no objection to Lady Somers being made a member of our party. Now, I know you ain't accustomed to keeping track of all these social comings and goings, but do give us a little advance notice next time, old boy—if merely to ensure there'll be enough room at the table, you know. As it is, I think we can just manage to squeeze you in next to me, my dear," he confided to Jennifer in a friendlier tone. "That is, if you think you could be satisfied with me as your partner instead of this handsome gadling?" he asked. Then, not waiting for a reply, he tucked Jennifer's hand under his arm and turned in the direction of the dining room.

This last description certainly didn't fit the Richard Avery she knew, Jennifer thought to herself. But then again, perhaps it did, because from Edward Rutland's perspective it must have appeared that in bringing her along this evening, Richard was trifling with his daughter's affections in a casual sort of way he didn't intend to brook. At any rate, Rutland clearly meant to keep a close eye on Jennifer and to monopolize her time insofar as possible, because he not only had her placed beside him at the table, as promised, but also kept her engaged in conversation throughout the entire meal. And in all probability, he meant that stratagem to provide a chance to heal whatever rift her presence might have opened between Abigail and Richard, Jennifer decided based on the frequent, covert looks he directed at the opposite end of the table where those two were seated.

Having thus deduced her host's intentions, Jennifer promptly endeavored to set his mind at ease regarding her own feelings toward Mr. Avery by acting so gay and charming and so generally unconcerned that by the time the last covers were removed, she had him thoroughly convinced of her innocence and pleasantly bewitched as well. Perhaps the meal had had something to do with the transformation, too, for the food had been lavish and rich, the wine plentiful, and everyone had partaken of what was offered until they were altogether satiated. Talk had consequently deteriorated into a somewhat erratic affair by this point, as most of the company struggled to accomplish the simple task of digestion.

That chore didn't seem to have slowed Edward Rutland down noticeably, though his remarks were a trifle more disjointed than they'd been earlier in the evening. "Doesn't make a damned lot of difference to me what a man's politics may be, just as long as I'm convinced that he has some," he now proclaimed grandly to the assembled company in a loud voice. "But it infuriates me when some blasted fellow just niminy-piminys around so you can't tell which way he's inclined. Don't you agree, my dear?" he asked Jennifer.

"Oh, indeed," she murmured obediently, wondering if he had someone particular in mind.

Mr. Rutland apparently wasn't troubled by the need for any logical thinking at the moment, however. Instead, he poured another glass of wine and generously wet his throat before observing ponderously, and rather obscurely, "You can't fight tradition, after all, and no doubt it will have the final say once all this fuss about war and loyalty and honor dies down." There was a short silence as his guests attempted to meditate on that odd pronouncement.

"You know, I must confess that I don't understand one piece of the picture," Jennifer ventured to say at last into the void. "I mean, despite the fact that I'm a British citizen and might be thought ready to defend my country's position, I can't help feeling that the case for declaring war against France is just as strong as that against England."

Richard shook his head. "Not entirely," he offered before anyone else could speak. "The argument, I believe, goes something like this: First, if the United States entered into war with France, it would have to do so as a satellite of England—because the two are already thus engaged—and that is a position particularly to be avoided. Second, the French aren't busy attacking ships destined for other than English ports, nor are they impressing foreign seamen, or apparently engaging in any subversive activities such as spying or trying to foment a civil war." He paused to accompany that statement with a significant look before concluding, "And third, the effects of French confiscation of American ships has been limited primarily to the commercial classes, although the effects of so-called English 'aggression' have been felt by the majority of people in this country—thus making the former a less universally popular enemy than the latter."

Edward Rutland stared suspiciously across the table.

"You explained that little point remarkably well," he noted. "Why, one would almost be inclined to think you agreed with it."

"Not entirely," Richard said again in a polite voice. "It's only that I believe one must fully understand a position or idea before one can discount it or even argue against it." He hazarded another glance in Jennifer's general direction.

She returned that look with a warm smile. In fact, she suddenly felt so charitably disposed toward the speaker for the admirable way he'd handled the preceding conversation that it was all she could do to keep from applauding him publicly then and there. How nicely he'd managed to explain a viewpoint she knew to be quite unlike his own and equally unlikely to find favor in this household. Could it be that he was ready to acknowledge the limitations of forever adjusting his words and actions to fit the image others had of him or to ensure retaining their good opinion? she wondered.

"I have heard that Napoleon's very much the military expert," Miss Rutland ventured, breaking into Jennifer's thoughts and thereby, she no doubt hoped, into the conversation as well.

"Indeed he is," Jennifer acknowledged. "My friend, Mr. Hartley, tells me that Napoleon studies strategy constantly and has even admitted reading a paper entitled, 'Rationale of Tactic for Mounted Rifleman,' written by Robert Johnson, a new member of Congress."

Mr. Hartley says this, Mr. Hartley tells me that, Richard fumed to himself, wishing that just for once he could think of Jennifer without automatically thinking of some other man as well. What's more, he was annoyed that her references to this particular gentleman had such power to irritate him and that he was apparently capable of feeling so unreasonably jealous at the mere mention of the fellow. Why, one would think her precious Mr. Hartley had private access to Napoleon's bedchamber, the way he seemed able to report every last thing the emperor thought or said. "Well, if—according to Mr. Hartley—Napoleon thinks us such a country of dunderheads, why is it—in Mr. Hartley's view, of course—that the emperor doesn't declare war on the United States?'' he asked Jennifer in a voice now heavily laced with sarcasm.

She hesitated, considerably thrown by the sudden, dramatic reversal of Richard's attitude toward her and unable at once to put her finger on the reason for it. ''Mr. Hartley wasn't sure,'' she began steadily nevertheless, ''but he did indicate that apparently nothing can shake Napoleon's belief that any nation that engages the United States in war will suffer grave damages in consequence. So even though, as a military expert, he knows the American tradition—in Mr. Hartley's words—to be one of gallant individual effort set against a backdrop of stupidity, disorganization, and selfishness, he still can't be persuaded by his generals to become the aggressor by declaring war.''

A rather long silence followed this exchange, though no one in the group was clearly ready to attribute that fact to the astonishing information that had just been so bluntly presented. ''Dear me, Lady Somers—any more and you'll have us frightened out of our wits,'' Miss Rutland warned her finally with an uneasy little giggle. ''Why, I wonder if I shall be able to close my eyes tonight or even to get a minute's worth of sleep. Here I've always believed that Napoleon was a bloodthirsty creature who'd snatch at the chance to murder us all in our beds without a second thought. Only now you try to convince us that he's a perfectly normal, rational man, and the real threat comes from our own foolish lack of preparedness. Well truly, it's enough to make anyone wonder why you're still here, if you hold such a lowly opinion of our country.'' Then, aware that she'd spoken far more sharply than she'd intended—probably more on account of being piqued at Jennifer's frequent allusions to Mr. Hartley and the threat they might represent to her plan than anything else—she promptly lightened this last statement by offering her guest the impersonal smile of a well-trained hostess.

''But I wasn't—and it isn't only my—'' Jennifer began, before deciding to give up the effort to correct the impression she'd made. ''I beg your pardon,'' she said quietly instead. ''I appear to have spoken out of turn.''

''Quite all right, my dear,'' Mr. Rutland told her. He

patted her hand in a consoling—or condescending—fashion, depending on one's point of view. "Well, bound to happen whenever you let a lady get hold of an idea. That's why we men are accustomed to discussing such things among ourselves, you see." He suited his actions to those words by rising and motioning for the rest of the gentlemen to accompany him to another room. "And anyway, I think you'd find we'd all much prefer you to concentrate on looking pretty rather than on learning to argue politics," he tossed over his shoulder in parting.

At that remark, Richard, who'd just begun to get up from his chair, couldn't help noticing that Jennifer's face assumed the expression of a young girl who's been severely reprimanded and then sternly advised to mend her ways. Seeing the uncomfortable predicament she'd landed in made him rapidly thrust aside his less than generous feelings about her and Mr. Hartley in favor of considering rushing to her defense instead. But since he couldn't immediately think how to indicate that he was sympathetic without also drawing further attention to her plight, he ended up following his host out of the room without offering any comment whatsover.

The departure of the gentlemen signaled the ladies that it was time for them to withdraw for a little chat of their own. But it was with a distinct sense of rebellion that Jennifer forced herself to accompany the others into the drawing room, sit down in a chair, and accept the offer of a cup of strong China tea. Then she took a reviving sip of that hot liquid and tried to gird herself for the examination she felt sure would follow. She had to own being rather surprised at the quickness with which Abigail had proven ready to enter the fray, Jennifer thought, watching that lady attend to her guest's needs. Actually, she'd wondered earlier if her hostess might not seize the chance somehow to cast her in an unflattering light in front of Richard during the course of the evening. But that that lady should have ventured so close to the boundaries of accepted behavior to do so was considerably more unexpected, Jennifer decided. Indeed, Abigail must feel very deeply about Richard Avery if she was willing to risk censure by being rude to his special guest in order to establish herself firmly as mistress of the situation and of their relationship as well, Jennifer concluded with a heavy heart.

Nothing, of course, could have been farther from the truth. Rather, Abigail's treatment of Jennifer stemmed from her curiosity about the person that lady had called "my friend Mr. Hartley," and then referred to often enough to make her wonder if the two weren't a good deal more than mere friends. And this suspicion had been strengthened when Richard Avery had also turned on the lady in what Abigail had easily identified as the sulky way a man responded to the news that his rival was making steady headway. Therefore, she now undertook to explore Jennifer's intentions regarding both gentlemen.

"You must forgive my sorry manners," Abigail began, turning toward Jennifer and smiling at her in a friendly fashion. "I shouldn't wonder that you think us a nation of incompetents when you've just witnessed an example of very poor behavior." She lowered her eyes for a moment in what might have been genuine embarrassment at having laid herself open to the charge of being neglectful of her social obligations. "But truly," she continued in a candid voice, looking up again, "it's no surprise that I'd bumble my way through a discussion of substance when talk of men and women and their simple doings is far more my normal sphere of interest, you know."

At this point, however, the subtlety with which Abigail had been preparing to make her inquiries was sacrificed as Sylvia Trask abruptly joined the conversation. That lady had been lounging on the sofa in a rather indolent fashion and steadily consuming what would have been for anyone else present an undecorous amount of cognac. "Good Heavens, love—such things may be your hobby, but they appear to be virtually Lady Somers's métier," she advised Abigail with a loud laugh. "Clearly Mr. Hartley is but one of her *many* admirers, and after tonight, I'd think it safe to say she's captured our elusive Mr. Avery as well—something we all know *you've* been trying to do for years." She smiled rather maliciously at her hostess and then settled back again in her corner and refilled her glass. "Indeed, you must tell me how you managed to accomplish those conquests without being obliged to compromise your virtue, because—as I'm sure all the 'ladies' here will readily attest—that's one little trick I never bothered to master myself.'' She raised her glass in a toast to Jennifer and then tossed off its contents with apparent unconcern.

Jennifer and Abigail had both flushed a brilliant red during the preceding speech, though for altogether different reasons: The former, because the danger to her reputation mentioned was precisely the one she'd barely avoided with Mr. Verplanck—an event she'd thought was destined to remain a secret; and the latter because the history of her relationship with Mr. Avery had just been so casually and brutally exposed to public view. Still, Abigail realized as she struggled to regain her composure, at least such bluntness would serve to take the edge off her own approach, wouldn't it?

She rose to refill Jennifer's cup. ''Pray, don't pay her any mind,'' she advised in an undertone, pouring the tea and then nodding in the direction of the sofa where Sylvia Trask was ensconced. ''Her own marriage isn't terribly successful, you see, and I'm afraid she isn't above going out of her way to stir up jealousies and to cause trouble for other people in theirs.'' She pulled a chair close to Jennifer's with the apparent intention of continuing to talk privately.

''Ah, but we aren't speaking of my marriage,'' Jennifer pointed out quickly in a firm voice.

''No, indeed—nor mine,'' Abigail agreed. She attempted to include Jennifer in a conspiratorial smile. ''Though you don't mean to tell me that some gentleman hasn't hinted he's considering making you an offer? After all, you and Mr. Hartley sound as if you've a lot in common.''

That observation caused Jennifer to pause for a moment in surprise before offering a comment. To be honest, she'd expected her hostess to prove interested in discovering where things stood with her and Mr. Avery—not with Mr. Hartley. But perhaps, she decided, this was only Abigail's way of determining that Jennifer was safely accounted for and thus represented no threat to her aspirations to become Mrs. Avery. ''Well, it's true that Mr. Hartley has indicated a desire to discuss the subject,'' she admitted, ''but I was forced to beg off. I haven't developed a lasting affection for him, I'm afraid.'' Now that was curious, she thought. Surely Abigail looked relieved at the news that she wasn't in love with Mr. Hartley, when Jennifer would have thought she'd react in quite the opposite way. And to make matters even more confusing, shortly thereafter Abigail appeared willing to leave off with their tête-â-tête and to widen the circle to include some of the other ladies. Talk shifted to such general concerns as the best remedy for influenza and the latest rage for sleeves decorated with no less than three rouleaux, and didn't return again to the foibles of one particular gentleman or another.

Nevertheless, Jennifer found her thoughts drifting repeatedly back to Richard Avery while she listened idly to the conversation flowing around her. She couldn't understand why Abigail had barely referred to him, unless it was that she was perhaps too well-bred to inquire directly if that gentleman had made her an offer, much as she might long to do so. And it was that very singular omission that caused Jennifer to wonder briefly if she hadn't somehow gotten the entire situation twisted around. Maybe Abigail didn't really wish to marry Richard, despite the rapid way she'd supported him earlier and clearly demonstrated that her sentiments were aligned with his. If only Richard had stood by her in a similarly stalwart fashion, Jennifer thought wistfully. True, at one point, he'd seemed on the verge of rising up to defend her. But then the gentlemen had withdrawn and he'd gone with them, leaving her to sort out her feelings alone. Still, the whole calamitous situation had surely been of her own manufacture, and she was now perfectly ready to take responsibility for it. Far more ready, in fact, than to have to deal with how Richard, as her escort, might feel about how she'd acted, in addition to what he, as her friend, might think about what she'd said. Jennifer sighed. And just how, she wondered, was she ever to go about restoring the comfortable relationship she'd once thought existed between them if she couldn't first reopen the lines of communication that somehow seemed to have been broken along the way?

It wasn't until she and Richard were seated in his carriage on the return trip to No. 30 Wall Street that she attempted to bring up the subject. "I believe I must apologize for my behavior this evening," she began a trifle defensively. "Apparently, I committed the unpardonable sin of having an opinion on something as unfeminine as politics and then actually daring to express it. But even so, I assure you I should never have said a word if I'd guessed that what I had to say would raise such a tempest."

"Oh, but I'm afraid that you seem inevitably to fill the role of gadfly," Richard pointed out lightly, "as someone who has tonight been called a gadling ought very well to know. And anyway, I can practically guarantee that in a few days no one present this evening will remember that little incident or even what you said at all, but only how you looked and what you wore—those being the paramount concerns of most people in any social situation, especially when confronted by a beautiful woman such as you." He hesitated for a moment before observing in a strictly casual voice, "Though from what you say, Mr. Hartley appears able to concentrate on more serious matters, even given the apparent distraction of your presence."

"Yes, that's true. It seems to me that after being surprised that a beautiful woman could have anything intelligent to say, most men promptly discount her words entirely," Jennifer said in a thoughtful tone. "But I think Mr. Hartley appreciates me primarily in an aesthetic fashion. Therefore, he merely listens without bothering to judge whether or not my opinions are, in fact, sensible or worthy of debate. Well, it makes me feel ridiculously liberated not to be forced to weigh each word three times before uttering it," she admitted, tucking a loose pin back into her topknot. "But like other men, Mr. Hartley still only sees a part of me, you know. It's as if everyone is bent on making me feel responsible for being attractive, and that seems to be about as reasonable as making you feel guilty for—for being tall!"

"Well, I must confess I never thought of it exactly that way before," Richard admitted, belatedly conscious of having adopted the very attitude she'd just described. He studied his companion speculatively for a moment. "But what about trying to play down your looks so that they weren't the focus of attention?''

Jennifer laughed. ''Oh, I've tried that tactic, and I promise you the response is even more absurd! Why, some people feel you're mocking the pains they take with their appearance when you've clearly chosen to ignore your own, and others think you utterly vain for being so confident in how you look that you can afford not to enhance it. I could go on, but I imagine you take my point?'' She smiled at her companion in a friendly way, feeling relieved that they were once again having a discussion in the congenial fashion that always made her hope it would go on forever.

''Yes,'' Richard agreed, and then paused as the same idea occurred to him. ''I must confess, however, that what I just realized is that this is the first time the two of us have talked about anything in a very long while, as you pointed out earlier this evening. And what's more, I have to admit that I've missed our talks a good deal, because unlike you, perhaps, I've no one else with whom I can discuss ideas.''

''Now that is too bad,'' Jennifer said honestly. ''But I'd have thought Miss Rutland would have been happy to provide you a ready audience.''

''And there you've put your finger on the heart of the matter,'' Richard admitted. ''You see, I sometimes think it's as if Abigail doesn't have any opinions of her own, or if she ever does recognize one, she immediately dismisses it as unimportant and certainly not worth mentioning. And then, too, she's eminently persuadable. Why, I can spend a half hour convincing her of one position, and then turn around and argue the opposite point of view, and she'll agree with that as well! So it isn't exactly as if we can have a real discussion when only one of us appears to have anything to say.''

''Indeed, though there are compensations, I'm sure. For example, Miss Rutland would doubtless never have landed herself in the basket as I did this evening on account of my incautious tongue.'' Jennifer followed this confession by attempting to look properly abashed.

''True,'' Richard said bluntly. ''But then, are you perfectly sure you'd really wish to trade that tendency for the dull, safe methods of someone like Abigail?'' He offered Jennifer a devastating smile that made her heart race madly in response.

Only if it could assure me of receiving other similar samples of your undivided attention, she promised herself fervently. But apparently there wasn't to be an opportunity to prolong such rediscovered intimacy tonight, for just then they arrived home and were forced to bring the evening to a close.

A similar thought had apparently struck her companion, because as they walked up the front steps he hesitated and appeared once again on the verge of speaking. Whatever he'd been about to say was lost, however, as the door swung open and Walters promptly stuck his head outside.

''Oh, I'm so glad you've returned, sir,'' he said at once in greeting. ''A man arrived here nearly two hours ago to see Lady Somers, and I put him to wait in your study. He refused to leave a message, but insisted on seeing her himself. He didn't seem the sort who might actually steal something, but I've been keeping a sharp eye on him all the same.'' He looked anxiously at his employer.

''And quite right, I'm sure,'' Richard said soothingly. He turned toward Jennifer and cocked an eyebrow. ''Not expecting a mysterious, late night caller, are you? No? Well then, I expect we'd best go see what the fellow wants.''

The visitor was a man of indeterminate age dressed in roughly woven homespun. He had the look of someone unaccustomed to being much indoors, for he was seated gingerly on a chair, peering in a hungry fashion out the window. When Richard and Jennifer entered the room, he rose and crossed toward them with catlike grace. Then he paused to look Jennifer carefully up and down, and particularly to stare at her hair for a few moments. This examination appeared to satisfy him, for he said at last in a relieved voice, ''Aye—you're the one, all right. I've a letter I promised to give only into your hands, miss.'' He reached in a pocket, drew out a soiled piece of paper, and held it out.

Jennifer took the sheet and unfolded it, wrinkling her

brow as she quickly scanned the contents. "Why, it's from my father!" she exclaimed in surprise.

Chapter 12

JENNIFER CONSIDERED the man standing before her with new interest. "How did you come by this, sir?" she asked him politely. Her hand tightened around the piece of paper, although she kept her voice low and steady.

"Mere throw of the dice, miss," he said with a casual shrug. "Quite a toss and tumble around Niagara lately, you see, and I'd a fancy to stick around and see if something mightn't shake itself into my lap."

Jennifer looked mystified by this statement, but Richard paused to examine the man's clothing, the way he stood, and how he seemed attuned to every sound emanating from either the house or the street. "You're a scout, aren't you?" he asked after a moment. "Working for whomever can pay?"

"Well, I ain't used to hanging a name on it myself," the man answered cautiously. "Let's just say I know the country thereabouts as well as a dog does its fleas. Once in a while, someone or other may get a hankering to explore the area and find a way to convince me to show 'em around, is all. Your father and I took a little trek together, miss. Only, him being a right curious sort of a fellow, he took a trifle too much interest in the goings-on, and then the redcoats and a few other folk began to take an even bigger interest in him."

"But he's a British subject, with a fortune and a title and—and everything," Jennifer protested.

"Maybe, but who'd ever guess—leastways, not when he dresses like any ordinary fellow and even talks like one, too. Oh, he managed to bring 'em around, all right—why, I swear that man could talk the shell off a coconut! Still, no one's too happy about the whole thing. He ain't in leg irons or anything like that, but until they decide to give the word, he's got to stay put. Anyhow, he thought you might have begun to fret about him by now, so he paid—er, persuaded— me to bring you the news and his note to confirm it. Can't read myself, but he promised there wasn't anything in it that would raise an eyebrow.''

Jennifer read the note through again. "No, there certainly is not," she confirmed with a little smile. She cocked her head to one side and looked hopefully at the messenger. "You're returning to Niagara right away, I take it?" At his quick nod, she inquired, "And you're prepared to wait until I write a reply to my father—are you not?—because I'm sure he's an anxious to be kept informed of my well-being as I am of his."

The messenger nodded a second time, though less enthu- siastically than before. "Aye—he said you'd be bound to want to send him a bit of a scribble." He bounced up and down on his toes for a moment before asking, "But, if you could be quick about it, miss—? I don't aim to spend the rest of the night anywhere but on the other side of the river, you see."

"Of course," Jennifer agreed promptly. With Richard's help, she located paper, pen, and ink, and then sat down at his desk to compose a note to her father. While her fingers flew across the page, she couldn't resist throwing a last question over her shoulder. "But could you tell me—how does my father seem?"

"Oh, very well, I promise. If you ask me, save for thinking you might be worrying about 'im, he appears to be enjoying himself no end. One day he'll be playing cards with a couple of soldiers, and the next day hobnobbing with the officers as if he's merely paying a call. And all the while he's nosing about looking at everything and asking question after question like, 'how does this work?' or 'what's this for?' until you're apt to give him the first answer that comes to mind so as to shut him up for a while!" This appeared to convince the messenger that he'd discharged his obligations, for he shifted closer to the door and, holding out his hand for the note, asked, "If there's nothing else—? Don't fancy cities overmuch, you know. Can't understand how a body could truly like being jammed next to someone else all the time," he confessed, shaking his head in disbelief.

Jennifer folded and sealed the letter and gave it to the messenger. Then she murmured a thank you and watched Richard escort the visitor to the door of the study. The two exchanged a few quiet words, and then Richard transferred something from his pocket into the other man's hand before the latter slipped silently from the room.

"Would you like to see my father's letter?" Jennifer asked, holding out the sheet to Richard as he crossed the room toward her.

He took the paper and began to read it, his expression becoming increasingly bewildered the farther he got: "Niagara has captured my attention by force! Nothing British has ever convinced me before of how the identity of beauty allowed the soul freedom to soar, yet kept one unable truly to leave worldly cares immediately behind, despite all best intentions, well carried out. Love, J.S." He hesitiated for a moment, clearly at a loss to know what to say about such a strange communication. "Well, I must admit that it appears unmistakably to be from Lord Somers," he began, before adding in a doubtful voice, "though I confess I'm not at all certain what to make of it. Apparently, he seems very much taken by the local scene, or should I say, by the grandeurs of nature—?"

"Oh, doubtlessly," Jennifer laughed. She leaned closer and offered him a conspiratorial smile. "May I tell you a secret?" she whispered. "There's really an altogether different message hidden in this letter. You see, when I was very young, before I began to accompany my father on his travels, we became accustomed to hiding our real news for one another in some harmless chatter in order to throw whoever might be interested off the scent. Of course, I'm not certain there ever really was anyone who cared to monitor our correspondence, mind you; the whole thing might have been merely a ploy concocted by my father to keep me amused. Still, that little trick has proven handy on some occasions, as you can imagine, and we continue to resort to it whenever we feel it necessary. The real message reads as follows: "Captured by British. Convinced of identity. Allowed freedom, yet unable leave immediately. All well, Love." She regarded Richard with sparkling eyes. "Can you figure out how it works?"

He scanned the letter a second time. "Oh, I see. It's sort of cipher, isn't it? Quite simple, really. You just read every third word and ignore the rest."

"That's right. And you can understand now why I wasn't more alarmed when our visitor couldn't provide too much information, because I already knew my father wasn't in any real danger at the moment, and in my reply, I indicated that I knew he was safe. From what he says, I take it that he'll merely have to bide his time until the British finally lose interest in him before he'll be able to make his way back to New York."

"Yes, I should think so," Richard agreed. "And truly, I don't think you need worry. Our visitor also told me that things are still quiet in the area, at least for the moment, and there's no question yet of the British being any more willing to exchange shots than the Americans, or of Lord Somers being awkwardly trapped in the middle." An amused smile began to creep over his face. "But can you imagine what a stunning blow your father must have dealt those poor fellows when he revealed that he was actually a titled gentleman conversant with the very cream of polite society? Why, I warrant they must have thought that he was—or, perhaps, that they were—quite unhinged, the way he was wandering about, apparently content to prose on endlessly about the meaning of Beauty."

"Ah, but don't forget that Papa's used to people believing that he's off his head, so it doesn't faze him in the least," Jennifer told him with an answering smile. "Besides, look how well it served him in this instance, since the soldiers surely saw the letter he wrote me but never thought to care two straws about it. And it isn't as if he's actually a spy, after all."

Richard shot a sudden, piercing look at his companion. "You're referring to Mr. Henry, aren't you? I can't pretend I haven't thought of him a time or two myself these past few weeks, but I still say I was right not to try and stop him, though I confess I'm no longer as certain that we shouldn't interfere eventually in some fashion. I just haven't yet figured out the safest way to thwart his plans, and keep the two of us from becoming embroiled in the bargain.''

"Excellent!" Jennifer exclaimed happily, much to the speaker's surprise. "Why, I find it entirely encouraging that you're a little confused! After all, how many people do you imagine honestly go about knowing exactly what they should say or do at every moment? Precious few, I assure you. I'm usually in a perfect stew myself half the time, so you can see that I'd find it a hopeful sign that you're finally ready to admit you are, too, and to understand that such a state is human and natural and not necessarily to be feared.''

"Oh, I understand it well enough," he admitted slowly. *And probably a good deal better than I shall ever understand you, my lady,* he thought to himself, scarcely daring to breathe and perhaps break the tenuous bond that had been forged between them. She was so close he could reach out and touch her. Why, his hand had already begun to move seemingly of its own accord, drawn to the soft knot of curls on top of her head. But even though he dearly longed to pluck out a pin and cause the whole mass to tumble about her shoulders in delightful disarray, he forced himself to push the pin firmly into place instead. "Still, I think it quite ungenerous of you to wish me to stumble about in the dark simply because you happen to be there also," he said lightly. There now, could that actually have been a disappointed look that flashed across her face for a moment and then was gone? he wondered.

"Yes, you're probably right," Jennifer said carelessly after a moment, in a tone that matched his. She turned to leave, but paused before she opened the door to offer a final remark. "And don't forget that I'm rather used to being accounted willful and selfish for always stating my opinions without hesitation and for having little patience with anyone who prevaricates.''

"Good God, what a coil the household should be in if we all began to do likewise!" Richard exclaimed in mock horror. That observation won him a grudging smile from his guest, which he found sufficiently encouraging to continue. "Not that Miss Danhope, for one, ever appears to need inspiration to speak her mind, though I must say that such a tendency probably isn't any great handicap to her so long as she is in *your* company. Do you know that she's already given me a trimming for allowing the Manhattan Company to serve its customers poorly by providing them with such an inferior product? Still, setting aside those considerations for the moment, I do think the twins have changed enormously since your arrival—in a positive way, I mean." He caught sight of the expression on Jennifer's face and admonished her. "Now, don't look so surprised—or did you think I hadn't noticed? Indeed, I believe you've worked a minor miracle by turning George and Caroline into two lively, inquisitive, thoughtful children, especially considering what you had to begin with. But come now—haven't you anything at all to say? Just because I may be guilty of being a bit of a lout myself at times doesn't mean I'd wish the same fate on anyone else, much less my own children."

Jennifer appeared taken aback at that notion and fiddled with the doorknob for a moment before replying. "I never truly imagined that you were such a heartless person," she admitted, raising her eyes slowly to meet Richard's. "It's only that for a while I think I must have been caught between recognizing that you didn't know how to act any differently and believing that you didn't wish to change. Then too, I probably concluded that since you were such a perfectionist you'd naturally devote all your time to correcting your behavior once you'd decided that that was what you wanted to do." She permitted herself a tiny smile. "So you can see that I'm as culpable as you, sir, because I insisted on expecting you to be perfect when you were already struggling—though perhaps not consciously—to be only human, and thus fallible."

Richard uttered a small groan. "Stop, stop," he pleaded in a feeble voice. "I can't continue babbling on about this any longer or I shall surely expire from relentless boredom or extreme self-consciousness, I'm not certain which. What do you say about giving our poor brains and everyone else's a rest and declaring tomorrow a holiday? It's been cold enough for a while so that the ponds have doubtless frozen good and solid. How about all of us bundling up and taking skates and a couple of sleds and heading out to Lispenard's Meadows for a day of physical, rather than mental, exertion? After all, isn't Miss Danhope always saying that we're both guilty of overthinking every last thing?''

Jennifer was caught so off guard by Richard's suggestion that she didn't pay very close attention to the rest of his remarks. "Oh, can you skate?" she managed to ask.

He looked aggrieved. "Surely you must realize that as a perfectionist, I'd scarcely be likely to suggest engaging in any activity at which I'm less than outstanding,'' he observed blandly. "Why, I warrant I'm already looking forward to demonstrating my prowess to you!''

Accordingly, the following forenoon, Jennifer, Richard, Molly, and the twins swathed themselves in numerous layers of clothing and piled into a huge sleigh already crowded with sleds, skates, and other necessary paraphernalia. Richard had at first been reluctant to use the sleigh, since the preceding evening his town carriage had still been quite satisfactory. But it had snowed lightly during the night, and the early morning sun had melted the powder into a treacherous sheet of ice that he'd finally been convinced would be best handled by adopting a wintertime mode of travel. Indeed, as they moved slowly up Broadway, they encountered several other souls who'd wished to venture out and been caught in a similar dilemma. They, however, hadn't made the same decision as Richard, and one carriage had ended up overturning while rounding a corner; another two had fetched up crosswise after sliding along the street. But the owners of these vehicles seemed to be taking their mishaps in stride, merely waving good-naturedly to the twins and loudly commending Richard for his forethought.

The trip was a reversal of the last portion of the drive Jennifer had taken with Gulian Verplanck. But long before they'd reached the bridge and causeway where the road crossed over the meadows and then continued on north to Greenwich, George and Caroline were demanding some sort of entertainment. How Richard came to be the one who suggested they start off with Christmas carols, Jennifer wasn't certain, but soon his pleasant baritone was leading them in one song after another.

When they finally reached the meadows themselves, the twins barely waited for the sleigh to draw to a halt before throwing themselves down and clamoring loudly for their sleds. Molly led them away to a nearby small hill and promised to keep the children nicely in check, as she put it. This left Jennifer and Richard free to wander about, enjoying the sight of so many city folks doing likewise, and to exchange commonplaces on the scene. The pond formed by the outlet of the stream from The Collect draining into a low-lying portion of the meadow was indeed frozen over, as Richard had predicted, and it was here that the majority of the pleasure seekers had congregated. Women in furs mingled with young boys dashing about on wooden skates. Along one side of the pond, vendors had gathered to sell hot cider, roasted corn, and warm, spiced gingerbread. Behind them was the hill that had been stamped smooth by eager feet where people of assorted ages were sliding down on all manner of conveyances—George and Caroline among them.

Jennifer and Richard watched the twins for a while, warming their hands around mugs of steaming cider. "This must be something like the Frost Fair on the Thames that my father enjoyed when he was a boy," Jennifer observed. "He said once in a great long while there'd be a big enough storm so the river would freeze and then London would virtually declare a holiday. Both banks would be lined with booths selling everything from books to ginger beer, and there would be tables where people could try their hand at such odd games as Prick-the-Garter or Teetotums, and a barge for dancing, and a huge cleared area for playing skittles and knock-'em-downs with a section set aside for skating."

"Well then, perhaps you're ready to give the ice a try yourself now?" Richard suggested hopefully. "I must confess that I'm beginning to feel more like a Jack Frost than a Jack-a-dandy the longer I stand here and let the chill steal its way into my bones."

"An excellent idea," Jennifer agreed. She smiled at him

in a challenging way. ''I believe you did boast of your expertise, and I confess that I'm altogether anxious to discover whether you're a truc dab or a mere dabbler, shall we say?''

Her companion didn't require any further prompting to don his skates and set off, though not without first checking the tightness of Jennifer's lacings and then escorting her to the edge of the pond. After promising to return in a few minutes, Richard stepped onto the ice, and before he'd taken more than half a dozen strides, Jennifer had to admit that he was without doubt the most expert skater in sight. His stroke was powerful yet effortless, and he moved so smoothly that it was impossible to tell where one foot left off and the other took over. What's more, he seemed to be enjoying himself immensely, and the boyish grin that had crept over his face together with the graceful motion of his tall figure was such a powerful combination that it made Jennifer's breath come in little gasps that she couldn't honestly ascribe to the cold weather. If only they could spend more time together like this, in harmless activities that allowed them to feel at ease with one another in a completely natural fashion they never seemed to manage otherwise, she mused as she stepped out onto the ice.

Jennifer's style tended to be as daring and erratic as the rest of her chacacter. She darted here and there, sometimes whizzing gloriously along and the next moment stumbling over a rough place in the ice that she hadn't been able to slow down enough to avoid. Nevertheless, she had a thoroughly good time, too, and when Richard came back to claim her, as promised, she was secretly loathe to trade her independent status for that of a partnership. Still, once they'd joined hands and begun to circle the pond, she had to admit that his nearness made her feel almost giddy, and the sensation of being steered smoothly along by his strong but gentle touch was as delicious as floating through the air. She was just on the verge of commenting to that effect when Richard surprised her by beating her to the point.

''Unparalleled feeling—ain't it?—gliding about as if there's not a cloud on the horizon,'' he observed. He smiled down at her in a way that mirrored his own pleasure at having her, for once, literally well in hand. "Do you know, the longer I skate, the less important all my worries seem, until I can nearly convince myself I haven't a care worth fussing over."

Jennifer had barely opened her mouth to ask what might be worrying him when she was drowned out by the twins' voices loudly beseeching their father to take a turn around the ice with them instead. The two were standing beside Molly on the bank, having apparently tired of their first activity and clearly ready to undertake a second. In response to Richard's questioning look, Jennifer shrugged her shoulders helplessly. "You'd best do as they ask, or we won't have a moment's peace," she advised in a tone of long-suffering. "Though, truly, I'd never have imagined that I should one day find myself competing for the attention of a handsome man with two such complete scamps—and apparently coming up with the short straw, besides." She patted his hand in a teasing manner. "But never mind. I suspect I shall recover eventually—particularly if I can succeed in locating a stronger restorative than hot cider." She flashed a mischievous grin over her shoulder and coasted to a fallen log to remove her skates.

A few minutes later, she meandered over to Molly's side. That young lady had steadfastly refused to be coaxed out onto the ice, despite Richard's assurances that he'd hold on to her tightly to keep her from falling and the twins' more physical attempts to pull her off the bank. In her own defense, Molly had muttered something under her breath about how if God had intended people to skate, He'd have invented something more substantial than only narrow slivers of silver or wood as the sole barrier between oneself and who-knew-how-many feet of water. Since Jennifer knew that the speaker was far from religious, this remark struck her as particularly humorous. But because she also guessed that Molly was sincerely afraid and probably reluctant to admit it in front of everyone, Jennifer refrained from pressing her to elaborate on this new dimension of her character.

The two women watched for several minutes as Richard led George and Caroline through a simplified version of intricate skating maneuvers. With both, Jennifer was pleased to note, he was patient and encouraging—not falling into the trap of mocking his son's timidity because he was a boy or limiting his daughter's explorations on account of her being a girl. Rather, he was so impartially gentle and considerate that it caused Jennifer to admit that he certainly appeared to have taken to heart her recommendation about mending his ways, and Molly actually to remark on that fact.

"Pretty picture they make, don't you think?" she asked. "Why, two months ago you could have knocked me over with a feather if you'd have told me I'd be watching a stiff-neck like Mr. Richard Avery willingly climb down from his high horse to satisfy the whim of a pair of nine-year-old brats. And now look at him," she said with a satisfied voice. "He's just as tickled as they are—and all three seem as happy as cows in clover."

Jennifer studied the group for a few more moments in silence. "Yes, they do look utterly content, don't they?" she observed, wondering why that realization didn't seem to make her feel quite as pleased as she suspected it ought to. In fact, it was having the effect of making her feel rather superfluous instead, and that emotion was entirely confusing. On the one hand, she was glad to have played a role in bringing that family together again, but on the other hand, she'd never realized that reuniting them might have the effect of excluding her, she admitted silently. If she'd stuck strictly to her plan of convincing Richard Avery to face his shortcomings and then take steps to amend them, all would have been well. But once she'd recognized that she was developing a *tendre* for the man—and her affection only appeared to deepen as she watched him grow to know himself better—she should promptly have shown the household a light pair of heels. Only she couldn't leave until her father returned, she reminded herself, trying unsuccessfully to quell a longing to be able to confide all this bothersome inner turmoil to that same gentleman.

Molly would never have claimed that she could be a substitute for Lord Somers, but she could easily see from Jennifer's expression that something was troubling her. So although she might not have nominated herself as confidante, she was kindhearted enough to know that, in lieu of any other audience, Jennifer would doubtless find her counsel welcome. Therefore, she sought to broach the subject she thought might be on her friend's mind, although in her usual blunt fashion. "Quite a catch, your Mr. Avery," she offered, "leastways, since he's shown himself to be a real flesh-and-blood man after all."

"Indeed," Jennifer said only in a noncommittal voice. "But why is everyone aways calling him 'my' Mr. Avery? I think you should rather call him Miss Rutland's Mr. Avery, if you wish to be precise."

"Oh, pish!" Molly gave one of her disparaging sniffs and decided to offer her friend a morsel of comfort. "Why, surely you can see the man don't care a fig for her?" And moreover, she added to herself, that fact doesn't bother Abigail a smidgen, now that she's set her sights on another target instead.

Jennifer raised her eyebrows in surprise. "Haven't we already talked about how 'my' Mr. Avery has been escorting that same young lady to every important function in recent memory? So why, pray tell, should he place himself so often in her company if his interest in her is as casual as you claim?"

"Convenience, for one thing," Molly said promptly. "Suppose he made it a point to attend such events in order to try to acquire a bit of the social polish you've been harping about him needing? Well, what's more sensible than that he'd decide he ought to mix in society a bit more and that he'd wish to be accompanied by someone like Miss Rutland whom he already knows well and who would be likely to agree to assist in that endeavor?" She hesitated for a moment, aware that the foregoing statement was a trifle too close to the real reasons she'd urged that Miss Rutland be selected, though for a somewhat different purpose. "Besides, even if the man might have wanted to look elsewhere and consider that it would be unexceptional to escort you to a few functions while you're under his protection, for instance, it ain't as if you've been sitting home counting the linen every night waiting for an invitation, have you? Why, you know perfectly well that your calendar's been so full that you've hardly set foot inside the house the last few weeks, which don't make it very easy for Mr. Avery to determine if you might enjoy his company. And anyway, I warrant the poor man doesn't shine in a crowd, and thus is scarcely liable to fancy being part of one—some men don't, you know.''

Jennifer appeared caught between wishing to ask Molly when she'd gained this sudden expertise about the male sex and whether she knew for a fact that Richard had been seeking to learn her whereabouts. Luckily for Molly, perhaps, Jennifer's curiosity was strong enough to distract her temporarily from pursuing either course as determinedly as she might have ordinarily. Instead, she merely inquired in a vague way, ''Oh, has he been looking for me?''

Properly concluding that the ''he'' in this sentence referred to their host, Molly smothered an impulse to answer truthfully that that poor man had been making every effort to try and keep Jennifer constantly in sight. ''Well, he's asked me a time or two where you'd gone,'' she admitted in all honesty. ''And if I were you, I'd begin to think twice about continuing to pit him against such opposition as the two puppies you've got barking at your feet at the moment. Why, if he don't tire of the noise, eventually he's bound to take off and track another scent altogether, in my opinion.''

Jennifer was so astonished first at discovering Molly again in the role of adviser and second, on hearing her speak practically in parables that she didn't respond immediately. ''Indeed, I never meant him to be forced to compete for my attention,'' she admitted at last. ''And in any case, he has nothing to fear any longer from Mr. Hartley, because that gentleman appears to have disappeared completely from the scene. He may even have gone to Washington to make a start in politics at long last, since I haven't seen him for a while now. And as far as Mr. Verplanck is concerned, there was never any question in my mind that he wasn't serious. Why, I should have thought that if anyone, Mr. Avery would certainly have realized that his friend was only interested in a casual dalliance,'' she mused, before calling herself abruptly to order. ''Surely, if he thinks otherwise, it can only be because of two things: First, that Gulian himself has said something to the contrary, though I can hardly believe he'd voluntarily relate the outcome of his suit—or should I say, "*pur*suit?" Jennifer indulged in a private smile as she recalled her last encounter with Mr. Verplanck.

"And second?" Molly prompted.

"I've endeavored to create the impression that I'm not interested in Mr. Avery, and now he believes I truly mean it. He must feel there's no future in pursuing the relationship any further," she said slowly. "What a bother it is that when one doesn't care overmuch about succeeding, one inevitably does! Now I suppose I shall have to go to great lengths to change his mind, and then I'll very likely botch it somehow in the end!"

"Oh, I shouldn't think it would be so awfully difficult to put things right," Molly said in a confident voice. She caught sight of the surprised look on Jennifer's face and hastened to invent a reason for having reached such a prompt conclusion. "Well, I mean, look at today, for example. Didn't he suggest this excursion himself and invite us along?"

"Yes, that's true—but it's not at all the same thing, being invited to form part of what you'll have to admit is really a family group," Jennifer pointed out. "Maybe he'd begin to think of me as a woman again if I acted more like an ordinary miss," she continued, half-aloud. "But how I hate all that simpering and pretending not to be able to string three words together and make any sense. Besides, he knows me well enough to be able to recognize immediately that such an attitude's merely a posture, so where will that get me? No, best keep things simple and honest," she decided, much to Molly's relief. She started to lift a hand to tease a curl in her customary habit of aiding her thinking, but her mittens prevented that action. Instead, she curled her fingers reflectively a few times and stared blankly down at her hands while she thought.

By this point, Molly had begun to feel increasingly uncomfortable about being caught squarely in the middle of what was turning out to be a thoroughly knotty situation. Indeed, it was all she could do to keep the various parties straight in her own mind. How she'd allowed first Miss Rutland and then Mr. Avery to persuade her to go along with their schemes was beyond reason, she reminded herself glumly. No, that wasn't entirely true. She'd undertaken it all—and gladly too—in the hope of helping her dear Jennifer find the happiness she felt surely lay in a certain gentleman's arms. Why, to relieve her friend's mind she'd come close to letting slip that Mr. Hartley hadn't disappeared at all; he'd merely taken up permanent residence at Miss Rutland's side. And the longer she was involved in all these maneuverings, the more Molly feared it likely she'd be tricked into taking a gross misstep, and thus be found out by one of the three parties involved. In fact, she was just wondering how she could extricate herself from the entire mess, and escape blame as well, when she was startled into emitting a little squawk as Jennifer suddenly clutched her arm.

"I have it!" her friend exclaimed excitedly. "I shall simply seize the initiative and ask Mr. Avery to escort me somewhere, thereby providing him with opportunity and encouragement at the same time! It's so simple I don't know why I didn't conceive of it sooner! It's altogether proper for him, as my temporary guardian, to spend a good deal of time in my company—and I intend to make the most of that fact! What's more, if I propose that he accompany me to some entertainment, he'll surely realize that I wish to enjoy the pleasures of his company and conversation, not those of Mr. Hartley or Mr. Verplanck, don't you think?"

Molly hesitated. "Of course, I ain't too certain about such niceties myself," she offered after a moment, "but it seems to me it ain't proper for a lady to invite a gentleman, and that's that. It's supposed to be the other way 'round—that's the way folks want it and that's the way it should be. You can't change the world just by wishing it so. And even if you could," she went on firmly, "I think you'd be straining your relationship as Mr. Avery's 'ward' to pretend that the two of you could go out alone together. He's not your legal guardian, after all, as everyone is quite aware, and even a man as poorly versed in social customs as he ain't about to think such a practice beyond censure. Therefore, you'd best agree to take me along, too."

She watched a familiar expression come over Jennifer's

face. "Oh, very well, but I don't see that either of those points is anything much to refine over," the latter declared stubbornly. "Besides, who's to know that I'm the one doing the asking, save the gentleman himself? Of course, I suppose you're right that when one is dealing with a person of such estimable good character as Richard Avery, one ought to approach the matter with extreme caution. That is why I plan to be so subtle and so ingenuous that he'll imagine he actually thought of the idea himself!" Jennifer waited for some reaction, and when one was not forthcoming, she asked, "Well, what's the matter? Don't you believe I can carry it off?"

"Oh, I've no doubt of it," Molly said sincerely. "If anything, I'd say your pride at gaining the upper hand might bring you grief in the end," she warned.

Jennifer merely laughed. "Probably true," she admitted readily enough. "Then I shall just have to make sure and hold myself on a short string in the hope of avoiding that pitfall, won't I?"

Molly continued to look dubious, though whether it was because she doubted that Jennifer could keep her word or because she thought they might have failed to take some other factor into account wasn't altogether clear. "Well, I suppose we'll have to wait and see," she offered at last.

Naturally, once Jennifer had made up her mind regarding how to approach the problem, she was all in a flame to begin solving it. And inevitably, she found several obstacles thrown in her path that appeared destined to prevent her from immediately reaching her goal. The first of these was a sudden—if, perhaps, long-anticipated—crisis at the Manhattan Company, which threatened to spell the end of the company's charter and demanded the majority of Richard's time for more than a week following the trip to Lispenard's Meadows. He alternated between meetings with the directors and interviews with the Common Council at which he'd been nominated to act as company spokesman. More often than not, he slept on the couch that had been set up in his office, returning to the house every day or so only for fresh clothing and to clean up before disappearing again.

It was endlessly frustrating to Jennifer that the person she most wished to see was only a short distance away but as inaccessible as if he were on the other side of the continent. And it was equally disturbing for her to be obliged to watch that man become increasingly haggard as the days wore on, and yet be unable to prevent it or even to show that she sympathized with his predicament.

Instead, she found herself with a second unexpected development on her hands. The twins, having at last gotten a taste of what family life might be like on their recent skating excursion, now refused to be satisfied with anything less. The fact that their father was again absent was merely a minor complication and one that they didn't seem prepared to tolerate for long. Whatever time wasn't spent on lessons or outings, George and Caroline now devoted to preparing for a family-style Christmas—a holiday that both children had suddenly embraced with the fervor of true converts. That attitude might have been suitable had they been more aware of the real spiritual significance of the day. When Jennifer asked George for details, however, he could only volunteer that the celebration marked the birth of a lady named Mary's baby boy, and this appeared to be the extent of either twin's religious knowledge. Rather, they were far more concerned with such secular inventions as decorating the house with holly and mistletoe, making a Yule log, and preparing for the arrival of Santa Claus.

They'd learned about the identity of Santa Claus from Molly, Jennifer discovered. Apparently she'd told them how the early Dutch inhabitants had continued to commemorate Saint Nicholas's feast day after their arrival in New York, and how he'd gradually become accepted by the city's English settlers as Santa Claus and the December 6 children's holiday on his feast had become confused with Christmas Day. Now the twins endlessly pestered Molly and Jennifer with questions: When would Santa Claus arrive? What did he look like? How could they be sure he would pay them a visit?

It was after one particularly trying afternoon some four days before Christmas that Jennifer finally reached the limits of her patience. In all honesty, however, she recognized that her own emotional state had had as much to do with bringing her to this point as had the children's excitement. And rather than become angry and blame them for something that was not their fault, she'd chosen to escape to the garden on the pretext of checking that the roses were protected against frost.

She was busy examining their burlap wrappings and humming mindlessly to herself when Richard Avery rounded the side of the house, lost in thought, and bumped squarely into her.

"Oh, I beg your pardon," he said, staggering a little before regaining his balance. "Er—I hope you don't mind my asking, but what the devil are you doing?"

Jennifer would have welcomed a few more moments to recover from seeing Richard for the first time in a week and a half, and at decidedly close range. As it was, her mind raced with the effort to decide what she should say first, even as her pulse raced at the firm pressure of the arm that had propped her upright. How exhausted he looked and how she wished he'd be moved to confide in her, she thought wistfully. And how she longed, too, to find a way to restore the friendly atmosphere of that afternoon on the skating pond when she'd felt at peace with the world and utterly contented with her companion. She explained her errand in a few quick sentences. Then, prompted by the thought that if she confided in him it might occur that he could do likewise, as well as by the desire to wipe the strained expression off his face, she proceeded to relate the reasons behind her sudden interest in horticulture.

"Good God—you mean to tell me that the twins are now expecting a visit from Saint Nick?" Richard exclaimed. He rubbed one hand tiredly across his forehead. "Well, I suppose that that wouldn't be any more difficult than some of the things I've been expected to produce out of thin air lately. The new pump engine still isn't functioning after almost a month, and the Council is demanding a satisfactory explanation for the delay or they'll revoke the company charter. What's more, there have been several outbreaks of violence, presumably by subscribers furious at having been without water for such an unforeseen length of time. If they only knew how much I sympathized with their situation—instead, as the company spokesperson, I've become their chief target.'' He sighed. ''If you ask me, I'd say it sounds as if the three adults in this house could use a vacation,'' he concluded with feeling.

The confidences she'd been hoping he'd offer and the opening she'd been awaiting having thus been presented, Jennifer didn't hesitate to make good use of both. ''Precisely what I think. You know, I'm told Mr. Cooke's performances at the Park Theatre aren't to be missed. And I warrant a little humor would be just the thing to perk us right up. Don't you agree?''

''Indeed,'' Richard said gratefully at once, ''and if you and Miss Danhope can manage, we can go as soon as tomorrow night. After all, I'd much rather watch *Much Ado About Nothing* than have to argue why that criticism shouldn't be applied to the activities of the Manhattan Company!''

The following evening, the Avery party set out for the Park Theatre, which was appropriately located on what was nicknamed Park Row, across from City Hall. They had earlier agreed that the three of them were looking quite handsome—Richard in full evening dress of knee breeches, white shirt, and snowy cravat; Jennifer in a simply cut grown of deep green crepe that showed off her hair and eyes to best advantage; and Molly in a fashionable new robe of white satin. What's more, they were all in a remarkably good humor, and consequently, the atmosphere was highly congenial—each person feeling free to comment or to remain silent, as the mood struck.

The theater itself was interesting enough to provide for a fruitful discussion. It was a huge, square building with a spacious lobby and seating for up to 1,200 people on wooden benches set up in the ''pit'' for men only or in the more luxurious but still sparsely decorated private boxes on three tiers. The stage was the most enormous one Jennifer had ever seen, measuring forty by seventy feet and providing ample room for whatever piece the manager had decided to stage. In fact, Richard explained, the theater appeared to be flourishing under the guidance of William Dunlop—at least when he chose to offer Shakespeare rather than the adequate, if uninspired, efforts of his own pen. Nevertheless, he couldn't be faulted for his choice of performers because he inevitably hired the finest English players, paid them well, and housed them generously in the appropriately named Shakespeare Tavern on Nassau Street. His greatest find to date, as Jennifer had mentioned the day before, was George Frederick Cooke, whom Dunlop had enticed across the ocean and who had proceeded to delight audiences with his astonishing performances and his rather eccentric private life.

All of this information was conveyed in snatches by either Richard or Molly during the time it took for the three to make their way to a reserved box on the fashionable second tier. It wasn't until they were seated, and Jennifer had had a chance to look around the interior, that they were able to hold a proper conversation.

"Well, what do you think of our bastion of culture?" Richard asked with a smile. "Tell me—how does this ugly monstrosity compare to a London theater?"

"Not very favorably," Jennifer informed him, her eyes twinkling. "I take it the acting must be quite exceptional to attract so many people to a place that clearly has little else to offer in the way of aesthetic pleasures?"

"Oh, yes, indeed," Richard said in a serious voice, "though I have heard it claimed that we reap the benefit of the very finest actors mainly to compensate for our having to suffer with bad acoustics, primitive scenery, and a veritable lack of amenities altogether."

Molly then chose to follow his remarks with one of her disparaging sniffs, and these two observations struck them all as so amusing that they promptly dissolved in laughter. In fact, it wasn't until several minutes had passed that Molly became the first to be aware that they were being watched by the occupants of a nearby box.

"Well, who'd have thought!" she exclaimed when she recognized the identity of their neighbors. "There, you see—he didn't go to Washington after all!" she exclaimed, poking Jennifer in the side in her usual fashion to attract her attention. "We appear to be gathering a bit of an audience ourselves, my friends—and only look what an unlikely one it is, too!''

Richard and Jennifer looked in the direction Molly indicated and found Abigail and Mr. Rutland and Benjamin Hartley staring at them with respective expressions of surprise, satisfaction, and embarrassment. Having more social presence than Molly, and at the moment apparently more tact than either of his companions, Richard smiled and rose in a half-bow of acknowledgment before thumping back down. "Not merely improbable, I'd call it, but inconvenient to boot,'' he complained in a loud whisper. "Now we shall have them watching us all night and yet not be able to learn the details of how that little couple happens to be together until intermission.''

"Oh, do you truly care?'' Jennifer asked curiously.

"Of course. Don't you?'' he asked in amazement. "Why, I'd have thought it the most natural thing in the world for you to wish to discover how one of your beaux should have now become the escort of my former, er, beloved, instead.'' He raised his eyebrows and smiled mischievously at Jennifer.

Former? Jennifer thought rapidly to herself. Then Molly had been right, she realized, catching a glimpse of the cat-in-the-creampot expression on her friend's face. "Perhaps,'' she admitted with a bit more spirit, "but how ill-bred of you to say so.''

"Yes, isn't it?'' he agreed blandly. "Still, no doubt I've only picked up the habits of the company I've been keeping lately.'' He grinned, glancing from one to the other of his companions.

Fortunately for the outcome of their evening, Jennifer was prevented from offering a further rejoinder as the lights dimmed and the curtain rose. The performance was excellent, as expected, and certainly sufficient to divert their attention for the next hour. The curtain had barely fallen, however, when Mr. Hartley presented himself at the entrance to their box and, without prompting, plunged into the very subject they'd been hoping to discuss with him.

"Apparently I owe you a heartfelt 'thank you,'" he said to Jennifer after greetings had been exchanged. "It seems that a few weeks ago, you and Mr. Avery attended a dinner party at the Rutlands' house, and I believe that somehow my name came into the conversation a time or two. Well, it appears that Mr. Rutland was curious to know more about the man to whom you so often referred, and shortly thereafter he invited me to call. What a disaster that was! We had an enormous argument, because as you know our beliefs are fundamentally opposed to one another. Nevertheless, for some reason he asked me to come again, and then again—and each time we'd end up in a pitched battle. But afterward, Abigail and I would talk together a little and now—'' He broke off and ran his hand nervously through his hair. ''Well you see—we've decided we're quite well suited, and even her father agrees.'' He looked over at the box where the aforementioned gentleman was smiling at him in a genial fashion as if he couldn't believe this reaction himself. ''In fact, he's willing to put aside our differences and even to support my political aspirations to a certain extent because that will please Abigail. So even though you, sir, should doubtless have been a more 'suitable' husband in some ways, I hope you'll trust me to provide Abigail with everything she might want in a marriage.'' He looked anxiously at Richard at the conclusion of this speech.

Without hesitating, that gentleman reached out to pump his hand enthusiastically. ''Capital!'' he exclaimed at once. ''My felicitations to you both!''

''And mine as well,'' Jennifer added, ''together with every good wish for your future happiness.''

Molly, for her part, merely smiled while she murmured a silent prayer of thanks that events had been resolved in a way that alleviated her fear of being discovered in the midst of scheming on Abigail's behalf. And this new development also hefted at least some of the burden she felt for making sure that things worked out right between Jennifer and Richard from her already weary shoulders, she thought happily.

A few minutes later, Mr. Hartley departed, looking enormously relieved at having discharged an errand he'd clearly been dreading. A not uncomfortable silence fell between the remaining occupants of the box. ''Well, don't that beat all,'' Richard observed calmly at last.

"You mean to say you don't mind?" Jennifer asked.

"Mind? On the contrary, I'm delighted! Why, the man's just performed the service of delivering me from a deucedly awkward situation. I never intended to make Abigail an offer, you see, despite the fact that everyone expected me to do so. But then, perhaps you, too, were expecting something a bit different—from Mr. Hartley, that is?"

Jennifer shook her head. "No. I find my own attitude perfectly matches yours."

"Really? Well, don't that beat all," he repeated in a pleasant tone. He smiled at her and then broadened the smile to include Molly as well. In fact, his honest pleasure was so infectious that secretly none of the three felt the least bit unhappy with how matters stood at the moment.

That state of affairs persisted throughout the remainder of what turned out to be a most enjoyable theatrical performance and drive back to No. 30 Wall Street. To be truthful, the whole group was so happily lost in the congenial feeling among them that they entered the front hallway and began to ascend the stairs before they were unexpectedly interrupted. "It's about time you returned," drawled a familiar voice. "And just where did you two love birds and your agreeable little chaperone fly off to this evening, I wonder?"

Chapter 13

THE COMPACT figure of Mr. John Henry detached itself from the landing and began to descend the stairs toward them. "Trust you don't mind my showing up so precipitously, dear fellow?" he said in a confident tone to Richard, smiling in that ingratiating way Jennifer particularly disliked and that caused Molly to bristle angrily. "The thing is, I'd have hung around the dock until sending advance notice of my arrival, but I couldn't really see the whys and wherefores of standing on such ceremony with you.'' Because he'd by this time arrived at approximately her level, he bent to kiss Jennifer's hand and then to press it rather overlong between his own moist palms before releasing it. ''How delighted I am to find you still in New York, my lady, and still ravishing as ever. Indeed, it looks as if you've all begun to get on famously during my absence. But then, proximity does seem inevitably to be the handmaiden of desire,'' he observed, staring through Molly as if she weren't even there. He paused to watch the response to this feeler with the detached interest of a man examining a couple of rare bugs before killing them to add to his collection.

Fortunately, perhaps, Richard was becoming so rapidly irritated by the presumptuous way the new arrival was treating him as a guest in his own house, that he brushed aside this comment as altogether beneath his notice. ''Quite right to come here straight off,'' he assured Henry politely as they shook hands. ''But let's not keep jawing away standing up like regular riffraff. Why not go up to my study for a bit of cognac and you can relate the details of your voyage in a little more comfort? And you'll join us, won't you?'' he asked, turning smoothly toward Jennifer. ''After all, I'm sure Mr. Henry would enjoy having something pleasant to look at after weeks of what's bound to have been a beastly fatiguing trip.''

Jennifer had just been on the point of excusing herself with Molly for the evening, not least because she personally found Mr. Henry's company offensive and his conversation generally distasteful. As they mounted the stairs behind Henry, however, Richard cast a look of such pure supplication in her direction that she promptly revised her decision. It pleased her to know that Richard obviously wanted her company.

After Molly departed for her room and the others had arranged themselves comfortably on chairs in front of the fire and been supplied with a glass of brandy each, Jennifer had little difficulty understanding Richard's intention. Mr. Henry, it appeared, hadn't waited for his host's return before beginning to toast his arrival in New York and was therefore already nicely primed—a fact that Jennifer hadn't previously noted, but Richard clearly had. And augmented by the smokescreen her presence should doubtless provide, he hoped to discover whether Mr. Henry's condition might not prove sufficiently precarious for him to play, unawares, right into their hands.

"I trust you had a pleasant journey?" Richard inquired as a start.

"That ain't exactly the word I'd apply to several weeks spent aboard a damnably cramped packet being forced to endure execrable food and even worse weather," Mr. Henry croaked, tossing off half the contents of his glass.

"Well, then, perhaps you at least found that it was, er, advantageous, if I recall your prediction—?"

"Not exactly in the way I thought it should be," Henry admitted, downing the rest of his cognac. "Oh, they treated me well enough, I suppose, and even gave me a membership at the Pitt Club. As if that trifle would fully compensate for all my time and effort! But then when it came down to counting out the pennies, they actually had the audacity to quibble over the amount! Let me tell you, there's no more closefisted person in all creation than a little clerk all puffed up with himself and as anxious to skin a flint as to pay you what you deserve!" He stared significantly at his empty glass, and Richard hastened to provide the necessary fuel for him to continue, wondering at the same time if they hadn't had this identical conversation before.

"Fact is, been referred back to Canada for further discussion of my situation," Henry went on in a bitter tone. "But I ain't such an innocent that I can't see the lay of the land by now. I imagine they'll merely try to shab me off again, dispose of the evidence, and then look for a way to keep me bent to their purpose." He paused to drink deeply once more. "I tell you, I'm through with the British once and for all—and with Craig and now Prevost and his lot in Canada, too! Why, I dealt with them in proper good faith and look at the thanks I've gotten. Well, they haven't heard the last of our arrangement, I promise! Just wait until Crillon and I finish laying the groundwork. We'll see what they have to say then about old John Henry!" This threat appeared to signify the conclusion of his tirade, because he called for another bumper and then lapsed into a silence broken only by occasional malevolent mutterings under his breath.

Jennifer was somewhat disappointed by the vague nature of the preceding disclosures—a turn of events clearly not aided by Mr. Henry's tendency to refer to himself in the third person when in his cups. Still, she thought it safe enough to question him about what she judged to be a more peripheral matter. "And who is this Mr. Crillon?" she asked in a casual tone. "I don't believe I recall your mentioning him before."

"A prime fellow," Henry said enthusiastically, if somewhat indistinctly at this point, considering the amount he'd drunk. "Met him first in London, and then he turned up at Ryde waiting to sail on the same packet with me. Comes of a well-known French family. Had to flee that rascal Napoleon, of course. Believe he left behind an estate in Lebeur near the Spanish border, and somewhere I recall hearing that his father was the same duke who besieged Gibraltar. Anyway, he's gone to Boston to conduct a bit of business on my behalf. Probably meet him yourself when he returns in a week or so—that is, if it wouldn't be inconvenient for him to stop here?" he inquired rather belatedly.

"Not at all," Richard said at once in a gracious fashion. "Happy to provide a roof for the man, if you like." Then, having quickly deduced Jennifer's drift himself, he moved to supplement it by inquiring, "I take it Crillon has acquaintances in Massachusetts, then?"

"Plans to wait on the governor," Henry related with obvious pride. "Thinking of going down to Washington, you see, and interested in securing an introduction or two before he arrives there. Damned good notion, too, 'cause I hear the capital's as tight a little enclave as you're bound to find anywhere. I'm told you can't even sneeze without someone across town asking if you've a touch of influenza! What's more, Crillon appears to be a veritable fountain of ideas, 'cause he's hit on a dandy scheme to help me out of the spot I'm in. Why, he might even come up with a way for you to be a part of the thing as well." He regarded his host fondly through bleary eyes, having more or less forgotten Jennifer's presence for the time being.

"Excellent," Richard said in a hearty voice. "But we've plenty of time to talk about that tomorrow or the next day. You must be fagged to death by now. Why don't I show you to your room and let you get some rest instead of hounding you with any more questions that can easily keep until later?" He helped Henry to rise from his chair—a feat that appeared to tax Richard to the limits of both his strength and his ability. Then he tucked a hand solicitously under Henry's arm and steered his guest out of the study and down the hallway in the direction of the same bedroom he'd occupied on his last visit.

When Richard returned, he found Jennifer staring meditatively at the fire, twirling her empty glass in one hand. Without asking, he refilled both their glasses with what was only their second measure, and sat down in his own chair to assume a similar pose. They continued to sit quietly in this fashion for several minutes, each apparently reviewing the foregoing conversation in an attempt to determine just how they should proceed.

"You realize, of course, that this means we've only a week or two at most to try and 'borrow' some of Henry's documents?" Jennifer began, as if picking up the thread of an ongoing conversation.

"Yes. I suppose when Crillon arrives it will be that much more difficult to get hold of the things," Richard admitted. "And then, depending on what this 'dandy scheme' is that the two of them have dreamed up, they may depart immediately thereafter."

Jennifer tapped the arm of her chair with her fingers in an unconscious imitation of her host which, when he noticed, made him quickly smile and then hide his mouth behind one hand. "I can't see any help for it but to conclude that we've simply got to get our hands on those letters again," she said in a resigned voice.

"It appears so," Richard agreed. "But we can't actually take them, since Henry would certainly notice their absence. I suppose that means we've got to copy them."

"Yes, because then no matter what happens, we'll at least

have something convincing to support our story.'' She paused for a moment before saying thoughtfully, ''Do you know, I can't help thinking Henry must have suspected all along that he'd be dealt a losing hand by his employer, and decided at the outset to protect his future by secretly amassing a case against the very people whom he was purporting to assist.'' She wrinkled her nose as if she'd suddenly encountered a nasty smell and then took a quick sip of cognac to wash away the odor. ''Not a very pretty picture, is it?''

''Not in the least.'' Richard hesitated while he cast about for the next piece of the puzzle, and then picking up the narrative, continued slowly: ''And now that Henry claims to be at odds with his former partners, and what's more, threatening to seek some sort of revenge, it seems safe to assume that he—or Crillon—will try to turn his evidence to best advantage. From what he says, the British apparently refused to 'buy back' his letters, and he hinted that if he returns to Canada, he thinks he'll be forced to give them up altogether. Therefore, I'd guess he means to peddle those documents in Washington to whomever can pay and presumably wishes to embarrass England by producing them.''

Jennifer regarded her companion with admiration. ''Precisely what I think!'' she exclaimed warmly. Now, why was he never so quick to nose out the sense of things that had to do with the heart instead of the head? she wondered, feeling just a tiny bit annoyed at that fact.

His companion's hard-won praise was certainly more to his taste than he'd hitherto been willing to admit, Richard thought happily. But why did it seem as if she was so hesitant to bestow it? he wondered, feeling a trifle irritated at that thought. He took a last, comforting swallow of brandy. ''What puzzles me,'' he admitted, ''is why Crillon would have gotten mixed up in all this business in the first place. The obvious answer that comes to mind, of course, is money. If Crillon had to flee France, as Henry claims, then he might very well be living in considerably reduced circumstances and naturally seeking some way to improve on that situation. And frankly, you'll have to admit that in this instance, he seems to have hit on the perfect combination of a highly lucrative commodity and a not overly bright partner—particularly when Mr. Henry has been tipping a few, shall we say? For that matter, have you figured out how it is we're to copy the damned things without becoming nicely blinded ourselves, if we have to bend the elbow as often as Mr. Henry does?''

''Not exactly,'' Jennifer confessed. She smiled teasingly at her companion. ''Though one part should be easy: You may recall that I had little difficulty in gaining access to his room before, once I was given the opportunity. So give me until tomorrow morning, and I promise I shall have contrived a plan that is bound to succeed and on which you won't hesitate to pin your hopes.'' She tossed this off with an airy confidence with which her companion was obliged to be satisfied.

It actually took Jennifer even less time than she'd expected to think up a way to keep Mr. Henry busy long enough for her to sneak into his room and copy at least a few of the more damaging letters and the cipher. All she had to do was to remember that the next day was December 24 and an obvious solution presented itself. Why not suggest that Henry disguise himself and play the role of Saint Nick? After all, the children didn't know he'd arrived yet and therefore wouldn't suspect the true identity of their visitor. What's more, she realized happily, the scheme should rather handily serve two purposes at once—provide the twins with the visit they'd been primed to expect, and account for a portion of Mr. Henry's time outside his apartment during which she could safely accomplish her task.

Unfortunately, what had seemed to her an ideal solution to their dilemma didn't strike her partner quite as favorably. In the first place, Richard wasn't convinced that it was wise to encourage what he still thought of as capriciousness on the part of George and Caroline regarding this Christmas "business," as he called it. And in the second place, he had to admit fearing that he wouldn't prove sufficiently adept at maintaining the subterfuge as long as might be required. Although he'd had some luck lately in letting his natural good humor break through his austere manner, he recognized that while he secretly continued to picture himself as a dashing and romantic figure, on the surface he still seemed a stuffy, pompous man. Although he now usually noticed when he reverted to his previous habits, he had discovered that trying to change them was more difficult than he'd expected. And somehow it seemed easier for him to cast off his old ways and adopt a fresh viewpoint when Jennifer was present. Whether he was primarily assisted in this by the example of the lady's own exuberant style or by the fact that she refused to allow him to escape without pouncing on his every relapse with deadly accuracy, he wasn't able truthfully to say.

For a few minutes, Richard allowed his thoughts to dwell on Jennifer in delightful disorder, not making the slightest attempt to sort out one from another. How wonderful it had been to see that they could work in such pleasant harmony as they had last night, he recalled, a little smile tugging at his mouth. Together, he was certain they were utterly invincible. Why, if she were going to be beside him, he'd even feel no qualms about playing a role in this ridiculous scheme of hers to entrap John Henry. Still, he was well aware that he couldn't forever count on her presence, so he supposed that at some point he'd just have to leap blindly into the dark on his own and hope for a soft landing. Though to be sure, he thought somewhat peevishly at the end of this digression, he didn't immediately perceive a vast difference between doing something because it was good for him and doing something because other people expected him to do it.

Nevertheless, since the first step in Jennifer's plan involved passing the bottle enough times so that Mr. Henry agreed to cast his lot with theirs, Richard felt fully able to participate in that activity. In fact, it soon appeared clear, as he'd suspected, that the real danger might lie in his trying to keep up with the immoderate pace at which Henry consumed all liquid offerings. By late afternoon, following a couple of hours of making sure that his guest remained hidden and enduring a good deal of negligible conversation and a somewhat greater quantity of purposeful drinking, Richard judged the time right to introduce what he had in mind.

"Wonder if you'd do me a favor," he began casually. "Tomorrow's Christmas, as you know. Now ordinarily, it ain't something that's uppermost in my mind. But this year the twins have had their heads stuffed with a bunch of foolishness, and now they tell me they're awaiting a visit from Santa Claus. Well, you can easily see that I can't expect to play that role without my absence instantly giving the whole game away. So I wondered, in that case, if you'd mind greatly filling those shoes? I should think we'd be bound to score a hit if you do, 'cause George and Caroline don't even know you're here and so won't in the least suspect."

This proposal seemed to strike Mr. Henry as inordinately funny, and he proceeded to laugh until his breath came in great whooping gasps and his face was as red as a persimmon. "You want me to play Santa Claus?" he got out at last. "Oh, that's famous! Well, and why ever not?" he wondered aloud, and to Richard's amazement, promptly agreed.

A few minutes before six o'clock, Molly executed her part by coaxing the children downstairs to the kitchen to sample some of Mrs. Booth's sugarplums. Jennifer and Richard then took the opportunity to smuggle a strange-looking figure into the schoolroom and to hide themselves in the corner near the door to await the twins' return. Mr. Henry swayed docilely in the center of the room where they'd left him, though if truth be told, he was probably far too sodden to do much else. He was dressed in a truly odd array of clothing that included a heavy topcoat that had belonged to the late Mr. Booth, a pair of Sydney's oldest boots, woolen mittens, and two scarves; his head and most of his face were obscured by a hastily assembled wig and a beard of rough cotton-wool powdered white and topped by the sort of red knit cap that sailors wore. But since George and Caroline couldn't be expected to know what Santa Claus was supposed to look like, it had generally been agreed that this curious outfit would probably serve the purpose.

And so it did—if the children's screams of delight on discovering their visitor were any indication. Jennifer, for her part, at once took advantage of the noise and hubbub to beat a hasty retreat down the stairs to Mr. Henry's apartment, which lay directly below the schoolroom. Despite her pleadings, Molly had steadfastly refused to divulge how to gain access to a locked chamber, although she had agreed to check herself and make sure the door would be open for Jennifer. Therefore, that young lady wasn't surprised when the knob turned smoothly under her hands and she was able to slip inside without any difficulty whatsoever.

Locating the packet of letters proved as easy as gaining entry to the room. Jennifer found the bundle in the same pocket of the identical coat where they'd been before—a fact that led her to wonder whether the occupant was so slow as to believe himself perfectly above suspicion or only too dull-witted to recognize the stupidity of his actions. Then she hastily thrust aside those thoughts and set herself carefully to copying.

She began with the cipher that Henry referred to in his correspondence but that she hadn't seen before. This she augmented with a letter dated February 10, 1809, to Governor Craig, in which Henry admitted having difficulty with the cipher and suggested using an index with numbers for every letter of the alphabet and for various phrases. Therefore, if he wanted to say "troops are at Albany," he explained, he'd use the number sixteen to stand for "troops," and the number 125 to represent "Albany," and then spell out "are at" with figures corresponding to the letters in those words.

Next, she hastily scribbled copies of the first few letters she'd read the last time that detailed the arrangement between Henry and the governor general and outlined both the scope of his mission and the objective for which he was to undertake his investigations, along with the credential he'd been issued. At this point, Jennifer paused to nibble delicately on the end of her pen. She didn't have sufficient paper and certainly not enough time to copy all of the remaining letters that comprised Henry's reports, and how was she to decide which ones to include? She read quickly through the entire batch and then chose a few that seemed most clearly to indicate how Henry's activities were meant to foster unrest within the United States. For example, in a letter from Windsor, the largest city in eastern Vermont, dated February 19, Henry indicated that although that state wouldn't stand alone against the wishes of the national government, it might unite with other states in a serious plan of resistance to the idea of war with England. And in a letter dated March 7 from Boston, he stated confidently that if war was declared, the legislature of Massachusetts would, in turn, declare itself permanent, invite a Congress to be composed of delegates from the other Federal—presumably, New England—states, and erect a separate government, "to protect their common interests and for reasons of defense." Against whom, Jennifer wondered—the duly constituted government in Washington?

The sound of a door opening upstairs and the noise of several pairs of feet milling about provided her with ample warning that it was time to quit the premises. She bundled the letters back together and replaced them in Henry's coat pocket. Then, after taking a quick look around to make sure all was in order, she slipped out of the room and closed the door firmly behind her. A brief stop in her own apartment to dispose of the evidence of her activities was out of the question, though, since she was afraid of an untimely meeting before she could reach that room. Therefore, she had to be content with darting into the study to stow letters, pen, and ink behind a thick volume of Chaucer which, it occurred to her irrelevantly, seemed rather unlikely reading material for someone of Richard Avery's tepid temperament.

Jennifer had scarcely closed the study door and begun to ascend the stairs when she promptly ran into that same gentleman and his companion. Mr. Henry was still dressed for his role as Santa Claus and leaning heavily upon Richard's arm while making slow work of the business of walking. "Just slipped out to check on the progress of our holiday feast," she invented. "But I promise I stayed long enough to know that your visit was an unqualified success," she informed Henry with a smile. "My hardy congratulations, sir, on a fine performance."

" 's pleasure," Mr. Henry mumbled. "Happy t'be of service."

Richard patted his companion encouragingly on the shoulder, keeping his other hand where it was to prop Henry upright. "A splendid effort, indeed, dear fellow. I'm quite in your debt. But now I'm sure you'd like to get out of those absurd clothes and rest awhile from your exertions, wouldn't you? Yes, I thought so. What?" He leaned closer in order to make out Henry's fading croak. "No—no trouble at all, I promise. I've still plenty of time to get in a little work before dinner." He made sure he was looking at Jennifer when he finished speaking, and then tipped his head meaningfully in the direction of his study.

She had little difficulty interpreting that message, and quietly let herself back into the room to wait until Richard had finished attending to Henry. He finally came in about fifteen minutes later. Without asking, he immediately poured them each a tumbler of sherry before throwing himself wearily into a chair. "I think I must be as muzzy as our poor guest," he admitted, "although doubtless in my case, it's purely the result of my nerves being stretched taut for too long." He began to smile a little, which eased the tiny lines around his eyes and mouth somewhat, Jennifer observed happily.

"But my God, I wish you could have stayed to witness that amazing spectacle," he told her. "I must say I don't know what ever put the notion into his head in the first place, but Henry apparently decided that old Saint Nicholas must have been a bit of a magician, or possibly he was too muddled to remember what it was he was supposed to be doing. At any rate, all of a sudden he started to tell riddles and then to perform a little sleight of hand. The twins thought he was beyond anything great, of course, and if I hadn't known what you were doing when this tour de force was taking place, I probably should have enjoyed it enormously myself." Jennifer began to giggle. "That's right, go ahead and laugh," he told her in a heavy voice. "After all, it isn't your children who now believe that Santa Claus is a consummate trickster!" He began to chuckle despite himself. "Still, it's a rather interesting new way to look at Christmas, ain't it? Well, I mean, if we're supposed to feel joyous and all, what's the matter with feeling like we're attending a certified farce?''

"Nothing that I can think of," Jennifer agreed promptly in amusement. "Save for the fact that such a feeling is altogether out of keeping with the true spirit of the holiday, which—as you're doubtless aware—is for some reason supposed to be solemn and holy, not just joyous. Still, it seems unaccountable to me that those attitudes have somehow become confused in people's minds. Why, the world will think us all heretics for performing such an irreverent display as the one in which Mr. Henry just played the leading role," she announced cheerfully.

Richard smiled at her, and then offered, "Probably—unless, of course, we undertake first to keep that little escapade a secret, and second to ensure that we conduct ourselves in public with our usual, er, decorum."

Jennifer smiled back for a moment. Then she rose and retrieved the copies of Henry's letters from where she'd hidden them earlier and tossed the packet into his lap. "Well, if you truly want to sober up, I'll wager these will bring you to your senses quickly enough. And lest you fall into the trap of dismissing Mr. Henry as nothing but a buffoon, these will remind you that he can also be properly bright-eyed when he chooses to be."

She sipped her sherry and watched as Richard read quickly through the copies she'd made, his face becoming more serious and concerned with each page. Finally, he came to the end of the last one and sighed deeply. He fussed about with the stack of papers for a few moments, tapping all the edges straighter so that they formed a precise pile as if to avoid commenting a little while longer. At last he said slowly, "These form a most convincing case against Henry—and against England too, for that matter. I'll admit now that when you first told me this story, I thought you were merely exaggerating in your own, ah, unique way. But with the evidence that you've amounted, it's hard to see Henry's actions as other than treasonous, and to agree that we've no time to lose in bringing the situation to the immediate attention—''

"Of whom?" Jennifer inserted. "Indeed, I've thought and rethought how we should dispose of our booty, and I must say I'm puzzled as to what we should do next. But it does seem to me that one thing we need to guard against is the letters being used to cause mayhem by one political party or another. Therefore, we ought to place them in more impartial hands—if we can find them. And don't forget that whatever we decide to do with our copies may prove irrelevant when Henry and his confederate also have copies that they'll no doubt peddle to the first interested person or group they encounter."

The two looked momentarily dejected by this reminder, and there was a short silence as they sipped their sherry and considered the prospect that all their careful efforts could still easily go for naught. "It seems to me," Richard ventured at last, "that we must try to discover whom Crillon intends to approach in Washington, and then either find some way to forestall his attempt or get to that person first. And how successful we may be will depend upon what this Mr. Crillon is like and just how skillful he shows himself to be at this little game."

They had the opportunity to form their first impressions of Mr. Henry's partner when Count Edouard de Crillon arrived in New York about a week later and promptly presented his card at No. 30 Wall Street. He was a thickset, balding man, with a bulbous nose that peeped out of a luxuriant black beard and whiskers. He seemed to swagger when he walked, either on account of his thick legs or because that was his preferred method of locomotion. What was readily apparent, however, was that Crillon was as astute as he was charming. Indeed, several hours later, after he'd unpacked his bags and been treated to a splendid supper prepared in his honor by his countryman, Monsieur Fouquet, and despite being plied with a daunting amount of liquor, Crillon still hadn't given the slightest clue as to the particulars of his background or to his immediate plans. In fact, after receiving one vague answer and then another to her questions, Jennifer had been forced to conclude that the man was a veritable master of ambiguity as well as ideas—always providing enough of a response to be considered polite and delivering it in such a personable way as to remain perfectly above reproach, yet never giving anything away. What's more, he didn't appear in the least susceptible to allowing wine or a beautiful woman to get the better of his wits, so that Jennifer and Richard were obliged to admit that Mr. Henry seemed to have chosen the ideal accomplice, given his own decided weaknesses in those same regions.

In fact, some two days later, the two men informed their host that they planned to depart the following morning on the stage for Washington. But when Richard sought to inquire where they planned to lodge, Crillon only tossed off in a disinterested fashion that one boardinghouse was much the same as any other to him. And Henry, perhaps taking a lesson from his companion, turned crafty as well, and merely allowed that since he wasn't certain of his final destination, he was terribly sorry not to be able to supply that information.

That evening found Jennifer and Richard sharing a quiet game of chess in his study. Their resources and energy clearly depleted for the moment, they'd agreed that some sort of diversion was called for in order to prevent fixing their attention once more upon Mr. Henry and his plans or reassigning blame for their failure in not yet having discovered how to thwart his schemes. Luckily, this pastime had proven more than minimally diverting to them both, once they'd found their skill to be nicely matched and their zeal for the game shared equally as well. In fact, about an hour after they'd settled down to play, Molly had stuck her head in the door to see if her presence was required, and observing that they were happily occupied, had promptly discarded all thoughts of propriety in favor of withdrawing again. And if she could have read their minds, she'd have been all the more anxious not to disturb them, for they were both thinking how peaceful they felt at that moment and yet how difficult it appeared, sometimes, to prolong that very pleasant sensation. Therefore, it wasn't surprising that neither heard the study door open some time later or noticed a figure approaching the table where they sat in front of the fireplace, staring at the chessboard, until he spoke.

"Good evening," Lord Somers said calmly, as ever. "Do tell me, Avery—who are those two gentlemen I just passed on the stairs? I swear I've seen the dark one in Paris sometime or other—though it escapes me exactly when—and I promise you he's not to be trusted!"

Chapter 14

JENNIFER GAVE a little yelp of delight. "Oh, Papa!" she exclaimed happily. "How very glad I am to see you!" She jumped up from her chair in order to throw her arms around her father and nestle her head against his chest as she snuggled close to him.

Richard had also risen and now walked over to pump his lordship's hand enthusiastically. "And I, too, am happy to find you safely returned, sir!"

Lord Somers appeared rather taken aback by the warmth of his welcome, and paused to detach himself from his daughter's embrace so that he could remove his traveling cloak and gloves. "But why ever wouldn't I be? Surely you received my note?" he asked in a puzzled voice. "I sent it by special messenger several weeks ago, and the man not only assured me that he'd delivered it, he also brought me one in return that was certainly writ by no other hand than yours," he said, looking questioningly at Jennifer. "Why, he even described you to a hair," he told her, smiling a little at this pun, "so I know he couldn't have been pitching me a tale. And you discovered my real message, did you not? Well then, I'm afraid I don't understand the reason for all this fuss and fervor," he admitted.

Jennifer tugged at his free hand to force him to look down into her face. "It's only that so much has happened while you were away that we're all aflame to tell you every last detail!"

Lord Somers cast another glance around at the cozy scene and took note of the comfortable, if not intimate, relationship that seemed to exist between his daughter and their host. He draped his cloak over the back of a chair before settling into it and crossing his legs. Then he smiled pleasantly from one to the other of his companions and prompted in a helpful fashion, "Now then—why not proceed from the beginning so you won't be tempted to skip any details?"

Jennifer perched on the edge of her own chair and regarded her parent earnestly. "Well, we suspected that Mr. Henry was a spy," she began at what was certainly not the beginning. "That is, I suspected it—and then I found some letters that seemed to prove he was in the employ of the Canadians, well the British, really. Only Richard didn't believe me, of course, so then I tried to steal the letters—actually, I only borrowed them for a while to copy, in order to have some proof, you know. But now we've learned that Mr. Crillon means to try to sell the letters and we don't know to whom. If we could just get there first with our copies—" She finally broke off, realizing from her father's confused expression that she'd been anything but systematic in her narrative and had only managed to muddle the whole story hopelessly instead.

"Perhaps I might try my hand?" Richard suggested, much to the evident relief of Lord Somers, who'd been expecting a different sort of revelation, judging by the atmosphere in the room when he'd entered. "John Henry is a business acquaintance of mine, you see—actually, I originally met him through a mutual friend. He's one of the men you saw on the stairs. The dark bulky fellow is a Frenchman named Edouard Crillon. I take it he's the one you thought you recognized?"

"Yes," his lordship said thoughtfully. "I'm almost positive it was in Paris, though the exact circumstances escape me. As I recall, he was very cozy with several of Napoleon's toadies. Doesn't he style himself a count, or some such nonsense?"

It was Jennifer's turn to look confused. "That's right—Count Edouard de Crillon. But why do you call it nonsense? Mr. Henry told us Crillon had a huge estate near the Spanish border and that his father was a well-known duke.'' She narrowed her eyes and thought for a moment. "In fact," she told her father, "he claimed that Crillon had to flee Napoleon, presumably for political reasons, so how could it be the same man you saw dawdling about with his underlings?"

Lord Somers shook his head sorrowfully. "Entirely possible, love. Don't forget that a title's as easy to invent as a name, and who ever bothers to check the particulars of a fellow's background? What's more, things were in a rare mess in that part of the world when I was there, so even if one had wished to, I doubt it would have been possible to verify Crillon's claims to either family or fortune—and surely it would be much more difficult now. Fact is, I'd lay you odds the man's a counterfeit and that whatever interest he has in this, Mr. Henry should be suspect as well."

Richard looked pleased. "Just what I thought, only I couldn't get a handle on what was making me feel so uneasy. But I fear we're straying a bit from our story, sir." Whereupon he proceeded to relate the following account in a fairly coherent fashion: How John Henry had initially aroused Jennifer's suspicion; what she'd discovered that proved he was in league with England to promote a revolution in America if war was declared; the manner by which Richard had been convinced that Jennifer was right and been led to reevaluate his own loyalties; and exactly how they'd ended up doing something as reprehensible as breaking into Henry's room to copy some of the most damaging of the letters for evidence. "Which brings us to our present dilemma,"he admitted. "Henry and Crillon depart tomorrow on the stage for Washington. Once there, we believe Crillon will try to peddle the letters to the highest bidder. Of course, we'd like to head off that possibility, only we don't know whom he means to approach. And even if we did, we wouldn't have Henry conveniently stashed somewhere nearby to corroborate our version of the situation and to convince the interested party to accept our set of copies as the genuine article."

"Hmmmm," his lordship said only when Richard had finished. "Yes, that last factor does seem to weigh things a little more heavily in their favor," he acknowledged. He thought for a moment. "Didn't you say that neither man actually knows anyone in Washington, and that at best Crillon has only a few letters of introduction?" he asked Jennifer, cocking his head to one side inquiringly.

She nodded. "Well, then, that should even things up nicely, if not give us the advantage instead," her father observed in what she promptly decided was an extremely irritating and entirely obscure fashion.

"What should?" she demanded.

"Why, me—that is to say, my acquaintance," Lord Somers told her. "Don't mean to brag, you know, but I imagine I could safely claim to be on the nod with everyone of any import in the whole of Washington—from Augie Foster, the British minister, and Louis Serieur, the French equivalent, to James Monroe, the secretary of state. In fact, the only person I fancy I haven't met is President Madison himself, though I'd very much like to. From what I hear, he's said to be about as amiable a fellow as one could ever hope to find."

At this point, Jennifer had to make an heroic effort to curb her impatience. "I'm afraid I don't take your meaning," she said, wondering how she could so quickly have forgotten her father's mode of circuitous discourse. "Just how will your acquaintanceship with all these people further our project?"

"By my calling on those connections and asking them to pay our claim special mind, thereby outwitting Crillon at his own game," Lord Somers explained happily. "Well, you must see that I'm the perfect person to represent you in this instance, since neither Henry nor Crillon know who I am or even saw me come in tonight. As a start, I can travel on the same stage with them down to Washington tomorrow and try to get a fix on their plans without their suspecting me in the least. Besides, no matter what they intend to do, it shall certainly take them a little while to be introduced around. And in the meantime, you see, I can quietly advise the appropriate people of my own arrival and be ready to pounce the minute those two make their move. Then, as soon as I discover what's afoot, I can safely send for you both to join me at once without having to be afraid your presence had prematurely sounded the alarm.''

''But you've only just returned, and now you propose to leave again so soon?'' Jennifer protested. *Why the last thing I want is for you to hie yourself off before I can solicit your help in sorting out all my bothersome emotions*, she added somewhat irritably to herself.

''I hate to admit it, but I think the idea's a sound one,'' Richard put in at this point. ''After all, you and I couldn't dog their coattails without one of 'em becoming suspicious. And what's more, we wouldn't be able to gain immediate entry to the highest circles the way your father would, which would only put us back at the same level as Henry and Crillon. So, I think you'll have to agree that we don't seem to have any other choice.''

''Well, I don't agree,'' Jennifer said stubbornly. ''There must be another way we haven't thought of yet. Besides,'' she added, looking beseechingly at her father, ''I don't want you to go when I've so much I need to . . . to discuss with you.'' Then, feeling that she'd allowed herself to stray perhaps a trifle too close to her real reason for not wanting him to leave, she forced herself to amend that statement. ''Well, I mean, we haven't even exchanged two words about your trip, and you were gone more than two months. And you know I'm not the sort who can be satisfied without at least demanding to hear an account of your adventures. What was Niagara like? And for that matter, how did you finally manage to get away from our own soldiers' watchful eye?''

Now, Lord Somers was fully as anxious as his daughter to learn what had transpired during his absence—particularly since he'd observed that her relationship with Richard Avery had clearly undergone a transformation and that she'd also been scrupulously careful so far not to allude to that change at all. Still, he decided, it was scarcely advisable to attempt to seek any information while the gentleman in question was also present. Therefore, he leaned back in his chair and offered casually, ''Oh, the last wasn't much of a trick once the officers in charge got over their astonishment at discovering a peer of the British Empire wandering happily around in the wilderness and then determined that I wasn't up to any mischief which directly concerned the government of either England or Canada. In the meantime, of course, I enjoyed myself hugely by poking into every corner and asking endless questions to feed my insatiable curiosity. Why, I daresay I made such a damned nuisance of myself that the poor fellows were very relieved to see me quit Fort George at last and depart for the other side of the river.''

His lordship paused to smile modestly at the success of what had apparently been a well-planned stratagem. ''As far as the phenomenon of the falls themselves is concerned, though,'' he continued after a moment, ''I doubt my thirst for knowledge could ever be completely quenched, shall we say? Picture an enormous cataract split into two parts: the American side stretching away for a thousand feet in one direction, and the Canadian side extending more than twice that distance in the other direction like an immense horseshoe.'' Lord Somers made a couple of excited, sweeping gestures with his arms, apparently to illustrate that spectacle. ''Good Lord, what I would have given to have been dropped even for a little while onto tiny Goat Island, which sits precariously on the very rim and divides the two sections!'' His eyes sparkled briefly at that notion before he gave himself a shake and attempted to recollect his present surroundings instead. ''But see here—I've rambled on far too long. Tell me: How have things fared these last few months in the more civilized part of the world?'' he asked, turning politely toward Richard.

That gentleman gave a crooked smile and said, ''Oh, we've managed to carry on well enough, though I'm not certain the term 'civilized' is the one I'd choose to apply to some of the activities hereabouts, of late. You see, the Manhattan Company only just finished installing a new pump engine and we're hoping to restore full service to our clients by next week. But during the time the water supply was interrupted for the installation, I'm afraid some members of the public grew rather restless. I hadn't yet had a chance to tell you,'' he continued to Jennifer, ''but two days ago someone took an ax to the front door of our offices, despite the presence of the private guard I'd hired to watch for such attacks. And last night, I learned, our reservoir on Chambers Street was smeared across the front with mud and garbage and the words 'liars' and 'thieves' painted on it in what we at last determined was pig's blood. And that, I'm afraid, is how I've been obliged to keep myself occupied, at any rate, while you were away,'' he concluded, fully aware that this statement wasn't entirely true. One or two things had also claimed his attention—not the least of which had been his lordship's only daughter—and he wouldn't have minded having the opportunity to relate those matters to that same gentleman at all, Richard realized.

Jennifer, whose thoughts had already been moving in a similar direction, now chose to press the point home. ''There, you see—ever so much has happened during only a few short weeks. Why, to be sure, I've a great deal I wish to tell you myself,'' she admitted, looking pleadingly at her father again.

Lord Somers reached out to stroke his daughter's shining hair tenderly for a moment. ''I know, my love. But surely those confidences will keep for a while—will they not? —whereas this contretemps won't, I'm afraid. And anyway, I think it's grossly unfair to let you two have all the fun and not allow me to play a part in this little adventure,'' he complained, in an effort to steer the conversation into other channels.

''That would be impossible,'' Jennifer declared in a firm voice.

''Perhaps,''he admitted meekly with a tiny smile. ''Will it help if I promise to send you a letter at regular intervals, so that you can keep abreast of what progress I've made and also be convinced that I'm not simply gadding about enjoying myself while you've been left behind to cool your heels? Very well then, let's say that I'll write once a week. And I think we may safely dispense with our usual precautionary measures and write uncoded letters for the time being, don't you agree?'' he asked. ''Excellent! Then it seems to me we've only to set our trap and wait patiently until our prey eventually discovers the bait and becomes snared in the bargain!'' he concluded with a relish that, in this case, his daughter couldn't help but find altogether disquieting.

* * *

Jennifer watched her father slip out of the house early the next morning only a few minutes after Mr. Henry and Crillon had departed to catch the stage for Washington. But if she hadn't known who he was, she'd never have recognized the man in the plain cloak and scuffed boots, carrying a small, worn valise, as her relative—and a peer of the British realm. She had to admit that he certainly appeared to be correct in asserting that people responded primarily to the trappings of class and to their expectations of what a lord should be like, rather than to the person himself. And without either the fashionable clothing or the haughty demeanor routinely adopted by members of polite society, Lord Somers blended perfectly into the background—a fact that he was surely counting upon to provide the ideal camouflage behind which to carry out his observations.

But her father's appearance and manners weren't the only things that were disguised, Jennifer reminded herself—or even the most important things, to her way of thinking. By now, if pressed, she would probably have admitted that the whole of her relationship with Richard Avery appeared to be only the slimmest of fabrications based on a series of increasingly dubious pretenses.

She twisted the curtain cord around her fingers as she reviewed their brief history. At first, they'd naturally assumed the roles that her father had assigned them and that they had all initially been convinced would carry them handily through the duration of his absence. Jennifer held the silk rope up to the light and watched as it was temporarily transformed into a stream of living gold. And yet, she thought, it hadn't been simply naiveté that had caused Richard and her to cling so tenaciously to the guises of employer and governess. Rather, they'd depended on these roles to provide a structure in which both of them could comfortably manage for a while.

She, however, was inclined to confess that that arrangement hadn't proven entirely satisfactory. Of course, their subsequent attempts at pretending to appear to be first casual acquaintances and then mere companions hadn't fared much better. But his latest fiction of being co-conspirators was by far the most unwieldy to date. Why not grant that it was only another ruse—a way to avoid admitting that they sought each other's company for reasons that actually had very little to do with treason or treachery? And although Jennifer told herself that she was perfectly prepared to concede a deepening attachment to Richard, she was also aware that his feelings about their relationship still remained as much a mystery to her as she would have guessed they did to Richard as well.

What's more, Jennifer decided, if one were to engage in any discussion of disguises, it certainly ought to begin with Richard Avery. After all, didn't he still seem bent on attempting to appear the very sort of man she was just beginning to perceive that he was not? Although he preferred to avoid such issues altogether, he hadn't been able to conceal the loving father lurking behind his dutiful and unforgiving exterior or the curious mind that hid beneath the dogmatic way he often expressed his views. It was these same dichotomies that intrigued Jennifer most and that she longed to bring to light and explore in turn as one might a series of rare and precious treasures. But so far she'd been unable to conduct such an examination.

She was delighted, therefore, when Richard came looking for her the next afternoon to make what sounded like a thoroughly uncharacteristic proposal. She was in the schoolroom putting things to rights after a particularly strenuous history lesson, during which she and her charges had reenacted the Revolutionary battle of Harlem Heights. Jennifer and Molly had represented British soldiers while George and Caroline played the Continental army. In the course of attempting to stop the English advance up the island of Manhattan, the children had become enthusiastic about ensuring that the redcoats received a "proper drubbing," as George had phrased it. The results of the twins' successful rout had been overturned furniture, a burst pillow, and the scattering of most of their toys around the room.

Jennifer was retrieving the latter items and stowing them in the toybox when Richard peered tentatively into the room. She offered him a friendly smile and continued to pile blocks and playthings into the wooden chest. Apparently deciding that her expression had been sufficient invitation,

Richard crossed the floor, bent to free a rag doll from beneath one leg of the table, and righted a chair before folding himself carefully onto its tiny seat. He paused to take in the chaotic scene for a moment. Then, because he also knew the general proclivities of the room's inhabitants, he returned Jennifer's smile and asked curiously, "Who won?"

"Oh, the Americans, of course," Jennifer assured him in a serious voice. "We may undertake to study history somewhat differently in our schoolroom, but I promise you we'd never consider changing the course of actual events. George and Caroline had the battle admirably well in hand from the start," she advised, and in a few sentences outlined the cause of the room's disarray.

Richard, whose attention had promptly wandered to a happy contemplation of the speaker's face and figure, called himself reluctantly to order when Jennifer finished. "I'm delighted to learn that we may still call ourselves an independent country," he told her with another smile. He looked down at the doll he was cradling in his lap and then held it at arm's length for a better scrutiny, before observing with a touch of regret, "Yet, if the children are spending their time playing soldier, then they probably haven't any interest in trifles such as this."

"I wouldn't say they weren't interested, precisely," Jennifer temporized, feeling suddenly interested herself in learning what had prompted Richard's observation. "It's only that their old toys are now being put to different uses. I'll have you know that you're holding one of the best scouts in the American army in your hands!" She examined the tattered doll again and then allowed, "Though I must say the poor thing does look as if it's long since had its day."

Richard attempted to plump up the doll's body where it had been squashed by its encounter with the table. He then straightened its plain cotton jacket, propped the figure on one knee, and stared at it for a moment. "Do you know," he said in a thoughtful voice, "I've had this very same subject on my mind recently—or since Christmastime, at any rate."

Jennifer could barely prevent her jaw from dropping open

in astonishment. "What subject—dolls?" she managed to ask finally.

"Oh, not just dolls—other toys too, naturally," Richard explained.

"Naturally," Jennifer repeated, She gazed at the speaker in fascination and begged, "Pray, do continue."

"It occurred to me that the children haven't received any new playthings for several years," Richard went on slowly, "and this doll is a perfect example of how they've outgrown or worn out what they do have." He hesitated, dropping his head self-consciously for a moment before raising it again and fixing Jennifer with a candid look. "You see, I've come to realize that one must actively foster the childlike side of one's nature in order to retain a viable perspective on life as one grows older. And what better way to help George and Caroline along the path on which, thankfully, you've already started them by ensuring that they're supplied with things that encourage their imaginations to soar and allow their sense of wonder to be unleashed? So I thought, perhaps, that we all might make an excursion with the goal of addressing the current lack of those crucial supplies." He gave Jennifer a shy grin. "Besides, I'd heartily enjoy the excuse to put aside my dry old papers for one afternoon in favor of stuffing my head with the possibilities of whirligigs and whimmy diddles."

"With *what*?" Jennifer squeaked.

Richard appeared amused by her response. "Traditional American toys," he explained, "to which I will see that you're shortly introduced."

A half-hour later, the twins and their three adult companions marched eagerly down the front steps of No. 30 Wall Street and turned in the direction of the waterfront. It was the kind of clear, cold day typical of New York winters, and the group was so well bundled that maneuvering along the icy streets required a concentrated effort. Even then, their progress was slow and their movements so jerky and comical that Molly was overheard to mutter that they looked like a family of ducks stranded on shore after misplacing their pond.

That image was appropriate to their destination, because

when they turned down the street leading to the wharf, they caught their first real glimpse of the enormous flock of seabirds who made that fascinating habitat their home. They threaded their way along the docks through hogsheads bursting with rice and tea from China, barrels of fine woolens from England, and chests of delicate porcelain from Italy. Enough flour and sugar to supply countless households for a year were being unloaded by sailors who swore colorfully in a half-dozen languages as they staggered under their hefty burdens. Along with these necessities were luxuries to match the most discriminating tastes in everything from wines and liquors to silks and linens.

Jennifer had just concluded that the French and English blockades appeared to be having little effect on trade when Richard chose to comment on the same fact. "Odd, ain't it, how normal everything looks," he observed. He tore a banana off an enormous bunch and tossed a coin to a grinning seaman. Then he neatly pulled down the peel despite his thick woolen gloves, took a large bite, and chewed appreciatively for a moment. "What do you say we forego all talk of politics and other serious subjects for the day? That's not the reason we came here, after all," he reminded her.

Richard stood smiling down at Jennifer. His dark head was bare despite the chilly weather, allowing the sun to pick out highlights as red as her own, and he had an unguarded, eager expression on his face. In fact, he looked so utterly appealing that Jennifer was tempted to promise that she'd gladly discuss anything he wished if only he'd fold her into his arms for a single, glorious minute. "Yes, I believe you said we were to look for whammy doddles," she forced herself to say lightly.

At this remark, the group promptly burst into delighted laughter. "No—that isn't exactly what I said," Richard said gently when he had caught his breath. "I said we'd try to find some whimmy diddles. *You* may feel free to search for whammy doddles if you like—though I'm afraid I don't have a clue as to what those may be!"

Molly looked quickly from one to the other of her companions, decided in relief that their romance appeared to be developing nicely without the need for any interference from her, and resolved to offer a different sort of assistance. "I think I know where we can find what you're after," she said, turning toward Richard. "The sailors sit down by the water and whittle when they've finished their work," she explained. "They make all kinds of simple wooden toys that they sell for a few pennies. If you ask me, though, just watching some of 'em carve is worth the price alone."

Molly's companions were soon able to agree with her claim. After leading them to where a row of seamen were bent over small piles of shavings, she pointed out one man who was expertly using his jackknife to turn a piece of wood into a whirligig: a figure of a man with long, flat arms shaped like paddles that fastened to his body with wooden pegs. Whirligigs were meant to be "Sunday toys," Molly told them. On that day, when children were forbidden to play noisy games, they could take the whirligig, hold it aloft, and run fast until the air made the figures' flat arms whirl around in the manner that had given the toy its name. Richard bought two that sported the painted uniforms of American soldiers, and the group moved on down the line of carvers

They found another sailor shaping the mysteriously named whimmy diddles. At first glance, this toy looked like nothing but two plain sticks: one stick was notched in the middle with a little propeller blade fastened to one end, and the other stick was smooth. To make the toy work, Molly grasped the notched stick in her left hand and, holding the smooth stick in her right rubbed it lightly across the notches until the vibration made the propeller begin to whirl. In some magical way, Molly was able to make the blades move first in one direction, and then suddenly stop and turn in the opposite direction. The twins and Richard and Jennifer took turns trying to duplicate this trick, but although they could start the propeller twirling, no one could make it change directions except Molly. Finally, she relented and showed them how touching the far side of the notched stick while rubbing made the propeller turn to the right, and touching the near side of the stick made the blades stop and then spin to the left.

After purchasing enough whimmy diddles so that they could each have one, the group moved on again. They watched other sailors fashioning wonderful jumping jacks from a couple of sticks and a few pieces of wood. For these, a carved figure or "jack" was suspended on a thread between one end of two sticks; by squeezing the other end of the sticks around a block and tightening the thread, the figure flipped over in the air like an acrobat.

They wandered around for some time, marveling at the ingenuity of the carvers and acquiring other samples of their skill. But after a while, Jennifer noticed that Richard lingered the longest beside those sailors who were making toy boats. He seemed to be looking for something in particular, she decided, because before leaving, he asked every man a question. Finally, she drew closer and watched him repeat this performance with a fellow who was just putting the last touches on an elegant wooden sailing vessel. This time, however, she made sure that she heard the answer to Richard's question.

"No—no canoes," the sailor told Richard. "Why, it ain't nothing grand to carve a canoe, and anyhow, there's no call for such simple things—leastways, not when folks can have something as fine as this frigate." He held up the carved ship for Richard to admire. Then, seeing that Jennifer was nearby and watching his customer closely, he jumped quickly to what seemed an obvious conclusion. "Why not buy this pretty gewgaw for your wife?" he wheedled, waggling his head in Jennifer's direction. Just then the twins ran up to try to persuade Jennifer to come with them. "Besides, if your lady don't fancy it, doubtless one of your children would," the sailor pressed again.

In the past, being mistaken for husband and wife would have proven disconcerting, if not highly embarrassing, to the two parties involved. But perhaps because of their strange circumstances or the agreeable feeling of enjoying each other's company, Jennifer and Richard were content merely to exchange a tolerant smile over the sailor's head. "Very well," Richard agreed, "we shall buy it. But even though you think it a small challenge to carve a canoe, I can tell you it's no mean challenge to paddle one." He dropped a few coins into the man's outstretched hand, took the boat, and presented it to Jennifer with a small bow. Then, offering the fellow a last filip, he grasped Jennifer's arm firmly and steered her away.

It took Jennifer a few moments to deal with the heady sensation of Richard's hand on her elbow and the fact that he'd just given her a first—albeit, rather strange—present. At last, she observed in what she hoped was a strictly casual way, "I didn't know you'd ever paddled a canoe."

"Actually, I haven't," Richard admitted bluntly, "though I've always wanted to. When I was much younger, I dreamed of taking a canoe down the length of the canal that runs from The Collect to the river." He colored slightly and added, "But I daresay the whole idea was nothing except a silly boyhood fantasy."

Jennifer gave him a long, searching look. "Oh, I wouldn't say that at all," she assured him. "But whatever happened to that dreamy boy of long ago?"

Richard stopped so abruptly that Jennifer bumped into his side. Apologizing for his clumsiness and giving her arm an unconscious little pat as if to assure himself that she was all right, he moved on. After a few more steps he paused again and then suddenly smiled down at her in a delighted fashion. "Why, I believe, with your help, that I'm just in the process of rediscovering him," he confessed happily.

Despite feeling heartened by Richard's revelation and glad to be in his confidence at last, Jennifer was still at sixes and sevens for several days following the excursion to the wharf and her father's departure. Much as she'd longed before Lord Somers's return to confide her feelings for Richard Avery to him, she soon discovered that she was strangely reluctant to do so in the few hours he'd spent at No. 30 Wall Street. Why she suddenly changed her mind, however, wasn't any clearer to her than the feelings themselves. Instead, she'd been content to trail after her father while he made the minimal preparations necessary for him to assume his new role, only sharing an occasional commonplace on either her activities or those of Molly and the twins. But far from putting him at ease on the question of whether it was advisable to leave her once more in Mr. Avery's care, Jennifer's comments were so clearly meant to obscure the real state of her mind—and her heart—that his lordship yearned to be able to have a few private words with Avery himself. What's more, he even had the distinct impression that Richard harbored the same wish but, because Jennifer refused to let him out of her sight, had had to give up any hope of accomplishing such a task. In fact, Lord Somers decided the three of them were like the misguided characters in one of Shakespeare's plays—each secretly knowing, or believing they knew, how the others felt until the whole thing was so thoroughly confused that only an open sharing of information would alleviate the total disaster that would surely result if they failed to do so. And having a good deal of sympathy for the two people he'd left behind in that unenviable state, his lordship took great pains to ensure that his first letter arrived less than a week after his exit from New York, thoughtfully sending it by another special messenger in order to lessen the time it would have taken to arrive through ordinary channels.

Jennifer had been trying to distract herself again with a little mending and had finally been persuaded to carry her basket and needle into Richard's study and to join Molly in bearing him company while he struggled to prepare yet another report for the Common Council. Thus, they happened to present an unusual picture of domestic harmony when Walters entered to announce in dubious tones that Lady Somers had a visitor. Upon being exhorted by her to produce the person at once, Walters returned a few minutes later with a man whose tiny stature made Jennifer wonder whether he might not at one time have been a jockey. This impression was supported by the fact that he barely glanced around the room before heading over to the windows and peering anxiously down at the street, presumably looking for his horse, Jennifer decided.

Whatever he saw—or didn't see, as it turned out—appeared to satisfy him, however. Turning away from the window, he looked from one to the other of his three hosts and offered, by way of explanation, "Just making certain that man took care of things, like he promised. Poor Harry's cold and tired and wants a warm mash and a rubdown.''

Hoping that the last remark did indeed refer to the man's horse and not to himself, Jennifer ventured, "I take it you've come up from Washington? Have you brought a letter from my father, perhaps?''

The man paused to gaze slowly around the room for the first time before staring even more closely at the speaker and then scratching his head. "Aye—I've a letter, all right. But I'm blowed if I'd of guessed that the man who gave it to me was your pa, miss. Why, I'd have thought he was this lady's father instead," he offered, looking at Molly. "He seemed a common sort of bloke, y'know—no fancy clothes or big speeches, just a plain man with a proposal to make and a bit of money to seal the bargain. Ordinarily, I work at the racecourse taking care of the horses, on account of I used to ride a little myself. But when winter comes, the races are over, and I have to look for a room instead of a stable. Usually, I find a job minding ponies at one of the coaching inns. I met your pa when he came in on the stage, y'see. Well, after a couple of days, we'd got to talking and he asks would I like to trot up to New York and deliver a letter for him, and I admit I might have a mind to take such a trip, and so, here I am.'' He leaned a trifle closer and confided, "The thing is, miss, stable work's awfully dull and a man can quickly get bored if he ain't careful. That's why, even if he hadn't paid me so handsome, I warrant I'd have been off like a shot anyways.''

Jennifer smiled at this artless speech and accepted the letter the man held out to her. Then she looked inquiringly at Richard, who promptly took her meaning that they ought to extend a little hospitality to the traveler. "If you'd care to go back downstairs, I'm sure my housekeeper, Mrs. Booth, would be happy to fix you up with a bit of supper and a bed," he offered.

Just as if they were playing house, Molly thought, looking from Jennifer to Richard and then wondering if the same idea had occurred to either of them. She watched the man toss his head vigorously up and down several times the way she'd seen a stallion do when passing a mare in heat.

"Well, I could use a serving of warm mash 'bout now, myself," he agreed, accepting her offer to show him downstairs with a grateful smile.

After they'd gone, Jennifer and Richard lost no time in drawing two chairs near the fire and unfolding the sheets of paper. Then, bending their heads close together—the better, they no doubt told themselves, to decipher Lord Somers's casual scrawl—they began to read.

"My dearest Jennifer: What an interesting career I believe I could make of traveling endlessly around America! One meets so very many curious individuals and feels perfectly free to reveal as much or as little as one wishes to one's fellow travelers, and yet still discover sufficient about them to remain perpetually amused. Take two of the men who were on the stage with me from New York, for example. One, a Mr. John Henry, described himself as a 'commercial traveler' and indicated that he was on his way south to conduct a little business. I think he might ordinarily have been a very pleasant fellow, except that he seemed unaccountably ill at ease—muttering under his breath a great deal and frequently resorting to a few sips from a pocket flask, which thankfully appeared to have a calming effect. Perhaps, it occurred to me, he was suffering from some sort of nervous condition."

At this point, Jennifer started to smile, and after a sidelong glance at Richard, they both began to laugh. "It's too bad that Mr. Henry's nerves seem to be plaguing him," she got out finally, trying without much success to look serious.

"Indeed," Richard echoed. "Possibly the poor fellow's in the wrong line of work."

"At any rate," they read, turning back to Lord Somers's letter, "Henry seemed on good terms with the other man, a Mr. Crillon, though both were a trifle vague about how they'd met. Still, the farther we got from New York, the more agitated Henry became and the more effort his friend had to exert to calm him down. In fact, the only thing that seemed to distract Henry at all was when Crillon began to talk about Castile St. Martine, his family estate in the south of France. How big was it, Henry wanted to know, and what did they grow up there, and could one live there year-round? Why, you'd think with all his questions he meant to leave at once and take up residence there himself.''

Richard looked thoughtfully at Jennifer for a moment. ''Do you recall my wondering just why Crillon had chosen to become involved in this whole affair? Well, I must say that given your father's information and his sentiments on the matter, the smell seems to be getting worse, to put it bluntly. I've no doubt that Crillon means to make a bit of money out of Henry—in fact, I wouldn't be surprised to learn that it was he who suggested trying to sell the letters in the first place, once he'd learned of their existence. But now I'm beginning to think that we might be asking the wrong question. Perhaps we should be wondering, instead, why Henry needs Crillon as his partner. After all, how can it be to Henry's advantage to be obliged to split the profits of this enterprise with someone else?''

''Well, I imagine he needs the man because he has neither the nerve, nor perhaps the connections, to be able to carry off the auction of the documents himself,'' Jennifer offered. ''And then, too, if Crillon did propose the idea in the beginning, shouldn't that be worth a little something?''

''Yes, it should. But what else does Crillon possess that appears to interest Mr. Henry? His estate in Lebeur—correct? And why should your father indicate that it seemed almost as if Henry were considering residing there?''

Jennifer thought for a moment. ''Because after his letters are made public,'' she reasoned slowly aloud, ''it will be revealed that he acted as a spy for both the British and the Americans, and he won't be able to remain in the United States any longer. And we already know that he can't return to Canada, and that he wishes at all costs to avoid England— particularly given as how the disclosure of his employment shall certainly make him a less than welcome guest on those shores.''

''Exactly. And therefore, wouldn't he be overjoyed to learn of the possibility of settling down on a large, quiet estate in France? And moreover, since the current owner of that estate is unable to make use of it—being an exile as he is—what would be more convenient for them both than for Crillon to offer the property to Henry in exchange, let's say, for suitable recompense from the sum Henry will realize from the sale of the letters?''

Jennifer looked only half-convinced by this argument. ''I imagine that's a possibility, of course, only we don't yet have enough information for me to think it more than flimsy at this point. Besides, what if he doesn't succeed in selling the letters after all? Then he won't be obliged to seek refuge in France or anywhere else, since there'd be no reason why he couldn't remain in the United States. And without the cash he expects to earn from the sale, he wouldn't be able to buy the estate from Crillon, if that's what he means to do.'' She hesitated. ''Still, Henry did seem confident of their ability to locate a ready buyer. And anyway, I can't see that it matters greatly if Henry leaves the country or not as long as we hold the whip hand.''

''Perhaps that's true,'' Richard admitted. ''It's just that I'm clinging to the hope that we can not only beat him at his game, but also find a way to punish him. But then, no doubt that attitude's merely a remnant of my old way of thinking that there's only one right way to do something—and in this case, the right thing to do would be to hold the miscreant accountable.''

Jennifer could think of no comment to offer at this point, and the two returned to Lord Somers's letter once again. ''At any rate, Henry left our company altogether in Philadelphia, where he hired a private carriage to continue his journey alone. Crillon seemed to have known of Henry's plan in advance, for he didn't appear in the least surprised. When I wondered aloud where his friend might be bound, however, he professed not to know. I subsequently enjoyed a pleasant chat with Crillon, who can be a most charming fellow when it suits him, and thus passed the duration of the journey in a very agreeable and productive manner. Crillon has made some very advantageous connections since his arrival in this country, and boasted to me of carrying a letter of recommendation from Governor Gerry of Massachusetts to President Madison himself. But even though he clearly expects to move in the best social circles, his personal finances are bound to be strained in order to permit him to do so. He lodges in a respectable but hardly opulent boardinghouse called O'Neale's Franklin House. As for me, I've taken a room at a small, quiet hotel near the Capitol, which seemed to offer more privacy than stopping with friends should have. Tonight, I shall surely rest well after my trip and tomorrow begin my explorations of the city, etc. Love, J.S.''

"Look, there's a postscript," Richard said, pointing to a scribble at the bottom of the page: "Water and feed Jeremy, please, and then send him on his way the day after you receive this, so I can turn him back around to New York with the next installment of my adventures within a week's time. His services have been engaged to ensure the safety of a frank correspondence, which I trust you'll agree is absolutely necessary."

Jennifer looked up at Richard and gave a wry smile. "Jeremy, I take it, must be our new courier, and Harry one of his horses. I wasn't altogether certain, you know. Well, at least we appear to be keeping up our end of the arrangement. Though I must say that merely standing about doesn't suit my temperament any more than it probably does poor Harry's. And I warn you that if we're to pursue this course for very long, I'm liable to become quite fractious and disagreeable, besides."

"Then I don't think you need worry," Richard said, returning her smile. "I imagine, you see, that neither Mr. Henry's nerves nor Mr. Crillon's pocketbook are prepared to support a very lengthy siege."

In this assumption, Richard was apparently correct, as Lord Somers's second letter, received a week later, testified. The three friends greeted Jeremy's arrival with a tableau remarkably similar to the one they'd assumed on the previous occasion. This time, however, Molly volunteered so promptly to escort the messenger downstairs that it caused Jennifer, at least, to stare thoughtfully after her for a moment as she disappeared in the direction of the kitchen, and then to wonder briefly if leaving her alone with Richard could actually be what her former chaperone had in mind.

"My dearest Jennifer," they read. "Although it is apparently fashionable to ridicule the lack of amenities in this nation's capital, I have taken a decided fancy to the city, for it has a certain style that I find at once unique and delightful. Where else, after all, would one find the following purely pastorale scene: cattle browsing happily near the White House, shacks hastily thrown up to house the burgeoning populace, fewer sidewalks than mud sloughs (if not virtual swamps) in damp weather, and partridge nesting comfortably on the Capitol steps? All of this, mind you, is in the midst of the beginnings of Pierre L'Enfant's grand design for this seat of government. Still, there are the usual diversions available to members of fashionable society, and both Mr. Crillon and I have been taking full advantage of the musicales, card parties, and dinners that abound. Indeed, Mr. Crillon appears to be cutting quite a dash, and is invited everywhere and widely sought after by one hostess after another, including Dolly Madison herself, I hear. I, too, am enjoying my share of invitations and, in fact, frequently encounter Mr. Crillon at such functions. But it is amazing what a perfect disguise is offered by one's choice of clothing: Don evening dress and a miraculous change is apparently wrought, and one's identity wholly converted. Why, when we were introduced a couple of days ago by Monroe's wife, Crillon gave me a perfectly blank look and then confessed quite honestly that he didn't believe he'd had the pleasure of meeting me before."

Jennifer and Richard paused to exchange a knowing smile before continuing to read: "It occurs to me, however, that Crillon may be a trifle out of his depth in this affair, or at least that his judgment doesn't always appear entirely sound. For example, it was whispered that he'd ridiculed the modest ten dollars per week price of his boardinghouse and insisted on paying twenty-five dollars instead! Such an action is doubtless only meant to create an impression and is negligible in the long run. Nevertheless, the fellow appears to have been careless in enough little ways to cause a few rumors to begin circulating regarding whether he actually is who he claims to be. And furthermore, someone was apparently seen making a few inquiries to that effect at his residence as well.''

"I wonder who authorized such an investigation." Richard mused. "If Crillon by this time has started to hint at his purpose for being in Washington, it seems to me it could be any one of several parties: the British, who might want to prevent his succeeding in selling off Henry's letters; the French, who might want to protect themselves, if they're considering becoming involved in the purchase; or the Americans, for similar reasons as the French."

Jennifer, who'd continued to skim ahead in the letter while Richard was speaking, now stopped to regard him in open admiration. "Precisely what my father thinks. He says that he made a casual inquiry along those lines to Foster, the British minister, but the man was totally disinterested and only wanted to tout about how his mother had just been promoted from mistress to wife of the duke of Devonshire! But when he raised the matter with the French minister, he got a rather different reaction. Listen:

" 'Ran into Serieur at a reception given Thursday by Mrs. John Van Ness, a woman reputed to be the richest heiress in the country. I'd forgotten what a melancholy-looking fellow Serieur is—a fact most of the matrons here loudly attribute to his unmarried state but which, he admitted to me, is due to his finding most American food completely indigestible. He told me that Crillon had approached him and confided a very strange story: Aboard ship en route to America, a Captain John Henry had become friendly and shown him letters proving that three years ago Britain had engaged Henry to foment a rebellion in Massachusetts. Now, Henry was apparently at odds with his former employer and willing to part with the letters for a consideration. Might France be interested in such a proposal, Crillon wondered? Serieur was ready to acknowledge that if evidence of subversive British activity in New England was put before the American public, it would doubtless create a furor beside which Napoleon's actions would pale. Nevertheless, Serieur is a very crafty fellow and far too cautious to commit himself to Crillon—or so he assured me, at any rate. He recommended that Crillon contact the State Department to discover if his information wouldn't receive a better reception from the Americans than it had from him. And then, perhaps seeking to demonstrate how eager France was to prove herself an ally of the United States, Serieur undertook to speak with Monroe directly about Henry's letters and Crillon's proposal, though damned if I was able to learn what Monroe's response had been to his story.' ''

Jennifer sat back and gave her head a shake as if to clear her thoughts, an action that sent her curls bouncing and caused one to tumble appealingly down over her forehead. ''It seems to me that matters are certainly proceeding apace, don't you agree?''

Richard nodded, dragging his eyes reluctantly away from that tantalizing curl and making an almost visible effort to pay attention to what Jennifer was saying.

''Let's sum up what we know,'' she went on, ticking the items off on her fingers. ''First, the British are clearly not involved, since presumably their minister would at least know if they were attempting to stop Crillon. Second, the French don't appear to be interested in doing business with him either. Which brings us to the third point—that it now seems likely our 'friend' will focus his attention on the Americans and, depending on his powers of persuasion, shall endeavor to make them his partners.'' She paused to scan the remaining half-page of the letter. ''Fortunately, Papa seems to realize this, too,'' she announced, ''for he says he means to try to have a private word with Monroe before he can be approached by Crillon. What effect this may have he doesn't know, since Monroe will doubtless still wish to speak with Crillon himself.''

''Yes, but even so, at least it will serve to set up his guard, I should think, so that he won't be tempted to agree immediately to whatever Crillon proposes,'' Richard said. He considered that idea for a moment. ''Indeed, I confess I don't see how the outcome of your father's intentions can be anything but to the good,'' he concluded.

On that note, the two parted for the evening. As Jennifer climbed the stairs to her bedchamber, however, her companion's last remark continued to echo in her head. There it was again, that notion of ''good intentions.'' Well, she simply didn't believe that merely because one meant well, the results of one's actions were always necessarily beneficial—and what's more, her experience seemed to confirm that conclusion. Why, she'd nearly begun to think that her father's real intention in traipsing off to Washington so precipitously had been to see if he couldn't manage to improve on his daughter and Richard having become conspirators by making them consorts as well. Certainly, he'd either overlooked or forgotten the fact that without his blessing, no formal agreement could be reached, and since he'd disappeared without bestowing it, matters were destined to remain at a standstill until he did. True, this little intrigue had served increasingly to throw the two of them together. Yet so far, nothing whatsoever appeared to have come from all this new-found intimacy that she could discover. For one thing, Richard hardly seemed the sort of man to be overcome by a passionate desire to do anything impetuous or unseemly. And for another thing, she admitted slowly, she doubted she'd have the slightest idea how to deal with him if he should suddenly decide to modify his approach. Why did it seem as if the faster events moved in the public arena, the more they dragged to a halt in the private one? All too often now she had to admit feeling as if she were in a state of suspended animation, waiting for some portent or divine act to awaken her and bring her back to life again.

Chapter 15

JENNIFER WASN'T alone in observing that her relationship with a certain gentleman appeared lately to have grown becalmed. Richard, too, felt as if matters between them had reached a certain point and there had become stuck—through neither conscious choice nor effort—waiting for some outside force such as a change in the wind to give them a much-needed push in a new direction.

In fact, in his own mind, he often likened the situation to a kind of ocean voyage. First, there had been all the bustling about in order to provision for the journey, the excitement of putting to sea, and a brief period of making steady progress. This had been followed by what hc thought of as a series of violent storms that had threatened to sink their vessel and had caused sufficient damage to require putting into port for repairs. When they'd set sail again, it had been with the mistaken impression that all was now well, so that they'd been caught unawares by a freakish squall that had wrecked the sails, broken the mast, and left them adrift on strange waters. True, things were calm enough for the moment, and they'd ample food and water to last for a while. But they were entirely at the mercy of the elements, and the uncertainty of not knowing in which direction land lay, plus the temptation to begin rowing nonetheless—if only to feel that he was doing something to extricate them from this helpless situation—was beginning to weigh heavily upon him.

There must be some special significance in the fact that he kept referring to water and trips to or on the sea, Richard thought idly to himself. First there had been his recollection of wanting to paddle a canoe down the canal from The Collect, then the excursion to the docks in search of toy boats, and now this ridiculousness. He looked down at the shavings covering the top of his writing table and at the inexpertly carved but unmistakable shape of a canoe that was at last emerging from the small block of wood. Then, recognizing that both his line of thinking and his present enterprise were completely uncharacteristic of the man most people knew as Richard Avery, he smiled broadly—something else he'd found himself apt to do at odd moments lately.

Odd too, he mused as he picked a splinter out of his thumb with the jackknife it had taken him several days to locate in a bottom drawer, but he just didn't feel the same as he used to. He laid down his knife and began to thrum his fingers on the table. But what could be wrong when he was happily closeted in his study as usual, free to be alone with his thoughts? His fingers paused in mid-air. Why, that was precisely the trouble, he realized slowly: he wasn't happy to be alone, engaged in some solitary pursuit and isolated from the rest of the world anymore. He was also growing tired of merely sitting around thinking instead of *doing*. And the longer he continued to remain indecisive, the more lethargic he began to feel—as if he were caught in a circle that tended to perpetuate itself.

Well, he decided abruptly, he was determined to break out of that pattern once and for all. But exactly how was he to accomplish that little trick? he wondered. Then by chance his eyes happened to fall again on the wooden canoe, and he began to have a clue where he might find the answer to his question.

Later that afternoon, Jennifer and Molly returned from a walk with the twins to discover a sealed note at each of their places at the table in the schoolroom. "Isn't this your father's hand?" Jennifer asked George and Caroline, examining the elegant writing that spelled out "Lady Jennifer Somers" on the front of her copy.

"I think so," George said, peering dubiously at his own "Master George Avery."

At this point, Caroline, who'd been the only one practical enough to open her letter immediately, breathed happily, "Oh—a party! But what's a 're-gotta'?"

Jennifer peeked over her shoulder. "A regatta," she corrected after a moment. "It's a boat race." She paused to scan the note, which was written in the same neat script as the outside. "Why, it *is* an invitation!" she exclaimed in surprise, and then proceeded to read the contents aloud: "Your presence is requested tomorrow afternoon at a Winter Festival in Lispenard's Meadows. Games! Refreshments! Main Event: a Grand Regatta! Everyone eligible! All entrants receive a prize! Vessels must be handmade and able to travel on ice. Festivities begin at 2 o'clock! Transportation will be provided!"

Jennifer sat back and looked at Molly. "What do you think of that fantastic message?" she inquired in a bewildered voice.

"I think we'd all best get to work making our boats for the regatta," Molly answered calmly. "Assuming, of course,

that you mean to enter one, for I promise you that I do.''
She emphasized her decision with a couple of loud sniffs,
and then sat back and offered Jennifer a mildly curious
smile, as if inviting her to find an objection to that response.

Molly's suggestion was soon seized upon by her companions, and they spent the remainder of that day and the first
half of the next designing what at least three of them
secretly hoped would be the winning entry in the race.
During all those hours, they didn't catch a single glimpse of
Richard Avery. This fact in itself wasn't particularly unusual, except that Jennifer had immediately suspected that it
was Richard who had dreamed up the Winter Festival to
cure their doldrums. And it wasn't long before she found
herself more interested in determining what had prompted
that gentleman to organize such an event rather than in
manufacturing a speedy vessel. It was only the pleas of the
twins that she enter into the spirit of the celebration and not
spoil their pleasure that goaded Jennifer, in the end, into
making a boat at all.

At exactly two o'clock the following afternoon, Walters
knocked on the schoolroom door to announce that a sleigh
had arrived to take them to the festival. When they trooped
downstairs, they found that it was the household's own
vehicle that awaited them. It had been so completely transformed by swags of colored bunting and bunches of straw
flowers, however, that the four guests applauded the cre-
ator's ingenuity. And Jennifer, for her part, immediately
began to wonder when she might next contrive to have a
private word with the gentleman who was surely responsible
for orchestrating what was already turning out to be a most
enchanting diversion.

Their arrival at the meadows promptly dispelled any
doubts about the identity of the aforementioned individual.
No sooner had the sleigh pulled to a halt beside the skating
pond than Richard Avery came forward to greet them,
wearing a distinctly proprietary air. He was also wearing
formal evening dress, Jennifer noted absently, despite the
fact that it was still daytime, and he looked so incredibly
handsome as he helped them out of the vehicle that her heart
gave a thump of pure joy just looking at him. A moment

later she almost thought that organ had decided to stop briefly altogether. Richard, perhaps carried away by the spectacle he'd created and only—or so he told himself, at any rate—thoroughly immersed in his role as master of festivities, had bent over her hand with a flourish. But then, unable to resist any longer, he'd pressed it to his lips for a lingering kiss that suddenly made Jennifer aware of how much she longed for this delightful activity to become a daily routine. And when he raised his head, Richard's face reflected such a transparent happiness that she couldn't refrain from giving the hand holding hers an affectionate little squeeze before slowly withdrawing from his clasp.

"Here now, sir," Jennifer chided in a gentle attempt to break the mood, "I warrant you're looking far too pleased with yourself for your own good. Do you mean to show us your creation or merely keep us standing still until we all become icicles, I wonder?"

Richard smiled good-naturedly at that jibe and shook his head. "No, we wouldn't want that," he agreed, "leastways, not when I've gone to such trouble to arrange this little entertainment." He led the group over to a smaller nearby pond. At one end of the bank there were two gaily decorated tables: the first held a tempting array of meats and cheeses and dainty cakes over which Ellen rather nervously presided, and the second was covered with the wrapped packages that they learned were the prizes for the regatta. A handy fire offered a way for the guests to keep warm and to enjoy a fragrant mug of hot chocolate or mulled cider. The surface of the pond had been marked off with the course for the boat race and an area for curling. In the latter game, Richard told them, participants threw round, smooth stones along the ice down the path indicated toward a point called the "tee." The goal of the game was to get one's stone closest to the stake marking the tee, and part of the strategy was to knock other people's stones out of the way in the process.

Even though these preparations were admirable testimony both to Richard's thoughtfulness and to his imagination, Jennifer was far more impressed by the fact that for once he'd also decided to invite others to partake in the day's fun as well. Shortly after their arrival, another larger decorated sleigh drew up crowded with a family boasting three boys and two girls.

Mr. Martin was a recent addition to the Manhattan Company, Richard explained as he introduced that slight, spectacled gentleman. But how had Mr. Avery known that they'd been so busy getting settled that they hadn't yet been able to get out much? Mrs. Martin wondered. And wasn't it nice of him to have planned an outing he knew the children would enjoy, she went on, smiling fondly at her offspring—particularly, she confided to Jennifer, when she'd had her hands full of so many domestic chores that she had had no time left over for worrying about whether her brood was happy or not.

"To be sure, it was excessively thoughtful," Jennifer agreed in all honesty, making certain that Richard was near enough to overhear that compliment. "Nevertheless," she warned with an impish grin in his direction, "I imagine the grown-ups ought to be prepared to find themselves fully as diverted as the younger members of the group."

In this assumption, she proved to be quite correct. What's more, the elder Martins turned out to be agreeable companions altogether ready to join in the fun. And their children were an unaffected, if rather energetic, bunch who generously opened their ranks to include George and Caroline.

The group started the afternoon off by trying their hands at curling, taking turns launching the stones provided toward the tee at the end of the course. Mr. Martin soon proved to be the champion at this endeavor. Despite his small frame and poor eyesight, he directed his throws with such deadly accuracy that his stone repeatedly landed closest to the target, knocking out any of his competitor's markers in the way with enviable consistency.

After stopping to partake of the refreshments, they learned that it was time for the Grand Regatta to begin. Richard herded everyone over to the racecourse and requested that the participants bring out their entries. Merely examining the strange collection of assembled vessels was sufficient to send the entire company off into paroxysms of laughter. The boats ranged from those that were easily recognizable as such, like Richard's wooden canoe, to those that with some imagination could still be said to be vessels, like Jennifer's carved bar of soap fitted with a miniscule sail. But the strangest entries were the ones that appeared to have little resemblance to boats at all and nothing whatsoever to do with sailing. And the most curious of those was unquestionably Molly's offering. That lady had simply removed the heel from an old slipper, replaced the lacings with red ribbons, and declared her craft ready to meet all comers.

At a signal from Richard, everyone ran up to the starting line and released their boats with what they hoped would be enough force to propel them the ten feet to where a set of flags marked the end of the course. To the surprise of everyone but its owner, Molly's entry won easily, for it was not only first across the finish line but it also traveled half as far beyond that line. She graciously accepted the winner's prize before confessing that the secret of her craft's speed lay in the thick layer of wax she'd melted onto the sole of the slipper the night before. Then, as promised, each of the other participants received a prize. Once he'd given out awards for such obvious things as most beautiful or most useful entry, however, Richard's inventiveness was stretched to the fullest to think up a category in which each person's craft could be accounted a winner. Everyone burst out laughing when he announced the prize for the greenest entry (Caroline's painted boat) and the prize for the boat-most-shaped-like-a-box (one of the Martin boys' little box with cambric sail).

Another hour of simple games like blindman's buff and cat-and-dog, which was played with a paddle and a block of wood, followed before the company moved to disperse. And when the Martins finally departed after repeatedly thanking their host and promising several times to return his hospitality as soon as they were able, Jennifer couldn't help joining them in regarding Richard in a decidedly favorable light.

Since she and Molly and the twins were all pleasantly exhausted, none of them felt obliged to converse much on the journey home. Richard had joined them, and Caroline immediately fell asleep against her father's shoulder while George also managed to snuggle up next to that gentleman with the excuse that the sleigh was overcrowded. Jennifer was quite content to divide her attention between stealing little sidelong glances at Richard and silently recounting all the hidden facets of his character that he had begun revealing during the afternoon and that were pushing her even closer to being completely won over than she'd heretofore been ready to admit.

As for Richard, he'd counted the afternoon a success when, upon holding up his handmade canoe, his eyes had met Jennifer's in a look of perfect understanding, and she'd smiled warmly at him in a way that made it clear that for once she approved of him without any reservation. How alive he felt, he realized, sneaking a quick peek at Jennifer to reassure himself that she still looked as contented as he had thought she did. Nevertheless, these feelings were probably short-lived at best, and the Winter Festival only a temporary solution to the dilemma posed by his growing attachment to Jennifer, he reminded himself glumly a few moments later. He then spent the remainder of the drive trying not to become too depressed at the unwelcome onset of cold reality.

Indeed, he recalled the next morning with a tiny sigh, his one earlier attempt to resolve his uncertainty by seeking an audience with Lord Somers, though not perhaps with the intention of formally making Jennifer an offer, had unfortunately been curtailed first by her presence and then by his lordship's own precipitous departure. And to be honest, before he'd concocted the previous afternoon's diversion, he had found himself counting the days with noticeable longing until he, too, could reasonably anticipate receiving the summons from his lordship to depart for Washington.

Both Richard and Jennifer were considerably relieved, therefore, when the arrival of Lord Somers's third letter allowed them each to cast their doubts temporarily into the shade. "My dearest Jennifer," it began. "How fortunate for our little venture that I should have been so easily able to schedule a friendly prose with my old acquaintance, Jimmy Monroe. Picture in your mind, if you will, a tall, powerfully built man in his mid-fifties with a craggy face, and you shall have imagined him to perfection. We reminisced a little about Paris, and I happened to mention casually that a man I thought I'd met at that time was now in Washington and apparently engaged in a most unusual sort of work. He knew instantly to whom I was referring, of course, and I daresay his quick response would satisfy those critics who dismiss him as intellectually inferior to the president. He must by far be the more worldly of the two, however, for he not only readily admitted that Crillon had already requested an interview with him but then also bluntly inquired what I knew of the whole business. I immediately seized the opportunity to lay our suspicions before him, and I warrant I made a fairly solid case for proceeding with a healthy dollop of caution. In any case, I believe he'll prove a formidable stumbling block to Crillon, if he becomes convinced that all is not right and tight about the man's proposal. Monroe values integrity above everything else, and sometimes his overwhelming sense of moral righteousness has proven his own worse enemy. It did in Paris, certainly, where he said he was positive that whomever he dealt with was in some way corrupt or stained—particularly, it seemed to me, if they appeared to deviate from his beliefs to any great degree. But I digress.''

Jennifer paused to share a companionable smile with Richard at this last remark, but his head was still bent over the letter and he was clearly lost in thought as his fingers patted out a little rhythm on his chair. ''I do think others must find it as odious for a man to feel virtuous for being pure in heart as for him to possess even an average number of shortcomings to which he's loathe to admit—don't you agree?'' he asked abruptly, coming as close as comfortable with this impersonal phrasing to referring directly to himself. He hesitated for a moment as the now familiar rush of emotions that accompanied Jennifer's nearness washed over him and made him wish to reach out and take her hand and press it to his lips. Instead, he raised his head and looked at her with an intensity that caught her squarely off guard and that made her feel as if her answer were vitally important.

''Perhaps,'' Jennifer acknowledged. After rapidly scanning Richard's face, she quickly deduced that his question wasn't quite as objective as it appeared, and that by asking it, he'd made himself vulnerable for once in a way she knew he disliked and even feared. And the fact that he'd done so anyway, and was apparently willing at last to trust her, stirred a strong, responsive cord, and she hastened to offer support for his effort. "I, for one, however, would always consider the circumstances before passing judgment based on what might at best be only a partial understanding of what had occurred."

That answer appeared to satisfy Richard for the moment, and the two returned dutifully, but with a conscious effort, to Lord Somers's letter: "Crillon, meanwhile, appears of necessity to have become a bit more cautious himself. I'm told he confessed to Dolley Madison that he'd received three—or was it four?—anonymous, threatening letters in the last week. He now talks of nothing but being surrounded by spies, possibly to divert attention from his own activities, and loudly denounces the rumors that he admits are circulating to his prejudice. This latest tidbit vies for attention with the antics of Betsy Bonaparte, whose marriage to the emperor's profligate younger brother, I learned, was promptly annulled by direct order of Napoleon himself. She runs around the city scantily clothed in diaphanous, low-cut gowns loaded with jewels, talks incessantly, and proclaims that she is 'wholly devoted to the pleasures of this life.' Fortunately, the lady is blessed with a faultless figure and considerable wit, since otherwise such carryings-on would soon become nothing but tiresome to her audience. Crillon, too, is one of her admirers and seems on altogether familiar terms with her, leading one to speculate whether their acquaintance might not, perhaps, be one of long standing. Still, those conjectures are doubtless best left to the gossip mongers with which Washington abounds. Therefore, I shall resolve to waste no more time recounting such things here, particularly when it appears that my real mission in this city may shortly be coming to an end."

In this assumption, his lordship proved to be entirely correct, because events were rapidly changing—picking up speed and bouncing crazily here and there like a stone rolling unchecked down a steep hillside. The next letter from Washington arrived so close upon the heels of the previous one that even had Jeremy not obviously begun to look done in, a brief calculation of the number of days that had elapsed since his last visit would have indicated that he'd been traveling at virtually a forced march. What's more, Lord Somers's habitual calm seemed to be threatening to desert him, for his message was couched in language that clearly showed he was ready to fly off in five different directions at any moment.

"My dearest Jennifer," it began as usual. "Henry has suddenly turned up and is stopping at an out-of-the-way roominghouse in nearby Georgetown! I should not even have known of his arrival, except that Crillon subsequently approached a lawyer I know named Archibald to request his assistance in arranging for the transfer of title to a large, landed estate he owns in France, which he claims is valued at 400,000 francs! Apparently, Crillon told Archibald that a friend—presumably Mr. Henry—had begged to buy the estate from him in exchange for a monetary settlement the friend expects to receive shortly. The amount Crillon is to realize for the land wasn't specified. When I expressed surprise, however, that a fellow of apparently modest means like Crillon should own such a valuable property, Archibald indicated that at first he, too, had been struck by that disparity but upon reflection had ascribed it to the vagaries of being an exile from one's own country. He did say that Crillon acted extremely full of himself and highly pleased with the arrangement, and paid the modest fee required for his services without question. He then went so far as to give Archibald a handsome bonus besides, dismissing his generosity as scarcely worth comment since he said that he fully anticipated becoming a man of considerable means before overlong."

Jennifer and Richard exchanged rather alarmed looks at this news. "But if Henry has arrived in Washington, it must mean that Crillon has received definite encouragement regarding the sale of the papers—don't you agree?" Jennifer asked in an anxious voice. "After all, his actions would certainly lead one to that conclusion."

Richard nodded and pointed a little farther down the

page. "Yes. You see, here your father, fearing likewise, says that he immediately called upon Secretary Monroe."

"Archibald's story could signify but one thing," they read on, "and that was that Monroe—despite my warning—had made Crillon an offer for Henry's letters. I went at once to learn if such was the case, and discovered to my horror that Crillon's asking price for the damned things was $250,000! Thank God, Monroe also thought this request absurd and gave him only a positive enough response to convince Crillon of the sincerity of his interest before putting forth several reasons to delay the matter for a little while. There were certain other conditions to the sale that Crillon indicated were not negotiable; these Monroe alluded to but did not detail to me when we spoke, other than to indicate that President Madison should have the final say on all particulars—a statement that for some reason caused me to feel decidedly uneasy. Still, Monroe has bought us a little space in which to breathe, though I don't doubt that he means to pursue the purchase of the documents nevertheless, since he claims they're far too important to forswear altogether, no matter how much it costs the United States—monetarily or otherwise. He has scheduled a meeting between the president and Crillon—at which Henry, also, is to be present—in one week's time. He has agreed that we may have such a meeting with Madison ourselves as soon as you arrive in Washington. Therefore, I urge you both not to lose a single day before setting forth, so that we may still be successfully able to cut the ground from beneath our devious friend Mr. Crillon."

Richard looked inquiringly at Jennifer as soon as they'd finished reading. "Could you be ready to leave as soon as tomorrow, do you think?" he asked in a brisk fashion, feeling greatly relieved that they were apparently getting under way at last. "My thoughts are that we could send Jeremy off first thing in the morning. Because he goes astride, he can travel far more quickly than we and can go on ahead and arrange for a fresh pair to be awaiting us at suitable intervals so that we can anticipate making speedy progress and spending only one—or at most, two—nights on the road. And because we don't know how long we shall be in Washington, I should think we ought to plan on a week's stay at the bare mimimum. I trust Miss Danhope would be able to look after the twins, wouldn't she? And because the household, as you know, is quite used to functioning in my absence, I don't think we need to worry a whit on that score, either.''

Jennifer could think of nothing to add to these arrangements except to pronounce them good and then to excuse herself to pack. It wasn't until she and Molly were busily selecting and folding garments from her wardrobe that it occurred to her that the trip upon which she was about to embark would be considered highly unsuitable by most people. And, in fact, it was Molly who finally raised that point just as she finished stuffing a pair of half boots into Jennifer's valise. "If you ask me," she sniffed, "you seem to have forgotten one very important thing."

Jennifer gazed about at the piles of clothing, trying to determine what she might have overlooked. "Then you do think I should take the extra mittens after all" she ventured.

That question appeared to put Molly a trifle out of sorts. "Pooh!" she scoffed. "It ain't like you to be such a pea-goose, I'm sure." Then, noting her friend's confused reaction to this remark, she relented somewhat. "Let me spell it out for you," she offered a little more kindly. "Who is to escort you on this expedition? Our host, Mr. Avery— correct? And who is to accompany you two: a footman, a maid, or perhaps a companion? No one—isn't that so? Well then, what do people ordinarily conclude when a decidedly eligible man and a highly desirable woman are discovered to have gone off together without a chaperone?''

"Why, that they've arranged an assignation or are actually eloping," Jennifer said in a puzzled voice. "Oh!" she exclaimed fearfully a moment later, staring at Molly in sudden comprehension. "You mean that that is what everyone will believe if Mr. Avery and I disappear from New York together?''

Molly nodded patiently. "Exactly. And although we shall know that such is not the case, no one else will be aware of your real purpose, you see.''

"Yes, and we can scarcely advertise our plans without

running the risk of jeopardizing the whole venture." A stubborn and sadly familiar look crept over Jennifer's face. "Well, I shall simply ignore any such attempt to sully my reputation because it shan't be the first time some well-meaning person has tried to call me to task for flying in the face of society's dictums!"

"All fine and good for you, I'm sure." Molly sniffed again. "We both know, however, that your companion isn't nearly as experienced in that particular realm. In fact, I wonder why the possibility that you might be doing something so improper in most people's eyes didn't occur to such an exemplary man as your Mr. Avery. Indeed, had it crossed his mind, I think it would surely have given him at least a moment's pause, if not reason to reconsider the decision altogether."

"Oh, doubtless it did," Jennifer said stoutly, unconsciously slipping into her new role of defending that gentleman to all comers. "But I imagine he only dismissed the notion of being censured for our actions as of little consequence compared to what disaster might result if we fail to act at all!"

In point of fact, Richard's mind was not on the propriety of the journey they were about to undertake but, as Jennifer had guessed, on the probability of their being able to accomplish their task in Washington. And because their chances for succeeding appeared to hinge on such inconsequentials as whether Mrs. Booth had sufficient money to see to the household needs and whether he could be spared from his office an entire week or more, his thoughts were wholly taken over by the need to attend to those concerns. What's more, he'd so readily become accustomed to spending considerable time alone with Jennifer—first in his capacity as her unofficial guardian and later out of a habit they'd both easily fallen into—that he'd long since come to think that practice entirely unexceptional himself. Even though he was well schooled in the strictures governing acceptable behavior, Richard had by this time literally forgotten that it wasn't right to go out alone with an eligible woman without a chaperone on even a simple outing, much less on a journey of the magnitude he was now planning. And since he'd also been used to living isolated from other members of his social set who'd have been quick to seize on such a lapse, he'd continued happily, if somewhat blindly, to feel that he was acting in a wholly respectable fashion. Indeed, he would have been greatly surprised if anyone had sought to point out to him that his actions in this instance could in any way be thought unseemly, particularly because he'd examined his own conscience and come to a fuller understanding of the concepts of obligation and responsibility—and one that didn't hinge on the mere outward appearance of doing what was proper.

Jennifer wasn't about to raise the issue herself once it became obvious that Richard's mind was occupied elsewhere. For one thing, she was delighted to note that his thinking appeared to have changed to such an extent that the first thing that occurred to him was no longer whether his actions were right or wrong. And her own emotions were confused enough regarding her companion and what she might wish their relationship to become that she didn't mean to call attention to that question and thereby be obliged to confront it herself.

Therefore, she steadfastly thrust aside any further consideration of the matter in favor of helping facilitate their departure. She listened to Richard as he related their requirements to Jeremy and then watched the latter depart on Oliver, a magnificent creature that had once been a broken-down thoroughbred he'd nursed back to health. Jeremy had a half dozen such animals with similar-sounding names who claimed the better part of his wages and upon whom he unstintingly lavished his care. In return, he told Jennifer, they lived up to every inch of their breeding and, as in this case, were perfectly suited to the task of carrying him on various errands that served to augment his income.

After seeing him go off, Jennifer went somewhat reluctantly to perform the task of bidding good-bye to George and Caroline. The twins, having only just been told by Molly that their companion was to leave that morning on a short trip and was taking their father along as well, appeared somewhat inclined to kick up a row at first. It was only once

Jennifer assured them that she fully intended to return, and then reminded them rather tartly that she wasn't in the habit of lying, that the children accepted her departure with the philosophical calm usually possessed by those more accustomed to being told what to do rather than consulted about it. Still, the two clung to her in such a tender and affecting way that Jennifer was secretly touched and struck anew by what a large and solid place they'd managed to secure for themselves in her heart.

Indeed, a sort of nameless happiness seemed to have settled upon Jennifer, and the sensation was so agreeable that she made no attempt to shake herself out of the mood. It did occur to her not long after they'd set out, however, that it was precisely the fact that she and Richard were alone together that she was mainly enjoying. And even though she paused to wonder if she didn't half hope their little escapade would somehow force his hand, she steadily resisted the need to analyze her feelings any further. That is, she was succeeding nicely in that endeavor until they turned off Broadway and headed toward the river. Then, just as they swung around the corner, they had the misfortune to pass Sylvia Trask and her husband, who were coming out of a shop on the side street. What's more, that lady clearly thought it worthy of notice that Richard Avery and his beautiful guest were bundled into a traveling coach loaded with several valises and making for the outskirts of the city. And she remained in view long enough for Jennifer to watch the speculative glance she'd first cast in their direction be replaced by a knowing, crafty smile. Well, if she'd harbored a single illusion about whether they would suffer any repercussions for their actions, the look on Sylvia Trask's face appeared to move that question from the realm of possibility into that of virtual certainty, Jennifer thought wryly. Richard, however, had been so busy handling the reins that he appeared to have missed the exchange entirely, and she hurried to compose herself so as not to call attention to the fact that she felt suddenly disconcerted.

Luckily, the first portion of the trip retraced the route Jennifer and her father had followed from Philadelphia across New Jersey to New York, but in reverse. Therefore, she was able to chat easily about her earlier experiences on the road as the ferry negotiated a careful path across the Hudson River. This precaution was mandated by the fact that a recent, unseasonable thaw had allowed the center of the river to flow freely again but had left the sides of the channel clogged with large pieces of ice that had to be pushed aside by men armed with long poles or circumnavigated altogether.

The unsettled weather hadn't been any more kind to the roads, which were in as sorry a state as Richard claimed ever to have seen them. Then, too, he'd only finally been persuaded to set off in the post-chaise rather than his roomy sleigh because it was well-known to be somewhat easier on the horses. He'd also realized that as they moved farther south, the ground probably wouldn't be frozen at all, and therefore considerations of speed and utility were likely to take precedence over those of comfort. Such had been the theory, at any rate, but for the first few hours the travelers found themselves proceeding at a snail's pace. They were continually obliged to climb down and lead the horses around one or another obstacle in the road or set their weight against the carriage in order to push a wheel out of the mud. After awhile, however, they found the going a bit easier, for the road had recently been ditched on either side and was consequently fairly dry and smooth. But by this time, they were caked with mud and so disheveled that Richard was prompted to observe jokingly that it looked as if they'd had to fight for their lives against a band of highwaymen.

Unfortunately, the landlord of the coach house where Jeremy had arranged for them to stop for supper and a change of horses appeared to reach an entirely different conclusion just as quickly. After one glance at the state of their clothing and a quick look that took in their baggage and the absence of male or female attendants, he tossed a broad, conspiratorial wink in Richard's direction. Then he promptly showed them into a private parlor and saw that they were provided with hot water so that they could clean up before their meal. He said he would serve their food himself, after which, he promised in a meaningful voice, he'd endeavor to see that they weren't disturbed.

"What a very odd fellow," Richard observed. He rapidly stripped off his cloak and gloves and began to wash, sniffing the air for a hint of the menu with a boyish eagerness Jennifer found utterly endearing.

She paused to unfasten her bonnet before agreeing nonchalantly, "Yes, perhaps. Though I fancy our host thinks that because of our appearance and our lack of companions, we may have recently been engaged in a fight for my honor, shall we say?"

Richard stared dumbly back at her for a moment and then exclaimed, "Good God, but that idea never occurred to me!"

Jennifer smiled at him in a friendly way. "I know," she admitted, "and I must confess I'm altogether glad that it didn't, since otherwise we might have found it necessary to alter our plans merely to comply with convention."

"Oh, but truly, I should have thought of how this little jaunt might succeed in compromising you," Richard assured her in a serious voice. "Indeed, it's quite unconscionable that I didn't anticipate the weight others might give to our arrangements and appearance alone together simply because I've begun to deem such things of little account myself, you see." He offered Jennifer a rueful smile in return.

"And a very good thing, too! After all, why ever should you fret over something for which I promise I don't give a jot myself?" she argued.

At this point there was a brief hiatus as the landlord arrived to serve their supper. First there was a hearty soup swimming with chunks of carrots and turnips; this was followed by a brace of rabbit, freshly caught that morning and nicely roasted, a side dish of boiled potatoes, and plenty of hot cornbread to be carved from a huge slab and then spread lavishly with new butter. This simple fare couldn't have looked more appealing, and for several minutes the two travelers occupied themselves with emptying the plates. Once they'd satisfied their appetites, Richard offered a choice between brandy or a hot rum toddy, and when his companion chose the latter, spent a little while mixing the liquor, sugar, and spices according to some personal recipe.

They'd pushed their chairs back from the table and were sitting silently watching the logs hiss and pop in the fireplace and sipping their drinks, when Jennifer was struck rather forcibly by a recollection of the last time she'd found herself in similar circumstances. Of course, the setting was doubtless the sole resemblance between the two occasions, she reminded herself, since before she'd mainly been concerned with fending off Mr. Verplanck's advances and now she found herself wondering precisely how she might succeed in encouraging them from her present escort. After all, she could scarcely throw herself at him, she reasoned, irritated both at the remnants of the conventionality that prevented her from initiating such an action and at the strength of her desire to cast prudence aside even as she longed to cast herself into his arms. If only some disaster were to befall them from which they'd have to be rescued, or she should succumb to some illness that would render her weak and pale and induce him to wish to take care of her. Oh, bosh, she thought to herself—there wasn't much likelihood of the second possibility occurring when she was as sturdy as a Welsh pony and twice as stubborn besides. And as far as the first was concerned, she imagined she was fully as liable to do the saving as the other way 'round. So much for romantic twaddle! She took a deep swallow from her steaming mug. Why, if she waited for events to occur to suit her purpose, she appeared destined to remain a miss forever, she decided.

Jennifer was so caught up in these unhappy ruminations that she'd quite forgotten her companion for the moment. Richard, therefore, had been left alone with his own thoughts, which weren't proving much more productive than Jennifer's—a fact that might have made him feel somewhat relieved, had he known of it. As it was, however, he found himself turning over the end of their previous conversation again in his mind. Was he really so awfully concerned that leaving New York without a chaperone might have irreparably damaged Jennifer's reputation, or wasn't it really that he secretly hoped he should now be obliged to make her an offer and thereby mend it? God, but he was lily-livered, he admitted with a grimace. He peered into his cup, wishing it were the sweetness of the drink that had made him flinch and not the thought of his own inadequacies. Hadn't he even hoped that setting off in such a dashing fashion might have prompted the lady beside him to view him for once as something other than an overcautious, unimaginative prude? And yet the only result of this attempt at spontaneity had apparently been to cover himself with mud rather than glory.

He rose from his seat to poke at the fire, and before settling down again, walked over to the table to refill his cup. When he turned around, he realized first that he was standing directly in back of Jennifer's chair and second, that her closeness was causing him to feel as reckless as he might ever have wished. Without his being conscious of how it came to pass, his hand stole out of its own accord to stroke her glorious curls as he'd often longed to do and then to rest for a second against the indescribable softness of her skin.

The warmth of the room and the abundant food and drink had lulled Jennifer into a semiconscious state, so that when she felt a touch on her cheek she didn't stop to think. Instead, she tilted her head to the side to trap the hand temporarily against her shoulder in a soft squeeze, and then turned to plant a kiss tenderly on the fingertips. The stillness in the room was abruptly broken as one of the occupants roughly caught his breath and then expelled it again with a little sigh.

"I beg your pardon," said a faint voice behind her. The hand on her cheek was slowly and carefully removed, much to Jennifer's infinite dismay. "I confess I must have let myself be seduced by our surroundings and allowed the moment to get the better of my judgment," it continued more strongly. "Otherwise, I'm certain I should never have dared to take the sort of liberties other men may frequently have been persuaded to attempt."

Quite probably true, Jennifer thought to herself bitterly. "I see," she said in a neutral fashion. "Then it's only that you lost your head for an instant—which, as you say, men are so often wont to do in these circumstances—and nothing more?"

"Precisely," Richard agreed without knowing in the least why he did so. He walked over to where he'd left his outer garments and began pulling on a glove with exaggerated attention—partly to hide the way his hands were trembling and partly to signify that the preceding interlude was at end. "Indeed, I urge you to put the whole thing out of your mind and forget that it ever happened," he said over his shoulder.

"Do you—truly?" Jennifer wondered in such a soft voice that Richard was unable to keep from turning back to face her. His eyes met Jennifer's almost reluctantly, and suddenly they were both lost in a look that was so powerful and so seemingly endless that when he finally broke away, Richard found himself standing next to his beloved, although he hadn't any idea of how he had gotten there. He felt Jennifer's warm breath on his palm as she reached out, took the second glove from his limp grasp, and then pulled it onto his hand, smoothing the leather over his fingers in a tender caress.

"Very well, I shall try to pretend that nothing happened and even that there is no attachment between us, if that is what you honestly wish," she said slowly. "But I believe we're both aware that that method hasn't been highly successful for either of us in the past, has it? Even so," she went on without waiting for an answer, "I promise I shall make one last attempt, but only if in return you will promise that there's in fact nothing else you wish to tell me now."

Richard stared down into the pair of emerald eyes that searched his face hopefully and felt his throat tighten. "You must know that as a man of honor, I can scarcely make such a promise," he blurted out before he could stop himself. Then he promptly gave up the effort to maintain his earlier indifferent façade, pulled Jennifer to his chest, and planted a half-dozen kisses among her curls. "I truly don't wish to deny the feelings I have for you any longer, my dear, but you must see that admitting them solves only half our problem," he said in a miserable voice. "Until we've untangled this coil caused by Mr. Henry and had time to consider how the tempest he's created may affect our lives, I don't feel free to say or to ask or to promise anything more," he finished as if it pained him. He pushed Jennifer gently to arm's length and then winced as he read the hurt in her eyes when she raised her head.

Jennifer opened her mouth as if to protest and then closed it again after seeing that the distress on Richard's face easily matched her own. By sheer strength of will, she managed to put on her traveling clothes and make her way out to the carriage, where a fresh team of chestnuts waited impatiently to be given their heads. Inwardly, however, she dreaded the thought of the long hours ahead alone with Richard in the coach—and the rest of the trip as well. If only he'd been able to declare himself plainly instead of giving her only the tiniest reason to hope, she wouldn't feel so desolate now, Jennifer told herself. But when he'd admitted that his emotions were of a deeper and more lasting variety than a mere temporary passion and yet still refrained from asking then and there if he could solicit her father for her hand, Jennifer had felt as if her heart had been ripped in two and left exposed so that the wound might never heal. And by this time, even the fact that Richard was clearly suffering as much anguish as she was counted, unfortunately, as only a small point in his favor in Jennifer's mind.

The strain of maintaining their composure proved considerable for the two individuals in question, and two days later, Jennifer had seriously begun to question whether she could hold out much longer. By then, they had reached the outskirts of Washington, however, and they lost no time in stopping to ask the direction of the hotel where Lord Somers lodged. Indeed, Richard had barely drawn the horses to a halt in the yard before Jennifer jumped down from the carriage and rushed inside to look for her father. But before she could inquire whether he was in, she spied his familiar figure descending the stairs in the front hallway. Whereupon, she ran headlong into his arms, and for perhaps the second time his lordship could remember, immediately burst into tears.

Chapter 16

"WHAT'S ALL this?" Lord Somers asked confusedly. He disentangled himself from his daughter's arms and pushed her far enough away so that he could gently force her chin up with one hand and examine her face. What he saw there didn't prove very comforting, however, for his eyes darkened and took on the cast of a mama bear protecting her cubs—a stance he'd been moved to adopt, if infrequently, after his wife's death. "Come now," he ventured, "surely being separated from me for the last month or so hasn't been sufficient to put you in such a taking?" This attempt to tease Jennifer out of her mood having had little visible effect, his lordship tried another tactic. "No doubt the trip here has merely walked you off your legs, even if Jeremy assured me he did his best to keep you mounted the whole way." This second effort was slightly more successful than the first because it at least caused Jennifer to shake her head back and forth, although she still didn't volunteer a word as to the cause of her distress. "Pray, do bear up a bit longer, love," his lordship urged finally in exasperation. "After all, if we don't wish to blow our own trumpet, we'd best beware of giving any of the tabbies hereabouts something to chew over, hadn't we?"

Despite the fact that the hallway was absolutely deserted at the moment, Lord Somers's advice appeared suddenly sensible to Jennifer when she observed that Richard had at last determined their direction and was now rapidly approaching. She hurriedly removed her bonnet and ran a hand through her curls to ensure they hadn't been crushed, and then pulled out a lace handkerchief and daubed at her eyes as if to show how much the reunion with her father had affected her. And if his lordship happened to note that his daughter's rapid change in demeanor seemed to coincide with Richard's arrival, he wisely decided to keep his own counsel on that point. Instead, he merely greeted Richard in a cordial fashion, inquired politely whether he'd found the stables to be adequate, and then suggested that they remove to his private sitting room.

Once they were settled, his lordship undertook to outline their immediate course of action. "We are to see President Madison tomorrow afternoon," he began. "When Jeremy trotted in this morning, he said he thought you might arrive tonight, if all went smoothly, or early tomorrow if you encountered some delay or other. Therefore, I thought it wise to allow a small margin, for safety's sake, and request that the interview be later in the day. Still, I must say I'm happy to see that you both appear to be in good health and that nothing untoward seems to have occurred during your journey," he added, looking from one to the other of his companions. A studious silence greeted this remark and prompted the speaker to wonder what exactly *had* transpired either in New York during his absence or on the trip to Washington—or possibly both. "Well then," Lord Somers continued somewhat more briskly, "let's discuss our strategy for tomorrow, shall we?"

"Indeed," said Jennifer at once in relief. "Do you know, I've been puzzled myself over precisely what it is we may expect to accomplish by turning up with our copies of the letters when for one thing, the Americans already know of their existence, and for another, seem inclined to persist in negotiating for their purchase."

"Yes, I'd wondered about that, too," Richard admitted. He turned to hazard a direct look at Jennifer for the first time. "One thought that occurred to me was that by coming forward, we provide a sort of independent corroboration of Henry's activities. After all, the letters could simply be a sham—part of an elaborate scheme he'd devised to try and strike back at those he felt hadn't dealt with him fairly. But we can offer verbal testimony that Henry freely confessed his treachery to us and actually tried to persuade me to join him and other like-minded souls in endeavoring to subvert the proper workings of the government."

"Yes, I've no doubt that such a story would be invaluable if Henry were to be put on trial for treason," Jennifer allowed, returning his gaze as calmly as she could manage. "Only that doesn't seem to be the end toward which the principals are headed. Why, if you ask me, every last person seems practically determined to reward that scoundrel by paying him an outrageous sum for his little bits of nastiness and then watching him walk away laughing at our stupidity." She paused to stare accusingly at her companions, apparently unconscious of how perfectly she'd just recounted Richard's argument of the previous week urging that Henry ought to be punished.

"Ah, but after all, this is politics, my dear, not real life," Lord Somers pointed out to her. "I doubt that you could prevent Henry from selling his letters for the highest price he can extract from the buyers. The French, for example, are still interested and only waiting to see what the Americans will do before seeking to place their bid. Serieur was quite clear on that head, and I imagine Monroe realizes how much more advantageous it would be for the United States to control how the documents are used rather than having to watch every instant to see which way the frogs will jump. And besides, I should think that having a second set of letters turn up would at least knock down the absurd amount Henry is demanding and bring it to within reason. With such results, I, for one, would be satisfied because I think we've as much hope of bringing Henry to justice as of seeing pigs fly!"

These very reasonable remarks appeared to signal the end of the discussion, and Richard excused himself shortly thereafter to retire to his room for a while before dinner. Scarcely had the door closed behind him, however, when his lordship turned roundly on his daughter and demanded in a skeptical tone, "Just what, I wonder, have you been up to these past few weeks, my naughty puss? And don't try to fob me off with some tale of merely having laid on the shelf all the time because if anything ever smacked of fakery, it would be the claim that everything is top of the trees between you and that gentleman!"

As a result of this accusation, Jennifer's shaky composure immediately crumbled and she began to cry again. Lord Somers greeted this unusual turn of events with dismay, staring at his daughter in a manner that vacillated between fascination and genuine concern. "Good heavens," he observed tactlessly after a moment, "I never knew you could be such a deuced watering pot." This remark only increased the flood, so in the hope of stemming it, his lordship hastily thrust out a large handkerchief to replace Jennifer's soaked piece of lace, and urged, "Here now—no need to carry on this way. Has Avery said something to upset you? No? Well, then, he didn't, er, try to force your hand, perhaps? It's not an approach with which I'd particularly credit him, but I've known of stranger things to occur when one makes the mistake of thinking one is dealing with a greenhorn. Why, I remember once—"

"He didn't do a thing, not a thing," Jennifer volunteered suddenly in a despairing voice. She snuffled unattractively into her father's handkerchief while he waited patiently for her to continue.

"And I take it that you wanted him to do something?" he prompted. His daughter nodded but remained mute. "Now see here, Jennifer," he threatened at last, "if you don't tell me this instant what is going on, I've a very good notion to spank you!" He paused to gauge the effect of this remark and then, having been struck by a certain possibility, regarded her again in a considering way. "It couldn't be that you actually wanted him to give in to a masculine impulse to carry you off, could it? What I mean is, you haven't gone and lost your head over the fellow, have you?" His daughter hesitated and then nodded again slowly. "Well, don't that beat all!" he exclaimed in a happy fashion and in such an uncanny imitation of Richard himself that Jennifer at once glared at him irritably.

"Well, you needn't act so infernally pleased," she snapped. "Or is it, perhaps, that you anticipated something of this very nature developing and are delighted to see that for once I've proven to be quite accommodating?"

Lord Somers shook his head. "The thought never seriously entered my head, as I believe I've assured you before," he admitted in all honesty. "I'm not at all surprised to learn, however, that you've fixed on the most unlikely of possibilities, since it is for that peculiar tendency that I reckon you're justifiably famous.'' He couldn't resist shooting a wicked little smile at his daughter to accompany this last observation.

Jennifer looked a trifle injured, but she still couldn't keep from asking in a curious voice, ''Do I truly always seem to pick the most difficult route?''

''Indubitably, but not in the way you think,'' her father replied. ''It seems to me that primarily the difficulties happen to arise only after you've set your course.''

''Do you mean, then, that I create them myself?''

''Not exactly. It's more that I think you can't believe things will work out smoothly and are forever prepared to encounter a few snags. And when you inevitably do find one or two, you immediately turn all your energy to trying to untangle things. Why, sometimes I wonder if your reaction isn't perhaps an unconscious way to avoid the experiences entirely.'' His lordship laced his fingers together and considered them for a minute before raising his head and shooting a piercing look at Jennifer. ''You see, when you approach life as a series of problems to be solved, you can at least be in control of the situation for the moment and have some say about what will happen. And to my mind, that's exactly where the problem—if I can use that term— seems to lie: The more you concentrate on what to do next, the less you're aware of what is going on now and how it makes you feel. And I think in some ways it's a very dangerous habit—and one, I fear, to which the male sex is all too often addicted—because it renders a person unable to identify emotions and to settle instead for living a life that may be complicated, but not truly full.''

Jennifer cocked her head at her father and marveled at him for almost a minute. ''How little one really knows of other people, after all! Indeed, I hadn't the slightest notion that you were so wonderfully insightful,'' she confessed. ''But how is it that if you've always known such things, you haven't seen fit to share them with me until now?''

Lord Somers shrugged his shoulders. ''They're only my own conclusions, you know, and perhaps I'm following an altogether false trail. But then, I suppose I imagined that some time or other you'd come to recognize this predilection of yours—as you so readily perceive similar weaknesses in others—and see how very often it trips you up, shall we say?''

"But I don't simply invent these dilemmas," Jennifer argued somewhat indignantly.

"And I never meant to imply that you did, love. Only, life always seems considerably more confused when you're around. You must admit that you're forever climbing out of one kettle of fish only to tumble immediately into another."

"True. Why, I'm in a perfectly horrid pickle right now—"

"And I'd like you to explain, if you will, how being in love with the same gentleman who's clearly enamored of you should in any way be an onerous situation," her father declared, pouncing on her statement with the enthusiasm of a boy for a plate of sweetmeats. "He is not already married, and neither are you; I have no objections to the match, if it's what you wish; and he appears more than able to provide for all your needs. So much for the immediate, if superficial, objections one might offer. And now to the more important points, at least in my mind: Do your temperaments complement each other sufficiently to allow you both to relax and to be yourselves? Are your beliefs similar enough—or generous enough—to coexist comfortably? And are you prepared to learn from each other, to laugh together, and to forgive the other person promptly and not hold his mistakes against him?" Lord Somers watched his daughter nod a trifle dazedly. "Well then, it appears to me that you can count on enjoying many happy years of married bliss. Unless, of course, there's some other reason that might prevent my shortly wishing you every happiness—?" He peered intently at Jennifer from beneath carefully lowered eyelids.

Her cheeks flushed a dull red. "Only that we haven't yet seemed to find the, ah, opportunity to discuss that topic," she admitted. "And anyway, you must admit that such a discussion would more properly be conducted with *you* than with me," she flared.

"No doubt. But surely you've at least been moved to confess your true feelings to the gentleman?"

"Well, in point of fact, no—not in so many words."

"And yet you still see fit to think you've landed in some

devilish tangle?'' her father said in amazement. ''Because, if so, I must tell you that this time it appears to be one solely of your own making, my dear. Why, as far as I can see, you've but to face the lion that you imagine lies in the path in order to beard the beast neatly in its den. And once you confront it straight on—precisely the advice you'd give someone else—I warrant you'll discover the thing's a mere pussycat.''

This esoteric speech proved to be Lord Somers's last word on the subject, for he took himself off to change for dinner and thereafter carried through the remainder of the evening without once again referring to their conversation. The interview left Jennifer in a rather subdued state of mind, however—either the journey had sapped her strength or she was feeling the results of fighting her deepest emotions for too long.

Upon meeting President Madison the following day, Jennifer decided nothing could adequately have prepared her for the plain-looking man of about sixty with a strong chin and lucid eyes who bowed politely over her hand. Washington Irving might indeed have described him disparagingly as that ''withered little apple-john,'' but she had no difficulty perceiving the quick intelligence that lurked behind his simple manner. James Monroe, his secretary of state, loomed in the background behind him, providing a notable contrast in both appearance and demeanor to the president.

Madison invited his guests to be seated and then rang for coffee. After the refreshments had been served, and the steaming pot placed close at hand, he turned to look directly at Jennifer. ''I believe you have a little story to share with us?'' he asked her in a mild but undeniably blunt way.

Jennifer had been feeling anything but altogether comfortable, and she couldn't in good conscience ascribe the sensation merely to being awed by her host or by her surroundings. The White House was certainly built on a grand scale, with a clearly admirable design and even more impressive proportions. But inside, it was actually rather cavernous, some of the rooms sparsely furnished and others still under construction. What's more, she'd learned that the roof leaked and in cold weather, her father had whispered, a terrible dampness clung tenaciously to the interior. Still, Jennifer had enjoyed her brief glimpse of the public rooms and admired the way many of them had been brightened by a sprinkling of what she'd been told were some of the Madison family's personal belongings. Yet, once their little group had been directed into the room the president used as his study, and she'd had a moment to reflect on their errand, she'd been seized again by doubts. However was she to explain how she'd come to take an interest in Henry's affairs without seeming to be anything but a common telltale? And how could she expect to convince her listeners that a British subject could voluntarily reveal information detrimental to her own country without wishing to become an exile herself?

Nevertheless, she obviously couldn't equivocate at this point, she realized. She stared nervously back at the two faces waiting patiently for her to begin, and then stole a quick look at the pair of faces beside her as if to draw strength from their presence. Then, thrusting her misgivings firmly aside and taking a few deep, steadying breaths, she simply and succinctly related her story, beginning with how Henry had aroused her suspicions, how she discovered the evidence of his activities, and concluding with their latest speculations regarding his partnership and plans and possible future courses of action. Whereupon, she produced their copies of the letters and offered them to the president for his inspection.

To her surprise, Madison made no comment whatsoever regarding the methods by which she'd obtained the documents. He observed with only a smile that she was certainly a redoubtable opponent and he dearly hoped that all her countrymen wouldn't prove similarly formidable. Because Monroe had already seen a sample of the goods Crillon was trying to peddle, Madison asked him to look the papers over first. Once the secretary had scanned the documents and pronounced them genuine, insofar as he could tell, Madison leisurely and with complete attention read through the entire stack. Then he sat back in his chair and for several minutes remained lost in thought. When he finally broke the silence to offer a comment, it wasn't quite what Jennifer expected him to say.

"You know, I believe it's this Crillon fellow who interests me the most," Madison admitted. "After all, Henry's motives for undertaking this venture are patently obvious: the wounded party—as I collect he fancies himself—attempting to hit back at the people he imagines have subverted his lofty principles and high purpose by being too closefisted. But why should Crillon become involved in his little scheme? For the money Henry has promised to share with him? Somehow, it doesn't strike me as very likely, or for that matter, sufficient recompense for his trouble."

"The same notion occurred to me," Monroe put in. "I couldn't help thinking that the man was attempting to promote more than his own self-interest, and it seemed possible that he might be representing France, because if the letters prove as volatile as we suspect they may, she stands to gain the most when we turn our attention toward England. When I sought to make a few inquiries, however, I discovered a most surprising fact." He turned toward Lord Somers. "Do you recall telling me that Crillon had received a few threatening letters and that someone had been asking a lot of questions at his residence? Well, I learned from our own sources that Crillon is indeed being watched, and that the men who are shadowing him are in the pay of that devil Napoleon! Therefore, it seems to me that Crillon could hardly be Bonaparte's agent if the emperor himself has given orders that he's to be kept under tight guard."

"Unless he's decided that, despite being in his employ, Crillon's not to be trusted to deliver as promised?" Madison suggested in a thoughtful voice. "Still, all of this is beside the point, because one of the stipulations to the sale of the letters is that Crillon is to be granted immunity for his role in this whole matter. Henry, too, is to be allowed to escape what most people would no doubt consider just retribution for his activities. In fact, we're being asked to promise that we won't even publish the letters until he has departed our shores."

"But that's infamous!" Jennifer exclaimed heatedly, forgetting where she was for the moment. "Surely you don't mean to agree to such outrageous terms when you have our copies of the same letters already at your disposal—and our testimony, besides?''

''Oh, but I fear we must,'' the president told her gently. ''We can't allow the documents to fall into unfriendly hands, you know—leastways, not in their present form. As you're well aware, Henry wasn't at all reluctant to include the names of those Americans who'd agreed to conspire with him, and publication of the letters as they stand will not only incriminate those individuals but once again promote dissent within the ranks of both parties. And my goal is, rather, to seek national unity, since a country divided internally will never be successful in waging war against another, and I've little doubt anymore that that grim prospect is what lies ahead of us.

''Still, I fancy I've kept my belief that war is inevitable as close a secret as I could manage. I was merely waiting for the proper time and the right provocation, shall we say, to promote the idea of declaring war. So, you see, Henry's letters offer the perfect tool both to bind the nation together and to bend everyone to a common, if decidedly deadly, purpose.'' He sank deeper into his chair and dropped his chin into one hand—the very picture of a man who has struggled with his conscience only to have reached a decision to which he can never be fully reconciled.

A brief silence followed the close of the president's speech. Finally, the secretary of state stepped into this breach by voicing the thought that was on everyone's mind. ''You needn't feel that all your efforts have been to no avail,'' Monroe told the three visitors in a kind voice. ''Indeed, your information and your copies of the documents were our reserve forces, should our attempt to hold a hard line with Henry—or with Crillon—have failed. As it is, however, we've succeeded in striking a bargain that we believe to be equitable, if not what one would call just, without having to involve any of you after all.'' He looked at Jennifer. ''Though perhaps I might suggest leaving your evidence behind when you depart today, since I warrant it can be of little further use to you and, being writ in your own hand, might prove only a source of embarrassment were it to turn up in unsympathetic quarters.''

These remarks apparently signified the end of the interview. The three visitors departed shortly thereafter, following the president's formal expression of gratitude on behalf of the county and a personal invitation to attend a reception for his birthday the next afternoon. But despite the fact that Madison's words were obviously sincere and his sentiments deeply held, none of his guests felt at all like putting a good face on their experience.

''Well, it appears that you were correct in what you advised we might expect to accomplish with our little subterfuge,'' Jennifer said heavily to her father as they climbed into the carriage.

Lord Somers didn't appear to take any more pleasure in having scored a hit than his daughter. ''So it seems,'' he admitted without enthusiasm. ''Do you know, I think I shall steer clear of politics entirely from this point on. Such entanglements just simply aren't to my taste anymore.''

''I quite agree,'' Richard offered in a decisive voice. ''Why, I'm sure I can't fathom why anyone would volunteer to become a philanthropist when no one seems to be of one mind regarding precisely what that means in the first place, and scarcely a single person seems grateful for any such efforts, in the second. But then again, maybe I've only found I'm too mean to do good simply for the sake of some abstract—and possibly misguided—belief that it will somehow profit humanity.''

''And I feel likewise,'' Jennifer confessed, feeling an abstract happiness at once again finding them so clearly in agreement. ''After all, how could one ever accept the notion that going to war could in any way be beneficial?''

The following day found Jennifer, Richard, and Lord Somers in a rather more sanguine mood. This transformation was no doubt due in part to their having finally discharged what each privately thought of as his or her responsibility in the Henry matter, and in part to the anticipation of soon being able to leave Washington—a city for which none of them had developed a particularly lasting fondness.

First, however, they agreed to attend the president's birthday celebration, if only to allow Richard and Jennifer to garner a little taste of the more enjoyable side of life in the capital. Accordingly, they drove over to the house on F Street that the Madisons leased. It was a commodious three-story structure set on a large lot and included such unique features as a cupola on the roof with a ladder that could be let down to the street in case of fire.

They were greeted immediately inside the entryway by Dolley Madison, and it was quickly evident from her warm welcome why she'd earned the reputation for being an excellent hostess. She chatted familiarly with Lord Somers and showed a friendly interest in Richard as well. She then complimented Jennifer on her beauty and her lovely gown, confiding that because she couldn't any longer boast of owning the former of those herself, she at least always endeavored to possess the latter. In fact, she was rather plump and unmistakably past forty, but she still retained the laughing blue eyes and flawless complexion that were rumored to have helped persuade Madison to propose to this Quaker widow with a small son when she was only slightly more than half his age. She was wearing a handsome frock of rose satin that showed off the rich tones of her skin, and a turban decorated with feathers, which his lordship later explained was virtually her signature accessory, finished off her costume. After recommending that her guests sample a bit of her homemade currant wine, she moved off to greet some other new arrivals, leaving behind a favorable impression of a woman with great personal charm and dignity.

Lord Somers promptly disappeared to carry out his hostess's advice, and Richard and Jennifer suddenly found themselves alone for the first time in several days. Given that their last solitary encounter had been the stop at the inn on their way to Washington, which had had such a disastrous outcome, and the fact that each held identical—if secret—expectations about the course their relationship might take, it would have been understandable if this development had made them both a little nervous. Surprisingly enough, though, neither appeared to feel self-conscious or even very ill at ease. Whether this shift was the result of their both being glad of some companionship in these strange surroundings or because of their having finally dispensed with the artifice that often exists between people who don't know each other well, probably neither could have said. They walked around for a few minutes, admiring the decorations and speculating quietly on the identities of the other guests. "Do you know," Richard confided after a while, "I collect I shall be very glad to go home—won't you?"

Jennifer sighed. "Yes," she admitted. "That is, I shall be happy to return to New York and be with my father again, though I'm not certain what he means to do now; we haven't yet had a chance to discuss the possibilities. I wonder, because it seems clear from what President Madison said that war may break out shortly, whether Papa thinks we should try to return home to England, or whether he wishes to—"

Whatever his daughter imagined he might be contemplating was interrupted by the headlong arrival of Lord Somers himself. Unfortunately, he'd been carrying three glasses of the aforementioned red currant wine, much of which he'd managed in his haste to spill on his snowy shirt cuffs so that he now looked as if he'd made a rare botch of slitting his wrists. He appeared totally oblivious to this odd condition, however, so anxious did he seem to share the reason for such intemperate behavior. He thrust a glass each at his companions and then fairly dragged them into a secluded corner. "Just saw Monroe when I was getting our provisions," he blurted out excitedly, "and what do you think? Today, according to his instructions, our friend Mr. Henry received a draft from the Bank of Columbia drawn from the Contingent Fund for Foreign Intercourse of the public treasury for $50,000!"

Chapter 17

THE ANNOUNCEMENT of Henry's triumph was greeted as vociferously by his companions as Lord Somers could have wished. Jennifer promptly tossed aside her upbringing and the conventions of her sex altogether in order to exclaim in a feeling voice, "Hell and damnation!" And as for Richard, he drew himself up to his full, impressive height, knitted his brows together in a scowl, and pronounced it a black day for democracy and then declared himself ready to fight any person who claimed otherwise. At least, the three derived a modicum of comfort from the fact that although they came from different backgrounds and held clearly divergent views, they'd all managed somehow to arrive at the same conclusion: War was a sickening prospect and those who advocated it or in some way—either consciously or unconsciously—sought to promote it were scurrilous criminals, at best.

"And that's not all," Lord Somers told them, neatly picking up the thread of his story again. "Henry has reserved a seat on tomorrow's stage to Baltimore and from there, I've learned, he plans to head east." His lordship regarded his companions expectantly. "Why, he must be bound for New York—don't you see?—for it's certainly either from there or from Boston that he'd expect to sail for the Continent," he explained, not having had the patience to wait until his listeners puzzled out his drift.

"Probably," Richard acknowledged. He looked at Lord Somers in confusion. "But I'm afraid I don't follow you, sir. I thought we were through with Henry and Crillon. We weren't able to prevent their plan from bearing fruit, so to

276

speak, so I don't really see what we can hope to accomplish by trying to keep them in sight now."

"Actually, neither do I," Lord Somers confessed readily enough, smiling a little at his own artlessness. "I imagine it's just too deucedly tempting, that's all. I mean, because there's a fair likelihood that Henry will turn up in the same city as we shall, where's the harm in taking a peek at the fellow now and again? For although it's true we can't any longer hope to subvert his plan, it seems to me that we may still discover something that would afford us the satisfaction of knowing he wouldn't simply bear away the prize. And I must say that that development would please me no end."

"And me," Jennifer chimed in. "But how about Crillon? Did Monroe indicate what's to happen to that ne'er-do-well?"

Her father shook his head. "Not precisely, though I doubt you ought to apply such a term to a man who may shortly be doing extremely well—in a financial sense, that is. Apparently, during the time in which Henry is readying to leave the country, the president is engaged in preparing a report to Congress to accompany his letters—the stipulation, as you'll recall, having been that nothing was to be published until Henry had sailed. I take it from what Monroe said that Crillon's agreed to remain in Washington for a while and even to testify, if required—but only before a closed committee in Congress and not in any sort of public forum. Still, it does beat all how everlastingly helpful that man is proving himself to be. Why, it's almost as if he means to dangle about long enough to ensure that the outcome of this little enterprise is exactly what he expects and nothing less." Lord Somers paused for a moment to consider that statement. "Do you know, I may just nose around a bit more before we quit this city and ask Jeremy to keep an ear to the ground for me as well. In fact, I believe there might even be one or two men in New York whom I fancy might be able to tell me a thing or two," he mused a trifle obscurely. "Perhaps we'll discover that we've been entirely too hasty in concluding there's nothing more to be learned about the mysterious Mr. Crillon."

"As I recollect, it was you who reached that decision," Jennifer reminded him, before adding in a dry voice, "And anyhow, you declared that you were finished with politics from now on, didn't you?"

Lord Somers widened his eyes innocently. "Did I? Why, I'm sure I can't recall. And besides, this ain't exactly the same thing, but only a little bit of hocus-pocus to keep things from becoming too awfully flat. Surely you'll grant me that innocent pastime?"

"How could I refuse when I believe I'm usually the one charged with forever being mixed up with some deviltry myself?" Jennifer said with a smile. "But pray, do take care to remain as inconspicuous as possible, won't you? It's only that I can't help feeling increasingly concerned about our position in this country, because once Henry's letters are made public, I wouldn't be surprised to find that a great many people suddenly thought it their business to discover what *our* business in the United States might be."

Lord Somers appeared momentarily insulted that his own daughter should have seen fit to caution him. "No need to fret, love," he assured her confidently. "I'll be a perfect slyboots, I promise you."

Three days later, just as dusk began to stretch its long fingers over New York City, the travelers drove up to No. 30 Wall Street and breathed a collective sigh of relief at the sight of that graceful abode. The return trip from Washington had ended up being a rather stilted affair, primarily because the feeling of camaraderie, which had grown during their pursuit of Henry and his letters, appeared to have dissipated once their quarry had been run to ground. Instead, that very agreeable sensation had been replaced by a new reserve between Jennifer and Richard, partly because of Lord Somers's presence and partly because both were aware of not being able to forestall coming to some resolution about their futures. And because the last matter was dependent on the outcome of several other questions—whether the Somerses would decide to sail for England, for example, and how the worsening political situation might affect that decision—neither of the principals looked forward to finding a particularly smooth course ahead. But if truth be told, what was causing these two the most discomfort was the realization that they'd now have to face the possible consequences of their little adventure and be ready to deal with the chilly reception usually afforded those who transgressed the boundaries of socially acceptable behavior.

Their initial welcome home was a gratifyingly warm one, at least. No sooner had they pulled the horses to a stop and begun to climb stiffly down from the carriage than the front door burst open and two small forms hurled themselves at the arrivals with repeated shrieks of delight.

Richard was so overcome by the children's obvious joy at his return that he promptly knelt down on the walkway, mindless of its usual coating of winter slush, and gathered George and Caroline into a fierce but tender embrace. Behind him, Jennifer and her father exchanged a satisfied look at the happy transformation that had been wrought in this little group during their sojourn in the city. A moment later, they found themselves suddenly pulled into the circle as the twins insisted on greeting them as if they were part of the family, too. The five stayed thus entwined for a few amicable minutes until Richard finally recovered a measure of his normal self-control and suggested that they move indoors.

But the twins were determined not to be gotten rid of easily, and nothing would do but that they all sit down to dinner together. Therefore, a half hour later, the dining room resounded with a clamor that Molly complained was sufficient to raise the dead, as the children proceeded to relate the details of the events that had occurred during their absence. At last, when they were all feeling well contented with their excellent meal, a pleasant silence descended on the room.

It wasn't long, however, before the peaceful atmosphere was disrupted when Molly finally volunteered an account of some of the other activities that had recently claimed the household's attention. "I'm sorry to tell you, but your departure apparently didn't pass without notice altogether," she said slowly, clearly reluctant to throw a damper on the celebration. She looked from Jennifer to Richard and then inquired dryly, "Or can you explain why else we were suddenly gifted each day by a visit from one interested person or another seeking your company when no more than a handful of souls cared a straw about your existence before? And the most persistent of those callers was none other than Sylvia Trask, who turned up on the doorstep not more than an hour after you drove off. What's more, she actually professed to have seen the two of you loaded in the carriage heading out of the city, and her hints about what such an event signified were hardly subtle and a good deal less than ladylike!" She paused to give a couple of loud sniffs. "Nevertheless," she went on a trifle defensively, "I was scarcely in a position to contradict her when I could neither say where you'd gone nor why you'd left together on a drive that was obviously not of a very brief duration. I tried to plead that you had urgent family business to attend to," she said, turning toward Richard, "but dashed if the lady didn't laugh in my face and then dismiss that notion by saying she knew perfectly well that all your family was right here in New York! Then she went so far as to speculate on whether it was true that the possibility of a new addition to a family often prompted a couple to decamp in the same precipitous fashion as you had!"

Jennifer stared at Molly, her cheeks flaming. "Why, what a horrible thing to say!" she exclaimed at last. Her anger grew as another thought struck her. "Good God—the woman's a terrible prattle, too, as we're all aware. Why, I daresay we shouldn't be surprised to discover that she's spread it around town by now that I'm shortly expecting a by-blow!" Then, belatedly remembering that the twins were present, she peeked quickly in their direction and was relieved to see that they apparently didn't understand what all the furor was about.

Molly shook her head firmly. "I don't think we need to worry about that. I'm certain my contempt at her suggestion was quite convincing, you see, and I imagine even the most dedicated gossip would hesitate to share what might turn out to be only a rumor with whomever will listen."

Lord Somers appeared torn between guilt and anger at

that possibility. "Indeed, I reckon I'm entirely to blame for not having considered at the start that leaving the city alone might make you both vulnerable to charges of impropriety," he allowed in a crestfallen voice. "Still," he warned, "I daresay we'd all be ill-advised to think we could treat the matter lightly and fail to respond at all, you know."

At this point, Richard intervened to say in decisive accents, "I quite agree. And if there's one thing everyone here will grant, it's that I enjoy the certainty of possessing a spotless reputation myself. Therefore, I shall make it my business to take one or two key people aside as soon as possible and explain to them in plain terms how Jennifer and I happened to quit New York together." He hesitated before adding with somewhat less assurance, "Though I confess I'd welcome suggestions from you on what excuse you think I should offer for our behavior."

Now, Lord Somers and his daughter had each privately taken note both of how familiarly the speaker had used Jennifer's name and how he'd openly solicited their assistance, for once, in an endeavor in which they had an undeniably large stake. These two facts clearly testified to how great a change Richard Avery had undergone in the last few months, and his former partners immediately longed to question him further. Before either of them could respond, something in the conversation finally seemed to hit closer to home as far as the children were concerned. "But now that you're back, you're not planning to leave again soon, are you?" Caroline asked with an anxious little frown, voicing a thought that was also on the minds of several of the others present at the table.

That question had the unhappy effect of reminding Jennifer what an awkward position she was in now in the Avery household. She had an extreme dislike of lying to children, however, because she knew that falsehoods were inevitably found out and ended only by giving the distinct impression that there was one set of rules that governed the behavior of children and an altogether different—and often far less admirable set—for grown-ups. Therefore, she felt obliged to admit honestly, "I'm afraid I'm not entirely certain. I should think, though, that it might be several weeks at least before we reach any decision, isn't that so, Papa?'' She cocked an eyebrow inquiringly at her father.

Lord Somers, however, either missed that cue or wasn't yet ready to fall in with it, for he only rubbed his hands together for a moment. ''We shall see, we shall see,'' he murmured in a tone that was either ominous or encouraging, depending upon one's point of view.

The next afternoon, Jennifer promptly sought out her father in an effort to discover what he'd meant by last evening's remark. She found him lounging comfortably in his host's study, poring over some new maps of the Western Territories that he'd obtained on his trip to Niagara. He was smoking a cigar—a practice he adopted on occasion when he felt completely relaxed—and the room was filled with clouds of bluish smoke that eddied and swirled when the door opened.

Jennifer walked over to where he sat and peered briefly over his shoulder. Then, after stepping back to admire the picture he made, she commented, ''Well, you certainly seem to be at home to a peg.''

Lord Somers removed the cigar from his mouth and expelled a little puff of smoke. ''And indeed, why shouldn't I?'' he asked pleasantly. ''After all, I collect the traveler's most valuable asset is the ability to feel at home wherever he may be.''

''I see. And do I take it that we're still to be considered travelers, then?''

His lordship paused to blow a perfect smoke ring before suddenly fixing his daughter with an intent look. ''Well, my dear, it would seem that that depends on you.''

''On me!'' Jennifer exclaimed in surprise.

''Doubtlessly,'' her father confirmed. ''It's all the same to me, you know, whether we remain here or return to England. Once war is declared, we'd surely be safer there, but also stuck for however long the 'hostilities,' as some people fondly call them, might last—and that could be several years. Whereas if we remain in this country, we've ever so many more options available to us,'' he observed, his eyes drawn longingly back to his maps. ''Of course, I warrant there's a certain risk involved in being British in a country that may soon be at war with England, but I daresay those risks are negligible compared to what I imagine you might see as the disadvantages of remaining here when you haven't yet resolved your feelings for Mr. Avery.

"I imagine, from the story Molly related, that we're none of us to be allowed the luxury of ignoring the conclusions that others may have drawn about the relationship between you and our host. And even though I know you fancy that *you* can live outside the rules of society, I sincerely doubt that that's true in the first place—and nor would I like you to discover that I'm right, in the second. Besides, don't forget that you are merely a visitor here and, if nothing else, you certainly owe it to the gentleman who makes this city his permanent residence to try and correct any damage a few malicious tongues may have caused to his household and his peace of mind.

"But if you think that you can avoid that situation by running away, or that I shall decide that we're to return home so that you needn't do anything about it yourself, then I must tell you, miss, that you've got the wrong sow by the ear! The fact is, I've determined not to lift a finger to help you out of this muddle. It's high time you faced what's in your heart, and to my way of thinking, the question of whether we're to return to England or remain here is a moot one until you do so." He leaned calmly back in his chair to observe the effect of this challenge.

Jennifer stared at him in dismay at the close of this little speech. "Surely you don't mean to abandon me?"

"Not at all," he assured her. "But you stated last night that we're in no particular hurry to decide one way or the other, and I, for one, have ample business to keep me busy for a while yet. Still, I don't think you ought to bide your time too long while the busybodies continue to make your activities the subject of their daily chats," he advised, before fixing her with a blandly curious look. "Indeed, I find myself wondering how it is you intend to fill all the hours ahead, and how long it may take before you feel ready to seek an interview with the very person whom I trust would be delighted to help you out of your dilemma..."

* * *

In fact, it took Jennifer nearly two more full days to succeed in reaching the decision her father had wondered about and to try to beard the lion in his den, as he'd once phrased it, by requesting a personal audience with Richard Avery. In the interim, she'd become increasingly irritable and inclined to be snappish, and had taken remarkably few pains to conceal that fact. She tried to excuse this behavior to herself, at least, as being the result of the treatment she'd received on the one excursion she'd made since returning to New York.

The previous afternoon, she and Ellen, the Averys' maid, had walked to a fashionable shop on nearby William Street to buy material to be made into some new dresses for Caroline. Inside, she'd happened upon one of the ladies she recalled meeting at the Rutlands' dinner party and nodded at her politely, only to be greeted by a cold stare in return and cut in such an obvious fashion that everyone in the shop promptly began to buzz about it. And it was only the timely entrance of Abigail herself a few minutes later that saved the situation from becoming even more uncomfortable. After taking a quick glance around and rapidly assessing Jennifer's predicament to an inch, Abigail at once saluted her in a friendly voice. Then, allowing a concerned look to steal over her pretty face, she drew Jennifer aside and inquired in a perfectly audible whisper how her Aunt Harriet was faring and whether the trip to Philadelphia had been a difficult one.

Jennifer hadn't the slightest idea why Abigail should have decided to come to her assistance. Nevertheless, she was quite willing to take the hand that was being extended to her. Therefore, she immediately volunteered that the trip south had been fairly tolerable and that her aunt was recovering nicely from a dangerous bout of pneumonia. But how, she'd asked in surprise, had Abigail known of her distress?

Oh, there wasn't anything mysterious about that, Abigail assured her with a laugh. Why, Sylvia Trask had been in a perfect rush to share how she'd spotted Richard Avery driving his guest out of the city. Only, when she'd sought to discover the reason, the silly thing had apparently gotten the facts all mixed up, Abigail confided, and had thought the "family business" on whose behalf the two had disappeared referred to Mr. Avery rather than to Jennifer. But after all, Abigail allowed, what else could one expect from a lady so fond of her sherry that she confused an emergency with an elopement? Thank heavens, she went on with a laugh, looking confidently around at the other ladies in the shop, they weren't all such pea-gooses as to make the same careless mistake. And at any rate, she promised as she patted Jennifer's hand in a kindly way, there'd been no lasting damage done to her reputation. Then, after inviting Jennifer to call as soon as she was settled, Abigail permitted herself a tiny, satisfied smile before sailing complacently out of the shop.

Unfortunately, Jennifer had been so caught up in her own thoughts since then that she hadn't stopped to take Molly into her confidence or even to consider how odd her behavior might appear to the casual observer. And her friend, knowing only that Jennifer had been closeted with her father a few days before—and also being fairly certain where that young lady's heart lay—had hastily jumped to the erroneous conclusion that Lord Somers had announced the two were shortly to return to England. That mistake in itself wouldn't have been so awful if Molly hadn't previously determined to assist the lovers in whatever way she could, and thus decided to waste no time in relaying her news to the gentleman involved.

Therefore, when Richard heard a knock on his study door at shortly after dinnertime, he settled his face into a polite mask and girded himself to learn the worst. Because he was something of a pessimist by nature anyway, his demeanor required very little revision. Still, he'd secretly hoped to be proven wrong in this instance, and Jennifer's immediate and passionate response to his one overture on their trip to Washington had given him temporary reason to hope that that might indeed occur. But save for the need to resolve the new crisis caused by their disappearance, it now seemed inevitable to him that reason would soon prevail and his life return once more to its stolid, predictable course. To be sure, he'd acted immediately to address the question of whether he'd compromised Jennifer's reputation—and rather cleverly, too, he'd thought—by embroidering on the story Molly had already invented for Sylvia Trask's benefit. Then, as promised, he'd taken Edward Rutland aside and confessed that the real reason for his sudden exodus from New York had been the unforseen illness of one of Lady Somers's relatives whom she hadn't known was in this country—a fact which, he explained guiltily, he hadn't thought it necessary to divulge before now. Mr. Rutland had been both relieved and sympathetic, and after chastising Richard briefly for the impression he'd so thoughtlessly created, had promptly agreed to see if he couldn't help rectify it. That was all well and good, Richard knew. Yet, to his view, all the gossip was only making his situation worse by pushing Jennifer and her father even closer to deciding to leave the United States. So prepared was he, in fact, to be told that they were now readying to depart, that without realizing it, his manner ultimately gave his visitor the distinct impression that that was exactly what he wished to happen.

"Good evening," Jennifer ventured. She crossed the room toward Richard's desk, but her first sight of the mountain of papers covering its surface and the owner's weary face proved somewhat daunting. "I wondered how you were faring in catching up with business. You didn't come to dinner, so I thought I would see if I could bring you a tray," she invented, seizing on the first excuse that popped into her head.

Richard was in fact very tired and hungry, and in this weakened state, Jennifer's gesture of concern and the friendly smile that accompanied it threatened to be his undoing. He suddenly longed to gather her onto his lap, bury his head in the soft, perfumed flesh of her neck, and beg her not to leave. Why was it that he seemed able to decide one thing in her absence, but the moment she appeared, his resolve invariably crumbled and he realized that whatever he'd concluded was not at all desirable and was often even ridiculous? Was it that he still insisted on thinking only with his head and steadfastly denying the dictates of his heart, which the sight of her then promptly brought to mind? Of course, once he recalled that tendency, he immediately resolved not to give in to it and then quickly made the mistake of moving too far in the opposite direction in order to compensate. "How thoughtful of you to inquire," he told Jennifer in a colorless voice. "Then, perhaps you'll be as relieved as I was to hear that the suit against the Manhattan Company has been dropped—apparently the Common Council decided there wasn't sufficient proof of negligence in the installation of the pump engine to warrant continuing to press for damages. But truly, you needn't have bothered about any other domestic details, you know. I'm sure such chores are more properly Mrs. Booth's responsibility than yours."

Jennifer bristled inwardly at the last statement. "Indeed," she forced herself to say politely. "I'm certain I never imagined that acting in a caring fashion toward someone else wasn't a suitable endeavor for any person to undertake. But possibly I don't understand what my 'proper responsibilities' are, and it would be helpful to us both if you delineated them for me."

This request caused Richard to become a trifle flustered. "That's not what I meant," he corrected hastily. "It's only that you needn't do such things—that is, unless of course you want to—and I don't expect you to do them, though naturally I very much appreciate it when you do— Oh, blast!" he exclaimed in frustration. "I didn't in the least wish to appear ungrateful, but clearly that's how I sounded. And what's more, I've no fixed notion of what your responsibilities are. Why, I'd have thought that that would have rather more to do with you than with me, because I fancy it's entirely your decision if you remain in this household at all."

Jennifer shot a penetrating look at the speaker. "Indeed?" she repeated, remembering how he'd once declared exactly the opposite. "I take it, then," she added casually, "that it doesn't matter very much to you one way or the other whether I return to England or stay in America?"

At this point, Richard suddenly dropped his eyes and began to exhibit a wonderful interest in the nib of his pen. "Oh, I don't think it would be entirely true to say that it wouldn't matter to me," he offered after a moment. His heart was pounding and he tried, albeit without much success, to approximate the same emotionless voice that his guest used. "And there are the children to consider, after all. Why, they've become so accustomed to you, I doubt they'd have the least notion how to get on if you left." *And nor would I*, he added forlornly to himself. "Though I certainly wouldn't expect a mere consideration of the twins' needs to persuade you to change your mind," he assured her. *And what about* your *needs*? Jennifer thought, beginning to tire of all this absurd shilly-shallying. *Why can't you tell me that you love me and don't wish me to leave?* she wondered, even though she'd nearly despaired of receiving an answer to that question by this point.

Good God, what is it that's keeping me from saying that I love her and don't want her to leave? Richard wondered somewhat desperately at nearly the same moment.

Unfortunately, this interlude was just long enough for Jennifer to have time to reflect on her companion's last remark again. "What do you mean, 'change my mind'?" she asked suspiciously. "How could you already know what I've decided when I only now came here to tell you that same thing myself, and I didn't even know what my decision would be until this very minute? In point of fact, I've decided to stay in New York a while longer," she announced suddenly. And despite there being no discernible reason for her to have reached that conclusion, she immediately felt vastly better once she'd voiced it.

Richard promptly started up from his chair, a smile of pure delight stealing over his face. "Do you mean it? But this is beyond anything great!" he exclaimed happily. "And here I was sure that you proposed to leave! At least, Miss Danhope told me that that was your plan, and I must say I'm overjoyed to discover that she was wrong!"

Jennifer had barely opened her mouth to inquire what else Molly might have told him when the door to the study burst open and Lord Somers reeled unsteadily into the room. Even if this performance hadn't advertised his condition, anyone who got within a few feet of his lordship would have detected with one sniff that that gentleman was a trifle up in the world, to put it politely. He stared in a muzzy fashion from one to the other of his companions before dropping heavily into a chair. "Just discovered Henry's in New York after all!" he crowed. "Turned up at the Mechanic Bank this afternoon to exchange his draft for cash! What's more, he then asked how he might go about sending the money to a friend in Washington! Why, fancy he's got the deeds to Crillon's estate in his pocket right now! Well, most natural thing in the world to expect him to show up at a bank first off—the only question in my mind was which one? Made a few inquiries here and there—in the light of possibly transacting a touch of business myself—and damned if our little game-bird didn't light down exactly where I'd spread the toils! Fine bit of detective work, don't you think? Been celebrating my success ever since, you see," he added as an afterthought. "Like to join me?"

Ordinarily, Jennifer was merely amused by her father's infrequent lapses into the bottle. This time, however, she felt unaccountably put out, and she wasn't prepared to say whether that fact was the result of his ill-timed entrance or because she'd no patience left with his determination to persist in shadowing Mr. Henry when all she wished to do was to forget the man and the visit to Washington altogether.

"It looks as if you don't need any assistance from us in feeling glorious," Jennifer observed in a tart voice, leaning heavily on the last word so that her listeners noted its double meaning. "As I was saying to Mr. Avery when you interrupted us, we've decided to remain in New York a while longer."

"We have?" her father exclaimed in surprise. "Well, damned good idea to face down all those silly chatterboxes and force them to recant, if you ask me," he continued the next moment, although no one had. "Don't have a clue what took you so long to make up your mind, my dear, but thank God you finally did." He offered Jennifer a benevolent smile of approval, which he at once broadened to include the room's other occupant as well.

To his amazement, Jennifer promptly blushed deeply, mumbled something about needing to check on the children, and fled from the room. That unlikely behavior only seemed to confuse Lord Somers further, especially since he'd already jumped to what he suddenly saw was an entirely wrong conclusion about what had led his daughter to decide to stay in America. "Aren't I to wish you both happy, then?" he asked Richard in a puzzled voice. "Well, naturally, I thought her decision was the result of her having received a declaration of love from you."

"It appears that your daughter doesn't wish to receive anything from me, I'm afraid, because she hasn't given me

the least encouragement to think that my suit would succeed," Richard said dryly. "And although everyone else
seems to know what her sentiments are, I've not yet been
privileged to hear them directly from the young lady herself.
Instead, I live only upon my hope, or I should say my
expectation, that she does indeed—or some day will—care
for me. In fact, until she announced that you were remaining
in New York, I'd begun to think you two would sail away
before I'd had a chance to discover firsthand what lies in her
heart and then to declare my own."

Lord Somers stared at his host in disbelief. "You mean to
tell me that you haven't yet given her anything more than a
hint? Good God, what a pair of milksops you are! Well, I
must say the two of you appear perfectly suited to one
another, though I'd never have guessed it, not if I lived to be
a hundred!" His lordship made a face at Richard. "Here now,
don't stand there gawking at me, my boy! Find us a drop of
something to steady our nerves and we'll see if we can't find
a way out of this coil. And just thank your stars that at least
one of us appears to have his head properly screwed on!"

At nearly the same time as her father was sitting down
with Richard for a masculine chat, Jennifer sought out
Molly in order to conduct a little tête-à-tête of their own. If
truth be told, however, part of her was secretly relieved at
the discovery that her friend had apparently been confiding
enough of Jennifer's state of mind along the way so that
Richard wasn't entirely in the dark regarding the state of her
heart. And certainly, she wasn't so mean-spirited as to deny
the man the sort of confidante that she enjoyed. As she saw
it, the problem was that the same person had been acting in
that capacity for both of them, and that fact in itself must
have occasioned at least some of the confusion they were
currently experiencing. If Molly had only kept strictly to
what she knew for certain, they might have escaped their
present entanglement, but in her efforts to be helpful, she'd
apparently volunteered speculation and supposition as well.
Jennifer gave a tiny groan. Now, thanks to yet another
instance of good intentions run amok, she would be obliged
to sift through this mountain of fiction and fantasy, if only to

determine how much—if anything—she needed to do to remedy the situation. It did occur to her briefly that her reaction was completely overblown and her latest errand only another form of prevarication. But she hastily thrust that thought aside and assumed the same self-righteous attitude she heartily disliked in others for at least the second time in recent memory.

She discovered Molly tidying up the schoolroom and singing a raucous tune to herself, each verse of which appeared to end with the refrain, "And he was a sailor from Bristol, and she much too young for a bride."

"Truly, I didn't realize you were so familiar with the subject of matrimony," Jennifer observed after a few moments in a pointed fashion that was clearly meant to refer to more than the song.

"Oh, I've had a brush or two with it," Molly said modestly. "Still, no doubt you're more familiar with marriage than I."

"Well, I won't be, if you have anything to say about it!" Jennifer exclaimed somewhat unfairly. "Tell me—just how long have you been feeding Mr. Avery snippets of information about my feelings for him? It certainly must have been for some little time now because he seems able to predict to a nicety exactly what I'll do on practically any occasion!"

Molly appeared a bit taken aback by this accusation, though rather more by its form than its content, it turned out. Privately, she seemed to agree with the fact that Jennifer's response was altogether out of proportion. "Why, I merely assured the poor man that he'd nothing to fear from Mr. Verplanck and Mr. Hartley as rivals," Molly said mildly. Whereupon, she proceeded to sketch in the outlines of her various conversations with Richard Avery since that first day. "And anyhow," she concluded, 'I'm sure I don't see what you're in such a taking about. It isn't as if I've invented the feelings you have for the man, so what's the difference if he learns of them first from you or from me?"

Jennifer was in the midst of trying to summon a response to that very sensible question when her attention was drawn by a noise outside. Peering down into the street, the two women observed that Jeremy had arrived and was hastily dismounting. As if by mutual agreement, they at once forswore any further discussion, exited the schoolroom, and began to descend the stairs in the hope of discovering what news that messenger might have brought from Washington. But they hadn't even reached the door of the study when a loud oath from within stopped them in mid-stride. "Confound the fools!" they heard Lord Somers bellow. "They're going to blow the gaff with their silly scheming, damned if they won't!"

Chapter 18

WHEN JENNIFER and Molly entered the study, they discovered a dramatic scene eminently suitable to accompany the dire prediction they'd overheard outside. Richard half stood behind his desk, leaning forward on both hands and staring in disbelief at Lord Somers. The latter, having apparently recovered some of his composure—or at least a measure of his balance—was poised in a decidedly theatrical attitude: legs spread, head thrown back, one hand holding up a few sheets of paper. And poor Jeremy was crumpled in the far corner, looking so dismal at the reception he'd been accorded that it prompted Jennifer to wonder whether he'd ever heard how bearers of bad news in ancient times were often beheaded for their effort.

These theatrics were sufficiently distracting to cast her other concerns into the shade for the moment. Thus, she was able to observe in a relatively calm voice, "Any particular reason for this row, or are you all merely seeking admittance to Bedlam—or, should I say, Bellevue?"

Lord Somers waved the papers he was holding until they rustled like dead leaves in a strong wind. "Got a letter here from Secretary Monroe in which, as a courtesy, he advises us of the current status of the Henry matter. Apparently, before he left Washington, Henry—presumably at either Monroe's or Madison's request—wrote a letter postdated February 20, which begins as follows: 'To James Monroe, secretary of state. Sir: I have the honor to transmit herewith the documents and correspondence relating to an important mission in which I was employed by Sir James Craig, the late governor general of the British provinces in North America, in the winter of the year 1809.' Well, I won't bother to read you the whole of the text, which Monroe has generously provided, but Henry goes on to say that he hopes the material will prove that no reliance should be placed on England's professions of good faith and that it will promote unity among all parties in America. The letter is signed by Henry and noted as being sent from Philadelphia.''

His lordship deliberately paused and looked around at his audience. ''Well, it's obvious to all of us, at any rate, that he couldn't have written the letter on the twentieth, as he says, because that's tomorrow—and he's not in Philadelphia but in New York, as we've just learned! So it appears to me that the letter is part of a smoke screen I'd lay odds was cooked up by Monroe to make it appear that Henry decided, for some unknown reason, to disclose his activities to the government voluntarily. Clearly, they don't mean to reveal that Madison authorized a payment of fifty thousand dollars for the letters because that might damage their credibility in submitting them as evidence of England's treachery.''

Jennifer was quick to perceive the difficulties presented by that strategy. ''But if they meant to keep the money a secret, they haven't been very careful to do so,'' she pointed out. ''I mean, Henry took a public stage from Washington, so it would be easy for anyone to discover how and when he left the city. What's more, he then turned up bold as you please a few days later at a bank in New York to exchange his draft for a considerable sum of cash, thus making it relatively simple to pin down his arrival here as being before the date on this last letter. Therefore, it seems to me, that rather than improve on the government's claim, this move will actually serve to damage the president's reputation, should the full scope of his machinations ever be disclosed.''

Lord Somers smiled approvingly at his daughter. ''Just

what I was thinking," he told her. "But there's no help for it now; the thing's done. I only hope they don't attempt any more foolishness, or they'll very likely get their fingers burned for their trouble."

Everyone present indulged in a short, private meditation on the unhappy prospect his lordship had just raised. Then their thoughts were interrupted by a knock at the door and the entrance of Walters, who hurried across the room toward his employer wearing a distinctly worried expression. "Mr. Hays is here to see you, sir," he advised Richard in a completely audible whisper. "And he told me to say that it was an urgent, official matter."

"What the devil—? Damned peculiar time to choose to conduct business!" Richard exclaimed. Then, recollecting his companions, he explained, "Jacob Hays is the high constable of New York, the mayor's chief assistant in maintaining public order, and a thoroughly repulsive little man altogether too greedy for power, if you ask me. No doubt he's come to tax me with some new transgression on the part of the Manhattan Company," he guessed. "But no need for you to leave. I promise I'll make short work of whatever he has in mind to discuss."

A few minutes later, the individual who Richard told them boasted that he knew every criminal in the city personally swaggered into the study, and without waiting to be invited, took the chair closest to the desk. He was the sort of man whose appearance would ordinarily lead him to be called nondescript, save for the fact that he felt himself to be so extraordinary that he tended to preen like a peacock in mating season. That attitude usually attracted attention for a while at least, and it was during this transient period that Hays always attempted to order the circumstances so that he could continue to dominate the situation after his audience inevitably became disillusioned. Therefore, he now allowed his glance to rove boldly around the room, skipping over Molly and Jeremy as clearly beneath notice, then pausing at Lord Somers for a closer—if rather condescending—scrutiny, and finally coming to light on Jennifer. This young lady he proceeded to examine in such an outrageously irreverent manner that she promptly began to blush, and her father and her host each began separately to contemplate a somewhat more decisive, physical response.

"I understand you've some business to transact that concerns me?" Richard said abruptly, in the hope of disposing of his guest as quickly as possible.

Mr. Hays was not prepared to be hurried along, however. "In due time," he told Richard firmly. "Must say I've never known you to be so remiss in your hospitality before," he chided in mock surprise. "Aren't you going to introduce me to your other guests? But wait—this couldn't be Sir Jonathan Somers and his daughter, Jennifer, whom I've heard so much about, could it?"

"Yes," Richard acknowledged briefly. "And frankly, I don't care what you may have heard, or from whom, about my visitors. All *I* wish to hear is what this 'official matter' is that you mean to discuss with me."

"Ah, but I'm afraid that that matter involves your visitors," Hays informed him. "You see," he said, tapping his coat pocket importantly, "I have with me a warrant for their arrest."

"Why, you insolent cur!" Richard exploded.

Hays continued to regard him with implacable calm. "Yes, so a great many people appear to think," he agreed. "Still, my own behavior is nothing to the point—it's that of your two guests that concerns us at the moment." He paused to look Richard up and down with ill-concealed amusement. "Good God, man—no doubt if you'd such a weapon at hand, you wouldn't hesitate to horsewhip me to avenge the lady's honor! Particularly when I understand that you're rumored to be on altogether cozy terms with these spies!"

"Spies—?" Jennifer echoed faintly, harboring a wild hope that she hadn't heard correctly.

"Indeed," Hays assured her. "And allow me to congratulate you, my lady, on your excellent performance in feigning surprise at those charges." He stood up and began to stride around the room in order to give suitable emphasis to his words. "Did you not, soon after your arrival in New York, take a trip to the Western Territories in order to ascertain the status of the American troops in the area?" he demanded suddenly, turning around to point an accusing finger at Lord Somers.

That gentleman looked puzzled rather than alarmed by this question. "Well, it's true I did travel up to Niagara, but merely with the intent of studying how one might harness the power of that amazing phenomenon. Besides, I was detained by the British themselves when I couldn't immediately prove that I was a fellow citizen, so that ought to be evidence enough that I'm not engaged by the Prince Regent or any of his cronies on some furtive business for England. And what's more, though it hardly seems necessary to remind you, I *am* a respected peer of the British Empire," he pointed out with a quiet modesty that his other companions found utterly persuasive.

Mr. Hays was apparently unimpressed by this argument. "Rot!" he scoffed. "God, but you must think me green indeed to fancy I'd swallow such a ridiculous story about your reasons for undertaking the trip! In the first place, no call why you shouldn't be detained by honest soldiers, because I warrant it wouldn't be the only time the tail didn't know what the head was doing. Why, a poor infantryman's scarcely likely to be aware of the plans some general or other may have laid! And in the second place, as far as your being a lord is concerned, I personally don't see how that title is in any way incompatible with the one of 'informer.' If you ask me, the former calling's a perfect disguise for the latter because it enables you to snoop around with relative impunity and to gain access to places that are usually proscribed." He paused to examine Lord Somers's genial expression for a moment. "And if that weren't sufficient, your dedication in acting the simpleton's apt to dissuade most people from considering you a serious threat or at least as anything more harmful than the poor noodle you appear to be," he finished scornfully.

"And what about me? Do you think me a mere goose, too, or something entirely more sinister?" Jennifer walked over to plant herself in front of Mr. Hays in order to stare him defiantly in the eye.

He smiled down at her with the sort of warped pleasure she imagined a snake might feel about a mouse right before it swallowed the creature for dinner. "Oh, you, my lady, I've been led to believe are the cunning mind behind the entire operation. You direct your father where to go—Niagara or Washington, for example—and you sit back and await his coded reports delivered by special messenger! Meanwhile, it's you who curries up to those gentlemen who appear to be the most powerful or in a position to feed you the information you require about the state of America's forces—you do remember your friends Mr. Verplanck and Mr. Hartley, do you not? And at the same time, you place yourself under the protection of a man so easily duped by the womanish wiles at which you're a master hand that he's ready to defend you against any challenge without even questioning the reason for it!" At the close of this little speech, Mr. Hays cast a look of such disgust at his host that that gentleman fairly itched to put his hands around the other man's throat and put an end to the string of half-truths and insinuations to which he and his guests had just been subjected.

In fact, Richard was so stunned by the events of the preceding few minutes that he didn't know whether to try and laugh them off or attempt to order Hays out of the house. The trouble was that the man's facts were basically correct, but it was as if they'd been tossed up in the air and then put back together in such a haphazard manner that the overall result was a gross distortion of the situation, at best. Still, Richard had to admit that the depth of the information Hays seemed to possess bespoke a long and careful study of both his household and its occupants, and one that wasn't easy to discount. And moreover, the question of who had undertaken that investigation and who had authorized it were no doubt also linked in some way to the identity of the person who had ordered the arrest, he reasoned rapidly.

"Who is it that laid these charges?" he demanded. "I insist you give us the name of the person at once!"

Mr. Hayes appeared only mildly interested in the reaction he'd managed to provoke. "Oh, but I'm afraid I'm not obliged to divulge that information—at least, not until the hearing, which I believe may be the first week in April when the court sits. Now, I realize that that's nearly a month away, but in the interim, I've arranged for a very nice apartment in Bridewell Prison to accommodate our new guests.'' His voice grew harsh and he stared arrogantly at his audience. ''This warrant's absolutely legal, I assure you, so don't bother trying to think up some way to escape. And if you don't mean to come peaceably downstairs to my carriage, I've two leatherheads with me who'd be glad to drag you through the streets instead, if that's the sort of justice you've a taste for tonight.''

Richard walked over to the window and peered down into the street. Sure enough, he saw two members of the city's night watch shifting miserably about on the front steps in an effort to keep warm. The leather helmets they wore denoted their official position and were also the source of the derogatory name by which even their own superiors referred to them. He looked across the room at Lord Somers and Jennifer and gave a small, resigned shake of his head. ''This is outrageous!'' he protested in an angry voice. ''I shall speak with Mayor Clinton about this matter first thing tomorrow. And you'd best have a care how you step in the meantime,'' he threatened Hays, ''because I shall hold you personally responsible for their safety!''

Hays broke into a rude laugh. ''No need to worry, then. They'll be safe enough in prison, I warrant! Come along, now,'' he said sternly to his prisoners. ''I've wasted enough time as it is. Treason's a hanging crime, and spying ain't much different, that I can tell. I'm bound to follow the law, all right, but I'm damned if I'm obliged to be polite as well!''

Richard hurried across the study toward his guests and then hovered anxiously beside them as they donned their outer garments, which Molly produced. ''Don't worry, sir, I promise I'll exert every effort to clear up this misunderstanding as soon as possible,'' he told Lord Somers, stealing a little sidelong glance at Jennifer as he spoke.

His lordship, however, continued to look basically unconcerned by this latest development. But whether he was truly not worried or merely affecting that attitude for the sake of his daughter, Richard couldn't tell. ''Thank you, my boy, I'm sure you'll do your best,'' he said. He reached out to pump Richard's hand gratefully. "How very fortunate indeed is the man who's been blessed with influential friends new and old, near and far," he observed with peculiar emphasis. "Then, no matter how great the distance, he can be forever confident that they'll stretch out a helping hand the moment they learn he's in need." He looked at Richard for a long, telling moment when he finished speaking, and then let his eyes stray around the room from face to face until they came to rest on Jeremy, as if by accident.

At this point, Mr. Hays appeared to waver in his conclusion that Lord Somers's foolish demeanor was purely counterfeit, especially because the foregoing random speech strongly seemed to indicate otherwise. He'd been entirely too patient in putting up with all their silliness, he decided abruptly. Whereupon, he promptly altered his behavior, leaving Richard time to do little more than press Jennifer's hand briefly between his own in a fleeting gesture of encouragement before she was bundled down the stairs with her father and into the waiting carriage.

What may have sounded like utter nonsense to his guest, however, had made ample good sense to Richard, for he recognized that Lord Somers had sent him a perfectly clear message regarding what he was to do next. He allowed himself to spend a few moments staring mutely out the window after Hays's carriage had driven down the street, rounded the corner onto Broadway, and headed north toward the prison. When he finally turned away from that dismal sight, Richard had a look of grim purpose in his eyes that his remaining two companions found moderately heartening. He strode over to his desk, took a seat, and with one broad sweep of an arm cleared a space in the middle of its surface. Next he located paper and ink, placed them close at hand, and then sat nibbling on his pen for a minute.

"Are you prepared to ride hard tonight?" he demanded suddenly of Jeremy, who was still slumped in a far corner of the room. "I've a notion that may work, but its success will depend on your delivering the letter I'm about to write to Washington as quickly as you can, and then bringing me the answer I require from there with similar speed."

Jeremy tossed his head up and down a couple of times in

his own unique way. "Aye. If it's to help his lordship, I can manage right enough, I reckon."

"Capital!" Richard said in thankful accents. "Then go find yourself some bait in the kitchen and a bed for a while. I'll see that you're wakened in a few hours, and this letter will be finished and waiting by the time you're ready to set out."

He and Molly watched Jeremy exit the room to carry out his suggestion. The latter individual, who'd lost none of her habitual calm during Mr. Hays's visit and never doubted for a second that the three principals involved would puzzle a way out of their present difficulty within a relatively brief amount of time, now offered a suggestion of her own.

"If it's all the same to you, I'll pack up a few things the two of them might be needing," she offered. "Bridewell ain't the meanest place they could have ended up, from what I hear, especially since they've plenty of pocket money to ease their way through the worst of what it may have to offer. Still, I warrant one jail's as cheerless as another, and they'll be glad to get whatever we can provide in the way of dainties. Speaking of which, if you've no objection, I'll have a word with your cook. Doubtless the man can put together a basket or two to tide them over for the short time they'll be staying in that place."

This last remark was clearly said with a bravado meant to convince the speaker, as much as anyone else, of the quick resolution they might reasonably anticipate. "A splendid notion," Richard told her warmly. It occurred to him to mention that his chef, Monsieur Fouquet, was scarcely likely to enjoy being referred to as an ordinary cook, but he decided such a thought wasn't worth a fribble compared to his other concerns. "Let's divide things up, shall we? What do you say if you look after our friends', er, physical requirements and I see to their mental well-being, so that between the both of us, they ought to be able to bear up tolerably well?" Whereupon, after receiving a nod of agreement from Molly, he dipped his pen into the ink and began to write.

* * *

The next afternoon, Richard and Molly, laden down with two small valises of clothing, several warm blankets, and a couple of baskets stuffed with such temptations as roasted capons, drove up to Bridewell Prison. The dark gray stone walls seemed to mirror his mood, Richard thought glumly to himself, for he'd spent part of the morning, as promised, in an interview with De Witt Clinton, the mayor of New York, in his office at City Hall in the building next to Bridewell. That gentleman had proven a good deal less than helpful, however. He'd responded to Richard's appeal for information with bare civility, and then promptly lived up to his reputation as a man who favored blunt action over tactful maneuvering. He'd flatly refused to divulge the name of the person who'd ordered the Somerses arrested. And he'd merely raised an eyebrow in silent disbelief at Richard's suggestion that they ought to be released into his custody until their hearing before declaring the idea to be entirely too irregular. Then, apparently having been swept up by the current wave of patriotic fever, he went so far as to denounce his guest for harboring such bothersome visitors of his own, and finally offered the unsolicited opinion that war with England would be a "most important public service."

This exchange had been altogether frustrating for Richard, first because it had failed in any way to ameliorate the Somerses' situation, and second because it indicated how strongly public opinion might be weighed against ordinary British citizens as the prospect of war loomed ever closer. What's more, it meant that he was now forced to place all his hopes on the outcome of the other course of action he'd initiated through Jeremy, and he already had strong doubts about whether or not it would succeed.

It was this latter topic that occupied his thoughts as he and Molly were let in through the gate and then led past the jailor's quarters, the solitary cells, and the Long Room for common prisoners, before being directed to the second floor of the prison. Here, those who could afford to do so kept private apartments while they either awaited a hearing or served out their sentences.

Lord Somers and his daughter had been fortunate enough—or, perhaps, been considered sufficiently important prisoners—

to command one of the largest of these chambers, which boasted a coveted narrow slit of a window. What's more, the two visitors found that the occupants had wasted little time in making themselves as comfortable as possible. Within a few minutes of their guests' arrival, his lordship was able to bespeak a modest tea, which was brought in by a young guard apparently as grateful for Jennifer's smile as for the coin her father slipped into his hand. The baskets of food Monsieur Fouquet had provided enabled them to augment the simple fare with some juicy apple tarts and a buttery pound cake, and for a few minutes they were able merely to chat about commonplaces.

Indeed, at least two members of the group found it especially comforting to have something with which to occupy their hands, since merely seeing one another in such depressing circumstances was proving rather disconcerting to their minds. The moment the visitors had entered the chamber, Jennifer had felt oddly comforted by Richard's presence, even though objectively she was aware that there was probably little he could do to alleviate the situation. And Richard, for his part, had immediately felt unreasonably happy at discovering that Jennifer was safe, despite recognizing that that emotion was quite irrational when he knew her father was perfectly capable of ensuring that she was well protected.

The business of having tea might have been sufficient to camouflage the foregoing reactions to someone less keen-eyed than Lord Somers. As it was, however, his lordship had no difficulty observing the way the two were clearly drawn to each other. And that discovery prompted him both to hope that Richard might at last have decided to act without awaiting Jennifer's permission to do so, and that his daughter might finally perceive how much Richard cared for her and be inclined to offer him some encouragement in return. In fact, Lord Somers found that prospect so cheering to contemplate that he was obliged to call himself to order when he discovered that Richard had introduced a more serious topic into their conversation.

"I should tell you, sir, that I've already taken action on your proposal of last night," Richard informed him. "Jeremy departed before dawn, and barring a change in the weather that might impede his progress, I'd imagine we could expect a response before the week is out.''

Jennifer stared from her father to Richard and then back again in confusion. "What proposal?" she asked, a trifle miffed at feeling suddenly on the periphery of the discussion. "I'm sure I don't recall anything being mentioned.''

"No, not directly, it's true," her father agreed. "But I hinted as well as I dared about what course I thought we might follow—near enough, at any rate, for Richard here to have taken my meaning. Well done indeed, my boy!" he congratulated him warmly. "If you think for a moment, you'll realize there's only one way to prove that all our skulking and stalking was for a commendable purpose, rather than the dastardly one of which we've been accused," he pointed out to his daughter. "Secretary Monroe—or, preferably, President Madison himself—will have to write to the mayor, explain our 'mission,' if you want to call it that, and request that the charges be dropped and that we be released. Ordinarily, we wouldn't expect to suffer any more than, perhaps, a week or two of cooling our heels in this charming abode before anticipating that our captivity would be brought to a speedy close. But instead, we just may find ourselves in a very awkward position," he admitted slowly. "Because of their previous agreement with Henry, the timing, you see, now appears to be the crux of the matter.''

"Good God!" Jennifer exclaimed, as the significance of her father's remarks became clear. "You mean that the same gentlemen whom we just assisted out of their trouble in Washington may actually find it beyond their power to assist us out of ours—or at any rate, not immediately? Why, in that case, we may be obliged to languish here until Henry sails for the Continent and his letters are made public, and who knows when that will be." She thought about that statement for a moment, and then began to giggle a little. "When I recall what a pretty pass I thought we'd reached before, it quite surpasses the imagination that things should have become infinitely worse now! Though truly, we've no one but ourselves to blame, you know. Well, after all, if we hadn't been so effective in our sleuthing, we wouldn't have provided the very information that's apparently also clipped our wings, would we?'' Her audience nodded their heads in unison at this question like obedient school children, causing Jennifer to laugh outright. ''Besides, we don't exactly seem to be enduring any great hardship so far,'' she observed in amusement as she cast a pointed look around the chamber. ''And in some obscure fashion, it almost seems to make sense that we're being kept here as prisoners because during the Revolution, I understand, the British troops that took over New York used these same quarters to house captured American soldiers.''

Richard shifted uneasily for a moment at this mention of war, though he made a pretense of it being on account of the hard seat he was occupying. ''Yes, well, no need to think of yourselves as permanent residents yet, you know,'' he told them in a too-hearty voice. ''Surely Madison will be able to think of some way out of this tangle that won't require you to rot away here for untold weeks. And in the meantime, I'll see if I can't take up where you left off, sir, and discover what our old friend Mr. Henry is about,'' he promised Lord Somers earnestly.

At this point, his lordship paused to wonder why Richard should be choosing to waste his time in such a a manner when it clearly had so little chance of improving their situation. He'd just opened his mouth to point out that fact when another glance at Richard and the covert looks he kept stealing at Jennifer served to remind his lordship that a person with too much time on his hands was invariably cast into the doldrums or fell into a scrape, or sometimes both. And since he suspected that Richard either needed some task in which to immerse himself while they were locked up, or the feeling of performing some feat by which he might accrue a measure of praise rather than blame, he decided not to mention that such a pursuit was bound to be profitless. Therefore, he merely smiled in his usual genial fashion and allowed, ''And for my part, I'm confident that you'll endeavor to keep our best interests in mind, as always, dear boy.''

In point of fact, Richard was feeling painfully responsible for the Somerses' current predicament. True, he realized that this position wasn't entirely reasonable, but that didn't alter the feeling that he'd gotten his two guests embroiled in the entire affair to begin with and that he was now somehow obligated to extricate them safely from the ruins of their joint enterprise. He should have talked Jennifer out of her crazy idea of copying Henry's letters in the first place, he thought bitterly as he and Molly retraced their steps out to the waiting carriage. Or at least he should have stood up for his belief that tampering in such a fashion with someone's personal possessions was definitely unseemly. But he'd been too weak-willed to do so, thought on the surface one would certainly have thought his principles were worth fighting for. Just how was it that he'd been convinced to compromise them? he wondered for perhaps the dozenth time. Only, he hadn't compromised his beliefs, he'd reevaluated them, and his actions, rather than indicating he'd thrown them over, actually showed to what lengths he'd gone to make them his own and to incorporate them into his life.

Moreover, in the back of his mind lurked a thought that was altogether at odds with the foregoing hodgepodge. Here at last—though he told himself he was reluctant to look at it in such a light—was a situation of dangerous proportions from which he might, by his bold and daring actions, be able to save Jennifer and at the same time show himself to be a man of heroic stature who loved her deeply. He groaned to himself. Indeed, how convenient it would be if he could somehow incontrovertibly demonstrate those things instead of being obliged to state them outright, because his previous essays in that direction had been anything but fruitful.

He'd give a good deal to know what Jennifer was thinking right now, too, Richard realized. Was she speculating about whether he was doing anything to help her out of her predicament or already imagining how he might only succeed in making matters worse, the way the trip to Washington had managed to do? And given that whatever he did had but a slim chance of having any effect at all, was she perhaps considering how heavily to weigh that fact for or against him when it came around to debating the merits of his suit? Or was she standing by the window brushing her wonderful hair while the setting sun made it look as if she were wearing a diadem of pure light? he found himself wondering, before hastily brushing that irrelevant thought firmly aside.

And having in this manner decided—temporarily, at least—to become a man of deeds rather that mere thoughts, Richard set about the task of seeing if he couldn't discover what John Henry's plans might be. To that end he enlisted Molly's assistance, reasoning that because she knew the city intimately she'd be likely to guess where the man might be lodged and know those haunts that he might be inclined to frequent. In this estimation he proved quite correct, for Molly was able to fix Henry's direction so closely that within twenty-four hours and after remarkably little difficulty, Richard had pinpointed the cheap roominghouse near the docks where his quarry had gone to ground.

The next several days Richard devoted entirely to shadowing Henry's every movement. Such constant attention was scarcely necessary because there were only a handful of ships presently at anchor in the harbor, and it would have been relatively simple for anyone of moderate intelligence to learn on which of these Henry proposed to set sail. But as Lord Somers had guessed, Richard relished the activity—unnecessary as it might be—in order to feel that he was doing something other than feeling frustrated at his inability to secure the Somerses' release.

He barely went into his office at all and managed to avoid seeing anyone but members of his household. Whether that evasion was studiously pursued or adopted only as a convenience, however, he was distinctly reluctant to say. Of course, isolating himself again in this fashion allowed him to avoid being questioned about the Somerses and to pretend that he could ignore the stories he knew were doubtless circulating both about the reasons for their arrest and about his response to it. And because he saw to it that he did nothing but lurk in shadowy corners, bundled into Mr. Booth's invaluable topcoat, watching Henry drink beer or rum in one waterfront tavern after another, he told himself he also had no time to think about what he would say to Jennifer if and when she ever got out of Bridewell. And because it suddenly seemed easier to put off that eventuality as long as possible, nearly a week passed after his first trip to the prison without him once repeating that act. In lieu of going himself, he sent Molly on daily visits there to convey the latest news of his investigation to the Somerses and to ensure that they wanted for nothing. And this substitution he continually excused by telling himself that his presence was clearly required elsewhere. In point of fact, however, he was secretly afraid that seeing Jennifer again would cause him to toss away his carefully laid plans in favor of rushing to her side. What's more, he then convinced himself that such an emotional response would be of no real use to her and that he was accomplishing far more good with his current activities. But what he sadly failed to consider was that in being so careful to shield his emotions from Jennifer by not visiting her, he succeeded only in creating the unmistakable impression that he scarcely cared for her at all.

It was with decidedly mixed feelings, therefore, that he finally discovered from a sailor willing to be primed with a few measures of rum that Henry was to embark the next day. Strangely enough, space had apparently been reserved for him in advance on an American armed vessel called *The Wasp*, which had the previous morning received orders to sail for France. And no sooner had Richard garnered that information than he realized he ought to convey it with all due speed to his former conspirators. He debated for a moment whether or not to go directly to Bridewell, but believing discretion to be the better part of valor, he opted to return to his house and change his clothes before calling on the Somerses. He had just finished making himself presentable and was fussing over his neck cloth when he head a clatter downstairs. And by the time he walked from his bedchamber to the landing, Jeremy was staggering up the stairs to thrust a heavy envelope with an impressive-looking seal into his hand.

The poor man appeared so done in that Richard half-dragged him into the study, pushed him into a comfortable chair, and then pressed a generous glass of whiskey into his hand. The niceties of common courtesy having thus been attended to, he tore open the envelope and anxiously scanned the contents of the letter it contained. "Thank heavens!" he exclaimed a minute later in a relieved voice. "Why, damned if I won't leave for Bridewell this instant!"

At that declaration, Jeremy rallied sufficiently to shake his head back and forth in an energetic fashion. "Oh, no—wouldn't do that!" he said firmly.

Richard gaped at his companion for a moment in surprise, and was on the point of demanding irritably just why the devil he wouldn't when the door of the study opened and Lord Somers strolled negligently into the room. "So glad to find you at home this afternoon, dear boy," he assured Richard, as imperturbably as ever.

Chapter 19

RICHARD STARED at Lord Somers in amazement for a moment, his mouth indelicately half open. "But how the devil did you get here?" he demanded, after he'd recovered from his initial shock. "And where is Jennifer? Have the charges been dropped?"

His lordship held up a hand to ward off a second flood of questions, smiling a little at how high the one regarding Jennifer's whereabouts had ranked on Richard's scale of major concerns. "Jennifer, I understand, is upstairs seeking a hot bath—an activity I shortly expect to partake in myself—and indulging in the luxury of a little privacy after a week of being thrust cheek by jowl next to her beloved father. And as to your other inquiries and the details of our release, didn't Jeremy recount the train of events for you?"

"I'm afraid I haven't given him a chance," Richard said apologetically. "But he only arrived a few minutes before you did."

Lord Somers's polished demeanor cracked a little as he allowed himself to sink tiredly into a chair by the fire. "I take it, then, that Clinton made you dangle around for several hours while he played first fiddle in arranging for our release from Bridewell and, no doubt also claiming credit for that accomplishment?" he asked Jeremy. "Well, and I'm not surprised. You received a note from the president yourself, did you not?"

"Yes," Richard admitted, nodding at the sheet of paper that was still clutched tightly in his hand. "But it wasn't very informative. ' 'My dear sir,' '' he read aloud, '' 'I have taken the necessary steps to secure the immediate release of your friends from that most unfortunate situation in which they now find themselves. I do most sincerely ask your forgiveness for any inconvenience this episode may have caused you or them. I can only repeat that you have performed a valuable service for your government, for which I am extremely grateful, and hope that you don't feel the unforeseen repercussions of the act in any way diminish its worth in my eyes. Although I doubt that anyone can truly be thankful for having been brought to the brink of war, time will prove whether we've reason to believe that our actions were at least beneficial in preventing what might ultimately have been a far worse catastrophe. Yours, James Madison.' ''

"Mmm—yes, I see," his lordship acknowledged. "Apparently, Madison wrote to Clinton ordering that we were to be released immediately and instructed Jeremy to see that he delivered that letter first. You'll recall that we worried about how such a feat could be accomplished without compromising the previous agreement the government had made with Henry?" he said, tilting his head to one side in a considering manner. "Well, it appears that we overlooked one crucial factor: The president of the United States isn't obliged to divulge the reasons for his decisions—unless he wishes to, of course. Therefore, he merely told Clinton that we were conducting an investigation in response to a direct request from him to do so, and nothing more. Why, it wouldn't even surprise me to learn that Clinton never actually knew the name of the person who'd lodged the charges against us in the first place, given how comfortably he seems to operate without sufficient evidence. Madison, however, was kind enough to fill in that particular gap in the letter he sent to us—''

"Oh!" Richard exclaimed suddenly, as he was thus reminded of the original reason why he'd been about to set off for Bridewell. "Why, I nearly forgot, but I've some news of my own to share with you!"

"Oh?" Jennifer inquired in a sarcastic tone, having entered the room just in time to catch this last remark. "Why, then it must have been something vastly too important to entrust to Molly, since you seemed perfectly willing for her to play messenger all week instead of even once coming to discover yourself how we were getting on! Let's see now—what could it be?" she wondered. Her eyes flashed while she pretended to study Richard's face for a minute, in an attempt to control her temper. "Perhaps you meant to inform us that you'd had second thoughts about associating with persons suspected of being in the employ of a foreign government?" she offered, promptly giving up that effort as fruitless. She smiled with satisfaction as Richard began to squirm beneath her scrutiny and relentless questioning. "Or possibly you intended to advise how we might occupy ourselves and at the same time keep from fearing that we'd been deserted by the one individual we trusted not to let us down!" Her smile turned frosty as she glared accusingly at the man she clearly held responsible for those sentiments.

"Do you know, I think I'll just see if I can't have that bath now," Lord Somers announced pleasantly at this point to the room at large. "Come along, old boy," he urged, propelling Jeremy out of his chair and then pointing him toward the door. "Plain to see we're neither of us needed at the moment," he whispered loudly, "so best to make our escape before the, er, banners are raised."

Their departure had remarkably little effect on the scene in the study, however. Jennifer continued to stare angrily at Richard, for she was altogether furious and not bothering at all to disguise that fact. He persisted in regarding her, in turn, with a good deal of confusion. Seeing her again after being separated for a week had made him feel positively giddy, and he was having considerable difficulty admitting first that Jennifer clearly felt otherwise and second that she was obviously not in the least delighted to see him at the moment.

Unfortunately, in addition finally to convincing himself that his reasons for not visiting the Somerses in Bridewell were unexceptional, Richard had then typically forgotten that Jennifer not only didn't know what those reasons were, but also that she might arrive at an entirely different conclusion regarding their validity, even if she did. "Whatever's the matter?" he asked somewhat plaintively now. "Aren't you relieved to be out of prison?"

"Yes, but no thanks to you!" she exclaimed with an irritated toss of her head. "How could you just leave us in that—that place and never once come to visit?" she asked, trying without much success to keep her voice from breaking. "Not," she continued after a moment in a stronger tone, "that we were exactly at a loss for visitors, you understand. Dear me, no! Why, most everyone of our acquaintance in town—from Mr. Hartley and Mr. Verplanck, to Miss Rutland and her father, and even Sylvia Trask—made it their business to stop by and see how we were faring!" She hesitated briefly at the expression on Richard's face before plunging ahead. "I see that Molly didn't think to share that fact with you. Well, I'm sure I don't know why she didn't, nor do I have any idea how the news of our detainment so quickly became public knowledge. But at any rate, all of our visitors seemed to find it singularly noteworthy that you hadn't even put in an appearance at our little cell. And coming so close on the heels of our eventful trip to Washington, that omission and your apparent neglect of us seemed in their minds to point to but one obvious conclusion: that you had indeed compromised my reputation and, having done so, had subsequently decided to throw me over altogether!"

She held up a hand to forestall a response from her companion. "True, I'm well aware that you took great care initially to amend that impression upon our return. Your recent behavior, however, appears once again to have cast a cloud over us both. And what's more, try as I might, I simply haven't been able to imagine what might have prevented you from coming to see us while we were trapped in that horrid place. Why, I felt as if I hadn't a friend left in the world,'' she finished, before dropping her eyes and beginning to sniff in a suspicious way into one sleeve.

Now, this candid little speech had been uttered in such a forlorn fashion that Richard promptly threw caution aside in his haste to cross the room and gather Jennifer into a tender embrace, as he'd longed to do since the moment she'd entered the study. ''But I thought I shouldn't be doing you any good by stopping in merely to pass the time of day, though I see now that it was utterly foolish to deny us the comfort of each other's presence,'' he admitted after a minute into her damp curls. He crooked a finger under Jennifer's chin and gently forced her head back until she was looking at him again. ''To tell the truth, I didn't trust myself not to break down in front of you from worry and frustration, and I confess it was quite selfish of me to make you suffer on account of my inadequacies. Still, in your heart you must have known I was thinking about you every second, didn't you? Why, I stayed away mainly because I needed time to find out what it was I wanted to tell you—''

''Yes?'' Jennifer prompted eagerly. She smiled up at Richard in a confident, intimate way that made it difficult for him to breathe.

''Only that Mr. Henry sails tomorrow for France, and on an American ship, besides!'' he announced proudly.

Jennifer looked as if her smile had become frozen to her face as she gaped at Richard in disbelief. ''*That's* what you wanted to tell me?'' she managed at last.

''Why, yes, of course,'' he said hesitantly in a puzzled voice, conscious that he seemed somehow to have made another mistake. ''How else should I have spent all those days you were locked up if not in making use of my own freedom to learn what Mr. Henry meant to do? As I recall, I even told you that that's what I intended at the outset.''

''So you did,'' Jennifer agreed bitterly, ''though I was fool enough to think that that was merely an excuse to have a while to reflect on what was in your heart and what you meant to do about it! But I see now that I was entirely wrong!'' She pushed him an arm's length away, as he'd once done to her, and deliberately plucked his hands one by one from her shoulders. "It may surprise you to learn, but I don't give a hang when Mr. Henry means to sail, except that I've a very good notion to join him! It appears,'' she said carefully, making a new and obvious effort to control her temper, "that I've no inducement to remain here any longer, even if I was sufficiently deluded at one point to have convinced myself that I did! And what makes it infinitely worse is that you know perfectly well what my sentiments are, and yet you choose not to acknowledge them, and certainly not to respond to them in an appropriate manner."

"I don't either,'' Richard argued hotly, conscious of sounding rather like a recalcitrant child. "Just when do you think it is that you've told me in plain language how *you* feel? Because if it were up to me to say, I could point to a handful of occasions on which, if I'd dared, I might have intuited those sentiments and yet never would have presumed to believe in their existence without receiving confirmation from you—a circumstance, that you must admit, you've been quite unable to guarantee!"

Jennifer appeared somewhat daunted by the force of this rejoinder. "Perhaps,'' she allowed slowly. "Though surely you'll agree that it isn't as if we've had what anyone would call a wealth of opportunity to discuss such matters, what with all this business about Henry's letters and then interruptions of one sort or another."

"Oh, hang Mr. Henry!" Richard exclaimed a trifle desperately, much as his companion had earlier. He reached out and took Jennifer's hands in his and pulled her close again. "You must know that you've turned my life upside down and made me see things in a whole new way—even forced me to deal with matters I'd just as soon have left undisturbed. And through it all, you've been right beside me to buck me up, if I needed it, and actually to pick me up, too, if it came to that." He gave Jennifer's hands a little shake so that she looked searchingly up into his face. "Why don't you believe that you've owned my heart for ever so long, and that I've only been awaiting an invitation from you to ask for yours?"

Jennifer felt the aforementioned organ give a delighted leap beneath her breast. She was just on the point of responding when the very thing she most feared and to which she'd already made sad reference proceeded, naturally, to occur. The door of the study burst open, and George and Caroline tumbled inside, followed a second too late by Molly. The latter cast a quick, anguished look at the scene they'd interrupted and promptly sought to apologize over the twins' insistent bids for attention.

Even Richard had to concede that their luck appeared as damnably bad as ever, and that the present situation now seemed ludicrous at best. Therefore, he sighed good-naturedly at Jennifer over the children's heads and then shrugged his shoulders. "By God, I believe you're right," he agreed, beginning to chuckle a little despite himself. "It's positively uncanny, ain't it? Oh, very well," he told the twins at last, "you may have her, for now. But I warn you that I can be rather impatient myself, you know," he promised Jennifer, "and I don't propose to forget that you still owe me an answer. You won't keep me waiting too long, will you?" He smiled deep into his companion's eyes when he finished speaking in a way that made her shiver deliciously before she was finally dragged—albeit with great reluctance—from the room.

Now, Jennifer never meant to make Richard wait too long once he'd made clear what he hoped her answer to his question would be. Moreover, Lord Somers was nearly beside himself to learn what had occurred between his daughter and his host, and dropped one unsubtle hint after another to show how much he longed to know what lay behind the temporary truce that had been declared between these two. His curiosity wasn't destined to be satisfied too quickly, however, for by the following afternoon, everyone's attention was riveted on another matter completely. The papers were full of the revelation of the "Henry affair," as it was already being called, which the president had apparently decided to make public on the same day the author of the letters took his leave of America. "President

Reveals Secret Plot!'' the *Gazette* screamed, and ''English Spy Turns Over Evidence!'' cried the *Advertiser*.

Silence was the order of the day at teatime, as the members of the household read through the stories in the papers. The presidential message to Congress accompanying the documents had been brief and to the point. Madison claimed the correspondence proved that, ''a secret agent of the [British] government was employed in certain states, especially in the seat of government in Massachusetts, in fomenting disaffection to the constituted authorities of the nation, and in intrigues with the disaffected, for the purpose of bringing about resistance to the laws, and eventually, in concert with a British force, of destroying the union and forming the eastern part thereof into a political connection with Great Britain.''

Only the fiercely Federalist *New York Post* sounded an early, dissenting note to the general outrage over this news of British treachery; ''Proof or Poofery?'' it asked in huge headlines. Lord Somers flicked the paper thoughtfully with one finger. ''This is going to spell trouble,'' he predicted in a worried voice. ''Madison's gone too far, I'm afraid. You see what he's done, don't you?'' He pointed to where the text of the letters had been reprinted in the newspaper. ''He apparently gave Henry permission to erase the names of all the Americans who'd agreed to collaborate with him before making the letters public; wherever one of those names originally appeared, there's now only an asterisk. I've little doubt that Madison felt it not to be in the best interests of the country to reveal the names of the turncoats among us. Still, in his fervor to pin the guilt solely on foreigners, it seems to me that he's threatened the outcome of his entire scheme.''

So it must have seemed to several other onlookers as well. The very next day, they read, a motion was introduced in the Senate directing the secretary of state to lay before it ''the names of any and all persons in the United States, and especially in the state of Massachusetts, who have in any way or manner whatever entered into or most remotely countenanced the project or the views for the execution or attainment of which John Henry was, in the year 1809, employed by Sir James Craig, then governor general of the British Provinces in North America." And newspapers other than the *Post* had now joined in questioning the government's wisdom and motives in purchasing the letters, for Madison had also apparently decided at the last moment to admit that he'd authorized the payment of $50,000 to Henry. But he'd stuck to his story that the disclosures had been made to him in that gentleman's letter of February 20, never indicating that he'd heard them personally some two weeks earlier, as everyone at No. 30 Wall Street was in a perfect position to know.

"Government Duped?" and "Master Stroke or Major Swindle?" sniffed the newspapers, one editorial going so far as to claim that, save for the few communiques bearing on the nature of his assignment, Henry's letters were merely full of titillating paraphrases that incriminated no one and revealed nothing of antigovernment sentiment not already published openly in Boston or New York. And this impression wasn't helped significantly by the report that James Monroe submitted in which, the newspapers noted, he claimed that the Department of State was "not in possession of any names of persons in the United States who have in any way or manner whatever entered into or countenanced the project or the views for the execution or attainment of which John Henry was employed by Sir James Craig."

The official English response came two days after Henry's letters were made public and took the form of a letter addressed to Secretary Monroe from Lord Somers's friend August Foster, envoy extraordinary and minister plenipotentiary of Great Britain. He'd first read about the incident in the Washington newspaper, the *National Intelligencer*, Foster insisted, and on behalf of his government had to disclaim "having had any knowledge whatever of the existence of such a mission, or of such transactions as the communication Mr. Henry refers to."

Partly as a response to British denial of any involvement with Henry's "mission," and also in order to address the increasing charges of complicity being leveled against it, the government promptly ordered the Committee on Foreign Relations to look into the matter. And to no one's great surprise in the Avery household, at least, the first witness to appear before the Committee was the ever-helpful Count Edouard de Crillon. Yes, Crillon admitted, being of a sympathetic inclination, he'd naturally agreed to assist Henry in arranging to meet with the proper American authorities. He assured the Committee, however, that he'd only acted as an intermediary in securing Henry an audience with those people in a position to be interested in the documents. He'd never actually been involved in Henry's investigations themselves, nor did he stand to profit in any way from the monetary agreement the man had apparently struck with President Madison, Crillon promised his questioners, in an obvious attempt to paint himself as the virtuous party.

"What twaddle!" Jennifer scoffed. She thrust the newspaper aside, took a sip of coffee, and then slammed the cup back into its saucer so vehemently that some of the contents sloshed over the rim and Richard and her father jumped in their seats. "Beg pardon," she mumbled. "But, indeed, it puts me quite out of patience to have to sit meekly by and watch the public being fed such a mass of fustian when we know that Crillon was never a disinterested participant in the whole affair because he was in the pay of the French government all along!"

"We do?" Richard squeaked, goggling at Jennifer in amazement. Now, until this point, the three of them had been enjoying a companionable breakfast, perusing the papers, and sharing various tidbits with each other from time to time as the impulse moved them. Actually, however, Richard had been pleasantly lost in a secret contemplation of his beloved, rather than absorbed in a copy of the *Columbian Centinel* that a friend had brought down from Boston the day before. It was truly unconscionable for her to look so beautiful so early in the morning, he'd been thinking rather irritably. His study took in the tender little shadows her eyelashes cast on her cheeks and the one beguiling curl that tumbled down her breast toward the neckline of her morning dress. And yet, he admitted wryly to himself, how easily a stray comment could still manage to alter his entire mood. "You don't mean to tell me the fellow's a spy?" he demanded to know.

"But I did tell you," Lord Somers said in surprise. "Well, that is, I meant to," he recalled, "only, er, something came up—if you remember—and what with one thing and another I never got back to the subject. You see, that was the point of the letter we received from the president before we were released from Bridewell. Apparently, Madison got a note from Joel Barlow, the ambassador in Paris, advising him in a timely way to beware of any dealings with Louis Serieur, whom Barlow understood to be working in concert with a man from Napoleon's secret service to try and propel the United States into active hostilities with England. The man Barlow referred to as a spy was really a citizen of humble birth named Soubiron, whose chief talents were gambling and deception and who, Madison related, was in the habit of styling himself a French count with an estate called alternately St. Martine or St. Martial! It seems that the revelation that Crillon was representing the French interest in the Henry affair didn't really alter things, as far as Madison was concerned, but he did feel that he owed it to us to share that news—by way of thanks, I suppose. And what's more, Crillon is not without friends in high places himself, because it turns out he was the person responsible for our being detained at Bridewell as spies!"

Richard paused for a moment to digest this information. "But that means that Henry has turned over the $50,000 to Crillon in exchange for the title to a nonexistent property, which he's just set sail to France to claim," he said slowly. "Then justice appears to have been served, after all!"

"Perhaps," his lordship agreed, "though not evenhandedly, I'm afraid. You see, the president also indicated that he doesn't propose to interfere with whatever arrangement Crillon made with Henry, but will allow him freely to depart after he finishes testifying—and $50,000 richer, besides. To do otherwise would again have the effect of diminishing England's sole culpability in the matter, and this Madison has already shown himself unwilling to do. Still, I must confess that it galls me to no end to think that we're among a mere handful of those who know the truth behind all this nonsense," he said, frowning at the newspaper. He shook his head in disgust. "Politics!" he announced darkly.

His two companions appeared to share this last sentiment, for both looked considerably subdued. And Richard was even ready to admit that any lingering romantic notions he might have held had by this point been banished completely from his head. "Good heavens," Jennifer observed, voicing the thought that was now uppermost in everyone else's mind as well, "I wonder what will happen next?"

It wasn't long before this question was answered, because by the end of the week the Committee on Foreign Relations had completed its investigation and submitted its report to Congress. The text of that vital document was reprinted in all the papers. And two days after the preceding conversation, when the four adults in the household gathered late in the afternoon in the study for a glass of sherry, they were able to derive some comfort by sharing what was sure to be depressing news.

" 'The transaction disclosed by the president's message,' " Lord Somers read aloud, " 'presents to the minds of the Committee conclusive evidence that the British government, at a period of peace, and during the most friendly professions, has been deliberately and perfidiously pursuing measures to divide these states and to involve our citizens in all the guilt of treason and the horrors of a civil war.' " There was a brief silence. "Well, that's not too surprising a development, I suppose?" he ventured.

Richard looked at him absently. "No, I daresay it isn't," he agreed with some reluctance. "Nor, I suppose, is this," he said, indicating the story that he'd been studying. "Apparently, Clinton and his ilk will soon be delighted to find how many others have been swept up by a new wave of patriotism. It says here that ever since the Henry letters were published, the White House has been fairly deluged with such a vast number of people jostling to pay their respects that Dolly Madison is reported to be quite overcome by this unexpected effusion of loyalty. Of course, if it were merely a display of public spirit that was the primary result of this whole affair, I shouldn't feel so apprehensive. But we all know that Madison had a far different—and considerably larger—purpose in mind when he made the letters public, and that was first to unite the country and then to join hands against a common enemy: England." He pointed to his newspaper again. "Well, it looks as if he has achieved that goal—at least, if this editorial is to be believed. It proses on at some length about the wrongs the United States has suffered at British hands, and then urges that the time has arrived 'when the rights and honor of our country must be asserted by an appeal to arms, or ignominiously surrendered to the dictation of a foreign power.' "

Richard scowled at the page for a moment. "It's emotional blackmail, that's the only term for it, and I simply cannot conscience its use, no matter for how grand a purpose! I warrant we'll see no end of tasteless attempts to keep the public whipped into a patriotic frenzy until Congress is finally moved to declare war."

"Oh, but that trend appears to have started already," Jennifer inserted, pointing to the front page of the paper she and Molly had been reading. "Why else would such prominent space be given to reporting that the British minister in Washington has requested the protection of the government because he finds himself and his household continually besieged by people asking when he's leaving the country and offering to buy his coach horses."

Lord Somers shook his head. "Poor Augie. Still, I suppose it won't be long before such humor turns a good deal more ugly and he comes home one day to find the windows broken in his house and we begin to hear of other attacks against British citizens living in this country."

The foregoing remarks played quite nicely into the plan that had rapidly been forming in Jennifer's mind as her father spoke. For the past several days, she'd had to admit that her attention, like everyone else's, had been temporarily distracted by the developments on the public scene. She couldn't entirely dismiss from her mind, however, the fact that her private affairs still begged to be resolved. Nor could she ignore that it was clearly up to her, at this point, to make a push to settle things between her and a certain gentleman once and for all. Yet how to discover the most advantageous time to address that matter, and also the means by which to introduce the subject, had heretofore brought her to a stand. But perhaps, she mused, she'd finally found the key to smoothing that path.

She allowed a tiny, worried frown to crease her brow. "Indeed, I wonder whether it was wise to decide to stay here," she began. She rose from her chair and walked over to the fire—consciously striving, as she rarely did, to strike a pose she hoped would prove irresistible. "Why, we might even have placed ourselves in a position to receive some sort of spurious attack directly ourselves, mightn't we?" she asked her father.

"We might?" he said in surprise. "Well, always possible, of course. Though, I daresay it won't trouble us overmuch, since it never did before," he pointed out comfortably—and most inconveniently, too, as far as Jennifer was concerned.

Her little scheme was not progressing quite as she'd hoped, she realized, starting to feel a little anxious for the first time. Best to help matters along more directly, then, she decided abruptly. "Still, I should think we'd be glad of the protection we'd derive from residing in an American household rather than setting up one of our own," she said meaningfully. She cast a beseeching look from her father to Molly and back again, praying that at least one of the two would finally take her cue.

Luckily, her friend—who'd been anxiously awaiting just such a chance to help matters along herself—promptly volunteered her support. "Oh, indeed," Molly said firmly. "Why, just yesterday Miss Rutland inquired whether I didn't think it advisable for you to seek a more permanent form of protection, given how events were proceeding, and I told her that I quite agreed."

Lord Somers, however, continued to regard Jennifer with a puzzled expression. "Perhaps so, but I thought you told me—" He broke off as he began at last to perceive where the conversation was headed. "Why, that seems a splendid notion!" he enthused hurriedly, in an attempt to amend the situation as best he could. "And much safer, to be sure—if Richard will have us, that is. I wonder that I didn't think of it myself!"

At this point, Richard, who along with Molly had easily

discerned Jennifer's tactic, even if his lordship had not, decided that he might as well get right to the point. "As a matter of fact, I fancy I recall broaching that very idea and having it airily discounted as being altogether unworthy of consideration," he said in a thoughtful voice, staring at an obscure spot on the ceiling. "But then, the man of foresight is so rarely recognized in his own time, much less rewarded— don't you agree?" He watched out of the corner of his eye as Jennifer began to squirm a little at that observation. "If I remember correctly," he went on, getting up from his chair and beginning slowly to circle his desk, "I even noted that because four walls could offer only a moderately secure sort of shelter, it would be far more preferable to choose the much stronger and doubtless more lasting protection of a pair of strong arms and an American name—if one chose to look at it that way. No, don't leave," he said suddenly to Lord Somers and Miss Danhope, who'd both started to rise from their own chairs. "I believe I may soon be wanting a couple of witnesses."

Since he'd by this time maneuvered within easy distance of his goal, Richard reached out to cup Jennifer's face gently between his hands so that she couldn't move away. "That is what I offered, is it not?" he asked softly. "And as I recollect, you promised to provide an answer before too long. So I wonder—do you have it ready for me now?"

Jennifer stared up into the brown eyes that twinkled at her with tender amusement and felt the last stubborn, irrational shred of resistance dissolve in the rush of happiness that swept over her. "Yes—the answer's yes," she whispered. She stood on her toes and, blissfully ignoring her audience, tried to wrap her arms around Richard's neck.

"Now, I should tell you that I've already taken the precaution of securing your father's blessing. And don't forget that we also have two people who can easily testify to what you've just promised," Richard warned her. He bent down a little so as to assist Jennifer's efforts. "In case you ever find yourself threatened with prison again or accused of not keeping your word," he mumbled, right before his lips were silenced by a long and apparently satisfying kiss.

Being a man of integrity, Lord Somers paused long

enough to verify that the agreement had been duly sealed by the two consenting parties and then allowed himself to smile inwardly as he witnessed the outcome of his own little plan. After all, there wasn't the least likelihood that he'd ever be called upon to certify to the arrangement, but it always paid to be perfectly certain, he reminded himself, as he and Molly finally slipped unnoticed out of the room.

Afterword

On June 1, 1812, President James Madison sent a message to Congress, in which he urged that the members consider declaring war against England, "since [it has] come into proof that at the very moment when the public minister was holding the language of friendship and inspiring confidence in the sincerity of the negotiation with which he was charged, a secret agent of his government was employed in intrigues having for their object a subversion of our government and a dismemberment of our happy union."

The bill declaring war passed by a vote of 79 to 49 in the House of Representatives on June 4, and a vote of 19 to 13 in the Senate on June 17. On June 18, the bill was sent to the president for his signature. Ironically, on June 17, the British government finally ordered the repeal of the Orders in Council, which had been a strong factor in convincing skeptics of the need to declare war. However, communication was so poor that the repeal had no effect on the passage of the foregoing bill, and it took nearly two months for England even to hear that the United States had "recognized that a state of war existed between the two countries."

Little is known of the fate of either Edouard Crillon or John Henry. Crillon sailed for Europe, presumably some $50,000 richer, on All Fool's Day (April 1), and thereafter dropped out of sight. Henry surfaced briefly as one of those employed to help rake up scandal for a divorce on behalf of George IV (formerly the Prince Regent), in whose employ he is listed as "the informer of the 'Henry letters' notoriety."

The plot of this novel accurately follows much of the chronology of the "Henry affair," insofar as it is known today. However, no second set of the letters ever existed, and nor was an attempt made to try and keep the original conspirators from successfully relieving the government of the United States of $50,000. This stratagem and other conjectures regarding the relationships of the principals involved are wholly the author's own invention.